THE ONCE AND FUTURE CON

Peter Guttridge

GW00320190

HEADLINE

First published in 1999
by HEADLINE BOOK PUBLISHING

10 9 8 7 6 5 4 3 2 1

British Library Cataloguing in Publication Data

Guttridge, Peter
    The once and future con
    1.Madrid, Nick (Fictitious character) - Fiction
    2.Detective and mystery stories
    I.Title
    823.9'14[F]

    ISBN 0 7472 7582 3

Typeset by
Letterpart Limited, Reigate, Surrey

Printed and bound in Great Britain by
Clays Ltd, St Ives plc

HEADLINE BOOK PUBLISHING
A division of the Hodder Headline Group
338 Euston Road
London NW1 3BH
www.headline.co.uk
www.hodderheadline.com

For my brother, Michael
And my sister, Sheila

With apologies to admirers of T. H. White's *The Once and Future King*, the Arthurian epic about *rex quondam, rex futurus* whose title I have so shamelessly travestied.

Chapter One

When the crumhorn player fell out of the minstrels' gallery Bridget finally began to enjoy herself. She giggled as the lute player and the bloke who'd been blowing up a furry animal's bottom dropped their chosen instruments and grabbed their colleague as he toppled headfirst over the carved balustrade.

Whilst the assembled black-gowned guests at the long tables below the dangling musician held their collective breaths, Bridget hooted. She could see what was going to happen. The crumhorn player was hanging over the balustrade, his loose-fitting green doublet shrouding his head, whilst his desperate colleagues scrabbled for any kind of purchase on his legs and waist.

One of them got a firm hold on the musician's red tights. He kept hold, even when the musician slowly slid out of them, mooning the dinner guests below with his skinny, spotty buttocks.

Bridget's laughter and the man's exposure set off the atavistic heartiness of the couple of hundred men and handful of women in evening dress assembled in the neo-Gothic dining hall below. They had been downing white and red wine with abandon all evening and were even now passing the port as if it were a party game. The men gave basso, jeering laughs and banged fists on the long waxed tables, making the cutlery leap. The women were less abandoned although some of them tapped their knives fiercely against their wine glasses.

I thought the crumhorn player had been playing off-key – though how can you tell with these medieval instruments? – but I didn't realise he was as plastered as the rest of the room until his two saviours managed to get a grip on his bare thighs and haul him back over the balustrade. He stood there swaying and gazing round blearily until they bustled him off the balcony.

Bridget had taken against the musicians from the start. Not just because they insisted on dressing in Elizabethan gear but because they took turns to introduce each piece of music in mock-Elizabethan, with lots of prithees and for-sooths. And because she was in a bad mood. Had been since we'd left London.

We'd set off late after she'd been held up at her new newspaper – we're both journalists, though Bridget went into editing several years ago. On the M40 we got stuck behind a convoy of ancient vans and cars spluttering towards the West Country to hear the Wiltshire Messiah's latest sermon on Silbury Hill.

Once we'd reached Oxford I'd abandoned the car in a parking space outside the Lamb and Flag and we'd hurried through the cobbled alley to my old college. Dinner had already started when we finally entered the mock-medieval dining room. We'd found our places on opposite sides of the long table. Everyone was sitting on long benches.

Bridget was dressed with her usual restraint in a figure-hugging little micro-skirted number. Getting seated had proved tricky and involved her showing a great deal of thigh and a flash of her knickers to my side of the table. In particular to the banker sitting beside me, a chubby man with razor rash on his jaw and a florid complexion. He had leered at what he saw. Bridget caught him looking.

When she'd got settled she wagged a finger at him. 'Know your limitations,' she said. 'Stick with the blow-up doll.'

Then she leaned across the table to hiss at me: 'Have you ever seen so many mid-life crises gathered in one room? Tears before bedtime, mark my words.'

The chubby banker overheard.

'Oh, I think there are a number of people here who feel quite content with what they've achieved,' he said, sitting back in his seat.

Bridget appraised him. Uh-oh. After a moment she said: 'I wasn't talking to you, lard-arse.' Which wasn't up to her usual standard of repartee but seemed to do the trick.

Bridget had settled down. It was the arrival of the medieval musicians that had soured her. I could see she was restless during the first jaunty little number.

'The man playing the crumhorn is simply marvellous,' said a man wearing one of those waistcoats patterned seemingly to look as if someone has vomited down it.

'Isn't he,' his companion, a woman with too many frills for a woman of her age, trilled.

'That guy blowing up an animal's bum?' Bridget said.

'It's a utriculus actually,' vomit waistcoat said, a superior smirk on his face. 'An ancient bagpipe – the bag is formed from the entire head of a sheep or goat, with the chanter fitted into a wooden stock at the neck. The drones come from stocks in the forelegs. The chanter has seven holes in front and a thumbhole behind.'

'Jesus H. Christ,' Bridget muttered, reaching for the port and pouring herself a generous slug. She leaned across the table towards me. 'I see why you've turned out the way you have,' she said.

'What do you mean?'

'With a poker up your bum.' I actually started to look before she said: 'See?'

When the musicians had finished Bridget busied herself with her cigar until the din died down then looked around.

'What a bunch of tossers,' she said, loud enough for those either side of us to hear.

The chubby banker put his hands flat on the table and leaned towards her, a tight smile on his face.

'Somebody had too much to drink, have they?' he said.

I held my breath. My amigo Bridget Frost, the Bitch of

the Broadsheets, drinks to excess, it's true, but rarely if ever exhibits signs of it – or indeed suffers the consequences. More to the point, her verbal ripostes can be life-threatening. She opened her mouth and exhaled, engulfing the banker in cigar smoke.

'This is Bridget sober, actually,' I said quickly. 'You couldn't handle her drunk.'

'Nick Madrid – my champion,' Bridget cooed, patting my hand.

'I'm damned sure I wouldn't want to,' the banker said huffily through the wreath of smoke. Which is when Bridget stubbed her cigar out on the back of his hand.

He yelped. She smiled sweetly. Always a frightening sight. 'So sorry,' she said silkily. 'I was aiming for the ashtray.'

The banker clutched his hand like a wounded paw under his double chin. He started to say something but was drowned out by the voice of the Warden from the top table. A short hunched figure, with sparse white hair and yellow teeth, the Warden bellowed an introduction to the guest speaker, Lord Williamson of Fleming.

The guests at the top table were so meagrely lit that little more could be seen of them than flashes of white shirt or faces occasionally emerging from shadow. Only when Williamson stood could I see him clearly – a tall, patrician-looking man with a thick shock of black hair and an aristocratic manner.

He was actually a docker's son from Newcastle, one of the government's life peers. He was a socialist millionaire who had made his money out of genetically modified foods and was now the head of one of the government committee impartially investigating the risks of said foods. Makes sense to me.

He was also chair of one of the numerous committees competing to save Venice from sinking into the sea. The college had long-standing links with the Italian city – in the first term of their third year, history students these days moved to the city to study the Renaissance there. At the risk of sounding old, there was nothing like that when I was there.

Williamson enjoyed his own voice rather more than his audience did. He spoke for an inordinate length of time. During the many longueurs of his speech I saw in the dim light thrown from table lamps another side to the atavism I had witnessed earlier.

The diners were sinking into melancholy, flicking bemused glances around them, gazing in an abstracted way at the smoke-darkened portraits on the brick walls and up at the remote rafters of the high arched roof. Thinking of lost youth and faded dreams. At least that's what I was thinking about. But then I was on the second bottle.

It was some fifteen years before that I'd first entered this Gothic Revival baronial hall. There was something dispiriting about coming back so many years later. Then, I'd been seated on these long, narrow benches as an undergraduate. I was shy and insecure. No change there then.

I wasn't quite sure why I had agreed to come to this reunion. I had never fitted in. And not because I'd been a punk. That was just another kind of uniform and passed away after the first term into billowing New Romanticism – no, nobody has seen the pictures. But I'd had a chip on my shoulder. My dad had just died – I think I got in on the sympathy vote rather than my academic excellence – and I was angry at anything and everything.

As I listened to Williamson's spiel I was watching a spiteful-looking man in his late thirties at the next table. He'd been late too. I'd noticed him outside in the quadrangle when Bridget and I arrived. He'd been talking earnestly to someone – I couldn't see who – in the shadowy entrance to staircase H.

The man was very tall, narrow shouldered, with long, thin legs. His body widened around the waist and hips so that he looked like a pear on stilts. His head was the same: narrow at the crown but widening into soft jowls and flabby neck. His hair was black and receding, slicked back and chopped off straight just above his collar.

His name was Jonathan Askwith and we'd loathed each other at college. He was a couple of years ahead of me but our paths crossed often. He'd had a thing about my girl-friend and was always trying to get her into bed. Now *that* we had in common.

During Williamson's speech he sat with his cronies, doling out port from his own bottle, thumping the table with the heel of his hand as commentary on the speech, twisting his mouth to make facetious remarks whenever the socialist lord stumbled.

A woman facing him leaned forward to address a remark to him but he ignored her, a contemptuous expression on his face. She was wearing a low-backed silk dress. She had good shoulders and short red hair and even though I couldn't see her face I knew exactly who she was. My heart sank.

At the end of Williamson's speech, which received only desultory applause, people began to move between the tables. Bridget nipped off to visit the loo. I was waiting for the woman in the low-backed dress to turn round to con-firm my identification when the thin, bespectacled woman opposite me, wearing a garish purple velvet number and a badge in her lap, leaned over and held her hand out to me.

'Camilla Witherspoon. 'Eighty-seven. And you are?'

I took her hand and shook it. It was like a seal's flipper. I mumbled my name.

'Have you come back to Jesus as He has come back to you?' she asked, smiling a little too broadly. I read her badge: *He's Back – And Better Than Ever*.

Ah. The millennium had a lot to answer for.

Half the world had of course gone bonkers at the time. For several million people lunacy took the form of follow-ing one of the many millennial Messiahs who popped up everywhere from Alabama to Vladivostock to proclaim their Second Coming. (The sad guy who obviously wasn't with the programme and had come back as Pontius Pilate lasted only a couple of days.)

Three of the Messiahs came from the United Kingdom. The one woman among them didn't survive the tabloid onslaught on her affair with her Mary Magdalene, even though she insisted that He had probably done the same the first time around.

The two remaining British Messiahs were both remarkably media-savvy. The one from Wiltshire – who announced his return on 1 January 2000 and used the slogan Camilla had on her badge – had been the first to get major sponsorship. He'd employed one of the big PR firms who'd got him the cover of everything from the *Sunday Times* magazine to *Hello*.

He seemed to know his scripture. He'd even done a 'modern recreation' of the Sermon on the Mount on Silbury Hill, near Avebury. It was a fundraiser – £10 a ticket for a day-long event with live music. And no loaves and fishes – overpriced food was provided by various pizza and soft drinks franchises.

He was due sometime soon to go on breakfast TV in front of an audience of priests for a debate with the other Messiah, the one who'd been discovered working for his dad in the building trade in the East End. The East End Messiah was more militant. The first newspaper report headline was THIS MESSIAH'S NOT FOR TURNING THE OTHER CHEEK. His slogans – *Don't Get Cross Get Even* and *Gethsemane – This Time We Fight* – encouraged a certain amount of anti-semitism. Synagogues and mosques had been attacked and Hassidic Jews beaten up in the streets.

There had been a lot of religious types at the college when I'd been here as a student. The college was famous for its magnificent chapel and Holman Hunt's painting of Christ as *The Light of The World* which hung in it. Since those days a rough rule of thumb through my life has been to keep the God-Squad at arm's length. I avoided the woman's fanatical eyes, therefore, mumbled something non-committal and excused myself. I glanced across at the pear-shaped man in time to see the redhead lift a long leg over the bench she was sitting on.

As she turned to get up she looked across at me and stopped, straddling the bench. She glanced back at the pear-shaped man then, smiling at me, hooked her other leg over the bench and came up to my table.

'Nicholas,' she said, holding out her long, slender hand.

'Faye,' I said, clutching rather than shaking her hand, my eyes scanning her face for any sign of ageing. She looked no different to the last time I'd seen her, years before. Except for the wedding ring on her finger, that is. There was an awkward silence. I couldn't think of a single thing to say. Meeting your First Love much further down the line is like that.

'I said to Jonathan –' she gestured behind her towards the pear-shaped man – 'that I bet we'd see you.'

I looked at the spiteful man and back to her. She was married to *Askwith*?

'You've cut your tresses,' I said, smiling nervously. She was the only woman I'd ever met to whose hair the word *tresses* might apply. I remembered a pale beauty with long, auburn hair and full lips. I used to tease her about her pre-Raphaelite appearance, her looks accentuated by the clothes she wore. Burne-Jones and all the pre-Raphaelites had been in fashion at that time and she had played it to the full.

She raised a hand shyly towards her head.

'A long time ago,' she said. Another silence, then she started to move past me. 'Well, nice to see you, Nick—'

'You're married then?' I blurted out. 'Children?'

There was a beat as she looked again at the pear-shaped man.

'Sometimes things don't turn out as you expect,' she said, and I didn't know if she was talking about children or her marriage.

'Hey, shagger! Look who I've just met!'

Bridget's bellow would have given the trumpet that blew down the walls of Jericho stiff competition. It had been known to strike terror in people three cities away. Her voice now was not particularly raised so there was no immediate risk to the walls of the college, but it was piercing.

'Hi Bridget,' I said, blushing, as Faye, mouthing 'Shagger?' and lifting a quizzical eye, moved on. Bridget glanced at her as she passed.

'This is Genevra Wynn. We were at school together. I just met her in the bog – haven't seen her for an age. We were best friends.'

My friend was arm in arm with a broad-shouldered girl in a man's dinner suit who, in her high-heeled shoes, stood about two inches taller than I did – and I'm six foot four. She had close-cropped black hair, a flat nose that looked as if it had been broken at some stage and a scar running down her top lip. It twisted her mouth slightly.

'Bridget and I were joint swimming champions,' Genevra said, following the direction of my gaze which was, only by chance I assure you, fixed on her impressive cleavage. 'Hence the tits.'

I blushed.

'You were at the convent together?' I said.

'No, later,' Bridget said. 'Must say, Gennie, I didn't expect to find you here with all these tossers.'

'But you're forgetting Rex was here. I've come with him.' She looked at me and smiled. 'You were here too?'

I nodded. Bridget nudged me. 'Gennie's brother Rex is a real hunk – and next in line for a lordship.'

'He has the title now,' Genevra said. 'Daddy died five years ago.'

'Rex is now Lord Wynn of Wynn?'

Bridget, I could see, had gone weak at the knees. She's always had a thing about the aristocracy. What I couldn't figure out was which school she'd gone to where she could possibly meet a lord's daughter. Divining my thoughts, she said: 'Genevra and I were at Holland Park Comprehensive together. I did my A levels there. Great place. Lords and layabouts, coronets and council housing, rock stars' children and the children of the dysfunctional poor.'

'Come over and say hello to Rex,' Genevra said.

As she strode ahead Bridget leaned in to me and said,

only theoretically under her breath: 'A cracker, isn't she? And she's available. I checked.'

Genevra was a striking-looking woman, I had to agree, but just then my head was full of Faye and the thought that she was married to that oik. Not that things had gone exactly smoothly between us when we'd been together. On the night we finished she'd torn a dress I'd bought her to pieces. With her teeth. Intense? I should say so.

Genevra had stopped beside an equally tall man with broad shoulders and long, curly black hair tied in a ponytail down his back. When he saw Bridget he grinned, gave her a shameless look-over and then there was a lot of hugging. I had a vague recollection of him at university but he'd been a couple of years ahead of me.

He had startling green eyes and an endearingly gummy smile. He shook hands firmly.

'Wynn,' he said. 'Most people call me Rex. So you and Bridget—'

'Good heavens, no!' Bridget exclaimed. I gave her a sharp look. We weren't lovers, never had been, but did she have to make the very notion sound quite so absurd?

Rex's speech was an odd mixture of upper-class drawl and the Estuary English beloved of rock stars who want to hide their middle-class upbringing. His attention was distracted by the sight of Faye's husband buttonholing Lord Williamson.

'That's my boy,' Rex murmured. He caught my look.

'This is a business opportunity. We're looking for backers for a big project we're working on. Jonathan there is our finance director. You could do worse than invest, old stick.'

'That presupposes I have some money to invest,' I said. As a matter of fact, I was skint. It's exhilarating being a freelance but not when the rent is due and you don't have any money coming in. I'd been freelancing for ten years and things had never been so bad.

The college's guest speaker left the room with Jonathan Askwith. I looked round but I couldn't see Faye anywhere.

'So you know Faye and her husband?' I said, for want of anything better.

'Rather. Faye's brother, Rafe, was a good friend of mine. Lord Williamson's too, for that matter.'

Rafe, I knew, was actually a Ralph with pretensions. I remembered him; he'd been as irritating as the way he insisted on pronouncing his name.

'How long have they been . . .?'

He looked at me shrewdly and smiled.

'Better ask Faye that kind of question.'

'What kind of project are you engaged in?' I hurried on.

'You were here, right?' I nodded. 'Did you ever do Frome's course on the Arthurian legends or was he, er . . .'

'He died when I was halfway through the course,' I said. 'It was my favourite course.' I'd really got into the Arthurian stuff. Then Frome, a legendary drinker and promiscuous partygoer, fell down the stairs outside his rooms in college and broke his neck. I remembered it clearly because it was the day before Faye and I had split up.

'Mine too, but given added interest because I happen to live in the West Country, right in the middle of Arthur's realm. There have been stories in the family for generations that an old motte and bailey castle on the estate is actually the site of Arthur's Camelot. As you know, he was a sixth-century British leader not a medieval king, so his castle would not have been the great one of the movies.'

'Really,' I said, unable to keep the scepticism out of my voice. People had been wittering on for years about Tintagel being Arthur's birthplace and possibly Camelot without an iota of proof for either contention, and there were half a dozen other places competing for the tourist Euro by declaring they were the true site of Camelot.

More recently, King Arthur had even come back to lead the Welsh. The most famous legend about King Arthur was that as *rex quondam, rex futurus* – the Once And Future King – he was simply sleeping and when he was needed he would return and lead his people once more.

Devolved power in Wales plus millennium fever had encouraged some guy from Caerleon-on-Usk to declare himself Arthur Returned, come to rule his old kingdom. He was insisting that the monarchy – his monarchy – be reinstalled in Wales. He reached the nationals (the tabloids, anyway) when he accused the Prince of Wales of usurping his throne and challenged him to single combat. He even suggested that he might go for the Prince's Cornish Duchy too. He'd been photographed riding a white horse.

Arthur was regarded as a bit of a local crackpot until he got financial support from other crackpots, i.e., Tory Eurosceptics. The newspapers had made much play of the fact that here was a wannabe Welsh king supported by Little Englanders. By now he had a few thousand followers among the millions of deranged people adrift in the modern world. Plus, he had a great website.

Rex smiled.

'I can see you're doubtful, but never mind. The point is that Britain is crying out for an Arthurian theme park, and that's what we're going to turn Wynn House into.'

I groaned. I was finding it very depressing that Britain was fast turning into Heritage plc. As far as I was concerned, the last thing the nation needed was yet another rendition of its past, with rides.

'I've set up a company – Avalon Offshore Trust. We're here primarily to look for backers.'

'Faye is involved?'

'Oh yes, everybody gets their hands dirty on this one,' Rex said with relish. 'Faye is our PR manager. She'll be handling the press when we're ready to launch.' He indicated Gennie, who was trying to out-screech Bridget as they recalled God knows what old school scandal.

'Genevra is our conscience. She's the one who's going to make sure we don't make the whole thing too disgusting.'

'And you think a theme park is what's needed?'

'Needed?' He laughed. 'Well, I wouldn't exactly say that, old stick. But sure, it will be a boost to the local economy.

12

There's stiff opposition from the other sites worried about their tourist figures, but the local council's on our side. As are English Heritage, within limits.'

He excused himself to go and talk to some prospective investors. Bridget was still busy with Genevra, both of them sucking on cigars and giggling. I dawdled in the hall, looking up at the old pictures on the walls, then slipped out onto the shadowy landing that separated the dining room from the library.

It was chilly and gloomy, lit only by an electric light set into an old, narrow-stemmed gaslight. The arched ceiling many feet above my head was lost in shadow. Diners passed behind me, their feet clattering on the steps as they moved from the dining hall to the bar in the cellars below.

As I reached the door of the library, Lord Williamson emerged, looking flushed. We almost collided. He muttered an apology and hurried past me down the broad flight of stairs.

I entered the library, closed the door softly and sank back against it. After a moment I made my way cautiously down the centre aisle between the cubicles, looking to right and left, conscious of the squeak of my shoes at every step.

When I was sure I was alone I sat down in the history section. Slowly I let my glance travel across the spines of the books on the shelves, savouring the smell of musty bindings and waxed wood. I looked at the ceiling for some minutes, summoning memories, then I heard footsteps.

A moment later, Faye's husband, Jonathan, shambled into view, stoop-shouldered, heading for the door. He had almost passed me when he noticed I was there. He paused, straightened, looked at me impassively.

'Too late to have regrets,' he said, slurring the words. 'We've done what we've done.'

He came closer, a bottle of port dangling loosely in his left hand. He swung it to his mouth for a quick swallow then offered it to me. I declined. What did Faye see in this man? He peered at me, swaying a little, then let his body fall

back against a pillar a few inches behind him. Leaning there
he smiled crookedly. 'Graduate, are you, old boy? What
year?'

The bastard didn't even remember me. Well, two could
play at that game.

'I am. Were you?' I said. 'I'm afraid I don't remember
you.'

'No need for fear,' the man replied. 'Askwith, Jonathan. I
was in the fast set from Winchester. You would only have
seen our taillights. A little shit like you.'

Askwith took another swig from his bottle. I contem-
plated taking it from him and inserting it somewhere from
where it would need to be surgically removed. Then I told
myself the man was drunk and was in any case of no
importance. Aside from the fact he was married to the
woman who had broken my heart.

He leaned forward to scrutinise me with bleary eyes. Then
he pulled himself away from the pillar and up to his full
height.

'Oh, it's you,' he slurred. 'The oik from Ramsbottom.
Never knew what Faye saw in you. I mean, what the fuck
did you know? About anything? You were of such little
consequence. And you haven't changed, I can see. You don't
know what day it is. Now fuck off.' He paused. 'Better still,
I'll fuck off.'

Askwith turned and shambled away. When he'd gone – I
heard the door open and noisily close – I sat quietly for a
second or two, my face burning, before I followed him from
the room.

There was no sign of Faye or her bastard husband in the
bar. Genevra, Bridget, Rex and another bloke were
ensconced at a table in a narrow alcove. I wasn't in the
mood to join them so I went out into the quadrangle and
walked around to the back gate of the college.

It was a crisp night and my breath plumed before me as I
walked to the car to get our things. Re-entering the quadrangle, loaded down with luggage (Bridget is one of the great

14

travel divas who won't leave home without her vanity case and a trailer-full of clothes), I saw Askwith heading my way.

I shrank back into the shadows – I had no wish to encounter him again – and he stumbled past me, heading in the direction of the chapel.

I looked around me. The college was a product of the Oxford Movement in the nineteenth century and at night in its Gothic grandeur was a sinister sight. Yellow light from narrow windows spilled onto the tangled ivy and the gravel paths below.

Bridget and I were sharing rooms – a bedroom each with a study room in between. I put her luggage in her room and opened the bottle of cheap fizz I'd bought in case friends came back here. Sprawled on one of the cheap plastic chairs by the window, my feet on the windowsill, I took deep swallows of the wine and indulged myself with memories.

As I watched, gowned and dinner-jacketed men straggled across the quadrangle. Those who were alone invariably paused to look around at the college, wanting by their concentration to make concrete old feelings and memories. I saw Faye drift across the lawn, gazing up at the stars. Shortly after, Lord Williamson crossed the quad and disappeared into a stairwell.

I fell into a doze which Bridget disturbed when she came in.

'You made a sneaky exit. We thought you were puking up in the lav. You okay?'

'Fine,' I said. 'Thought you'd be with Rex.'

'Sharing rooms with Gennie. Didn't seem right.'

'Did you and he ever . . .?'

'We had a fumble at a party once. You sound jealous.'

'Me? Not at all,' I said. Though, bizarrely, I was.

'So who was the Nicole Kidman lookalike? Your first shag?'

'Who?'

'The broad who slipped away when I came back with Gennie.'

'You noticed.'

'I miss nothing, pal, you should know that by now.'

'We never did actually.'

Bridget poured a glass of wine and plonked herself down in the sagging armchair. She yawned. 'Tell me all about her then.'

So I did. The whole sad story. For some reason I remembered every detail. Looking out of the window at the quad as I used to do during my time of greatest upset, I told Bridget things I thought I'd forgotten, holding nothing back. She didn't interrupt once, the sign of a good listener. She did, however, snore rather loudly, within moments of my starting, which is not such a good sign. I told her anyway – it *is* good to talk – and when I'd finished I got a blanket from her bed and tucked her up.

I hauled myself into bed, leaving my dinner suit, shoes and starched shirt in a tangle on the floor. Our scout – the college name for the servant who looks after the rooms – woke us at nine the following morning with the news that Jonathan Askwith had been found in the chapel in front of Holman Hunt's *Light of the World*. Dead in his own vomit.

Chapter Two

'It was murder, of course,' Bridget said as we drove back to London. I glanced across at her. We'd both been pretty subdued for the past hour. I was thinking about Faye; Bridget had a hangover the size of the traffic jam we encountered once we reached the M40/M25 intersection.

'The guy choked on his own vomit,' I said patiently. 'You think someone induced it – by sticking their fingers down his throat maybe? I can think of easier ways to off somebody.'

'If he'd passed out it would be easy enough,' she said.

'The guy was a boozer – you should have seen the way he was putting away the port. Happens all the time to big drinkers and druggies.'

'That's what you're supposed to think.'

'Bridget, I know together we've seen more than our share of deaths by violence, but why are you so insistent this was murder?'

'Something was going on with him. You saw him when we arrived lurking in that doorway talking to someone.'

'I saw him; I didn't think you had.'

'Men in dinner jackets, remember?'

Bridget had a thing about men in dinner jackets – she found them irresistible. The effect had been muted the previous night because everyone had been wearing gowns over their jackets, but Askwith, when we saw him outside, had not yet put his gown on.

'The fact he was talking to someone doesn't mean he was

murdered. He was talking to me in the library later but I didn't kill him.'

'What about?'

'Nothing substantive – he was pissed.'

'*Nothing substantive* – that place really got to you, didn't it?'

Bridget hadn't been to university. She was brighter than most people I knew and better at arguing – or maybe I mean more argumentative – but it rankled with her, I knew. However many qualifications you get later, it never makes up for missing out straight from school. Add the fact that this was Oxford we were talking about and it made her really edgy.

'I just like to use the right words.'

Bridget snorted and looked out of her window.

'I wonder if they have a time of death?' she murmured. She saw my questioning look. 'I thought I saw someone coming out of the rectangle—'

'Quadrangle.'

'Whatever – next to the chapel when I was coming back to our room.'

'Did you tell the police?' I said.

'What, and be kept waiting for three hours? I've got a hot date tonight. Anyway, I didn't see his face.'

'Do you want to come back to my crib first?' I said.

'Your crib?' Bridget said. 'Aren't you a bit old for a cot?'

I blushed.

'I'm trying to get hip,' I said.

'I think that went out with the Sweeney, dear,' she said. 'Can't – I've got to get to the gym.'

Sex is the only exercise you need, Bridget used to say, and indeed, exercise other than that involved in her regular shaggathons had always been anathema to her. She took the piss out of me no end for the exercise I do – sadly, sex is not the only exercise I need, not the way I do it, anyway. So I do a vigorous kind of yoga called astanga vinyasa that attracted tabloid attention some time ago when

18

Madonna took it up. Admittedly, because of my height, I
usually look like a giant spider suffering convulsions while
I'm doing it, but I've never found anything better for
keeping in shape.

But here was the new and staggering thing about Bridget
– she had begun to exercise. We'd been in South America
the previous year and she'd been toying with the idea of
plastic surgery, partly because she'd been going out with
men younger than herself and was feeling self-conscious. I
couldn't see why. She's only in her thirties and in good if
slightly overweight shape.

Then she had started using the gym almost as soon as
we'd got back from Colombia. I couldn't figure out if it was
some peculiar method of shutting out the fact that she'd
killed a man at Machu Picchu in a rather gruesome way. She
had never talked about it, seeming more concerned that on
that same trip she'd slept with a murderous madman believ-
ing him to be someone else. She'd silenced me with a glance
when I'd observed it wouldn't be the first madman she'd
slept with.

I hadn't seen much change in her except firmed up arms.
Since she had already been able to fell most men with a
single blow – the benefits of that early convent education – I
dreaded to think what havoc she could wreak now.

I dropped her at Shepherd's Bush tube so she could go
over to her gym in the Barbican. It took me half an hour to
find somewhere to park that was in the same borough as my
flat. My car is a soft-top Karmann Ghia. It had belonged to
my dad and I used it maybe six times a year; the rest of the
time it was under tarpaulin.

It would have been easier for me to take the train to
Oxford from Paddington, but since it had been raining
pretty much non-stop since Christmas – almost six weeks –
I was worried that the car would simply rot under the
tarpaulin if I didn't take it for a drive.

In my apartment – okay, joke, studio flat – okay, room – I
dug out an old photo album from my university days and

looked at Faye and me. There were a few pictures of us on punting picnics. I was smiling but with a wary look in my eye.

I'd gone to university only a few months after my dad had died of a heart attack – although basically he'd really died because his body was clapped out after years of drink and drug abuse. Oxford was a culture shock. I was a working-class punk from a single-parent dysfunctional family, and the only middle-class person I knew was the family doctor.

I met Faye in the first week of my second year. We were both taking history, though in different colleges and years. She was in her first year at Lady Margaret. I don't know what it was that drew me to her. Well, aside from the fact she was a knockout. She was a quasi-hippy – a deeply unfashionable thing to be then – and I remember I had my dad's record collection, which was basically an A – Z of pop music from 1963 onwards.

I lent her old albums by the Incredible String Band, Love, Alan Stivell and Fairport Convention, and she plaited her long pre-Raphaelite hair and mooned around looking pale and winsome. Her skin seemed almost translucent – you could see thin blue veins pulsing beneath it.

Her brother, Ralph/Rafe, was up at the same time – he was two years older but he was staying on to do a doctorate. He was gay and heavily into the whole Brideshead thing. The TV adaptation of the Waugh novel had a profound effect on young men and women at the time. Oxford was thronged with languid Sebastian-clones clutching teddy bears, experimenting with being gay. The young men, that is, not the teddy bears.

These posers were quite happy to hang out in big woollies and college scarves wherever there were cocktails. If they had lighted sparklers sticking out of them, so much the better. You could get cocktails like that too.

Faye had a boyfriend on the Welsh Borders – she was always nipping off at weekends to Hergest Ridge up near Offa's Dyke – so I could only pine from afar, especially as it was difficult to cross over that friendship/lover divide. It

20

wasn't until the final term of the second year that we really got together.

I went to stay with her family in Somerset during the long vac between my second and third years. They lived in the gatehouse of some big stately home. They treated me very warmly. I remember sneaking along the landing, trying to avoid the creaking floorboards, to get into Faye's bedroom without alerting her parents. Not that we did very much. Getting together was only an approximate term.

She said she wanted to wait until she was married. I don't know if she was really a virgin but she was very strange about sex. She'd kind of freeze up, so we'd only go so far. We slept together and we carried on what used to be called 'heavy petting'.

I stayed a week but didn't see her again that summer – I was working in a bread factory over in Bradford. We wrote a lot and phoned, of course, until she went off to Italy for a month with her mother and some other friends.

In my third year, her second, I lived in Summertown with three girls. Yes, that's what I thought, too, but it didn't work out that way. Faye moved into a flat in Parktown, a mile down the road, with her brother Ralph. I got to know him a bit better. Moody, intense but occasionally very funny. He tolerated Faye, who was appalled by his gay lifestyle. He called her Mother Hen.

Although I was nuts about Faye it was a frustrating time for me, especially as there were plenty of other girls around more amenable to a lusty young man. Or even me. A hundred times I was tempted and a hundred times I resisted. Well, ninety-nine times – nobody's perfect.

The coroner concluded that Jonathan Askwith had died accidentally, passing out from an excess of alcohol then choking on his own vomit. I didn't go to the funeral but I did send a donation to the charity of Faye's choice, a child abuse organisation she was involved with.

Two weeks after the funeral Faye phoned to invite me down to Rex and Genevra's place at Montacute in Somerset. She sounded brisk and not at all like a grieving widow. I expressed my condolences then said: 'Montacute – isn't that National Trust?'

'Montacute House is, but Rex lives at Wynn House on the other side of the hill.'

'And what is this, a kind of house party?'

'Kind of. We want to offer you a job, but I don't know how it would fit in with your other freelance commitments,' she said. 'It would mean you coming down to the West Country for a few weeks.'

A few weeks in the West Country with Faye. Hmm.

'That's possible,' I said casually. 'What's the job?'

'Avalon Offshore Trust has a deal with a publisher to write an account of our discovery. We wondered if you'd like to do it.'

'What discovery? I thought you were building a theme park.'

'Did Rex not tell you? It's focused on something we've found here.'

'I'm a bit rusty on my history—'

'This isn't a history text – we need a journalist who can give it maximum impact. It will form part of the marketing strategy for the Avalon Project.'

She mentioned a figure – a generous one.

'What have you found exactly?'

'I can't tell you that. We're announcing it at a conference at the start of next week. But it's big news.'

Arthurian finds always were.

'It's not like that piece of slate they found at Tintagel, is it?'

In the summer of 1998 archaeologists had found a slate at Tintagel in Cornwall with an inscription on it that included the name 'Artognov'. The more credulous pretended that this was another way of spelling Arthur and that it was proof he had lived there. It wasn't, of course.

'And, if you've found the Grail, I'm going to have to say no. Even I have my standards.'

'But you're a journalist. What's your problem with the Grail? I know you never used to believe in God, but—'

'It's nothing to do with religion, it's to do with the fact that the Holy Grail as a chalice containing the blood of Christ is an invention of the Middle Ages. In the original stories the Grail was a horn of plenty or a big stone. And as for that Joseph of Arimathea shit—'

'Hey, okay, Nick – it's only history, you know. People like those stories.'

'Sorry. I'm old-fashioned. Way I was taught my history, you can't know where you're going unless you know where you've been.'

'So?'

'So if you invent the past you're distorting where you've been.'

'Nick, who cares about the past, about what really happened? It's a pageant. People don't want detail, they want colour, drama, gory deaths and big love stories. Who cares if Richard the Lionheart was a lousy king and Bad King John was the good guy? Who cares if Richard III's successors painted the hump onto his portraits and framed him for the death of the Princes in the Tower?'

'Or that King Arthur was no medieval King in a turreted castle jousting his days away but a sixth-century pig stealer and would-be rapist who was at most a petty tyrant?' I said. 'I care. I care that nationalism gets based on such bad history.'

'Nick, please. It would be so good to have you here. And you can tell the story as you see it. But when you see what we have you'll realise there's no need to lie or exaggerate.'

Her voice had gone low and breathy. If I'd had any sense I would have been cautious – she'd given me a real emotional mauling the last time around – but my motto is: once bitten, twice bitten.

As if reading my thoughts, she said: 'Nick, I gave you a

hard time all those years ago. I was callow. I didn't realise how vulnerable you were after your father's death.' She was almost breathing the words into my ear. 'I'm sorry. I'd like to try to make it up to you.'

I moved the phone away from my mouth so that I could gulp unheard.

'Where would I stay?'

'On site.' She paused. 'I live in the gatehouse.'

'The one your parents had?'

'That's the one. They moved to Australia years ago.'

So Wynn House was the big house I'd glimpsed through the trees when I'd gone to visit Faye that summer.

'Nick, it would be really great to have you here. This isn't an easy time for me.'

So I agreed. To be honest, aside from my feelings for Faye, I couldn't afford not to. Since Bridget and I had come from South America where I'd been covering the Rock Against Drugs Tour I'd found the freelance life increasingly difficult. Newspapers go through upheavals every so often where they get in new young editors who naturally enough want to bring in their own people – their own young people.

I never imagined I'd be over the hill in my mid-thirties, but that's how I was feeling. To pay the mortgage on my bijou residence I'd taken a job with an Internet company. They handled hundreds of acclaimed sites and my job was to write copy for them. I was the oldest there by a good five years.

Hack work, but at least I could walk to work – the office was just across the other side of Shepherd's Bush Green. And, of course, given that it was the Internet's Brave New World it wasn't essential that I go into the office. I could e-mail copy from home.

But the work was depressing me. It was so banal. When Faye phoned I was trying to find something interesting to say about a site devoted to looking after your teeth. I'd got as far as the headline: Dentally Does It. Well, yes, I did think that was good.

I'd got another site to write about that day. On the Celebs Solve It site E list celebrities dealt with 'gritty human dramas' sent in by members of the public. The latest was: What do you tell your daughter when she wants to have her tummy button pierced? As I said, gritty.

After three months of this introduction to the future I couldn't wait to go back into the past.

I started packing that night. When I phoned Bridget she laughed.

'I'm not sure what the accepted waiting time is before getting your leg over a grieving widow but I think two weeks is probably at the lower end of the scale. You're still stuck on her?'

'We ended badly,' I said quietly.

I'd told Faye about my infidelity. I felt it important to come clean – perhaps in the hope that it would spur her to be more amenable herself. Well, it had worked for Jude the Obscure. I remember I told her on my birthday. It was Friday the thirteenth. That should have warned me. She went nuts – excuse the technical term. That's when she tore the dress in half with her teeth.

We'd lost touch after university. I remember meeting for a drink in London a couple of times. She was working near Blackfriars, so we met in that Arts and Crafts pub that had been done out with gold foil like the interior of a basilica and with frescoes of friars and monks.

'Hello? Anyone home?'

Bridget's voice brought me back into the present.

'Sorry, miles away,' I said. 'What did you say?'

'We can travel down together.'

'I don't think I'm supposed to take anybody.'

'I've been invited too, you pillock. By Rex.'

'He wants you to work for them too?'

'Darling, *you're* the hired help. *I'm* a friend. I've seen Rex and Gennie a bit in London. So at Askwith's funeral I chatted him up for an invitation.'

'You talk about me behaving inappropriately with the

25

widow and you got off with Rex at the funeral! That's rich.'

'*He's* rich, darling. I think I could get used to his lifestyle – remember *Brideshead Revisited*?'

'The house isn't that big. How does this house party thing work exactly? Do I wear plus fours? H.G. Wells used to go to these big houses and have sex with anything that moved. Do we do our own thing?'

'I'm going to do Rex if I get a chance. Don't understand how I missed him before.'

That Friday, Bridget came over to Shepherd's Bush just after lunch for our drive out to the West Country. When I opened my door to her my jaw dropped. As did hers.

'What do you think you look like?' we both said simultaneously.

She was wearing court shoes, a pleated tartan skirt, pink cashmere twin set and, yes, pearls. Not to mention a Hermès scarf hiding her hair and knotted under her chin. She only needed a couple of dogs and a shooting stick to complete the ensemble.

'What are you trying to do?' I said, ushering her in.

'You can talk,' she said. 'Since when did you start wearing blue blazers, cavalry twill and cravats?'

I touched the cravat at my neck. 'I've had this for years. And cavalry twill is very hard wearing.'

I wasn't quite aping the nobs. I'd always liked the idea of a cravat, and in fact I'd got the idea from a young cockney drug dealer who looked like Leslie Howard and always wore cravats and cashmere sweaters.

I'd been on a bit of a shopping expedition for this trip. I'd drawn the line at the brightly striped City shirt worn without a tie and the highly polished leather loafers worn with neatly pressed denims. Even I have my standards. But when I came to look at them, these blazers – double-breasted, two lines of metal buttons – were quite stylish.

'Yeah, yeah,' Bridget jeered.

'But Bridget, this isn't your style. Why?'

'I'm trying to blend in.'

'With whom? Sloanes? If Rex likes you it's for who you are, not who he wants you to be. He's a man, not a woman.'

'What does that mean?'

'You know – women get a man then want to change him even though they risk losing the qualities that drew them to him in the first place. Men just accept the woman they've got.'

'Which magazine did you get that particularly insightful piece of information from?'

'I do have ideas of my own, you know.'

She looked at me.

'*GQ*. But my point is, you should just be yourself. If he doesn't want you as yourself then he's not worth it.'

'He's worth £16 million.'

'Have you got a spare headscarf?'

My plan was to drive down through Chiswick and on to the M4, but when we got there Chiswick roundabout was backed up to the High Street.

'I always think of traffic jams as an aid to contemplation,' I remarked cheerily to Bridget. 'The still moment in the rush of city life.'

Bridget peered at me. 'Hope you're not breathalysed.'

'You know I'm not drinking at the moment. I'm serious. It's an opportunity to see the familiar for the first time. To look properly at buildings that you barely registered when you were passing at speed.'

'After all, you've missed your meeting, your career is in ruins – what else is there to do? So I suppose Madonna's given up drink too, has she?'

'Bridget, I was doing this yoga long before Madonna took it up. I've stopped drinking because I'm about to start the second series and I need to purify my system.'

The yoga is split into six levels of difficulty. Most people are happy to stay on the first level, known as the Primary Series, but I'd finally, after about six years, got the hang of it enough to go on to the second series. To do it properly I'd decided to give up alcohol and be very sure I ate only organic food. It made me a pretty exciting date, but since I hadn't been dating lately it didn't matter.

I surveyed the traffic ahead. There was the obligatory taxi driver wedged across two lanes, thanking his passengers for not smoking whilst polluting the air with his mundane hatreds, holding down his bile beneath a lifeless bonhomie.

The traffic began to move. Before long we were heading west down the M4. It was still raining. It had been raining pretty solidly for weeks and there was flooding in Lincolnshire, East Anglia and parts of Somerset, where we were headed.

There was also a hint of flooding inside the car.

'How's work?' I said to Bridget, to distract her from the rainwater dripping through the canvas roof above our heads. Her latest job was as part of an editorial team charged with repositioning an Old Fogey newspaper. The editor-in-chief and editor were two of those people who were failing upwards – they would be headhunted for a newspaper, fail to reverse its decline, get fired, get hired by the next newspaper.

This paper's circulation had been sliding, so the new editorial team decided to make a brash appeal to the youth market – just as every desperate newspaper had been doing for twenty-five years. The paper launched a campaign to legalise cannabis. Teenage models were signed up as columnists. Political pundits put pop lyrics into their columns. Bridget's first splash was a double-page spread on a gay wedding in Timbuktu. Within weeks, the circulation was in free fall.

The problem was the usual one. The editors were ignoring demographics. There were more old people than ever, they were living longer and the grey pound was more important as each year went by, but still they chose to target young people.

But Bridget was happy there. The expenses were good and it did still have those links to the toffs. I thought she had been joking when she'd said she could meet some blue blood and get married, then put her feet up for the rest of her life. Apparently not.

'As it is, Rex says I can stay as long as I like, so I've taken some leave,' she said airily.

'But Bridget, you hate the country. Remember when you visited me in Sussex when I was down for that Aleister Crowley story – you couldn't wait to get back home.'

'Nick, there's the country and there's the country. I don't anticipate spending much time on Rex's allotment, you know.'

'No, you'll be in his theme park. If he's worth £16 million, why does he want to go ahead with this scheme?'

'Sixteen million doesn't go very far these days. Wouldn't get him into the five hundred richest people list.'

'I can't believe you just said that. I mean, I know you like spending, but even you can't imagine getting through £16 million in your lifetime.' I glanced at her. 'Can you?'

She winked. After a few more minutes she yawned and said: 'He seems keen on this King Arthur stuff. History – yech. I suppose you've been swotting up.'

'I've done a bit of reading,' I said.

'You'd better fill me in. All I know is Arthur became king by pulling a sword out of a stone although he also got one from some bint who lived in a lake. One or other of these swords was called Excalibur. He formed the Round Table at which all knights were equal, except he always had the last word. Marries Guinevere and they live happily in Camelot until Lancelot turns up, shags Guinevere, then all the knights go off looking for the Holy Grail. I forget the rest.'

'You've got the main lineaments of the story—'

'*Lineaments*? I say, thanks awfully.'

'But you missed out that at the start Arthur is born in Tintagel Castle, Cornwall, the son of Uther Pendragon. Whilst Guinevere is having an affair with Lancelot, Arthur sleeps with his sister Morgan le Fay and they have a son, Mordred. Later Mordred challenges his father's power.

29

Arthur kills him then, mortally wounded himself, is carried off to Avalon, a magical underworld from where he will return when his country needs him.'

'Hang on – he sleeps with his sister?'

'She's his sister in some versions. In earlier stories Mordred kidnaps and rapes Guinevere – his mother, see. Classic Oedipal stuff.'

'And all this is based on fact?'

'Hardly. Geoffrey of Monmouth made most of it up in the twelfth century in his *History of the Kings of Britain*. Medieval French and German Romance writers took his epic story and embellished it – they changed the name of Arthur's sword from Caliburnus to Excalibur. They did without his lance altogether. That was called Ron.'

'I can understand that. But there was a real King Arthur?'

'There is some early written evidence for a historical Arthur, yes.'

'*There is some early evidence for a historical Arthur, yes.* I'm hearing my friend turning into a pedant before my very eyes.'

'I think you mean before your very *ears*. Do you want to hear this stuff or not?'

She scowled.

'No, but if I'm to impress Rex I'd better.'

'Why is it women always feel obliged to pretend an interest in a man's interests – at least until they've got him?'

'Nothing like a good generalisation about women, is there? I don't know why – except that in this case the answer is £16 million. Now tell me more, prof.'

'If Arthur did exist it was as a British war leader, living somewhere between AD450 and 520, fighting against the Saxons when the Romans abandoned Britain. The Britons won a breathing space in about AD500 by winning a major battle at Mons Badonicus. Arthur may have been the British leader. Then again he may not have been – a historian writing only forty years after the event doesn't mention him at all.'

30

'But why could this theme park be such a money-spinner?'

'The Arthur industry is big business, that's why. I've been checking. There are over sixty books about him in print at the moment. Hollywood films the story every so often. Not bad for a pig-stealing petty tyrant who murdered his own son.'

'Where do you get that from?' Bridget said, stifling a yawn.

'You look at the Arthur in the early Welsh poems and in eleventh-century saints' lives – he's very different. There's a reference to Arthur's two sons, one of whom, like Mordred, he kills. In one poem Arthur spends all his time trying to steal a pig. In one hagiography he's a "certain tyrant from foreign parts" who tries to steal a bishop's tunic. In another he has to be dissuaded by his men from raping a girl they're supposed to be rescuing from her abductor.'

We were almost at Swindon. The traffic on the motorway was heavy and I was getting fed up having the car deluged every time a lorry went through a puddle. I suggested we divert off down the A4361 through Avebury.

'I've always liked the henge here,' I said.

'Of course you have, dear,' Bridget said with a laugh. 'What the fuck is a henge?'

'A stone circle. You know, like Stone-henge? This one's about four and a half thousand years old but, as usual, nobody knows why it was built. It's very atmospheric because the village is within one of the circles – there are two circles and also long processions spread over twenty-eight acres. In fact, most of the houses are built from stones taken from the circle and broken up a couple of centuries ago.'

We passed a sign saying WELCOME TO CROP CIRCLE COUNTRY and within a few miles the road ran through the outer bank of the Avebury stone circle. I pointed out through the heavy rain the large standing stones to left and right as we drove through. Bridget shrugged. I pulled into the car park of the old pub, almost in the centre of the stone circle, and we made a dash for the entrance.

The pub was pretty much deserted inside. Classical music was playing on the sound system. The walls were covered with photos of crop circles. We took our drinks over to a glass-topped table. It was actually the glass cap on an ancient well, some six hundred feet deep. The pub had run electric cables down to the water and set up a light there so you could see the old walls, lichen and moss growing from them, and the black water below.

A notice on the glass top stated this was the old village well and that many villagers had been toppled to their deaths in here for misbehaviour of various sorts.

'Seems a bit short-sighted,' Bridget said. 'What did they drink once the bodies started putrefying?'

'It's more theme park history,' I said sourly. 'Lowest common denominator stuff. Got to make it exciting for the family.'

I looked through the window.

'Fancy going to look at the stone circles?'

Bridget glanced at the rain falling in thick sheaves.

'Very funny,' she said.

'Do you?'

'Are you off your trolley? It's pissing down.'

'I've got waterproofs.'

'And a rubber sheet too, I hope. Nevertheless, no. You go if you want. I'll stay here listening to this rubbish.'

'It's Erik Satie. It's beautiful.'

'It's classical music, isn't it? Enough said.'

'I've got two lots of waterproofs in the boot.'

'Do the words "Fuck" and "off" mean anything to you? You want me to tramp across the fields in this weather to look at big lumps of stone? I think not.'

So I tramped off on my own. I walked across the road and wandered among the stones. It was very soggy, parts were almost under water and pools of water lay in the ditches. I climbed up the bank on the south side for a look at Silbury Hill rising out of the flat landscape in the near distance. The inverted pudding basin is man-made, but nobody knows why. It looked today to be rising out of the sea, for the fields around it had flooded.

On top of the hill, where until the nineteenth century they still held Mayday dances and cricket was once played, I could see tents and large groups of people. Followers of the Wiltshire Messiah, no doubt.

I walked to the outer edge of the bank and glanced down into the field below. You know that scene in *Zulu Dawn* where the British are looking for the Zulu but can't find them? Actually, you probably don't, but I'll tell you anyway. Then they come to the top of a hill and find them swarming like insects around a water hole just below them.

Well, spread below me for as far as the eye could see (which because of the mist, I have to admit, wasn't very far) were tents and tepees and yerts – I think that's what those Afghan things are called – hundred and hundreds of them.

At least these people didn't chase me with their assegai. I came down off the top and walked back to the pub, the rain rolling off my waterproofs. I figured Bridget would be happily getting into her next triple vodka so I diverted off to look at the church. I remembered reading it had a really nice rood screen and I wanted to see it – mostly because I didn't actually know what a rood screen was.

'A rude screen?' Bridget said when I told her what had delayed me. 'Did it insult you in some way?'

'Rood. It's a—'

'Save it. I really don't want to know. And then you spent twenty minutes looking at gravestones.'

'I thought maybe we could have a quick look at the West Kennett long barrow – it's just beyond Silbury Hill. It's one of the most impressive Neolithic burial chambers around.'

'Fascinating. Gravestones in a churchyard; burial chambers. Nick, why do you like this stuff?'

33

'The dead are much more interesting than most live people.'

'I don't want to know about your sex life.' She thought for a moment. 'I used to know a necrophiliac.'

'Was that when you were going through your Young Conservative phase?'

'Cheap. You know very well the one thing the Tories have always known how to do is fuck ordinary people good and proper. He was an actor, actually. Could only do it if you didn't move.'

'Well, unless you were dead, of course.'

'He wished I was dead by the time I'd finished with him.'

She peered down the well, lost in thought.

'That must have been difficult for you – the not-moving, I mean.'

'How do you know I move around when I shag? For all you know – and ever will know – I might be totally passive.'

'You, passive – the only time I can imagine you passive is if you pass out.'

The weird thing was I'd been thinking of Bridget in that way lately. Not passed out, sexually, I mean. Hearing her whingeing about all the men who treated her badly or were selfish in bed made me want to show her how nice it could be. The problem was I wasn't the right person to show her. As she was forever reminding me – based solely on the say-so of one old girlfriend – I wasn't much cop in bed. I took the waiting out of wanting.

'Do you want another drink?'

'What, here? No thanks. This fucking pub can't play decent music. You got a problem, dikko?'

She was looking beyond me. I turned to where two New Age caricatures were standing in hobnailed boots, worn cargo trousers and heavy jackets, their long hair drawn back and faces adorned with a lot of metal.

'Wondered if you might be heading Glastonbury way. And if so if you might give us a lift.'

'My car's only a two-seater,' I said. 'Sorry.'

'It's very important and we've got no other means of getting there.'

Bridget has never been what you'd call a hippy. She likes her creature comforts – she's the only person I know who took a matched set of Louis Vuitton luggage down the Amazon – but, bless her, she did try to engage them in conversation.

'On your holidays, are you?' she said.

The one with the ginger beard stared at her. The one with the rings through his lips shook his head.

'Crop circles,' he lisped. He had a ring in his tongue too.

'Bit early, isn't it?' I said, glancing out at the sodden fields.

'We came for the millennium and stayed,' he explained.

'So do you make them or worship them?' I said.

The one with the beard and fierce eyes almost snarled.

'Nobody makes them,' he said, 'except a higher power.'

I saw Bridget roll her eyes.

'What's in Glastonbury for you?'

'We heard there was to be a discovery,' said the lisper. 'Maybe the Grail.'

The guy with the beard and fierce eyes dug him in the ribs.

'Well, I'm sorry we can't help.'

There was a narrow bench seat in the back of the Karmann Ghia but Bridget had colonised that for some – just some, mind – of her luggage. It had taken an age to get all her stuff in the car. When I complained that the boot was already full of her luggage and I couldn't get the rest in, she replied with endearing ignorance, 'Can't you use a roof rack?'

'Bridget, it's a soft top.'

'So?'

Endearing is not, by the way, a word I would dare use of her in her hearing.

When we set off again, the rain was bouncing high off the road. Having seen the cars ahead aquaplaning, I crawled along. The rain had lessened by the time we reached

Midsomer Norton. We drove on to Ilchester. From there it was only ten minutes by various small roads to Montacute.

There was a hairy moment when I thought we weren't going to be able to get through a ford. Soon after we passed a familiar-looking gatehouse and drove up a winding drive to the front of a Tudor manor house.

I leaned forward to look past Bridget at the façade.

'Nice crenellations,' I said.

'Saucy,' she said, pushing up her bosoms. I gave her a quick look.

'Have you been watching *Carry On* films again?'

I was expecting a butler, but a young woman in a pair of jeans and a rollneck jumper answered the door.

'Rex and Genevra are both out,' she said in an East Coast American accent. 'I'm Mara. Rex's secretary.'

'Is Faye around?'

'I think she's over to Glastonbury right now. Lord Williamson is here somewhere.'

'Who else is coming down?' I said, trying to hide my surprise that the Labour Lord who had been the guest of honour at the college dinner was another of the guests.

'You're about it,' Mara said with a shrug. 'So okay, let me show you your rooms.'

We reached Bridget's first. There were fresh flowers and a bottle of champagne in a bucket on a side table.

'You want to walk round the grounds?' I asked her as she went in.

She didn't answer straight away. She dropped her bag – don't worry, the Travel Diva had left the rest for me to bring up – hooked up the bottle of champagne and a glass in one hand and headed for the en suite bathroom.

'What I fancy is a long soak in the bath with a packet of fags and this bottle. See you later.'

Mara pulled the door to and continued her walk down the corridor.

'Crazy lady,' she said, shaking her head.

'You don't know the half of it,' I said. 'See you later.'

Mara shook her head. 'I'm on vacation as of this afternoon. Enjoy your stay.'

My room was at the far end of the corridor with a view over the flooded fields to the north. I could see the remains of a small motte and bailey castle by a river some three hundred yards away at the bottom of the sloping lawn. There was a landing stage about twenty yards to the right of it and a chapel actually set in the side of the motte. From the house I could just see its squat tower. A hundred yards or so to the left of the chapel was a boathouse.

The river wound across meadowland. It had flooded its banks and formed a lake some two hundred yards across. I half expected an animatronic Lady of the Lake to stick her arm out of the water and wave a greeting.

Instead I saw a surreal sight. Around twenty swans were floating on the meadow, sleeping, dipping their heads into the water, crying harshly to each other. Some of them glided quietly between cows and horses, which were nibbling grass on the patches of higher ground, up to their forelocks in water.

I noticed a boat with something lying in it drift out from behind the motte, moved by the river's slow current.

There were piles of wellingtons and a sheaf of umbrellas by the front door. I found a pair of wellingtons that fit me and squelched across the grass towards the landing stage. The rowing boat, without its oars, nudged the jetty and stopped there.

I was curious to know what was in the boat. I made my way over to the jetty, lifting my knees high with each step, sinking almost to the tops of the wellingtons in the quagmire. I hoisted myself onto the jetty and looked down towards the chapel. I thought I had seen something move. The boat's oars were on a low knoll.

I looked into the boat. A woman lay there, her eyes closed, her hands folded neatly across her stomach. She was in jeans and a waxed jacket. She could have been sleeping but I had the certain feeling she was dead.

37

Chapter Three

I looked back towards the house. Faye, in waxed jacket and wellingtons, was making her way across the swampy lawn towards me. I looked beyond her and thought I could see a tall figure standing at the French windows leading out of the drawing room. I had an indistinct impression of a long white face peering down at me.

Faye raised her hand in a little wave as I walked towards her. She was about to call something when she saw my solemn face.

'We need to get an ambulance and the police.'

She looked beyond me.

'Is somebody injured?'

'I think she's dead but I can't be sure.'

'You go to the phone,' she said. 'I'll check. I know first aid.'

She strode past me.

I used the phone in the hallway then hurried back outside. Faye, her back to the house, was leaning over the woman in the boat. She straightened and turned as I squelched close. Her mouth was tight. She slipped her hands into the pockets of her jacket and took a step towards me.

'Dead?' I said.

She nodded.

'Do you recognise her?'

'Oh yes,' she said, glancing back over her shoulder for a moment.

'And? Who is she?'

'Lucy Newton. She is . . . *was* the archaeologist for the project.'

'Ah,' I said.

'She's the one who made our discovery.'

'How long has she been working here?'

'About a year.' She looked at me. 'Why?'

'It must be awful for you seeing her dead when you've got to know her so well. Especially after . . .' My voice trailed away.

'She was a scheming little bitch,' Faye said. 'Rex was planning to get rid of her. She was obsessed with him. But he'd done with her anyway.'

'Done with her?'

'Rex puts it about a bit. Noblesse oblige and all that. He's diddled everybody round here so he's had to start shipping them in.'

I realised she was referring to Bridget.

'Bridget can look after herself,' I said quickly. 'And did you say *everybody*?'

She smiled thinly and pointed to the raised bank below the motte.

'The oars are down there.'

'I know, I saw them. I suppose we'd better leave them for the police to look at,' I said.

'You mean they're clues? You think Lucy was murdered?'

'It's the kind of thing I've come across from time to time.'

She looked up at the sky and shook her head.

'That's just what we need.'

It was dark by the time the police had finished. They took statements from Faye and me and arranged for any other people in the house to give statements the next day. Everyone else seemed to be out, even Bridget, who I'd thought was in the bath.

I was surprised by Faye's harshness but I put it down to grief at the death of Askwith. I sat with her in the drawing room whilst she paced it in a proprietorial sort of way.

40

'So you've known Rex and Genevra since childhood?' I
said.

'Sort of. Their father didn't let them mix with anyone else
round here. They were sent off to school when they were
four or five. But when they were teenagers I got to know
them a little better.'

'When Rex was diddling everything in sight?' I said, and
immediately regretted it. Faye looked at me but said
nothing.

'Rex and my b-brother got to know each other at Oxford.
They were in the same social group.'

'Askwith too?'

'No, he wasn't part of that set.' She looked down.
'Occasionally on the fringes.'

We heard the doorbell chime.

'We lost contact over the years, but then when Rex
inherited the title he started spending more time down here
and we saw him quite a lot. That was mostly at weekends
until he decided to turn some of the outbuildings into a
conference centre or artists' studio kind of place. Then he
was down more often – he had to do a lot of work –
inventorying and one thing and another. And that's when
they discovered – well, I'll let him tell you.'

I'd noticed her hesitation when she'd referred to her
brother.

'How is Ralph?' I said.

'*Rafe*,' she said automatically. Before she could say more,
Mara knocked and entered the room.

'There's a King Uther Pendragon to see Lord Wynn. I
didn't know whether you might wish to see him. He doesn't
have an appointment.'

Faye looked at me.

'Word's got out about us. He's the third one this month if
it's not one of the others coming back.' She turned to the au
pair. 'Is he the short fat one with the long red beard and an
Excalibur almost as long as himself, or the large bald-
headed gentleman with the stutter?'

'Neither. D'you wanna see him?'

'This isn't a very good time, Mara. Suggest that he phone and make an appointment.'

'Sure, only he said he's come all the way from Asgard.'

'That makes him Odin, King of the Gods. Tell him he needs to brush up on his myths and legends.'

'I'll be going now too, by the way,' Mara said. Faye nodded.

When Mara went out there was a slight commotion in the hallway then Bridget and Genevra barged in. Bridget had on a waxed jacket and a pair of thick green socks.

'I walked into the village and bumped into Genevra,' she said. 'We've just walked back.' She looked at my expression. 'You have a problem with that?'

'The notion of you *walking*? *Anywhere*? No, no.'

She gestured back through the doorway.

'Who's your friend with the big sword who was going out as we came in?'

'Lucy's dead,' Faye said abruptly to Genevra. 'Rex needs to be told. Where is he?'

Bridget and I fell silent.

Genevra put her hand to her mouth and touched her scar. 'Lucy dead? How?'

'May have been a drug overdose,' I said. I described how I had found her.

'Suicide?' Genevra said. 'But why?'

I glanced at Bridget. She was mouthing, 'Who's Lucy?' at me.

'She was pretty keen on Rex, I understand,' I said.

'Killed herself for the love of my brother?' An odd expression crossed Genevra's face. 'I don't think so.' She walked over to the window and stood there for a moment, hugging herself.

'Who's Lucy?' Bridget said aloud.

Faye told her tonelessly. When she'd finished Genevra turned back to face us. 'I don't know where Rex is. We had lunch and then he got a call on his mobile and had to go

42

off.' She looked at her watch. 'Look, we've got drinks at seven. The others will be back. We can talk about what to do then. I'm going to get changed. I suggest you all do the same.'

She started to leave the room. As she passed me she paused to squeeze my arm lightly.

'Good to see you again, Nick.'

I didn't follow the others upstairs. Instead I went into the library. Something had been nagging at me about the way Lucy's body had lain in the boat. Formal, almost ritualistic. I found the book I was looking for and sat down in a wingback chair with it. It had a chapter list but no chapter details on the contents page, so I had to go through the thick work page by page, looking at the chapter headings to find what I was looking for. When I found it I began to read.

Everyone else was already gathered when I went in for drinks. I'd given up the cavalry twill and blazer and was wearing instead a rather fine Hugo Boss suit with a Fred Perry underneath. Rex, in rollneck and dark blue cords, was standing by the window looking earnest whilst a bony-faced man with thin grey hair plastered down on his scalp was talking insistently to him.

I looked round the room. Genevra saw me and waved me over to where Bridget, Faye and Lord Williamson were in conversation. I started over but Rex intercepted me.

'There you are, old stick. Please you could make it down and sorry I wasn't here to greet you. Sorry too about your bad experience. Come over and meet Neville.'

He took me over to the bony-faced man. He was about fifty with a military bearing. There was a tuft of whisker under his nose that he had missed whilst shaving. He wore another kind of uniform now, one that said Countryman: a drab green jacket, check shirt with a soft collar, a green knitted tie with a tiny half Windsor knot. His navy trousers were an inch too short, showing green socks. His sturdy brown shoes were highly polished.

'Neville's my estate manager. Been with the family for years. Great fellow. Don't know what I'd do without him. Nick here is a journalist, Neville.'

The look of distaste that crossed Neville's face suggested somebody had broken wind.

'A dirty job but somebody has to do it,' I said, grinning cheesily.

We were joined, not a moment too soon, by Faye, Genevra and a large man in roomy trousers and a V-neck cashmere sweater. He had an expensive haircut and smelt of some posh aftershave.

'And this man is my aide-de-camp in this project,' Rex said. 'Lancelot to my Arthur. A marketing genius – the man who wrote the paper on Britain as theme park, our heritage turned into an industry.'

'Who's Guinevere?' I said, watching Faye. She and Genevra exchanged glances.

'Well, the parallel isn't that exact,' Rex said, grinning.

The large man stuck his hand out.

'Buckhalter, name and nature.' He had a twangy American accent.

'Oh I see. As in . . .'

'As in the buck stops here, buddy. We don't make the money, my neck is on the block.' He looked around. 'And believe me, they got axes here can do the job. You can call me Buck.'

'That's your nickname, eh?'

He frowned.

'No, that's my first name.'

'Your name is Buck Buckhalter?'

'You have a problem with that?'

'Not at all, it just sounds like something out of fiction. You know, Milo Minderbender, Hubert Humpert.'

'Never heard of them. Buck is short for Buckminster. My parents were big Buckminster Fuller fans. I got off light actually. They loved the gardens of Capability Brown too.'

Lord Williamson joined us.

'Reggie Williamson,' he said, shaking my hand. He looked at me intently. 'I gather you're the one who found poor Elaine. Terrible thing. Sweet girl.'

'Elaine?' I thought her name was Lucy?'

'Lucy Elaine Newton,' he said. 'When I knew her she preferred to use her middle name.'

'She used to be Reggie's researcher,' Genevra said. 'When he was an MP, before he moved into the Lords and became a junior minister.'

'Damned good at it she was too. Hated to lose her.'

'What did she leave to do?'

'Work here, of course. Archaeology graduate, wanted to get back into it. Rex poached her. Brought her down here, told her what he was planning.' He shook his head sorrowfully. 'I was looking forward to seeing her today.'

We went into dinner soon after. I was seated between Genevra and Faye, directly opposite Rex.

'Buck did cutting edge stuff with nuclear power stations back in the States,' Rex said.

'Really?' I said. I hadn't taken to Buckhalter. He had a laugh that showed he had no sense of humour. He wanted to engage, knew he should be laughing, knew laughing was good, but laughed in the wrong places because he didn't know what was funny. An alien, in other words.

'I came over to do the same here but you limeys are a bit more cautious,' Buckhalter said.

'What did you propose?'

'I proposed we attack people's fear of radioactivity head on – you know, you familiarise people with something and they don't worry about it so much. They were willing to go so far but backed off the merchandising – glow-in-the-dark jackets and the like. They were nervous about the slogans too, said they might be misinterpreted.'

'What were they?' I said.

'*Nuclear power – it's a blast*, and *We can light up your life*.' He shook his head. 'So we moved on. But I like what I see here in Britain. You're just ripe for some serious marketing.'

'Buck's been working with the Wiltshire Messiah. Came up with his slogans.'

'I did a lot of work on him, then he ditched me, the ungrateful sonofabitch, But this heritage marketing, it has a lot of potential. You know the three golden rules of heritage marketing?'

'Location, location, location?'

'That's house-buying,' Faye said, smiling slightly.

'You got me then.'

'Don't give information, provide an emotional experience; stories, not histories; show, don't tell. You know, Britain is museum mad. A new museum is opening up almost every week. And they're meeting a demand too. Do you know how many millions of people visit open quotes historical close quotes destinations in Britain?'

'What do you mean by open historical close quotes?'

He looked puzzled.

'I mean I'm putting the word *historical* in quote marks.'

'I know *that*. I meant what constitutes historical?'

'Everything from a theme park to Tintag— Sorry, mustn't mention the T word, bad vibes. Everything from a theme park to an ancient monument.'

'So how many?'

'How many what?'

'How many millions of people?'

'Well, I don't carry those kind of figures around in my head, but it's a lot, I can tell you.'

There was silence for a moment. I'd been aware that Bridget had been getting restless – I suppose it was staring up at the ceiling and tapping her fingers on the table that was the giveaway.

'Nick tells me Arthur slept with his sister, Morgan the whatsit,' she suddenly said, to no one in particular. 'Incest – very modish. Plus you save on fares.'

I noticed Rex, Genevra and Faye all exchange swift glances.

'Morgan le Fay. The historian Geoffrey of Monmouth

named her as the ruler of Avalon,' Rex said. 'Chrétien de Troyes first identified her as Arthur's sister in his romance *Erec* in the middle of the twelfth century. Later stories had her stirring up trouble between Arthur and Guinevere and claiming she learned her magical powers from Merlin.'

There was another silence.

'Are you involved with the Avalon project?' I asked Lord Williamson. He put down his knife and fork and turned to me.

'I'm putting money in, yes. But I'm by no means the only investor. Rex and I are friends from way back. We were at university together.' He surveyed me. 'And you are going to be writing the book of the find.'

'Possibly – when someone tells me what exactly it is you've found.'

'Has Faye not told you yet?' Rex said.

'You told me not to, Rex – you wanted to show him yourself.'

'Of course. Look, why don't we give Nick the show after dinner. We need to check it works anyway for the conference on Monday. Bridget, you'll enjoy this too.'

'History?' How thrilling,' Bridget said, a lopsided expression on her face. I think she was trying to smile sweetly, but sweetly had been out of her repertoire for rather a long time.

After dinner Rex and Genevra led the way into another vast room. There were desks at one end and a conference area at the other. We sat at the conference table and looked towards a large screen on the wall before us. Buckhalter sat to one side in front of a computer. He began pressing keys.

'The audience for live arts and even the cinema in this country is outnumbered both by the audience for historical houses and for museums and galleries,' he said. 'There are almost two thousand buildings and ancient monuments open to the public. And that's not counting churches. It's a multi-million pound industry.

'But these days you've got to go one further. It's not enough to visit the past – people want to live in it. So here at Avalon Offshore Trust – we haven't got the name of the theme park itself yet – that's what we intend to give them.'

'If there's a Ye or a Yore in it – as in Days of Yore – I'll throw up,' I whispered to Bridget.

'Sssh,' she said, giving me an irate look, then directing her attempt at a sweet smile at Rex again.

'At our facility we intend to offer an authentic medieval experience.'

'Scrofula, leprosy, plague and high infant mortality?' I said.

'Not that authentic,' Genevra remarked mildly.

'Are you presenting Arthur as a genuine sixth-century war chief or as the Hollywood version?' I asked.

'Are you nuts?' Buckhalter's voice went up a register in disbelief. 'We give the people what they want. And they certainly want a Camelot they recognise – all that cloud-capped towers shit in Tennyson.'

'I think that was Shakespeare.'

'Huh?'

'The cloud-capped towers, the gorgeous palaces, the solemn temples, the great globe itself – it's from *The Tempest*.'

'Right, I meant the topless towers of Ilium.'

'That was Troy. Christopher Marlowe.'

'Okay, them dreaming spires then.'

'Oxford.'

Buckhalter reddened. Bridget dug me with her elbow.

'What's got into you?' she hissed in my ear.

I didn't know why I was feeling so peevish. Maybe because a girl had died and nobody seemed to care. Buckhalter turned to face me.

'Let me educate you here. We did some market research among tourists coming to Nottingham. Eighty-five per cent of them were disappointed that the castle wasn't the medieval one they'd seen in all the Robin Hood movies. We proposed the town pull down their existing castle – have you seen it? It's a pile of nineteenth-century shit – and build a medieval castle in its place.'

'A fake castle?'

'Give the people what they want. The city fathers didn't go for it. Philistines. Got no vision. Especially as they're at war up there and don't even realise it.'

'Kind of war?'

'There are about six different sites all competing to be known as Robin Hood country. They won't work together so they're tearing what could be a sweet scene apart. I suggested all the marketing guys should get together and settle it with an archery competition. Take turns at having an apple balanced on their heads to be shot off. The one that survived—'

'But surely that was William Tell?'

'Whatever – they got their crossbows.'

'Hang on, the Merry Men wouldn't have been seen dead with crossbows. The whole thing about Robin Hood and the Saxon against the Norman thing is environmental warriors versus environmental destroyers. Robin's men used long-bows because they were environmentally aware—'

'What about slaughtering the king's deer and using dye to make Lincoln Green and burning wood?' Genevra said, smiling. 'Doesn't sound too environmentally conscious.'

'Culling, vegetable dye and . . . okay, but two out of three ain't bad. They could make longbows without need-ing any industrial process. The Normans though were all early industrial process – a lot of smelting needed for chain mail, helmets and the metal bits of the crossbows.'

'Smelting?' Bridget said. 'Sounds like a sexual practice.'

'What's your point?' Genevra said to me.

'Well, nothing really. Just thought I'd be Barthian. You know, like the meaning of haircuts in the film Julius Caesar.'

'Barthian?' Bridget muttered. 'More like barking.'

'Can we keep to the text here?' Rex said, a hint of impatience in his voice.

'Sure, sorry. So what are you planning?'

Buckhalter tapped some more keys and an aerial shot of Wynn House came up on the screen. Triumphal music swelled from speakers on the floor.

'Here we go,' Buckhalter said. 'What we've got here is a computer model of the theme park.' As the different images came up, he talked on. And on.

'Look, Arthur is up for grabs,' he said. 'Nobody knows for sure where the real Arthur had his lands – in the west, in the north or in Wales. There are so many sites in Britain traditionally linked to him it's become a joke. But it means money. Tintagel is English Heritage's fifth most visited site. You get 150,000 people a year down there. You get a quarter of a million visiting Glastonbury, which sells itself as the real Avalon and the resting place of the Holy Grail.

'Here we are in Somerset, officially known as the "Land of Legend and Arthurian Adventure". But there's nothing drawing all this together. And that's where our theme park will come in. We need to come up with a name for it soon, by the way.'

'You're not using Camelot?' I said, surprised.

'Aside from the fact the name has links with a lottery provider, there already is a Camelot theme park up in the north. Totally different to what we have in mind but we want to avoid confusion.

'We have a three-phase development. Phase one you got the theme park centred round the castle we rebuild on top of the hill there and some rides linking that with the Grail Chapel. We'll have animatronics doing all kinds of shit and live actors doing their bit. There'll be jousting and sword fights and The Grail Experience. The Sword in the Stone test. And there'll be a cocktail bar.'

'A cocktail bar in the Middle Ages?'

'Yeah, well, we'll make sure it blends in. And a big banqueting hall called the Tuck Inn.'

'Friar Tuck's out of Robin Hood.'

'Whatever – it's all history, isn't it?'

'Not the way you describe it. What's Stage Two?'

'Stage Two, yeah. You ever see that old film *Westworld*?' I nodded. 'Remember how you could live whatever life you wanted? Well, we offer the medieval experience.'

'If I recall correctly, in *Westworld* the robots ran amok and killed everybody.'

'Hey, every innovative project has teething problems. Besides, that was just a movie. And we don't need to use robots – why use robots when you can use people? We get the people who come to stay to play the medieval parts. It's beautiful because then we've got them in character when the day tourists come and visit.'

'Won't the people staying here want a little medieval nooky?' Bridget said.

'Well, that's something we can look at for Stage Three: our specialist holiday.'

'You want to make it into a medieval brothel?' I said.

'Tell you the truth, we haven't finished Stage Three yet,' Rex said, with a warning glance at Buckhalter. 'We've also got a licence to have the Camelot Casino. We'll be trying that out in a week or so. That's when we plan to launch the project with a medieval banquet here.'

'He looked at me.

'So what do you think, Nick?'

'What do I think?' I pointed at Buckhalter. 'I think he's the Anti-Christ. It won't be long before the whole country becomes one big open-air museum: you just enter it when you get off the plane at Heathrow. Fucking heritage centres are destroying our past, not preserving it. They don't tell it how it was – that might be boring. They select the most exciting bits, blank out the unpalatable bits. Heritage is bogus history.'

'So what's wrong with that?' Buckhalter said, rising from his seat. 'Look, heritage places are not just a UK phenomenon. They're a worldwide one – Japan, the US. Know why I left the Wiltshire Messiah? He didn't have the vision to realise all the possibilities of his position. Lack of vision in the Son of God is quite a handicap, wouldn't you say?'

'What couldn't he see?'

'That he could spread His Word best by opening up a theme park.'

I snorted. Buckhalter ignored me. He was getting pretty messianic himself.

'Think of the rides you could have. Just riffing I could see the one about the Devil taking him up to a high place, offering him the world or pitching him down – that's a rollercoaster ride from Hell, baby! Twelve stages of the Cross – walk that Jesus walk!'

'It's grotesque,' I said.

'Grotesque? You know what the third most popular tourist attraction in the US is after the Disneylands in Florida and California? An inspirational theme park. All 2,300 acres of it. Check it out – Heritage USA, in Carolina. It's the centre of the Praise The Lord fundamentalist Christian television network, that's what. There's big money in religion.'

'Oh man oh man,' I groaned, looking to Bridget for support. She seemed unduly interested – even for her – in the bottom of her glass.

'Look,' Rex said, standing. 'I think it's time Nick and Bridget saw what is going to be the centrepiece of all this, what's going to make all this happen. Let's take them over to the chapel.'

I looked out of the window at the rain still falling.

'It's okay, Nick, there's a tunnel goes from the cellars right into the back of the church.'

As Rex led the way out of the room, Faye fell into step beside me.

'Nick, please stick around. I need this to work. Askwith sank all our money – my money – into it.'

'But this is the kind of thing I loathe,' I muttered.

'Wait till you see what Lucy found.'

'Yeah, and I don't see much grieving about her either.'

'You don't know the full story.'

'So tell me.'

'Later,' she said, as we progressed down a well-lit sloping corridor to a narrow Norman doorway. We all grouped together as Rex inserted a large key into the lock.

We entered a small chapel, very simple, smelling badly of damp. Rex led the way to a much shorter, narrower door behind the altar. This had modern locks and bolts on it.

When he had released the locks, he ushered us down a short flight of stairs into a well-lit crypt. A jumble of coffins lay around us.

'Okay,' Rex said, his voice reverberating oddly in the confined space. 'We'd decided to have the theme park and we knew we were going to have the Grail Quest adventure. Where better for the Grail chapel than a genuine old Norman chapel? Better still – its crypt. Lucy, God rest her, was to catalogue whose remains were in here. That hasn't been done for two hundred years – since Victorian days we've been burying kith and kin in the family crypt in the village church. This one is too near the river. We've done a lot of work on the outside recently because it used to flood all the time.'

He walked over to a black marble sarcophagus. It's lid had been propped up against the wall and a sheet of glass fitted in its place.

'And what does she find here?'

Rex's eyes glittered with excitement as he turned to me. I shrugged.

'The tomb of King Arthur and Queen Guinevere.'

Chapter Four

'Yeah, yeah,' I said, looking round at the ring of faces all watching me keenly. 'Pull the other one.'

'Hey, I thought this guy was supposed to be working with us here?' Buckhalter said to Rex. Rex gestured for him to be quiet.

I looked down into the sarcophagus. Lights had been rigged up at either end of it to illuminate the collection of white and discoloured bones. Little attempt had been made to sort the bones. There were two skulls, one pelvic girdle, one very long shin bone. Other bones and fragments of bone lay jumbled together.

'It's true, Nick,' Faye said.

'How come they're buried here?' Bridget said, puzzled. 'This place really was Camelot, then?'

'There was no Camelot, here or anywhere,' I said. 'And this sarcophagus is medieval. No way would a sixth-century warlord have been buried in a marble tomb – he'd be put in a long barrow somewhere.'

'It's the sarcophagus from Glastonbury Abbey,' Faye added patiently. 'The one that used to sit in the quire.'

'Again?' I said.

'Wynn's ancestors nicked it at the dissolution of the abbey. Lucy tracked it down in the Wynn family records. The abbey was dissolved in 1539 and everything was sold off or stolen. I guess Rex's ancestor either wanted the remains of Arthur and Guinevere or wanted to use the marble tomb for his own family.'

I must have been looking blank, although I was actually trying to dredge up my history.

'Don't you remember?' Rex said. 'The monks at the abbey stumbled upon Arthur and Guinevere's bodies in 1191 when they were doing some digging near the Lady Chapel. There was a lead cross identifying them, although Guinevere – spelt Wenneveria – was referred to as his second wife. We don't know when the lead cross was separated from the tomb but we know it was in the possession of a Chancellor Hughes of Wells in the 1830s. It hasn't been heard of since.'

'Hang on,' Bridget said indignantly. 'Back up a bit. I've never heard anything about Arthur and Guinevere's bodies being found. How come there's all this stuff about whether Arthur existed if everyone knew where he was buried? And how come everyone seems to have forgotten it since?'

'I vaguely remember this,' I said, scratching my head.

'The two sites – where they first found the remains and where they were removed to – are marked by signs in the ruins of Glastonbury Abbey,' Rex said. 'Their remains were removed in the presence of King Edward I and Queen Eleanor to a black marble tomb inside the abbey in 1278. On 19 April, to be precise. The tomb remained there until the dissolution of the abbey in 1539. Nobody knew what happened to it after that. Until now.'

'So why do we get all this old bollocks about whether he really existed?' Bridget said.

Rex shrugged.

'How do you know it's really the sarcophagus purporting to contain Arthur and Guinevere's remains?' I said. 'Or that these aren't the bones of someone in your family?'

Rex's smile looked a little forced. 'Look at the lid. *The Red Book of Bath* reported in the fifteenth century that the monks wrote an inscription on it.'

I walked across to the lid. There was a light directly overhead and I could clearly see the incised letters in the pitted black marble. I read out the inscription.

'*Hic iacet Arthurus, rex quondam, rex futurus.*' I looked at

Bridget. 'Here lies Arthur, the once and future king.'

'So is this King Arthur or not?' Bridget said.

'You bet,' Buckhalter said.

'That's the wrong question,' Rex, Faye and Genevra said, more or less together.

Rex continued: 'What we have here is a great story that deserves to be told. Right, Nick?'

I didn't say anything for a moment. Buckhalter scowled.

'Thought you were going to join us in our endeavour. You better get with the programme, buddy.'

'Has any attempt been made to date the bones?'

Rex waved airily. 'Carbon dating isn't accurate enough to tell us precisely whether these bones are sixth century. Lucy, God rest her, decided it wasn't worth it.'

'What's your problem, Madrid?' Buckhalter said.

'It makes no sense that Arthur and Guinevere would be buried in Glastonbury.'

'It does if Glastonbury was the ancient isle of Avalon, as is claimed,' Rex said.

'But it wasn't,' I said stubbornly.

'Prove it,' Rex said. He grinned and put an arm round my shoulders. 'That's why you're here, Nick. To write it as you find it. I don't want you to lie. And let me tell you something. Personally I don't much mind whether it's really Arthur and Guinevere or not. It's still a heck of a story and it will get a lot of customers through our gates.'

He looked at Bridget.

'Did you ever hear about the Cadbury dig back in the sixties?' She shook her head. 'Locals had been claiming for centuries that it was the site of Camelot. It was actually originally an Iron Age fort and certainly a very important site. A group of archaeologists wanted to excavate there but they needed funding. Now I'm not saying they deliberately misled would-be backers but they chose to call the dig the Camelot Excavation.

'Money poured in because people assumed that these chaps were going to dig up the Round Table. Needless to say

they didn't. They found no proof at all that the place had
been Camelot and I doubt they ever expected to. When the
excavation report finally came out – almost twenty-five
years later, in the nineties – I don't believe there was even a
mention of Camelot or King Arthur.'

We trooped back into the house. I was hoping to have a
talk with Faye – well, to be honest, more than a talk – but
she slipped away before I had a chance. Rex and Bridget
went into a small reception room for a nightcap. Genevra
and Buckhalter went their separate ways.

I wanted to know more about Lucy. In any case, I would
need to look at her papers for the story I was going to write. I
was impatient to get started. I assumed one of the desks in the
room we had visited earlier was hers. Tomorrow, I decided, I
would go into Glastonbury and check out the things Rex had
said about the tomb of Arthur and Guinevere.

I went to my room and pondered all that had happened
during the day. I'd brought the book from the library up to
bed. I read through the section I'd found again.

I slept late. By the time I'd done my yoga and showered it
was almost eleven. I went down to the library to return the
book and see what others they might have to help me with
the historical research about the tomb.

I found Bridget there.

'You're late up – how'd you sleep?' she said.

'Alone. How about you?'

She merely raised an eyebrow. She was sitting in a wingback leather chair, blowing smoke rings in the air, *Country
Life* open on her lap.

'Bridget, do you know your Holman Hunt?'

'Didn't know you were into rhyming slang,' she said
sleepily.

'It's not rhyming slang, you berk.'

'That is.'

'He's an artist – berk is rhyming slang?' I thought of the
possibilities: Turk? Perk? 'For what?'

'Berkshire Hunt, you Charlie.'

'Never knew that. Listen, there's no easy way to say this so I'll just say it.'

'I'm agog.'

'I think there may be a serial killer at large with a thing about King Arthur and/or Pre-Raphaelite paintings.'

Bridget burped, rather elegantly.

'Wouldn't mind some more fizz,' she said, stretching her left foot out then frowning. 'Need to re-do my toenails. What's Pre-Raphaelite?'

'It was a brotherhood of painters.'

'Wooftas?'

'No, just because it's a brotherhood doesn't make them gay. Men can just like each other, you know.'

'Okay, don't get nervous.'

'They shared a philosophy about painting. In the nineteenth century. And they painted a lot of pictures inspired by the Arthurian legends.'

'Do you think you could speed this up?' Bridget said, closing *Country Life*. 'I thought serial killers were defined by the fact they've killed more than one person – hence a series or serial. We have one unexplained death in a boat. Skip the middle bit and let's get to the nittyo-grittyo.'

'Holman Hunt was one of the Pre-Raphaelite painters, obsessed with realism. He once painted the Scapegoat of the Bible on site on the shores of the Dead Sea using a live goat tethered to a stake. The goat died of heatstroke but—'

'Nick—' Bridget warned.

'Well, he painted this picture, *Light of the World* – Jesus holding up a lantern in a gateway. It hangs in the chapel of my old college. It's the painting Fay's husband was found lying beneath.'

'Askwith. The accidental death.'

'Yeah, okay. But then I find this woman in the boat.'

'So?' Bridget was prowling round the room now, opening cupboards and cabinets. 'One of these must be a drinks cabinet,' she muttered.

'Another Pre-Raphaelite painting is of *The Fair Maid of Astolet*. She died for love of Lancelot. Of a broken heart.'

Bridget laughed.

'A man wrote about her, right? Maybe the feminists are right – instead of history maybe we should start writing her-story.'

'That's not the point.' I opened the book I'd found in the library. 'This is Malory's *Le Morte d'Arthur*. Book XVIII, chapters nineteen and twenty. The death of the Fair Maid of Astolet. Listen. "And so when she was dead the corpse and the bed all was led the next day unto the Thames and there a man, and the corpse, and all, were put into the Thames; and so the man steered the barget unto Westminster." '

'How touching,' Bridget said, stifling another yawn.

'The barge was covered with black samite, whatever that is, and she was "covered to her middle with many rich clothes and all was of cloth of gold." Astolet was actually Guildford, by the way.'

'You think this bint we found yesterday was meant to be the Astolet woman – what was her name?'

'Lucy Newton.'

'I mean the Astolet woman.'

'Elaine le Blank.'

'Elaine le Blank from Guildford.' Bridget rolled the name round her tongue. 'Sounds just like the woman my ex-husband ran off with.'

'The thing is, Williamson knew her as Elaine – I didn't know you were married.'

'Knew who as Elaine? Elaine le Blank? Well, he would, wouldn't he?'

'Lucy Newton. Knew Lucy Newton as Elaine. When were you married? And how come you've never mentioned it before?'

'The past is another country, as I'm fast discovering.'

'The past is another country – what does that mean?'

'Search me. I heard Rex say it yesterday. Thought it

sounded quite good. So let me get this straight. You think Lord Williamson is a serial killer? I know you don't like politicians, but even so, aren't you pushing it a bit?'

'I'm not saying it's him,' I said impatiently. 'I'm just thinking aloud.' I could see a putdown trembling on her lips so I hurried on. 'Listen, Tennyson wrote a poem—'

'That Sherpa bloke wrote poetry?'

'Not him. Alfred, Lord Tennyson. "Charge of the Light Brigade"? Long beard? So absent-minded his wife insisted he carry a piece of paper with his name and address on it when he went for a walk because he used to forget where he lived?'

Bridget shrugged. 'Vaguely.'

'Well, he wrote a poem about the Maid of Astolet except he called her the Lady of Shalott—'

'As in onions? Strange man.'

'Holman-Hunt, Waterhouse and, I think, others, all painted her – Waterhouse painted her in a boat. I think they bunged William Morris's wife Jane in a tin bath for the drowned effect. Hang on – no, that was Rosetti's mistress for Millais's *Ophelia*.'

'Nick!' Bridget warned.

'Anyway – you see the link.'

Bridget stopped and turned to me.

'Okay, I'm getting there. I've read these serial killer novels that sell for big money. The serial killer always has a high concept – the twelve apostles, the four horsemen of the Apocalypse, the seven dwarfs – no, strike that last one. So you're thinking, what – the Pre-Raphaelite Poisoner? The Camelot Killer? How'd the Arthurian lot die?'

'I need to check on that, but yes, it seems possible that there's someone out there just starting on a series.'

'And you want to include Askwith's death in this?'

I scratched my head.

'It seems too much like coincidence – but then again I can't see the significance of his death.'

'I'd better tell Rex.'

'Let's not.' I saw her expression. 'Hey, nothing against the guy, but I'd rather we kept this to ourselves until we have a bit more information.'

'We?'

'Well, you're going to help, aren't you?'

'I'm here to snare a husband, poppet. I'll leave the sleuthing to you.'

'But, Bridget, we're a team!'

'And I love you dearly. But as I've already told you, Rex is worth around £16 million and counting. I need to focus full time on the job in hand.'

I left Bridget a few minutes later and wandered gloomily down to the conference room, unable to believe that my feisty friend had turned into a gold-digger. It was empty except for Faye, who was sitting behind a desk looking in a drawer.

'Hi,' she said, standing and closing the drawer. 'Would you care for a walk in the ha-ha?'

'Sure,' I said, my gloom suddenly banished.

She walked round the desk.

'Although I could do with a laugh, we'd drown,' she said. 'It's flooded.'

Since I didn't actually know what a ha-ha was I couldn't make any comment on this. She came up to me.

'I'm going over to Glastonbury,' she said. 'Do you want to come?'

'Sure. But I need to look at Lucy's papers first.'

'Lucy's papers? Why?'

'I need her version of finding the sarcophagus – did she keep any kind of record?' Faye's eyes were on me. 'For the book,' I added. 'I want to get the immediacy of it. If she kept a diary that would be even better.'

'I have no idea if she kept a record. I don't know that she would have *needed* to write anything down. I think we assumed that you'd interview her.'

'I would have,' I said. There was a small silence. 'Did she have a desk here?'

Faye pointed back at the desk she'd just left. She flushed slightly.

'There. I was starting to sort through her stuff when you came in.'

'Perhaps I could do that?'

I found a box and emptied all the papers in the drawers into it.

'What about her room?' I said.

'Oh, she didn't live here at the house. But won't the police have all her stuff for their investigations?'

'Probably,' I said.

I nipped up to my room with the box and got dressed for going out. When I came out of the house Faye was sitting in one of a small fleet of four-wheel drives parked on the gravel.

'If you ever need to go anywhere,' she said as I climbed in beside her, 'use any one of these. The keys are usually left in the ignition.'

'Trusting.'

'Probably foolish,' she said with a smile, turning the vehicle and sweeping down the drive, past her house and into the road outside.

'I'd like to see your home again after all these years,' I said.

'I expect you will,' she responded casually, her eyes on the road ahead.

We were heading down on to the Somerset Levels when I plucked up the courage to ask her about Askwith.

'Do you mind if I ask about your late husband?'

'Depends what you want to ask,' she said cautiously. Did I see alarm flare in her eyes?

'Did he have any enemies? Anybody who might have wished him ill?'

She looked across at me quickly.

'That's a strange question since his death was accidental. He could be very abrasive but I don't think there was anyone who would have wished him harm. Why?'

'What happened that night?'

'Nick, you're not down here as some private detective investigating recent deaths, you're here to write an account of the rediscovery of Arthur and Guinevere's tomb.'

'Faye, I'm sorry. It's just I observed a couple of curious things that night. I hoped you might be able to shed light on them.'

She flared her nostrils. 'Well I can't. That's Glastonbury Tor over there. Where do you want me to drop you in the town?'

I looked out at the Tor. The fields around it were flooded. Approaching Glastonbury from this direction the Tor looked remarkably like an island, surrounded as it was by wide stretches of water. There was a sign at the roadside. 'Welcome to the Isle of Avalon.'

Faye guessed what I was thinking.

'Does look like it, doesn't it?' she murmured. 'Though at this time of year the countryside usually looks more like the Waste Land.'

'Do we have a Fisher King?'

She looked out of the window.

'Not any more.'

A storm was brewing when we came into Glastonbury. There had been a glimmer of sunshine but now the sun was smothered by the build-up of clouds. The streets took on an unreal appearance, bathed in yellowish light. The wind dropped. The town seemed to be holding its breath. Then, as we parked the vehicle and went our separate ways, the air stirred slightly and rain spilled from the swollen clouds.

Faye and I had arranged to meet in an hour in a nearby pub. I hurried down to the abbey, dodging puddles. Gutters overflowing, sheets of rain falling, bouncing high. Everything shiny, glistening, fluid brown. It was like a scene from an old gangster movie, listening for the hit car to round the bend and scythe the street with machine-gun fire. Instead, a bus drove by and fanned water from beneath its tyres across the pavement, drenching me.

64

The rain stopped almost as quickly as it had started. Shaking water off my overcoat, I walked up past the abbey shop and bought a ticket to see the impressive ruins. I expected to be alone in the grounds – the sky was lowering and there was a sharp wind blowing – but there were maybe twenty people scattered around the site.

By accident I fell into step with a tall Japanese man in a long brown overcoat. We smiled at each other. We parted when I stopped in front of a rectangular sign stuck in the earth and he went on towards the circular abbot's kitchen some two hundred yards away.

I was on the south side of the Lady Chapel. The sign read: 'Site of the ancient graveyard where in 1191 the monks dug to find the tombs of Arthur and Guinevere.'

I was pondering it when I became aware of someone standing close by. I turned. A tall old man with a bony face and a shock of white hair was staring at me. He was wearing an old tweed suit and carrying a gnarled stick, but I was immediately reminded of an Old Testament prophet. I stepped back as he raised his stick and jabbed it at the sky.

'The king will come on a white horse,' he shouted, fixing me with a wild, bloodshot eye. 'He will have a bow in his hand and a crown shall be given him by God so that he shall have power to compel the whole world! He will have a great sword in his hand and will strike many down.'

I nodded appreciatively.

'Thanks for sharing that,' I said, keeping an eye on his stick as I tried to step round him. He lowered the stick but blocked my way. His eyes boring into me, he spoke, quietly but fiercely:

'He will reign for a thousand years and the heavens will be opened up to his people. He will come in a garment white as snow, with white hair, and his throne will be as fire, and a thousand times a thousand and ten times a hundred thousand shall serve him, for he shall execute justice.'

65

I suppose I shouldn't have been surprised. Glastonbury is full of religious nutters of various persuasions. Half the sun worshippers who'd gone down to Cornwall for the 1999 eclipse had only made it back as far as here. I smiled cheerily at the old man and strode purposefully past him.

He called after me in a perfectly normal, very cultured voice: 'Couldn't spare the price of a pint, I suppose?'

He was standing slightly pigeon-toed, clutching his stick with both hands, a sheepish look on his face. I fumbled in my pocket and pressed a couple of quid into his open hand. His fingers were twisted with arthritis.

'Thank you kindly,' he said with a nod.

I nodded back, turned and walked away. He started to follow me. I increased my pace and went down to the abbot's kitchen. I went inside in the hope of shaking him off.

I was half expecting to see the Japanese man but the circular building – full of refectory tables and a mock-up of the old kitchen – was deserted. I lurked there for a couple of minutes then sneaked a look outside. There was no sign of the religious nut.

I walked back over to the ruins of the north transept. There was a bigger sign here headed: 'Site of King Arthur's Tomb'. It recounted how the bodies of Arthur and his wife were 'said to be found' in 1191 and how, as Rex had said, they had been put in the marble tomb and survived there until the dissolution of the abbey in 1539.

I wandered round the site for another half hour. There was something at once awesome and desolate about the jagged, incomplete walls of the huge abbey. And in the background, wherever I walked, I could see the old church tower pointing at the sky on the summit of the Tor, dominating the northern skyline.

Faye was already seated in the pub when I arrived. I'd been delayed looking in the windows of the various New Age shops that had blossomed in the town centre.

She didn't seem in the mood to talk. My heart sank at the thought that I'd blown it with my crass questions. We sat

66

side by side, sipping our drinks. I glanced at the side of her face. I was very conscious of her: the light down on her cheek, the curve of her cheekbone, the fullness of her lips. For her part, she was totally oblivious of me.

I was listening to her slightly unsteady breathing. I'm into breathing. Yes, I know, so is every living thing. But I mean that the yoga I'm interested in explores the power of different sorts of breathing. I hung out with some free divers once and saw how deep they could go on one lungful of air, doling it out very slowly because they'd lowered their heart-rate by breath control and didn't need to use as much.

My guriji in Mysore knew swamis who could bury themselves alive for a weekend or survive in cold temperatures in a pair of cotton pyjamas, thanks to the power of their breath. Why they should want to was, of course, another question.

Just at that moment, I wasn't thinking about those feats of endurance. I was thinking about a less lofty breathing trick. It's been proved – don't ask me to get technical with the proof which, frankly, will go straight over your head, just trust me on this – that you can seduce a person by matching your breath exactly to theirs. It's true. Breathe exactly in their rhythm and seduction is one hundred per cent guaranteed. Well okay, ninety-nine per cent.

'Why are you puffing like that?' Faye said, looking at me anxiously.

'Because you were,' I said absently. 'That's to say, it's special yoga breathing. I've taken up yoga since we last met. In a big way.'

'I know, Bridget was saying. Is it really true you inhale a washing line up your nose and pull it out of your bum then pull on either end to floss your entire inner body?'

'Not entirely, no. I tried to explain to Bridget about a purification rite I need to do over the next couple of days but you know her attention span – I think she's rather twisted what I said.'

'You always did have some strange habits,' she said.

I thought back, trying to imagine anything I used to do that could possibly match this distortion of a perfectly healthy and sensible yoga practice.

'Oh – that,' I said, blushing. 'That was just a phase.'

'Yes – that,' she said, pushing me lightly on the arm. She looked solemn. 'I'm pleased that you were able to come down. It's – it's—'

'You don't need to say it,' I said huskily. 'I feel the same.'

I leaned across and tilted her head towards me to go for a lip synch. Instead I got poked in the eye with a sticky-out bit on her large, dangly earring as she turned her head abruptly away.

'It's, er, great to see you,' I said heartily. She looked flustered.

'You too,' she said, 'though I was going to say it's enormously helpful.'

'Oh sure, that too,' I said quickly, nodding a lot. 'It's strange being together after all these years,' I burbled. 'Almost like old times.'

She smiled faintly.

'Almost,' she said.

'Faye, you know I still care for you an awful lot. I wondered—'

'It's too soon, Nick. Jonathan . . .' Her voice trailed off.

'I can wait,' I said.

After all, I thought, I've waited fifteen bloody years.

To be honest, I didn't know what I felt about Faye. I was thinking I wanted her in my life big time, but I didn't know how much of that was finishing off unfinished business. I was resentful that whilst she'd kept me in a state of frustration for two years she'd then gone off and married *Askwith*. Given the state of the adipose deceased – before he was deceased – my pride was hurt.

I know I hadn't my yoga-honed body back in those days – I'd looked a cross between a stick insect and a runner bean – but hey, in Woody's words, thin is fun.

As we left the pub Faye caught sight of something and her expression changed. I followed her look to a New Age shop across the road. Standing in the doorway was a tall, incredibly thin man in a shabby, tight-fitting black overcoat that came almost to his ankles. He had a black homburg perched exactly in the centre on his head and a long, straggly beard. He must have been in his late twenties. He was watching Faye without expression.

'Nick, let's go,' Faye called, hurrying towards the car. I got in the four-wheel drive beside her. She moved off very quickly, her eyes focused dead ahead. When I looked the man was no longer outside the shop.

'Who was the undertaker?' I said.

'You don't need to worry about him,' she said airily.

I laughed.

'I wasn't worrying, I just wondered.' I frowned. 'Are there things worrying you?'

'Global warming, the collapse of the world economy and the rise of hoodlum states in Eastern Europe for starters. Whether I've got enough petrol to get you to Wynn House for another.'

I waited a moment.

'So who is he?' I said.

She gave me a small smile.

'A knight of the Brotherhood of the Holy Grail.'

'Aren't they the blokes who chased Indiana Jones all over Venice when he was looking for his dad?'

'That was fiction, Nick. These people, however unreal, actually do exist. They've heard rumours about our find and they're hanging around in case it's the Grail.'

'They?'

'There are about thirty of them. That man seems to be their leader. The rest all look like accountants. But there's something freaky about them.'

'So word has got round about your discovery?'

'We think Lucy told some people, yes. This kind of thing attracts a lot of interest. You know, since the millennium

69

half the country is barking anyway – so many drifters now.'

'I know. I saw an encampment near Avebury as I drove down. A mix of followers of the Messiah, people there for the crop circles and a gang so stoned they're still heading back from the Cornish eclipse.'

Faye pulled up at a zebra crossing to let a group of people cross. Among them was my religious nut. He looked in through the windscreen of the car. I shrank down in my seat. When I looked Faye had shrunk down too.

'You're trying to avoid him too?' I said, when we had started off again.

'Who?' she said.

'The religious nut with the stick.'

'You met him?' she said, flashing a look at me.

'We had a chat.'

'What about?' she asked with what sounded like forced casualness.

'How He was coming back soon. Why? What does he talk to you about?'

She gave a little laugh.

'Oh, the same.'

When we got back to Wynn House I checked out the Arthurian books in the library. Rex and Genevra had a pretty good collection. I took a pile over to the sofa and settled down for a couple of hours. Around three Genevra came in. She was wearing tight-fitting jeans and a baggy jumper and her face looked scrubbed and healthy.

'How's it hanging, Nicholas?' she said, bouncing down beside me and leaning over to see what I was reading. I inhaled her perfume and watched her as she read the book I had in my lap.

There was something intensely sexual about Genevra. She didn't flaunt it but there was a physicality about her that made you – okay, me – want to take hold of her whenever she came close. Maybe she sensed what I was thinking because she suddenly moved away from me. Smiling crookedly she reached and touched the tip of my nose with her finger.

'So are you going to write about all this?'

'You bet.'

'And what do you think about our find? The real thing?'

'Well, I gotta tell you, Genevra, this abbey's monks were notorious for being a bunch of fraudsters who'd do almost anything to get the tourist buck.'

'They had tourists back then?' Genevra said.

'Sure – they called them pilgrims. Pilgrims could even get package holidays. You could book a passage to the Holy Land and your payment included sea-crossing then guides and accommodation at the other end.'

'Hmm. Buckhalter will be pleased to know we're working in an honourable tradition.'

'Who said it was honourable?'

She laughed, her scar twisting her top lip and tilting her grin. She saw me looking and put her hand up to her mouth, blushing a little. I reached over and moved it gently away.

'What happened?' I asked, nodding at the scar.

'Car accident.' She dropped her eyes. We both looked at her hand still held in mine. She raised her eyes. It was my turn to blush. We started to lean towards each other . . .

Just then the door opened. Genevra hastily withdrew her hand and we both turned to see who was in the doorway.

'Madrid, good to see you're hard at work,' Buck Buckhalter said. 'Genevra, you, me and Rex got to have a get-together.' He smiled thinly. 'If you'll excuse us, mister.'

'I'd like to see the sarcophagus again,' I said.

Buckhalter shrugged.

'Go ahead. Genevra?'

I retraced our steps of the previous evening. I'd been reading a contemporary account of the discovery of Arthur's grave written by Gerald of Wales, who seemed to have been an eye-witness back in 1191. According to him, the body of King Arthur was found deep down in the earth. The coffin was a hollow oak. The tomb was split into two parts. Most of it was allotted to the bones of the man, while the remaining third towards the foot contained the bones of the woman. There was a piece of the woman's yellow hair in the tomb but a monk grabbed for it and it turned to dust.

There were two other distinctive features about the man's body. One was that he was a much bigger man than was usual in those days. His shin bone reached a good three inches above the knee of the tallest man. The eye-socket of the skull was also a good palm in width. The second was that there were ten wounds on the skull. All were scarred over except for one, larger than the others, which had made a big hole and was obviously the death blow.

I looked down into the sarcophagus. I could see the long shin bone. And I could see a hole in the skull and other marks across the top of it. I gazed down at the jumble of bones laid loosely side by side, trying to puzzle out which bone was what. I have no idea how many bones there are in the human body but there were more here than I would have imagined.

'I'm Nanny,' a disembodied voice said and I jumped three feet in the air. I looked round to see a tall, middle-aged woman, dressed in a long black dress, her grey hair pulled back in a tight bun. She had thin lips that pursed into the narrowest of smiles.

'Guilty conscience?' she inquired with a slight tilt of her head.

'Always,' I said. 'But you also startled me. I didn't hear you come in.'

'That's because I was already here,' she said. 'I like to spend a little time in the crypt every day.'

I looked round at the coffins laid out in rows, the shadows falling oddly because of the low electric lighting, the spiders' webs hanging everywhere.

'I can understand that,' I said – which must constitute my *most* untruthful contribution to the long history of male untruths. And I wasn't even trying to get her into bed. I looked at her long white face and the word 'vampire' sprang unbidden into what passes for my brain.

I smiled cheerily.

'Well,' I said, rather too loudly. 'Must be going. I'm expected, of course.'

'I'm Nanny,' she repeated.

'Of course you are,' I said. 'I'm pretty slow off the mark myself.'

Yes. I know. That was a stupid thing to say too, but she'd made me very nervous. For a moment I assume 'nanny' was some local dialect word for two coffins short of a funeral. Then I twigged.

'Oh, *the nanny*,' I said, too enthusiastically. 'I'm the journalist. Nick, I mean. Pleased to meet you. Do you have a name other than the nanny?'

'I am not *the nanny*, I am Nanny.'

Hmm. Maybe I was right the first time.

'Don't you have any other names?' I said cautiously.

'What a curious child you are,' she said, scrutinising me openly. 'Nannies in *good* houses' – she emphasised the good – 'are only ever known as Nanny.'

'Yes,' I said excitedly. 'I know. They wear black and live to a very old age in the servants' quarters in the attic – though how they're supposed to get up the stairs I don't know.'

She reached out her hand.

'Let's go back into the house, shall we?'

I agreed. I wanted to nod that agreement but it was difficult, given that she was leading me back out of the crypt by my left ear, gripped as it was – rather tightly too – between her thumb and forefinger.

Chapter Five

The next morning Genevra was horrified when she saw me. Not because of any lasting damage Nanny had done to my ear – that was only Nanny's idea of a joke. Ha ha. No, Genevra was horrified because she found me sitting cross-legged on the Persian rug in my room with three feet of surgical gauze spilling out of my mouth.

'Hnngh,' was the best I'd managed when she'd knocked on the door. She took it as an invitation to enter. When she saw the gauze hanging out of my mouth, she rushed over and started to pound on my back.

'My God, Nick! Are you okay?'

'Hnngh, hnngh!'

I shook my head wildly and tried to roll away from her – an action hampered by my having me feet folded up on the tops of my thighs in the full lotus position. I put my hands up to push her away.

'But you're choking!' she said. And, thanks to her, I was, since what she didn't know – how could she? – was that the three feet of gauze she could see was attached to a further six feet which lay coiled in my stomach.

Who's a pervert? This practice is called Dhauti and it's one of my yoga kriyas – hygiene duties to you. Figuring I had a couple of hours on my own I'd taken a long piece of gauze, around three inches wide, and soaked it in warm milk. I'd then swallowed it, slowly and carefully. The first couple of times I'd tried this I'd retched a bit. But by relaxing my throat I could now easily keep it down.

The idea was that you left the gauze in your stomach for fifteen or twenty minutes – any longer and the strip would begin to pass through the body – and then slowly draw it out, bringing with it all the toxins and bad things in the stomach.

Genevra had other ideas. Seeing me turn purple in the face she started tugging at the gauze. This was not a good idea. My throat constricted. That had two consequences. The first was that I turned bright red. The second – of more immediate importance – was that I did start to choke.

Genevra didn't immediately notice. I think she was stunned to find out how long it was. (If only.) She gave the gauze a strong tug and, as my tonsils popped out, fell back a step, drawing it out hand over hand. Only when the last bit flipped from my mouth did she look down at the pile of phlegmy material coiled at her feet. She wrinkled her nose in disgust and wiped her hands clean in my hair. Thanks, Genevra.

I brushed my tears away.

'That could have been very nasty,' I said hoarsely.

'A pretty stupid thing to be doing, wasn't it?' she said, genuinely angry. 'If I hadn't come in we could have had another corpse around here.'

I forbore from pointing out that she had precipitated the crisis. She looked quite splendid, her eyes flashing, hands on hips, bosom heaving. My, was it heaving.

'It's quite straightforward actually,' I whispered.

'But what were you doing?'

'Soaking up phlegm, bile and other impurities in my stomach.'

'Yuk,' she said succinctly, giving me the once-over as I stood up. I was suddenly very conscious that I was only wearing a pair of designer knickers – it's all you wear to do my kind of yoga.

'You should see what the advanced practitioners do – on second thoughts, maybe not.'

'Go on,' she said, watching me with undue attention as I slipped on a dressing gown.

'In Bahiskrta you stand in water up to your navel then draw out the long intestine—'

'No, stop. I don't think I do want to hear this—'

'—wash it with both hands, then put it back.'

'I was right.' She wrinkled her nose in disgust. 'And you do that?'

'Do I look like I do?' I said, though it was a pretty pointless thing to say.

She sat down in the one chair in the room not covered with my clothes. 'I'm not sure what people look like who play with their own intestines. But on the present evidence . . .'

I sat down on the bed.

'Yeah, yeah. So how can I help you?'

'We wondered if you wanted to come down to the conference to announce our discovery and the opening of the Avalon project. Thing is, we'd need to go today.'

'Who's "we", what conference – and why me?'

'Rex and I are "we". It's a heritage industry thing. A symposium – Is there a Future for the Past? It's in, appropriately enough, the King Arthur Hotel in Tintagel. All the heritage Centres are going to be meeting there.'

'When do you intend to open?'

'Next weekend.' She must have seen my incredulous look. 'It's just the banqueting rooms – they're in the big barn alongside the house. There's very little needs to be done to them. We already have planning permission.'

'Bridget coming to Tintagel?'

'I think she's staying here to keep Rex company.' A smile flickered on her face. 'He has to talk to the police some more about poor Lucy.'

'Are they saying how she died?'

'Strangulation,' she said, looking away then, catching sight of the pile of gauze, looking back again.

'So it's a murder investigation,' I said, almost to myself.

Genevra shuddered slightly and got to her feet.

'Are you going to come?'

'Buckhalter going to be there?'

She grinned crookedly.

'Sure. But you don't have to travel down with him. He and Faye are going down in the morning. We're to see them there.' She looked me straight in the eye. 'You'll be travelling down with me.'

I affected nonchalance. Shrugged.

'Suppose that sounds okay.'

'Why are you squeaking?' she said.

As I packed an overnight bag I was thinking about my classic male response. On the one hand was a woman I believed I had been in love with for the past fifteen years – Faye. Here, on the other, was a stunning woman – Genevra – who, if I didn't miss my guess, had a sexual interest in me. Was I intending to be loyal to Faye? Not if I could possibly help it. Thank God I could blame it on my gender. Otherwise I'd get to thinking I was a real shit.

I called in on Rex before we set off.

'Nick, come in. Gennie tells me you're going down to Tintagel for the conference. That's great news. It's good that you're seen as part of the team from the off. It'll help reassure Buckhalter that you're on message.'

'That depends what the message is.'

Rex grinned his gummy grin.

'Of course, of course. Whilst you're down there check out the shops to see if there are any products we can make use of ourselves in our castle shop. Camelot chess sets, plastic Excaliburs, that kind of shit. I've already commissioned a Grail board game to complement the Grail Adventure Park we'll have in the woods and in the fields in the south east of the grounds.'

'You seem to have thought of everything.'

'Almost – but in fact there's something you can help me with.' He put his arm round me – this was obviously his way of being companionable – and led me towards the long windows. 'I want some names of meals and drinks.'

'That's not what I do. I'm a journalist. You want a copywriter.'

'What about *Dentally Does It*? What's that if it isn't a piece of copywriting?'

'You hired me to write the story.'

'Sure, but now you're part of the team. We go for multi-tasking here, or what used to be called all hands to the pump. You got a problem with that?'

He squeezed my shoulder. I shook my head.

'It has to be alliterative – something like King Ban of Ben Burgers.'

'Sure, I can do that,' I said. 'First rule of subbing. Headlines have to be alliterative.'

'I thought the first rule was that they had to pun.'

Know-all.

'You're right. Alliteration: second rule of subbing.'

'So get busy and I'll see you when you get back.'

Genevra and I set off around two in her Range Rover. The rain was holding off for the moment but it was a gloomy day, the sun faint in a murky sky. We figured to reach Tintagel by about seven. On the way I tried out various ideas on her.

'Okay, I got the wines sorted: do you want the TH or the Book of Bath?'

'Huh?'

'I've got to come up with some Arthurian names for stuff. So do you want TH or the Book of Bath? You get it? White or red? TH is for T.H. White – you know, the guy who wrote *The Once and Future King*. Disney made a cartoon of its first part, *The Sword in the Stone*.'

'Yeah, I got that one, it was the other one passed me by.'

'That's the red.'

'I figured that out, but why the name?'

'There's reference to Arthur in *The Red Book of Bath*.'

'Aha.' She glanced across at me. 'I'm not sure you've quite caught the popular line there. If our clientele were all PhD students we'd be well away.'

Genevra pulled into a service station and filled up with petrol. A white transit van followed us in and four men got out whilst the driver pumped the petrol. They could hardly take their eyes off Genevra. I could understand that. I was just thinking I was going to have to deal with them – aaaaagh – when Genevra got back in and we set off again.

The rain held off but I was reading the map so inevitably we took a wrong turning and ended up on the A30 going across Bodmin Moor.

'I need a pee,' Genevra said. 'Fancy a drink?'

'I'm not that kinky. I've heard about you aristos.'

She barked a laugh.

'Do people still say *kinky*?'

'Only saddos. What about cocktails named after Arthurian writers? Two Malorys and a Tennyson on the rocks, please, waiter?'

'Make mine a Von Essenbach. Maybe you should move on to food – look, there's a sign for Jamaica Inn. You ever been?'

'I thought it was just a book.'

'Used to be one of my favourites,' she said. 'You are now in Daphne Du Maurier country, you know. What's the betting the bar staff are dressed as smugglers and wenches?'

'Peas Perilous? Gawain and the Green Salad? How do you want your steak? Joan of Arc – that's so well done it's burned – or maybe Burned at the Steak and Chips.'

'Enough already.'

Genevra pulled off the road and we followed a curving lane up alongside Jamaica Inn, a group of gloomy grey slate buildings. The wind was blowing hard when we got out of the car. We entered beside the Daphne Du Maurier museum and walked past a waxwork Squire in nineteenth-century costume.

Genevra was wrong about the clothes of the bar staff, but the place had definitely been themed. We passed through a long food hall into the pub proper. Nearby was an enormous granite fireplace – think Stonehenge with a fire-grate

– burning what looked like half a tree. Seventies disco seemed to be the preferred music.

The place was packed with the biggest bunch of dodgy people I'd ever seen in my life.

'D'you think they still do smuggling from here?' I said, nervously looking from one hard-bitten face to the next.

'What do you want to drink?' Genevra said. 'I'm buying.'

'Mineral water,' I said, mindful that my body was a temple for the time being. A massive bloke with a shaved head and biceps like tractor tyres overheard. He curled his lip.

'In a dirty glass,' I added in my deepest voice.

'You here for the festivities tomorrow?' the barmaid asked cheerfully.

'Didn't know there were any.'

'I think that's why everybody else is here. I don't recognise a single regular in here tonight. It's our February Fair. Lots of good, healthy fun – it starts off with the local lads taking part in the tossing the cowcakes competition.'

'Sounds great,' I said, backing away and looking round for somewhere to sit. 'Where do you want to go, Genevra?'

She surveyed the room.

'Back to the car?'

There was a middle-aged vicar with a shock of white hair sitting in an alcove near the fire talking to another man of a similar age.

'Let's go on the other side of the table to those two guys – they look reasonably normal.' I led the way over. 'May we join you?'

'Of course you may,' the vicar said, a pleasant twinkle in his eye. 'I was just mulling over with my friend here a question concerning bestiality – what is and is not legal? My friend is of the opinion that, whatever the pros and cons of it as a satisfying experience – and personally I have my doubts – sex with a turkey does not fall within the definition of animal in the appropriate act on the statute book.'

So much for normal.

''S right,' his companion muttered.

81

'My contention is that not only fowl but also fish are regarded as animals for the purposes of the act. Which is to say that if you are caught with, let's say, a sea skate stuck on the end of your love prong you are committing an offence within the meaning of the law. The very point, incidentally, that I made quite forcibly to our touring fishmonger – to little effect, I regret to say.'

'Love prong?' Genevra mouthed at me.

'But is it rape?' the vicar's companion asked in a petulant voice.

'Now that is entirely another matter and one that I am not sure you can readily answer – the willingness or otherwise of the animal being difficult to ascertain. Accepting a handful of feed pellets does not in itself constitute consent, surely?'

'Wow, that fire certainly throws out a lot of heat, doesn't it?' I said grinning cheesily and starting to get to my feet. 'I think maybe we'll go and stand by the bar, thanks all the same.'

'No, no, I insist you join us,' the vicar said, putting out a restraining hand. 'It's not often we get strangers here in this little way-station in winter. And, believe me, despite the eccentricity of my conversation, you're much safer with me than with those badger-baiters at the bar. I am what passes for an intellectual in these parts.'

I sat down again.

'You certainly don't talk like a vicar,' I said.

'And why would I wish to?' he said. He touched his dog collar. 'Ah, you are making assumptions based on the clerical collar.' He smiled cherubically. 'But tell me, what is your particular bent?'

I flushed.

'Oh, I'm just a straightforward guy,' I said.

Genevra turned to face the man wearing the clerical collar. 'How come the collar if you're not a vicar?'

'I find the clerical collar encourages woman to confide in me,' he said, leaning over to squeeze Genevra's knee. 'And, as you know, a secret shared is guaranteed sex.'

I looked at him sharply. That is, after all, my line. He met my look and smiled.

'When I asked your bent it was not your sexual customs that interested me – although if you fancy a peccadillo with the parrot I should caution against – it has a foul temper. I was curious about the particular line of work that has brought you to this unique place.'

'Unique?'

'Why yes, look around you and you see modern life at its most depressing. The gentlemen by the bar are the badger-baiters – you may have heard their dogs barking in the back of one of the numerous white vans in the car park as you came in. They will be going off shortly to commit acts of great barbarity against our badger population in the name of sport.

'They are talking to the people who are gathered for the bare-knuckle fight that will take place later in a secret place on the Moor. See that large man with the shaved head you were standing beside? He is the undefeated champion. A great deal of money will change hands in attendance fees and side bets for the privilege of seeing him attempt to knock another man into the next millennium.

'In the corner over there are some crop-circle makers. They are waiting for a forward planning meeting with some local farmers. They'll be ready to make shapes to delude the foolish once spring is here. Farmers hire them because they can make more money charging people to come and look at the new marvels than they can selling the crops they've grown.'

'Who are they talking to?'

'That shady group are the Beast of Bodmin men.'

'They're trying to catch it?'

The man chuckled.

'They've *augmented* it – they'll slaughter a lamb in a barbaric way then leave the odd paw print and spoor that looks like that of a big cat.'

'Augmenting it – do you think it really exists?' Genevra said.

'Well, it may do. Certainly I wouldn't be going down to Dunmary Pool to look for Excalibur after dark, if I were you. That's supposed to be one of its watering holes.'

He shrugged expressively. 'People in the country have so much time on their hands and sex can only take you so far, especially in a small community. These dark nights encourage nonsense.'

'What was that you said about Excalibur?' Genevra said.

'Dunmary Pool – half a mile up the road here – is the lake into which one of the Knights of the Round Table threw Excalibur before Arthur went off to Avalon.'

'I'm surprised there are no horse mutilators on your list of ne'er-do-wells,' I said, trying to get into the spirit of the conversation.

'They come out of the cities sometimes. They're child molesters, aren't they? We like them – we geld them if we catch them.'

The parrot squawked loudly. I looked over just as the pub door beside its cage opened and four short, broad men came in. I watched them troop to the bar with a sinking feeling. They were the men from the service station.

I leaned over to Genevra. 'Don't look now but four guys have just come in who – don't look!'

Genevra looked.

'What, those guys at the bar?'

She spoke loudly, just as there was a lull in the general conversation. Every man at the bar turned to see who was speaking and who was being referred to.

'Oh, those men,' she muttered as the four men spotted us. 'I saw them at the service station.'

'Great talking to you,' I said to the would-be vicar and his surly friend. Taking Genevra's hand I headed for the food hall. We were halfway through it before the four men made their appearance behind us. I passed Genevra the car keys.

'Get the car started, I'll distract them.'

'You're not going to sing, are you?' she said, squeezing my hand and running out into the car park. I could hear heavy footsteps a few yards behind me as I hurried past the entrance to the museum. I glanced at the waxwork squire sitting there, a pewter tankard held out in front of him. I grabbed him by the arm and swung him round.

He was lighter than I expected, so when I reached the limit of my swing I let go of him. As he flew through the air his head separated from his body and the tankard came out of his hand, but all parts of him hit our pursuers.

Genevra was pacing beside the Range Rover when I got into the car park. The white transit van was parked deliberately across the front of our vehicle. A car pulled into the car park, headlights blazing, broodily silhouetting our four pursuers.

'What do you want?' I said.

'We want her,' the nearest one said as, to my left, I heard the door of the transit van slide open.

'It's only fair to warn you,' Genevra called out, indicating me, 'this man does yoga.'

'Cripes,' the one nearest to her said – he'd obviously had a Billy Bunter upbringing. 'I'm shitting me pants.' Perhaps not.

When he threw back his head and laughed I was certain. It was one of those underclass laughs – too loud, too long and definitely not amused. Except this one didn't go on for too long because Genevra hit him in the throat with her elbow.

I tried to think of an appropriately martial looking yoga posture with which to frighten the others. The lotus position wouldn't do. Then I thought of t'ai chi – I used to do a thing in that called stroking the bird's feathers that I always remembered as washing the duck. I crouched down a little and did the hand movements, rather smoothly I thought.

'Looks like he's the one shitting his pants!' a guy with an Elvis quiff, standing next to the one whose windpipe Genevra had crushed, said.

'He does yoga,' his friend mimicked. Genevra kicked that one in the balls and when he bent double kneed him in the face.

I'm not a fighter. You guessed? I don't know how to punch. However, I know enough to know that if you can't punch, make sure you're nifty with your feet. Or look as if you are.

I can bring my foot up straight-legged higher than my head, although the last time I tried it in a fight I looked like a Tiller Girl. This time I raised my knee to my chest.

'Who do you think you are, Rudolph bloody Nureyev?' said Elvis.

In answer I kicked out my foot and straightened my leg, catching him full in the chest. He fell back with a pleasing force, sending the fourth of them sprawling. Genevra looked beyond me. I followed her glance to see half a dozen more men, in donkey jackets and jeans, debouch from the transit van. They circled us.

We went back to back, circling with them. I would have surrendered – I was always taught that if you hit someone there's always the chance they'll hit you back harder so why take the chance? – but I could see Genevra was made of sterner stuff.

That's when the pub door opened and the vicar and his friend led out the badger-baiters.

'These men are trying to kidnap this woman,' I shouted.

'Look, stay out of this,' the tallest of the gang before us warned in a strong Welsh accent. 'We're Celts just like you. We're knights of King Arthur and this woman is a risk to the realm. You should join us, not oppose us.'

'A knight?' The vicar's friend leered. 'I'm a five times a night man myself. Anyway, you're Welsh, not Celtic.'

'Knights of King Arthur?' the vicar said. 'What, you're from that loony up in Wales? You're a long way from home, aren't you? What's your name, son?'

The tall man looked slightly embarrassed.

'Sir Bedevere.'

'Well, Sir Bedevere, I'm no Celt, I'm Cornish. Welsh, is it? Look you, boyo, *rrr*ugby, eisteddfod, the valleys, singing, *cha*-pel, Tiger Bay. There you go that's Wales done for you.'

'Look, we don't want any trouble,' Bedevere said. 'Just let us take the woman and we'll be on our way.'

'Go get the dogs,' one of the ferrety-looking men said as the bald-headed bare-knuckle boxer came out of the pub followed by the crop-circle makers. The boxer came forward and without warning punched Bedevere in the nose. Bedevere went down.

The two opposing forces squared off but what followed was a massacre. The crop circle implements were fiendish, the dogs were up for tearing anything apart, the bare-knuckle fighter loved a punch-up. It took about eight minutes before the knights of the Round Table were stretched out in various states of disrepair.

I went over to Bedevere, who was slumped against the white van, his jacket and shirt soaked with the blood that was still pouring out of his nose. He was holding his proboscis – steady now – as if it was about to fall off. Seeing the force the bare-knuckle boxer had put into the punch I could understand that.

'Who sent you?' I said to Bedevere.

'King Ardur, who do you dink?' he said.

I was wondering if these people were the ones who had killed Lucy, my serial killer theory notwithstanding.

'What do you want with Genevra?'

'A bargaiding chib,' he said.

'Say again?' I was aware that Genevra had come up beside me.

'Leberage. King Ardur wants you to abandon the whole idea of publicising the discovery of the false grave.'

'So you were going to kidnap Genevra? That's a major criminal offence.'

'So call the cops. I don't fugging care.' He rummaged in his pocket for a handkerchief and, wincing, pressed it to his nose.

87

'No, Nick,' Genevra said quickly. 'That won't be necessary. I'm okay. They've learned their lesson. Let them go on their way.'

I looked at her and shrugged.

'If that's what you want.'

I looked across to where the badger-baiters were gathered with their dogs. I'd bought them all a drink by now. I walked over, thinking to try something James Bond had done in *From Russia With Love* to get the 'Girl Fight' stopped.

'Now that we're buddies, can I ask you a favour?' I said to the lead badger-baiter. 'Call off the badger-baiting for the night.'

'Go fuck yourself,' he said, without even pause for thought.

It was getting dark as we reached the hills above Tintagel. I was driving. Genevra was asleep in the passenger seat, her long legs cantilevered, her face gentle and untroubled, although occasionally she gnawed at her lip unconsciously.

The road took us past long lines of modern windmills, ghostly white, trooping off into the darkness. The narrow main street of Tintagel was deserted except for a tall man in a long brown overcoat mooching around outside King Arthur's Great Hall, the folly built in the 1920s by an eccentric custard millionaire. It was the Japanese man again.

We drove past King Arthur's Arms and a shop called Merlin's Cave. The centrepiece of its illuminated window full of astrological tat was a huge two-handed sword with an ornate gold handle. Fifty yards further along the Tintagel Toy Museum had plastic Excaliburs on sale – for a pretty reasonable price actually. The road curved past the Country Club, which didn't quite live up to its name: a coach was disgorging a slow queue of pensioners for the Bingo Night advertised on a poster on the outside of the unprepossessing building.

'There isn't as much Arthur stuff as I thought there'd be.' Genevra had woken up twenty minutes or so earlier. 'Given it's all they've got.'

Until the 1920s Tintagel's economy had been based on agriculture and the quarrying of roof slates. Genevra was right. Once that had gone, what was left?

'There's nothing other than Geoffrey of Monmouth's twelfth-century account of Arthur's magical conception and birth to link him to Tintagel at all,' I said. 'The castle is picturesque, it's ruined – but it was built six hundred years after Arthur is supposed to have lived and died there.

'Another piece of tourism hype. Tintagel became a tourist destination in the late nineteenth century, when first Tennyson's poems about Arthur then the Pre-Raphaelite paintings of droopy Arthurian maidens and doe-eyed knights brought a revival of interest in him. And Geoffrey's statement that Arthur was conceived there got changed, first, into the claim that he was born there, then that he lived there. It wasn't even called Tintagel until relatively recently.'

'What do you mean?'

'The village's real name is Trevenna. In 1900, when the telegraph arrived and the postal system was updated, it was quietly changed to Tintagel – a flash of marketing genius modern day practitioners would be proud of.'

We followed the road onto Fire Beacon Cliff. William Taylor's enormous King Arthur Hotel lay before us. Visible for miles around, it's often mistaken for Tintagel Castle because of its imposing appearance. Taylor, a pioneer of Cornish tourism, built it in the 1890s. It looks like a railway hotel – it was intended to be. He'd hoped to get a tourist branch line of the London and South Western Railway run out between Camelford and Delabole. He even adapted a set of terraced medieval fields to make a golf course in anticipation of the arrival of tourists.

'What about the latest find, though?' Genevra said.

She was talking about a small piece of greenish-grey slate, 35 cm by 20 cm, inscribed with the word Artognov, which

89

had been found at Tintagel in early August 1998. The stone was dated to the sixth century by the style of the inscription and the broken pottery and glass found with it. It was discovered on the edge of the cliff overlooking a cavern traditionally known as Merlin's Cave.

The inscription reads: '*Pater Coliavi ficit Artognov*', which has been translated as 'Artognou, father of a descendant of Coll, has had this made (or built).'

'Everybody is excited by those first three letters, A-r-t,' I said. 'But Artognov is no variant of Arthur and the slate is no proof he was here. We know there was a large settlement in Tintagel – there are piles of Mediterranean pottery to prove it. It was either a trading post or the palace of some important leader.'

'So why couldn't that important leader be Arthur?' Genevra said as we drew up in front of the hotel.

I shook my head.

'Nobody knows the identity of the leader who lived here. Me, I don't think it was Arthur.'

We checked in and had a look round. The dining room was hung with cardboard shields and heraldic banners. Several people waved at Genevra. The bar was full of people, many of whom greeted Genevra warmly.

'Nick and I have just arrived,' she said to the most effusive. 'We're gonna get unpacked then we'll come back down.'

'How come you know so many people?' I said, as we lugged our baggage up the stairs.

'I've been doing this kind of thing for a while,' she said. 'I used to work for the National Trust, then English Heritage. You get on the circuit.'

My room was first. Genevra paused by my door.

'I've got a bottle of Scotch eager to be drunk,' she said. 'Do you want to drop off your stuff and come down to my room?'

Ulp.

I was there in two minutes.

'That was quick,' she said with a grin as she ushered me in.

Her room was enormous, with long windows overlooking the sea and the ruins of Tintagel Castle. We sat side by side on a sofa beneath the windows. You know those sofa-scenarios? Given our proximity there was a definite tension in the air and I, for one, was observing the body language closely. Her legs were crossed facing away from me. Not a good sign.

'So you and Bridget never?' she said.

'What?'

'Had sex.'

I looked at her and shook my head.

'Strange really because we've both been round the track a bit,' I said.

'Yeah, but she says you're useless in bed so she hasn't bothered getting excited about the prospect.'

'She said that?' I said, unable to keep the hurt out of my voice.

Genevra leaned over and kissed me on the cheek. Her legs remained crossed the wrong way but her breath wafted gently against my ear as she murmured: 'Only as a joke. Why – is it true?'

I sighed.

'I'm not sure this is the kind of conversation we should be having – can we talk about this conference? And why you're going along with this. You seem like you really care about archaeology and the truth of the past. How can you distort it like this?'

She retreated to her half of the sofa.

'It's all a story, isn't it? What does it matter what the truth is when people believe the legends? I know all the slogans – the past is another country, history is written by the victors, to understand the present you have to know the past, to plan the future you have to understand the past. But the one I believe is that history is the story of great men – and who is greater than Arthur?'

'Er – Nelson Mandela?'

'Good point.'

I took a big swig of my whisky. She sipped hers. Re-crossed her legs. Leaned over. Her voice was suddenly very throaty.

'It's been a long, stressful day, Nick. What do you say to a bit of rumpy-pumpy? I want to see what Bridget's been denying herself all these years.'

For a moment I wondered what Faye was doing. But only for a moment. Then I leaned into Genevra's embrace.

Chapter Six

We never did get down to the bar.

Next morning, whilst Genevra was still asleep, I stood by the window of her room and looked down on Tintagel Castle and the sea beating against the rocks in Tintagel Haven. The jumble of ruined buildings spread across the mainland and on Tintagel Island seemed to be clinging on, especially the perimeter walls plunging down to the wild sea.

'Well, that wasn't so bad at all,' Genevra said. I turned. She stretched under the sheet, her eyes fixed on me. 'Ten out of ten for effort. One or two things to work on but not a bad start.'

'You sound like a school report.'

She sat up, the sheet dropping away from her. She grinned.

'School's out.'

The Conference had already been going for two days. Later that morning – much later – we reported in for the final day. Plenty had already happened, as we discovered talking to the gossipy person registering us.

She was from the Florence Nightingale Theme Hospital somewhere in Northumberland so was dressed as a nurse of the mid-nineteenth century.

'It's been chaos, dear, chaos,' she said to Genevra as she adjusted her wimple. 'There have been *breakaway movements.*'

'What do you mean?'

'Well, Catherine Cookson Country, The James Herriott Highlands, The Bronte Moors, Heartbeat Hills and, er, Sabden Treacle Mines suggested forming their own Northern Chapter. But as for the rest, it's a bit like the Middle Ages. Except that instead of feuding warlords you have feuding theme parks disputing their right to titles on land. This is George Orwell Country. No, it's not, it's Ragged Trousered Philanthropist Land. That kind of thing.'

She handed us name badges.

'And as for the gentlemen from the William Wallace Freedom Park, well!'

'I don't know that one,' Genevra said.

'You do,' the woman said. 'There was all that controversy when the staff were accused of bullying English customers. It's the one where visitors start off pillaging a replica York – they use a model village they bought cheap – and end up hung, drawn and quartered. Anyway, they formed a flying wedge with Rebus World and the Ettrick Shepherd theme pub and tried to take over the meeting yesterday. They didn't quite have enough clout, thank goodness.'

She shook her head.

'Mark my words, there'll be a few sore heads this morning.'

'There was actual fighting, then?' I said, surprised.

She looked at me pityingly.

'I meant the drinking in the bar last evening. Went on well into the night. Although there was almost a scuffle on the first day when three competing Diana Worlds had a row.'

I was tutting appropriately when I heard a familiar voice call, without enthusiasm: 'Madrid.'

I turned to see Buckhalter in loud check trousers and a gold pullover with the insignia of two crossed swords on his left breast. He was standing with Faye, who was wearing a neat black two-piece, at the top of the steps leading into the vast conference room at the rear of the hotel.

Faye smiled at me. I felt guilty – but not that guilty. I resolved not to say anything to her about Genevra and me. I often do make the same mistake twice, but this time I thought I'd resist the temptation.

'When are we on?' I said.

'*I'm* on at the end of the day,' said Buckhalter. 'Then we're outta here.'

Buckhalter and Faye went through to set up. Genevra and I went into the bar where the delegates were having a coffee break. The Excalibar. Genevra and I were being discreet, determined not to give our relationship away by gesture or glance. We separated, therefore, although I looked over at her occasionally from across the room.

I joined a group of people around a large coffee table. The person sitting to my right, a bloke with floppy blond hair and a too-tight suit, stuck his hand out.

'Hi, you're the guy shagging Genevra, aren't you? I'm Jefferson from H.G. Wells World. Down near Piltdown? Here to talk about our new Time Machine ride. Can I introduce you to some of the conference's other Literary Experiences? Fred here is from Brighton Rock – simulated razor fights a speciality. Eamonn is from Joyceland – he manages the flower shop there, Leopold's Blooms. He started out at Finnegan's Funeral Parlours.'

Jefferson looked up as a pretty woman in slacks and a bright orange cardigan approached. She stopped between us.

'Janet, how lovely.' He turned to me. 'Janet's from Canterbury Tails. That's *T-a-i-l-s*.'

'Hi,' I said. 'I'm—'

'The guy Genevra is shagging,' Janet said. 'I know.'

'Has there been a public announcement or something?' I said, a little peevishly.

'Well, if you could keep your eyes off her it might not be such a giveaway,' Janet said, smiling sweetly.

I sighed. Genevra was, I had to admit, intoxicating.

'What's Canterbury Tails?' I said.

'Tableaux of scenes from Chaucer using stuffed animals.'

'Naturally,' I said.

Janet looked at a young man in a dark blue suit who was perched on the end of his seat clutching a big ring-binder file. 'Sorry, I don't know who you are.'

He muttered something, hanging his head.

'Sorry?'

'I'm from Duck Land,' he said, blushing.

'Ah yes,' Janet said. 'Good slogan.'

'Go Quackers at Duck Land!' Jefferson declaimed.

'It's my first job,' the man said quickly. 'I don't intend to be there long.'

'So what's with the Avalon theme park?' Jefferson said. 'Sounds like a winner. Genevra was saying last time we met you've got added value. What is it?'

'I can't say,' I said politely. 'You'll have to wait for the last session.'

'You're going to do a Jorvik?'

He was referring to the Jorvik Viking Centre in York. Since it opened back in 1984 it had remained the standard by which other heritage sites were judged. It was a twelve-minute ride through the recreation of a tenth-century village, complete with smells of livestock, food and, the big novelty, latrines.

'Along those lines,' I said.

'Hi, guys.' A sober-suited man in his fifties had joined us. He had a salesman's smile. 'You heard the latest? The Cymru Centre is planning to open up another of the Welsh pits. As a total mining experience.' I said, 'What, you mean visitors get emphysema, rickets, arthritis and white finger?' He laughed. 'The idea definitely has possibilities. You could have a great ride – it ends by crashing into eighty-five tons of nutty slack which slides down to smother a toy village.' He moved away. 'Crazy idea, crazy people.'

'What's the next session?' I ask Jefferson.

'Economic benefits of heritage tourism – transport, accommodation, catering and retail all benefit.' He winked and got up to go. Genevra was standing beside me.

'Buck tells me I have to go back tonight,' she said. There was a gleam in her eye. She lowered her voice. 'Why don't we skip this session?'

'If you insist,' I said.

'You're squeaking again. I've just got to talk to Buck. Wait here until I get back.'

I nodded then went over to the long window and gazed down on the ruined castle. It looked magnificent as the sea raged around the base of Tintagel Island, throwing up great plumes of spray. I'd forgotten how steep the flight of steps was which led from the Haven up to the gatehouse perched on the island's cliff top. I saw a figure in a bright orange anorak trudging up them. I squinted to get a better look. It was Faye.

The steps wound out of sight round the cliff-face. Faye disappeared from view then re-appeared a minute or so later at the gatehouse. She followed the path into the castle remains. As she walked past the ruins of the main hall I noticed a man loitering in the shelter of a half-standing wall. It was very windy, I could see by the way his coat and her anorak were billowing, and I thought at first he was sheltering from the wind. But he turned abruptly away when she happened to look his way and then I had a darker thought.

The Camelot Killer.

Faye walked towards the top of the island. I groaned as I saw the man following her, some hundred yards behind.

There was an old-fashioned telescope on a stand on the terrace of the hotel. I rushed outside. A couple of kids were messing with the telescope, pretending it was a machine gun. A quick clip round the ear took care of them. In my dreams. Cost me a fiver to wrest it from them.

I focused on Faye just as she reached the summit of the island. She stopped beside the walled garden and looked out over the sea, totally oblivious to any danger. I swung the telescope onto the man who was following steadily behind.

As I watched his back – I couldn't make out his features – I saw him pat his pocket.

A gun? I cupped my hands and bellowed Faye's name. The wind blew it back at me. I vaulted off the terrace onto the path and set off at a run towards the castle.

To get there from the hotel I had to descend by a steep path into the bay – Tintagel Haven – then climb up the steep flight of steps Faye and her pursuer had used. Even as I ran I knew that if the man did wish her harm I would never get there in time.

Getting down to the beach was easy, the incline speeding my progress. I had to go more slowly as I picked my way through the rusted remains of the derricks and capstans that had been set in place here a hundred and fifty years before for use in the slate cutting trade. And getting up the steep steps onto the island was a nightmare.

I was out of breath after the first twenty steps. Gasping I hurried on, totally winded by the time I ducked through the Norman archway into the castle. It took me another five minutes to get to the kitchen garden on the top of the island. The wind howled around me and when I stepped off the path I sank up to my ankles in the boggy ground.

I doubled over for a moment, struggling to catch my breath.

There was no sign of either Faye or her pursuer. I looked round wildly. The ruined chapel – one wall still standing – was a hundred yards in one direction, a man-made tunnel, almost like a grotto, a hundred yards in the other. If any harm had come to Faye, it would be in the grotto, out of sight.

I approached it with an unwise lack of caution but it was empty, the cobbled stones glistening with the water dripping from the arch above. I hurried to the eastern edge of the cliffs and looked down, my heart pounding, frightened of seeing an orange anorak floating on the water. There was nothing.

I followed the cliff edge round the upper rim of the island. When I had almost returned to the inner ward and

the steps by which I had reached these heights, I caught
sight of the orange anorak, slipping behind a pile of rocks
on the edge of the Haven. I shouted again but now I had the
boom of the sea to contend with as well as the wind gusting
around me.

I took the steps two at a time. When I reached the level
ground just above the Haven I glanced to my left, towards
Merlin's Cave. The Cave was a cavern the sea had hollowed
out that linked Tintagel Haven with the beach in the next
bay. It was accessible at low tide, submerged at high. I
glimpsed someone going into it.

I was pretty sure it was the man who had been following
Faye. I looked down at the water rushing into the Haven.
The tide was coming in. Quickly. I estimated it would cut
the cave off in about ten minutes.

It took me four to reach the entrance to the cavern. I
stepped in cautiously. The booming of wind and sea was
muted here. I clambered over rocky outcrops, peering into
the gloom for a sight of the man I thought I had seen
enter.

I was about halfway through the cavern – I could see a
sliver of light and a glimpse of the other bay some twenty
yards ahead – when I heard a noise behind me. I whirled
round and someone or something hit me. Very hard.

I went down. And stayed down.

I had this dream. (I know, I know. I hate them too, but I
really did – and at least it wasn't one of those dreams in
italics. I *really* hate that.) I was lying naked in a field. And a
snake came out of my stomach and coiled itself around me.
Then a woman came to me. A real looker.

She lifted me up and took me to the top of a high
mountain. She placed me on a wheel on which there were
seats, some rising and some falling. I looked to see where I
was sitting and I saw I was at the highest point of the wheel.
The snake had gone, by the way.

She said to me: 'Where are you?'

'I'm on a high wheel,' I said, to show she wasn't dealing with a fool. 'But I don't know what kind of wheel it is.'

'What can you see?' she said.

'I think I can see the whole world.' Which was also true. (This is a dream, okay?)

But when I next looked down I could see deep black water squirming with snakes and hideous coiling creatures. And suddenly I felt the woman push the wheel. I fell and fell, down among the snakes and coiling creatures. They wrapped themselves around me. And far, far away I could hear someone calling my name as the creatures dragged me deep into the boiling ocean.

I woke vomiting water, Genevra tugging at me and screaming my name.

'Nick! We've got to get out of here before the tide comes in any further!'

Still vomiting, I tried to stand but my knees buckled. I sank to my waist in the water.

'Nick – come on!' she cried, dragging me through the water. I tried to stand again and this time I was more successful. We struggled out of the cave. The waves were rolling in, quick and fierce. There was a thin strip of sand they had not quite reached.

We waited for a lull in the water's inward progress then waded across the near lagoon onto the dry beach. I slumped to the ground but Genevra pulled me back onto the path.

'What happened?' we said simultaneously.

I barked a laugh. She cradled me in her arms. It felt good.

'You know,' she said. 'When I asked if you wanted to skip the next session I was sort of assuming you'd spend the time with me, not go off for a walk on your own.'

'I wasn't walking, I was—'

'Looking for a place to toss yourself off – so to speak. I know. I spotted you wandering along the cliff edge peering over. Doesn't do a lot for a girl's self-confidence when she proposes a second helping of rumpy-pumpy and the guy immediately dashes for the nearest cliff-top.'

'I'd seen Faye up here—'

She squeezed me. Hard.

'I don't think I want to hear this – now it's former lover time.'

'Some bloke was following her. I think he had a gun. Where is Faye? Have you seen her?'

I shuddered. I suddenly felt very cold, but then I was sitting in a howling wind, soaked to the skin, in the middle of winter. To make my day complete, the heavens opened again.

'Let's get you back inside,' Genevra said, helping me to my feet and hugging me as she led me up the path back into Tintagel. 'Faye's fine. I passed her on the way down here. I was just in time to see you go down to the Haven. I came looking for you just as the tide was coming in – I didn't know if you knew it filled the cave.'

'I knew,' I said, my teeth chattering. 'Did you see anyone else? The person who hit me?'

'Somebody hit you? I didn't see anybody but if they went out on the other side then I wouldn't.'

I touched the back of my head gingerly, expecting to feel blood. Genevra put her fingers gently in the same place.

'Some egg you've got there.'

We were both sodden by the time we got back to the King Arthur Hotel. The session was still in progress so there was nobody about. Genevra took me straight up to her room. She stripped off her wet clothes unselfconsciously then, wearing only pants and a bra which stood no hope of holding in her lovely breasts, proceeded to strip me.

'You know, I don't feel as bad as I did,' I said as her left breast brushed across my cheek for the third time.

She ignored me and went into the bathroom to run a bath.

I stood in the doorway, a towel around my shoulders, and watched her as she sat on the rim of the bath, leaning over to splash bath salts in the water. Ulp.

'I said I was feeling a bit perkier,' I said.

She glanced at my face then looked down my naked body. 'So I see,' she said, shutting off the taps.

She turned, reached out and drew me to her with the nearest part of me that came to hand.

We joined the others in time for the final session. Our session. Buckhalter was sitting with Faye at the front of the room. The computer screen was set up.

Without preamble the presentation I'd already seen unfolded. When it was over Buckhalter stood up. He preened a little then intoned: 'It's the job of everyone here today to save yesteryear for tomorrow. But how we do that has to meet people's expectations of historic sites.'

He looked directly at me.

'Nostalgia ain't what it used to be,' he said, though I wish he hadn't. 'The Avalon project puts the future – in terms of the latest technology – in the service of the past.'

'Yeah, but what's the added value?' someone called from the back. I thought I recognised Jefferson's voice.

'Good question. And I'm going to answer it.' Buckhalter stuck his chest out. God, he was an asshole. 'You know there are at least half a dozen rival sites claiming they were Camelot. There are contenders in Cornwall, at Bamburgh and Alnwick in Northumberland, at the Mote of Mark in Scotland – and in South Wales at St Govan's Head and Dinas Powys.'

He smirked. 'Any one of them could have done what we've done except they don't have our added value.' He paused. 'They don't have the remains of King Arthur and his Queen Guinevere.'

There was uproar in the audience.

Buckhalter shouted above it: 'The tomb containing the bones of Arthur and Guinevere will form the centrepiece of our Avalon theme park.'

He stood smirking in his silly pullover as a wave of applause swept over the audience and a barrage of flash-bulbs suddenly went off. Faye sat beside him, a small smile on her face. Genevra looked at me and shrugged.

A long-haired white guy in a yashmak – a yashmak?? – stood up in the third row.

'All very interesting, Bucky,' he shouted. 'But I'm here from the Hengist and Horsa Experience in Kent to announce that we have found the *real* body of King Arthur, buried with his horse on the site of the battle of Camlann, his final battle.'

Buckhalter pursed his lips and glanced down at Faye, who was maintaining her smile, as further uproar washed around them. Buckhalter had been using a stand-up mike. Now a woman in an ankle-length flowered dress strode to the mike, her dress billowing around her like a tent, and took control of it.

In a hectoring tone, as more flashbulbs went off, she declared a double whammy: a farmer on the outskirts of Glastonbury had found the Holy Grail *and* the body of Joseph of Arimathea.

There were no further attempts to outbid Buckhalter, though had someone declared they'd found Lancelot's retirement home, a wattle and daub bungalow called Dunjoustin', I wouldn't have been surprised.

Whilst journalists and other delegates clustered around Buckhalter, the guy in the yashmak and the woman from Glastonbury, I went over to Faye. Sitting nearby was the young man from Duck Land, flicking glumly through his ring-binder of illustrations of unusual ducks.

'How are you doing?' she said. 'Shagger.'

'It's,' I began, but she squeezed my arm.

'She's a lovely girl. Much more—'

'But it's you I want!' The words burst out before I could hold them back. 'Always has been.'

There, I'd said it, although I was surprised to hear myself say it – and so vehemently. I looked round guiltily to see if Genevra had overheard.

'Nick . . .' Faye squeezed my arm again.

'Never mind that now,' I said, drawing her to one side. 'What happened on Tintagel Island?'

'What do you mean, what happened?'

'Did you meet a man there?'

An odd expression passed across her face.

'I thought you were in danger – I saw a man following you. Why were you there?'

She looked bewildered.

'I wanted a walk. I'd never been there. Why are you asking?'

'I was attacked.'

'You were attacked?'

'And left to drown in Merlin's Cave. If it hadn't been for Genevra I'd be sleeping with the fishes now.'

'And you think it was this man you say you saw?'

'Say I saw?' I touched the back of my head. 'Somebody clobbered me, that's for sure.'

'But you don't know if it was the same person who was following me. Nick, we have all sorts of people homing in on us. King Arthur brings out the fruitcakes. Remember that man we saw in Glastonbury. Could it have been him following me?'

'No way,' I said. I wondered whether I should tell her my theory about the Camelot Killer. 'Faye, some cranks tried to kidnap Genevra on the way down. And after what happened to Lucy, you should be especially careful.'

'Rex thinks she was the victim of some nutter passing through. You think it was one of these cults that are hassling us?'

Before I could reply Buckhalter joined us.

'Is the feeding frenzy over?' I said. He ignored me. No change there then.

'We've got to get back, Faye. Gennie's coming along too. Madrid, you're going to stay on here and check the place out, see if there's anything we can use.'

'Whoa, cowboy. I don't take orders from you and I'm a journalist, not a researcher.'

'Tsk, tsk – multi-tasking, remember?'
I frowned as I watched Faye walk away.
'How can I forget?'

They left me Genevra's car, which was good. But I had to check out of the hotel, which was bad, given that out of season there weren't many places in Tintagel to stay.

I was directed to a guest house a couple of miles along the coast road. I parked in front of an unprepossessing thirties bungalow, its garden stacked high with gnomes. A sign declared THERE'S NO PLACE LIKE GNOME WORLD. Two doors down a sign in front of another bungalow announced STRAW'S CORNISH ZOO. The guest house was the one in between.

A young woman in tight jeans, check blouse and pink fluffy slippers opened the door. She was cradling a baby.

'Quite a little theme park on this street,' I said as she let me in.

'We're the official guest house for Straw's Cornish Zoo. Visitors can come and use us as a base for their visit to the zoo.'

'You could do a double ticket with Gnome World,' I said.

'No, that's rubbish that is. They make me laugh, they do really. One day they're doing B & B like everybody else. The next day *he* comes home with a job lot of smoke-damaged garden gnomes from a fire sale in Penzance. They plonk a plastic pond in the back garden, take down the clothes line, stick a sign on the garden shed saying Pixie Grotto and start up as Gnome World.' She looked down at her baby.

'Ooh, she likes you. She's clicking her tongue. You have to click back.'

I smiled stiffly. I'm impervious to babies. 'Sorry, I never learned tongue clicking at school.'

'Oh go on,' she said. 'Look how she's grinning at you.'

'Straw's Cornish Zoo is better, is it?'

'Well, Beryl's back garden is bigger for one thing. Her late husband Dennis Straw started it up. He had an eye for a business opportunity – he was what you might call an entrepreneur. They had a couple of garden sheds that were just used for storing junk. Dennis did them out as an Aviary and a Snake House. He had half a dozen snakes he bought cheap along with some exotic birds when Tropical World in St Austell went bust. Then there were a couple of calves, a goat and a donkey for kiddies' rides. They do all right.'

The baby was beginning to sound like a metronome. I looked at the grinning little thing. It did look quite nice. Steady, Madrid. You have enough trouble looking after yourself.

She led me up a flight of narrow stairs, her big bum swaying above me in the too-tight jeans. Feeling self-conscious, I called after her: 'You've not thought of doing something similar yourself?'

She half-turned her head.

'Not likely. Well, would you like it? People with peeling faces and pacomacs under their arms poking round your back garden. You'd never have any privacy. There'd always be someone peering through the kitchen window, catching you in your curlers. Beryl hated it at first – the snakes gave her the willies, the birds made a terrible racket and the goat ate half of her smalls off the washing line.'

She opened a door at the top of the stairs.

'It's en suite,' she said as I squeezed past her and the baby into the room. 'Will it be a full English breakfast?'

'Muesli and herb tea will be fine'

'Herb Tea?'

'Do you have any?'

'Yes, we've got Earl Grey or Darjeeling.'

As bloody usual. The room was okay. Sort of. It was full of those bizarre things you see advertised in the back of Sunday magazines. For instance, there was a large furry thing like an elephant's foot by the bed. It had a zip down the front. It was to put your feet in to keep them warm.

In my en suite bathroom – little more than a converted cupboard – there was soap on a rope and the spare toilet rolls were in a knitted tube with a toadstool cap on them.

106

The woman's husband was a would-be poet. The walls were covered with his poems, displayed in exuberant typefaces. He was very fond of the semi-colon; shame he didn't know how to use it. It was song lyric stuff. One began: 'I have rode the highways'. Above my bed was an 'Ode on the Anniversary of Diana's Death'. Aaagh.

I dumped my stuff and immediately drove back into Tintagel, parked the Range Rover and walked slowly along the windswept street. When I saw a bloke in a ten-gallon cowboy hat and chaps go into the King Arthur Arms I wondered if the bump on my head had been more serious than I thought.

I stepped into a shop that was selling a range of Arthurian clobber, standing aside to let a man go by. A Japanese man. The same one or another?

'Get a lot of Japanese tourists round here?' I said to the big man behind the counter. He was dressed circa the launch of breakfast TV – a brightly patterned pullover with bobbles hanging off it.

'It's the chivalry thing,' he said in a strong American accent. 'It links to the code of honour of their whatsit – Yakuza?'

'Samurai?'

'Samurai, right. I love that Seven Samurai – you probably never seen it, but it was the basis for a big Hollywood movie – you know which one?'

'Magni—'

'*Seven Brides for Seven Brothers*,' he said.

'No, no,' I protested. 'That was *The Rape of the Sabine Women*.'

He frowned.

'That's not a Japanese movie I ever heard of. But I don't mean *Seven Brides for Seven Brothers* either. Damn, my memory's definitely going. No, Seven Samurai became – *The Dirty Dozen*? Can't be right. If it only took seven Nips you think it's gonna take twelve of our boys to get the job done?'

I thought it was time to change the subject.

'Interesting shop. All these swords.' I was looking at a glass cabinet in which a dozen long, carefully decorated broadswords were displayed side by side. They each had names. There was Excalibur but there was also a Lancelot, a Guinevere, a Viking and even an Ivanhoe.

'Do people actually buy these?'

'You bet. Had an old guy in the other day, lives in a bungalow in the next village. He bought the Excalibur, said it would look terrific over his mantelpiece. But most of them are bought by re-enactors. They buy them with scabbards, of course.'

'Re-enactors?' I queried.

He pointed to a poster on the back of his door advertising a three-day re-enactment of Arthur's last battle in Tintagel at Easter.

'But nobody knows what happened—' I started to say, then my attention was diverted by the appearance of a cowgirl in jeans, plaid shirt, cowboy boots and stetson at the other end of the shop. He followed my glance.

'My wife,' he said.

'You're from Texas or somewhere out West?' I said, puzzled.

'New York,' he said, looking equally puzzled. 'As I was saying, there are re-enactors from every age. Roman legionnaires, Norman knights, medieval jousters, round-heads and cavaliers, veterans of the Napoleonic Wars, troops from the two World Wars – though by law World War II people can only wear German or American uniforms in this country.'

His wife tottered over on her high-heeled cowboy boots.

'Bunch of weirdos they are,' she said in a strong Welsh accent. 'Dressing up to play games.' She cocked a thumb at her husband. 'Him and his mates are bonkers for it.'

Somebody tapped on the window. There were a half-dozen more cowboys and cowgirls peering into the shop. I looked from them to the American's wife.

'There's a lot of demand for battle re-enactments,' he said, giving his wife a dirty look. 'We've done film work. And we do weddings. Wherever anyone wants a fight basically.'

'He's off in the woods every chance he gets,' his wife said with a snort, sticking her hands in the back pockets of her jeans.

'Just an ordinary bunch of men getting together. We hold pagan feasts, sing songs around the campfire and have trials of strength.' He gave me a sincere look that reminded me of Hughie Green in his heyday. 'Please ignore the popular rumours. We do not flay sheep over the fire or paint ourselves in blood.'

'So you say,' his wife said. 'I'm off. See you later.'

I watched her walk out and totter down the street with the other cowhands. They were all wearing finely-chiselled cowboy boots except for one man who looked rather sheepish in a pair of trainers.

'Every week we have kit-making sessions,' the shop owner continued. 'We use templates of Saxon clothes and old methods wherever possible. Some people cheat and use sewing machines, but I sew everything by hand. Hand-dyeing too, with things like onion skins.'

I indicated the glass cabinet.

'Where do you get the swords from?'

'Toledo, Spain. Rolled steel. The real thing. The hilts are either gold or bronze. They're produced by old established sword-smiths who make ceremonial swords for navies and other branches of the military around the world. They have spare capacity so they started these as a sideline. Sell them all over – re-enacting is big in Scandinavia and Germany too – all that rape and pillage.'

'And you've got one?'

'Of course. But to be honest I'm more interested in the acting than the actual battles.' He smiled coyly. 'I do a pretty good impersonation of a bloated battlefield corpse.'

'I'm sure you do,' I said politely.

He leaned over conspiratorially.

'I'm in big demand. And I think it's important to do it properly because it encourages the others. One of the problems with re-enactments is that hardly anybody volunteers to fall.'

'To fall?'

He mimed taking a sword in the stomach, his face contorting in agony. He wasn't bad actually. As suddenly he straightened and jerked a thumb at the poster.

'That's why it takes three bloody days. You can understand it really. Why get all dressed up to lie hot and still – or, worse, to freeze your nuts off – for most of the afternoon? But it means the battles can go on for an absolute age. Tempers get quite frayed. "I just killed you, you're dead." "No, I'm not, it was only a flesh wound." "My sword went right through your body." "No, really, I feel fine." '

I backed out of the shop soon after and crossed the road in the rain into a cosy-looking pub. A log fire was burning and the first bar was pleasant enough, if you could ignore the photos of Lester Piggot on the wall.

I wanted some time to review matters. I'd also brought with me a couple of books to find out more about Arthur's tomb. My main preoccupation was to wonder if I had survived an attack by the Camelot Killer. I was trying to recall if there were any pre-Raphaelite paintings to do with drownings. Maybe it was enough that it was Merlin's Cave. I recalled a Burne-Jones painting about Merlin bewitched by Nimue.

As I sipped my orange juice and mineral water – a pint, mind, nothing effete about me – I wondered too about Faye. A strange look had crossed her face when I'd spoken about the man following her. Could she have been meeting somebody?

That reminded me of the sight of Askwith, her husband, talking to someone in the shadows at the college the evening he died. And that, of course, reminded me that I'd seen Faye drift across the quad on her own.

My Faye involved in murder? I couldn't believe it. Not, that is, the Faye I used to know. But it was some years since

I'd seen her and I'd been struck at the time by how cool she'd been when Lucy died.

I thought about Lucy. The Fair Maid of Astolet had died for love of someone. Lucy had had a fling with Rex, according to Faye, but I wondered too about Reggie Williamson. He was married with kids, but didn't researchers always have affairs with their MPs? I decided that I couldn't use such tabloid presumptions as the basis for my investigations, journalist or no.

Thinking about Lucy reminded me that I'd brought her papers with me. I wasn't feeling tired. As a matter of fact I was feeling amorous and wishing Genevra was here. (I was also missing Faye. Go figure.)

I resolved to take a look at Lucy's things when I got back to the guest house. For now I ordered a vegetarian dish and sat in the corner of the pub for an hour examining the history books I'd brought with me.

I drove back to the guest house around ten, got the box out of the boot and started to let myself in. The door swung open. My landlady was standing there, dressed as a cowgirl.

'People still do line dancing down here?' I said, as I edged past her again.

'Still?' she said, puzzled. 'It's only just got here.'

When I got to my room I put the TV on. A debate was taking place between the Wiltshire and the East End Messiahs. I tipped the contents of the carton onto the bed and opened the first folder.

As I leafed through the papers – lists of births, deaths and marriages – not sure what I was looking for, the debate got pretty heated. There had been unconfirmed reports in the tabloids that the Wiltshire Messiah (or the Wiltshire Dipstick as his rival referred to him) was a jobbing actor who had learned his scripture in touring companies doing *Godspell* and *Jesus Christ Superstar*. It was further rumoured that he took the 'Suffer the little children' bit of his preaching too much to heart and that he had a criminal record for assaults on under-aged girls.

111

I'd just opened the second folder and drawn out a sheet of University of Nottingham letterheaded paper when violence erupted in the TV studios. The apostles of the East End Messiah had begun singing 'Thank Heaven for Little Girls' and the Wiltshire Messiah's own apostles had gone for them.

I got up to turn the TV off as the programme was brought to a hurried end and the credits started to roll. I took a step and fell over. I reached down with one hand and unzipped the elephant's foot. Well, it was a cold room.

I realised I was still clutching the letter, now rather crumpled, in my hand. I shuffled back onto my bed and began to read. It was from a technical lab at the university and concerned the delivery of some bones for dating. The letter itself was dated the previous December.

I lay back cautiously, aware of the lump on my head. December was the month when Lucy had discovered Arthur and Guinevere's tomb. But surely these bones couldn't be from there – I distinctly remembered Rex saying they'd decided against carbon dating the bones. Had he been lying?

At nine the next morning I phoned the university and got through to the labs. I explained to the woman who answered the phone that Lucy had died and I was trying to make sense of her papers. We spoke for ten minutes. When I turned off my mobile I sat in the jeep and looked out to sea.

Curiouser and curiouser. Lucy had sent a sample of half a dozen bones for testing. She told the university only that they were from a crypt, although she indicated that she was curious about one bone which did not look the same as the others in terms of discolouration and other signs of antiquity. The lab had analysed the six bones. Five were from two people who had died at roughly the same time, somewhere between 2000BC and AD1000 – nothing like a margin of error when you don't want to be tied down. The sixth bone was from a third person. That there was a third person buried with Arthur and Guinevere came as a surprise, although I remembered now thinking, just before I was disturbed by Nanny, that there were an awful lot of bones in the sarcophagus.

That this third person had been buried with them within the last fifty years was even more of a shock.

Chapter Seven

Driving back to Montacute I thought again about Lucy's death. Although I couldn't find a second letter from the university in her files, they had written to Lucy only the previous week. She would have got the letter the day she died. That and my re-reading of Malory got me puzzling over another letter.

Elaine, the Fair Maid of Astolet, had written a letter that had been found with her body. It explained why she had taken her life. If a serial killer were really copying the manner of her death wouldn't he too have left a letter?

My phone rang just as I was approaching a lay-by. I pulled in. It was Faye phoning from Montacute.

'Nick, what you were saying yesterday about someone threatening our lives,' she said without preamble. 'I've just been talking to Bridget. She says you think there's a serial killer on the loose. You're not going to go public with this theory, are you? Because I think that would be very foolish and could cause immense damage to our project.'

I sighed and touched the back of my head.

'Bridget blabbermouth, eh? I have no proof. It was just an idea.' I saw again Lucy lying in the bottom of the boat. Then I had an image of Faye leaning over her. Of her turning and thrusting her hands deep into her pockets.

'You know when we found Lucy's body?' I said. 'You didn't take anything from it, did you?'

'Like?'

'A letter?'

'Why would I do that?' she said coldly.

'I don't know,' I said carefully. 'I just wondered.'

'Let's talk when you get back,' she said, and rang off.

I switched the phone off and started the engine. She was making a habit of deferring conversations. You might say we'd been deferring one for the past fifteen years.

When I got back to Wynn House Buckhalter was holding forth to Rex and Faye.

'If we get into bed with local developers we can put in big stores, smaller shopping units, hell, the Camelot Casino – and parking for seven hundred people.'

He noticed me out of the corner of his eye – and gave me a sour look. Rex saw me too.

'Nick, good to have you back. Come and give us your view of the PR implications of Lucy's death.'

'Well,' I said, taking a seat. 'I'd say the PR implications aren't good.'

'And they'll be even less good if you start mouthing off with harebrained theories about a serial killer on the loose,' Buckhalter said.

'It's a possibility I don't think we should ignore,' I said calmly. I looked from one to the other. 'Look at it this way. If it wasn't a stranger – then she was killed by someone she knew.'

Rex sighed and shook his head.

'What a nightmare,' he muttered.

'What do you think about the rival discoveries?' I said.

'We don't have to worry about the Arthur found buried with his horse,' Rex said. 'A terrific find but it isn't Arthur. Burials like that were particular to the Saxons, not the Britons.'

'Who's Joseph of Arimathea?' Buckhalter said.

'He's supposed to be the bloke who lent his tomb for Jesus to be buried in,' I said. 'In the twelfth century some storyteller decided Joseph had got the beaker used at the Last Supper and filled it with Christ's blood, brought it over to Britain, founded Glastonbury Abbey and buried it here.'

116

'So this farmer could have dug up the Grail?'

'No, no,' I said impatiently. 'There's no proof that Joseph of Arimathea came here. There's no evidence whatsoever that he even existed. And he certainly didn't bring the Grail over. The Grail originally was a horn of plenty or even a flat stone in Celtic myth.'

'Who gives a fuck?' Buckhalter said. 'If it brings more tourists into this area it can only be good for us. No problem.'

'You do have another problem though,' I said. I looked over at Rex. 'Didn't you say you hadn't had the bones dated?'

'That's right,' he said absently.

'Well, Lucy did.'

He looked at me sharply.

'How do you know?'

'I found some correspondence between her and Nottingham University.'

'The results?' he said, leaning forward in his seat.

'No, but I phoned the lab and got them.'

'And what does it say?' Buckhalter asked.

'Oh, given the margin of error they're more or less the right age. Well, most of them.'

'Most of them?'

'Analysis shows that there was a third body in the sarcophagus, one that wasn't nearly so old.'

Rex frowned. Faye looked puzzled, Buckhalter impatient.

'I don't know what you're saying,' Buckhalter snapped.

'I'm saying that a dead body – or most of it – was put in that sarcophagus somewhere between fifteen and fifty years ago.'

'Most of a body?' Buckhalter said. 'What the hell does that mean?'

'Well, there's no skull, for one thing. I don't know what other parts of the skeleton are missing.'

'So why couldn't some other bones have got mixed up with our King and Queen by accident?'

'Because the crypt hasn't been used for burials for over a century', Rex said slowly. He smiled grimly. 'So if there are any bones there it seems likely they are a result of—'

'—of foul play,' Faye said, relishing the phrase though her face was even paler than usual.

'Somebody's bumped someone off and dumped the corpus delicti in Arthur's tomb. Jesus.' Buckhalter looked at me. 'Well, if this is your serial killer and that's his killing rate, at least nobody is in immediate danger.' He rubbed his eyes. 'So what do we do? Toss 'em in the river?'

'Not a chance,' I said. 'We tell the police.'

'We have to tell the cops?'

I nodded. 'You bet. If we don't, the university will. We hand all the bones over for analysis. There's no way for us to know which are the new bones, which the old.'

'Shit,' Buckhalter said. 'This could delay the opening.'

'True,' I said. 'But every problem is an opportunity, so I'm sure you'll sort that. And there is a more intriguing matter.'

'And that is?' Buckhalter said fiercely.

Faye cleared her throat.

'Whose bones are they?' she whispered.

I needed fresh air so I went to the chapel by the outside route. Once in the crypt I looked down at the bones laid out in the sarcophagus. No wonder they were piled haphazardly – fitting three lots of bones into two skeletons would have taken a lot of imagination.

I had a torch with me and I shone it into the shadowy recesses of the crypt. I was half-expecting Nanny to be sitting there but this time I was alone.

I was wondering if there could be a way the newer bones had got into the tomb by accident. Among Lucy's papers I'd found notes in which she'd described her discovery of Arthur's sarcophagus. When she'd begun the crypt had contained some thirty tombs and wooden coffins. After years of flooding, the coffins were scattered all across the floor.

Some were on their sides, others piled haphazardly on top of each other. Several stone tombs had lost their lids, which lay in pieces on the floor. There were bones scattered everywhere.

The lid of the black marble tomb had lain across the sarcophagus at an angle, exposing either end. There were fragments of cloth rotted by immersion in flood water, which suggested Arthur and Guinevere's remains had originally been carefully wrapped. But when Lucy found them, their bones were scattered across the bottom of the sarcophagus.

So it would have been easy enough, when the crypt flooded, for other bones to have got mixed up with them. Except that, as Rex had pointed out, this crypt had not been used for some hundred years. There was no reason for more recent bones to be there, unless they had been put there under suspicious circumstances.

I sighed. The bones could have been anybody's. I went back up into the chapel and when I left walked the short distance to the flooded river. I looked to the east. The oars from the rowing boat were, I noticed, still lying on the grass. I looked over at the boathouse.

When I walked back up to the house I bumped into Genevra and Bridget. Genevra was wearing an anorak with its hood up. Bridget was dressed in a Country Life catalogue. She had on a long waxed jacket that reached down below her polished green wellingtons and a waxed hat that looked as if it should have corks hanging down from it. She was carrying a walking stick. She also had on some giant hoop earrings and full make-up, although her mascara had run.

She had a fixed smile on her face. Uh-oh.

'Just been showing Bridget the estate,' Genevra said. 'The heavens opened – good job we were prepared for it.'

'Nick!' Rex called. I looked over to the big old barn. He was standing in its doorway. He waved me over. 'Come and meet Mort Darthur. You guys too.'

119

PETER GUTTRIDGE

'That irritating little prick,' Genevra muttered. 'Not bloody likely. I should have a bath instead if I were you, Bridget. See you later, Nick.'

'Mort Darthur?' I said as I reached Rex.

'A pun on Malory,' Rex said, raising an eyebrow. 'He's a court jester. Leads a bunch of travelling players. We're going to be using them on various projects around the theme park. I thought you might like to meet him and check out the banqueting hall.'

He led the way into the barn.

'Wow,' I said.

It was the size of a small cathedral. Broad rafters, vast timber struts and cross beams held everything in place. The walls had been decorated with large shields and painted pennants. More shields hung from the upright timbers. Long trestle tables were stacked neatly against one wall. At the far end, on a raised dais, was a gilt throne. Someone was sitting on it. Buckhalter stood beside this person, a towering presence.

'We're ready to run with this whenever,' Rex said as we walked down the barn towards the throne. 'The kitchens are set up, lavatories provided and so on. We can do banquets here. We can also do jousts down the middle whilst people eat at the sides.'

The guy on the throne was tiny, his feet not touching the floor. He had a pair of red-rimmed glasses and a blond fringe. He looked like Brains from that old puppet thing on the telly. He was wearing a doublet and bright yellow hose, which put him a few centuries out. He stood up. It didn't make him any taller.

Rex did the introductions.

'Another one of your university chums?' Mort said.

'Sort of,' Rex murmured.

'University of Life, me, mate,' Mort said, though I wish he hadn't. 'With a First in the Bleeding Obvious.'

He suddenly plunged his hand down into his codpiece and brought out a business card then held it out for me.

120

'Thanks,' I said, taking it by one corner.

'Whatever you want, we can do,' Mort said. 'Roman, Saxon, medieval banquets. Jousts. We can provide you with wenches, musicians –' he shook his rattle – 'jesters – jongleurs if you will. The full service.'

'Mort was just suggesting that for our spring promotion we have Guinevere riding naked through the streets,' Rex said.

'Wasn't that Lady Godiva?' I said.

'It's all history, isn't it?' Mort said. I groaned. Not another one. 'Then there's the let-them-eat-cake bit.'

'But that was Marie Antoinette!'

'So? We haven't had that many queens so we've got to pool what we know about queendom – queendomness?'

'Queenliness.'

'Queenliness.' He sniffed. 'Nobody likes a clever dick, you know. Then we get Arthur burning the cakes. Or trying to make the sea turn back. Or getting an arrow in his eye.'

I started to speak.

'Before you say it, we know that's Harold,' Buckhalter said. 'But it's all history.'

'I was going to say that it wasn't Harold, it's just that on the Bayeux tapestry his name is next to that bloke. In fact Harold is the one lying on the ground—'

'So what?' Mort asked, giving me a filthy look.

'I'm going to leave you to it,' Rex said, clapping him on the shoulder. 'Be seeing you.' He turned to me. 'Nick, walk with me.'

As we walked through the old barn he said: 'Nick, I admire your integrity, I really do. And I understand your desire for historical authenticity. But unfortunately this world doesn't work that way. The bottom line is profit. I'm backed by some pretty serious heavy-hitters and they don't care about historical niceties. They see Stonehenge generating six million visitors a year, Glastonbury attracting almost two million. They want a slice.'

He pulled open the barn door.

'I hear you ran into a couple of bits of trouble in the West Country.' He glanced across at me. 'I hope you're not linking that to this serial killer theory of yours.'

I shook my head. We started to cross towards the house, both of us leaning into the wind.

'So do you have a profile of this guy?' he called.

I shook my head.

'It's just a theory,' I called back. 'One that I hope isn't true.'

'Me too, old stick. Me too.'

There was a bulky, bearded man in jeans and an anorak standing in the entrance hall talking to Nanny. Hanging down his back was a long double-edged sword.

'Oh, Rex,' Nanny said. 'There's an Uther Pendragon to see you.'

'Another one?' Rex said mildly.

The man held out his hand.

'Lord Wynn?' he said in a strong Birmingham accent. 'Please call me Uther.'

'Pendragon – that's Cornish isn't it?' Nanny said as we walked into the drawing room.

'I'm the father of King Arthur and a knight of his Round Table,' Pendragon said, his solemnity slightly undercut by the Brummy rasp.

'Uther Pendragon may never have been Arthur's father, whatever Geoffrey of Monmouth says,' I said. 'Geoffrey probably misread Arthur mab uthr – Arthur the Terrible – as Arthur, son of Uther.'

Pendragon gave me a fierce stare.

'I've seen photographs of you with Excalibur but you look different,' Rex said, smiling politely.

Pendragon growled.

'That's an impostor who has been going round for years claiming to be me. I am the real thing.' He reached behind him and with both hands pulled his long sword up over his head then placed the point on the floor in front of him.

122

'And this is Excalibur. I keep it always near.'

'Is it one of those made in Spain?' I asked.

He gave me a baleful look.

'This is the *real* Excalibur.'

'I would have thought King Arthur would be the one to keep it near.'

Uther looked slightly uncomfortable.

'We take turns,' he said, adding, after a moment, 'It was mine first.'

'Of course it was. But how did you get it back from Sicily, I wonder?' Rex said silkily. 'Or is that where Arthur has been sleeping all this time, as some stories suggest?'

Pendragon frowned.

'Sicily?'

'Did you not know that Richard the Lionheart presented Tancred of Sicily with Excalibur when he visited Sicily on the way to the Third Crusade? He claimed it had been discovered in the grave of Arthur and Guinevere in Glastonbury along with their remains – the remains that we now have here.'

'Those remains are the reason for my visit. I come with a message from my King, Arthur of the Britons. He demands that you announce his so-called dead body to be a fake and that you give up your plans to open an Arthurian theme park here.'

'Let me get this straight – the man who claims he has been sleeping in a cave under a mountain for the past fifteen hundred years is calling my things fake. And what about you? Even supposing that were true of Arthur, where have you and the rest of the Round Table been kipping?'

'I have been given the honorary title of Uther Pendragon just as my fellow knights have their honorary titles.'

'So what's your real name?'

'I no longer answer to my real name. I have been reborn.'

'You must think the rest of us have just been born too,' Rex said.

'You'd be well advised to listen to Arthur's demands.'

'Or you'll try kidnapping again?' I said.

Pendragon looked puzzled.

'A group of your knights tried to kidnap Lord Wynn's sister, Genevra, two nights ago,' I said. 'Hardly a chivalrous thing to do.'

'By what name went these knights?'

'The leader went by – was called Bedevere.'

He shook his head.

'I didn't know and nor, I'm sure, did Arthur.'

Rex looked at his watch.

'I believe you. And I'd love to chat some more, Uther, but there are a hundred and one things to do around here. Don't rush, though. Nanny will look after you. Nick?'

As we left the room, leaving Pendragon awkwardly leaning on his sword, I heard Nanny saying: 'Would you care for a glass of mead? I'm not sure what it is, but I think I have some I picked up in the National Trust shop in Wells.'

'A bit provoking to Uther, weren't you?' I said to Rex as he walked me over to the west wing of the house.

'What am I supposed to do? I knew they were going to be trouble. This guy is claiming he is the returned Arthur – the last thing he wants is for Arthur's body to be found.'

'You can't think anyone's really going to believe he's Arthur Returned. People aren't stupid.'

'Thousands of people believe in these fake Messiahs that have sprung up in recent months. And thousands believe crop circles are visitations from space despite all the evidence pointing to them being man-made. Fifteen million people in the UK read their stars every day. World-class organisations hire people partly on analysis of their handwriting and lay out their offices along feng shui lines. Millions of people believe that Jesus Christ was the Son of God and that his mother was a virgin. So yes, I believe people are stupid enough or trusting enough or needy enough to believe virtually anything.'

We'd reached a set of double doors. He pressed a light switch then opened them.

'And this will be our casino. The licence is being sorted.'

'When is this due to open?' I said.

'Same time as the banqueting hall, though I anticipate the clientele will be different.' He looked at me, seemed to be sizing me up. 'I could do with some front-of-house help when all this starts.'

'Multi-tasking?'

He grinned.

'Right.'

I didn't mind. I quite fancied swishing about in a tuxedo pretending I was in a Bond movie.

I left Rex shortly after and went along to Bridget's room.

'Just coming!' she trilled in answer to my knock. Bridget trilling?

'Oh, it's you,' she said sourly when she opened the door. That was more like it.

She'd got her dressing gown on. She walked across the room and poured herself a large vodka from a vacuum flask. She caught my look.

'I'm bracing myself,' she said. 'I have to pass the Nanny test.'

'The what?'

'You know these upper-class types – the only love they had as children was from their Nanny. She lives after retirement in the attic somewhere in the big house. Anyway, I've been invited to tea with her. Gennie tells me it's a sort of rite of passage – if she approves, I'm all but part of the family.'

'I've met her. Tell her you like sitting around in crypts and you'll be well away.'

I sat down.

'Isn't all this a bit quick? Have you and Rex actually done it yet?'

'Like rabbits. And you forget I've known him for years.'

'Well, after a fashion.'

'Besides, my biological clock is ticking – the alarm's just gone off in fact.

'You mean children?'

'I mean old age, you stupid git. If I leave it much longer I'm not going to be able to get anyone decent.'

'Is that what feminism is?'

'No, but it's my understanding of post-feminism. We're officially allowed to covet frocks and lingerie and lipstick then use our womanly wiles to get them.'

'The biological clock?' I repeated.

'Absolutely – it's been telling me just how long I've been working.'

'How long?'

'Too bloody long.'

The people at Glastonbury Abbey had told me that most of the ancient documents relating to the abbey were now housed at Wells Cathedral. Later that day I borrowed Genevra's Range Rover and drove into Wells. I parked in the cobbled square outside the entrance to the Bishop's Palace. The square was almost deserted although there were a couple of middle-aged women going into the National Trust shop. I started to walk towards the entrance to the moated Bishop's Palace then changed my mind and swung past the NT shop towards Penniless Porch.

Somebody coming in the other direction also seemed to have changed his mind. I was vaguely aware of a tall, thin man in a long black coat and homburg turning back into the porch. When I reached it a hopeful traveller in a bedraggled duffel coat was sitting cross-legged on the marble seat playing an out-of-tune guitar very badly. His dog, rope lead coiled around her, lay slumped at his feet. When the young man began to sing the dog gave a little yowl. I half expected it to put its paws over its ears, but it got to its feet and for a moment I was tangled in its rope lead.

Even at this time of the year there was a score of people

126

on the long grassy area in front of the cathedral taking photographs of the tiers of monumental statues, each one in its own niche, on the magnificent western façade.

At this time of day, between services, the cathedral was quiet, although still filled with that odd refraction of sound vast buildings generate: a vague background susurrus combined with the sharp immediacy of doors closing, wooden seats clattering, rubber-soled shoes squeaking on the waxed floors.

That's how I became aware someone was following me. As I walked down the right-hand nave I was conscious of a squeak of shoes somewhere behind me. When I stopped before the sign in front of the library telling me that it was closed for the afternoon, the footsteps also stopped.

Ordinarily I would have thought nothing of it – would not, indeed, have noticed it now had I not had my bad experience in Cornwall. I peered round the corner back down the aisle I had just walked up. Nothing except an old woman with a bunch of flowers at the very far end.

I followed the aisle past the main altar to the Lady Chapel at the far east of the building. Again the footsteps. When I paused before the Lady Chapel, the footsteps stopped. I crossed the Lady Chapel and headed west back down the side aisle that ran parallel to the one I had just walked down.

I walked quickly, my feet slapping loudly on the stone floor, then stepped sideways into a tiny chapel. I heard a pair of hurrying feet, then another. Two people wanting to run but unable to do so walking as fast as they were able. I shrank back against the wall, pressing my cheek to the cold marble of a large plaque.

A boy and a girl in the uniform of the Wells Cathedral school scurried past. I breathed a sigh of relief until I heard in the silence the rubbery squeak of those familiar footsteps, patient and deliberate.

I peeped into the aisle. Nobody in either direction. I went out into the aisle and came within a few yards to a sign for the

Chapter House. The way lay through an old oak door. A sign on it said *Private* but I lifted the latch and went through, closing it carefully behind me. There was a worn flight of cream stone stairs in front of me leading to the bridge that connected the cathedral to its school. The walls were of light sandstone and the whole place seemed light and airy.

I started up the flight of stairs. I had gone about twelve steps when I heard the door below me creak open. I dived into the Chapter House to my right. It was a circular room with a high roof. Nowhere to hide. I tiptoed across to a pillar beside the flight of steps and flattened myself behind it. I heard the squeak of shoes approaching. Then they stopped.

I held my breath and listened intently. I was cursing myself for coming out of the public parts of the cathedral. After a couple of minutes I heard the door again. Somebody leaving or someone else coming in? I stayed where I was and continued to listen. Nothing. I checked my watch and forced myself to stay where I was. For five minutes I heard nothing.

Phew. I stepped out and started back down the stairs. A man was standing two steps below, his shoes in his left hand, a walking stick in his right.

'Aagh!' I yelped.

'Spare any money for a pint?' the white-haired, wild-eyed madman from the abbey ruins said.

I sank down on the step behind me.

'What the fuck do you think you're doing?' I said. 'Why are you following me –' I gestured at his shoes – 'in your stocking feet?'

'So you wouldn't hear me,' he replied in a puzzled voice. The wild look came into his eye again.

'You are manipulated,' he said in a low, intense voice.

'Story of my life,' I said. 'But okay – who's manipulating me?'

'Who else but an Anti-Christ sprung from the wrestlings of incubus and nun?'

I got to my feet.

'Hey, is that the time? Gotta go. Great talking to you. It's good to know care in the community can chalk up another triumph.'

As I stepped past him he dropped his shoes and grabbed my sleeve.

'Merlin, that old trickster,' he hissed, spraying the side of my face with his spit. 'Merlin the Duality.'

'Merlin's manipulating me.' I pulled my sleeve free. 'That's valuable information, thank you.'

I set off down the steps. He shouted after me: 'Merlinus Sylvester, wild man of the woods, ran gelt mad from the din of battle when the heavens parted and voices struck him insane. He ran to live with the beasts, like Nebuchadnezzar – his nails became talons, his body grew feathers, he was sustained by grass and grubs.'

I turned back at the door.

'Are you working from a script or is all this just off the top of your head?'

He looked suddenly bewildered. I felt like a shit for mocking him. He really was another poor bastard with a screw loose and nobody to take care of him. Except that his high-flown language did sound like he was quoting and his Arthurian obsession was . . .

I watched him as he slumped onto a step and pulled on one of his shoes. His Arthurian obsession. Could he be the Camelot Killer? I dismissed the thought as quickly as I had it. If Askwith had been murdered I couldn't imagine this man doing it without anyone noticing him. And how would he have got to Oxford? He didn't look as if he had two shillings to rub together.

I went back up the steps and slipped a tenner into his top pocket. When I left, he was sitting on the step, gazing blankly at the shoe he still held in his hand.

I walked out through the south cloister so that I could take a look at the moated Bishop's Palace. I walked over the bridge across to the massive gatehouse. A couple of swans were idling beneath the bell that used to ring when it was their mealtime.

I did feel manipulated, by everybody. And out of my depth. I looked up at the black sky. More rain soon. I walked back to the car in the cobbled square. Faye, in her orange anorak and black jeans, was leaning against it. She levered herself upright and waited for me to reach her.

'Thought it must be you,' she said. 'Can you give me a lift back? I came in with Buck but he's going to be here for hours yet.'

'Sure,' I said. I looked at her strained face. 'As long as you tell me what's going on.'

'Nick, I can't talk.'

'You can. I'm the guy you used to tell everything to.'

She looked at me as if trying to remember, an odd little smile on her face.

'Did I?' she said. 'It's so long ago.'

'Well, you did. Remember that long talk we had before we split. You told me your innermost secrets.'

She turned her head away but nodded slowly.

'It's sort of linked to that – to that time, I mean.'

I put my arm across her shoulder. She shivered.

'Can we sit in the car?'

When we were settled I looked at her.

'Well?'

'Nick, there's something you need to know. My brother disappeared some years ago.'

'My God. What happened?'

'The thing about people disappearing is that you don't know what has happened, Nick.'

'Of course. But you haven't seen or heard from him in all that time?'

She shook her head.

'He'd talked of going to Canada. At first when he left I kept thinking I'd seen him in different places. I hoped he would write but he never did. Then, after a while, I forgot to hope.'

130

'So for all these years you haven't known if he's alive or dead.'

She shook her head and looked at me. She seemed to be expecting me to ask her something.

'How long ago was this?'

'Fifteen years.'

'When we split up?'

'Around that time, yes. But now I think I may know where he is.'

'Well, that's great,' I said.

She gave me an odd look.

'Hardly.'

I was obviously being slow on the uptake. Then it clicked.

'You think those other bones in Arthur's tomb . . .?'

'He was in the vicinity. He left his car at the Gatehouse.'

I frowned.

'What are you thinking happened to him? An accident? Suicide?'

'Or murder?' she said, voicing my unspoken third option.

'But why?'

'I don't know why. Just a feeling.'

'Can you remember the last time you saw him?'

'Of course. Your birthday. Friday the thirteenth.'

'The day we split up,' I said quietly.

She nodded.

'It will be well nigh impossible trying to track his movements that week after all this time.'

'Don't you think I tried then? He just disappeared.'

We said little on the drive back to Montacute. I dropped Faye off at the Gatehouse and drove up to the main house. I walked round to the back and across the sodden lawn and into the boggy meadow beside the river. I sank into soft mud.

The earth seemed bloated with water. The light was failing rapidly and the absolute silence and the freezing wind seemed to separate me from our own time.

'Can't you see him?' a familiar voice called from across the river.

I looked across and he was standing under a tree about thirty yards away on the other side of the flooded fields, near a track that led over the hill north east towards Glastonbury. The man I'd left behind in Wells only a couple of hours ago. He must have used my tenner to come straight here. But why?

'See who?'

'Ducks bellorum.'

Puzzled, I looked at the swans gliding across the meadows.

'Arthur.'

Ah. *Dux* bellorum. Arthur's sixth-century title of warlord.

The man waved vaguely at the ground beside him. He didn't seem so wild-eyed now. 'Bearded, muddy, savage, huddled with a small band of men in tattered cloaks around a smouldering rain-wet campfire.' He seemed as if he could see them, as he spoke, his voice summoning them. 'The wind beating at their backs, they look into the flames with tired, empty eyes. The resistance to the Saxon invasion. Brutal men with blood on their clothes and hunger in their bellies.'

I nodded. He continued to stare at me.

'Are you often here?' I called.

'You mean did I see the Fair Maid of Astolet drift to Westminster?'

I started.

'She was rowed according to Malory,' I said.

His face was split by a huge smile.

'That she was. Fair Elaine. She was a grand girl.'

'You knew her?' I said.

'Knew her. Know you. Knew her secrets. Know yours.'

He looked beyond me, saw something he didn't like, turned and started to shamble away. I looked round. Caught vague sight of someone stepping back at the side of the house. Turned back to him.

'Wait – can we talk some more?' I said.

He carried on walking.

'So did you see anything?' I shouted.

Without stopping, his head down, he thrust his right arm into the air and pointed at the sky.

'Signs and portents, for those who can read them.'

Chapter Eight

I actually looked up at the sky – that's how desperate I was getting to find out what was going on.

'Great,' I muttered as I watched him go. 'That's all I need – an Old Testament prophet as a potential witness.'

But witness to what? What had happened and where? The police had been back asking more questions but I got the impression they thought it was a random attack by someone who happened to come across Lucy on the towpath. I decided not to share with them any serial killer theory. No point *everybody* thinking I was an idiot. They'd spent a couple of days examining the towpath – the bits that weren't flooded, that is – but I got the impression they hadn't come up with anything.

I climbed up the side of the motte and sat on a fragment of the old wall. The oars had gone – back to the boathouse, I presumed. Why had they been lying there, just below the motte? Was that where Lucy had been attacked and loaded into the boat? It was a part of the towpath that couldn't be seen from the house.

But what was she doing there in the first place? I looked at the chapel standing some thirty yards away in the lee of the mound. Perhaps she had come to examine the bones. She would have got the letter dating the three sets of bones on the morning of her death. It made sense that she would hurry over here. Did she go to Rex first?

I didn't think so. I got the impression that she had sent them for testing secretly, perhaps even against his wishes –

Rex had told me they weren't going to bother. I guessed he didn't want to know how old the bones were, probably felt it was better for the project if they weren't dated.

But perhaps Lucy felt she had to tell him? She was, after all, obsessively in love with him. And he was angry to discover that not only had she gone against his wishes but there was also this added complication of the third set of bones. Got so angry he—

No, that theory wouldn't fly. If he'd killed her, he'd hardly draw attention to the fact that she was obsessed with him by making explicit reference to the Fair Maid of Astolet. And, if my serial killer theory were to hold, why did he kill Askwith?

Anyway, I couldn't imagine Rex as a killer. He seemed too easy-going, too *normal*. I imagined somebody ruthless, somebody who also had a lot to lose. Somebody called Buck Buckhalter?

A thought struck me. How did I know that Lucy was obsessed with Rex? It was only on Faye's say-so and I suspected Faye wasn't being entirely open with me.

The sun was almost gone now, the swans spectral figures gliding away downstream. I needed to talk to Bridget, my old amigo. But was she the same person I'd known and loved for all these years? I felt a twinge of jealousy about Rex. Why should I be jealous of a good-looking guy born with a silver spoon in his mouth worth £16 million who was bonking my best friend?

I grimaced. Was I sick in the head? I was pining for Faye, my first love who had broken my heart; lusting for Genevra, whom I couldn't keep my hands off; and getting jealous pangs about my best friend because she was sleeping with someone else. Still acting like a typical man, then.

When I came back into the house Rex was standing in the doorway to a small room beside the main drawing room.

'Old stick, do come and have a stiff one – so to say.' He ushered me into the room. 'My little den,' he said.

Some den. It was about twice the size of my flat in

Shepherd's Bush. The ceiling was some forty feet above us. There were books on three walls, a large assemblage of photos, plaques, painting and other memorabilia on the fourth.

He mixed a couple of gin and tonics, passed one over. What the hell – I couldn't stop drinking for ever. He sat down behind his desk and composed his face into a stern expression.

'So. How are you enjoying my sister?'

I blushed. Of course I blushed. But I was about to tell him to go screw himself when he grinned his gummy grin.

'Just joshing you, Nick. Wishing you two lots of happiness. She's great, isn't she?'

'One in a million,' I said, face still burning.

'And she gets better the better you get to know her.' He grinned again. 'You know I have to admit to a bit of jealousy. Genevra and I have always been close. *So* close . . .'

He had a curious expression on his face. I didn't know if he was giving me some kind of blessing or some kind of curse. I wondered if he'd had a head start on the drinking. I walked over to the wall of photos and other memorabilia.

'This Africa?' I said, pointing at a sepia photo of a group of men wearing creased linen suits and holding a range of hunting rifles. It was the black servants that gave it away.

'Grandfather was one of that Happy Valley lot in Kenya.'

'The one who got off with Greta Scacchi in *White Mischief*?' I said, only half-succeeding in keeping the envy out of my voice. I've always had a thing about Greta.

'You mean the person Greta Scacchi played? No, actually. But he lived that lifestyle, frittering away our money.'

'*Our* money?'

'Don't you know how it works? No, why would you? What's your background? I'm not asking for class reasons, old stick. Well, actually, I suppose I am.'

I sat down again.

'Working class, single parent.'

'Well, I venture to suggest you have no sense of duty. This house . . .' he waved his arm languidly to indicate, I guessed, Wynn House. 'We hold it in trust. It's not ours. It's not a pleasure to be here, it's a responsibility.'

'Yeah, I've heard that,' I said cautiously, resisting the temptation to say I wouldn't mind that kind of responsibility. He seemed to guess what I was thinking.

'Don't imagine most people could handle it. I was raised for it. Trained for it. My entire upbringing was designed to prepare me for this . . . this responsibility to the nation.'

'What about the rock bands?'

Bridget had told me that Rex used to manage various rock and roll bands. He reached back and touched his ponytail, perhaps for him a tangible memory of those early days.

'We're all allowed youthful rebellion. But I always knew my responsibility lay to the nation. And so did my grandfather. In frittering away my inheritance my grandfather was frittering away the nation's inheritance.'

The temptation to put my finger down my throat was almost overwhelming.

'Look, Nick, I don't expect you to understand, but an independent, property-owning landed class was for centuries seen as the right and natural ruling class. But power and privilege bring duties too.'

'I can imagine. Or rather I can't. But I do know one thing. If I lived in this house I wouldn't turn it into a theme park. Why are you doing it? Is it just the money?'

He raised an eyebrow.

'*Just* the money? Forgive me, but people who say that kind of thing usually don't have any. The tradition of opening great country houses for visits from the public goes back to the eighteenth century. However, this century the stately home is not enough. You need to give added value. The aristocratic pioneers knew that.

'The Marquess of Bath who opened Longleat to the public in 1949, introduced lions. Lord Montague of Beaulieu opened his house in 1952 and added his vintage car collection, whilst the Duke of Bedford, who opened Woburn Abbey in 1955, began a tradition of music festivals.'

He hadn't answered my question but I had a more important one.

'Do you mind me asking whether you saw Lucy on the day she died?'

'I don't mind you asking but I don't understand why you're asking.'

'I was just curious about her movements that day. I think she got a letter from the university about the dating of the bones that morning. I'm assuming she would have brought it to show you.' I paused then added casually, 'Or Buckhalter.'

Rex frowned.

'I think you're going some way beyond your remit concerning yourself with Lucy's unfortunate death. My view is that she was attacked by some madman on the towpath. I also believe that the police are quite capable of investigating her death without any assistance from you.' He got to his feet and walked over to the drinks cabinet. 'Focus, if you will, please, Nick, on the question of Arthur's tomb. Nothing more.' He held the gin bottle out. 'A top-up?'

That night, in bed with Genevra, when I'd got my breath back, I asked her about Rex's motives.

'Why is Rex doing this? He's worth millions, he doesn't need the money. Why is he fucking up his home to make a few more?'

'You can never be too rich or too thin,' Genevra said, smiling and cupping her full breasts. 'One out of two ain't bad.'

'No, seriously,' I said. 'And if he is so rich, why does he need investors?'

'You never risk your own money, surely you know that,' she said. 'That's how you stay rich.'

'Who are the investors?'

She suddenly sat up, breasts jiggling with the sudden motion – ay, Chihuahua! – and nipped my arm. Which hurt, actually.

'Listen, buster, when I invite you into my bed for a spot of rumpy-pumpy I don't expect to be quizzed about my family's finances, thanks all the same.' She reached under the sheet. 'If you can't think of anything else to talk about, put that to work instead.'

It would have been churlish to refuse.

Two tall people making love can get complicated because of the need to get your long limbs sorted out. I don't want to give away her intimate secrets but Genevra liked to get her legs up and over my shoulders and cross them behind my neck.

'I usually do this on my own,' I murmured.

'Pervert,' she gasped. 'Would you rather?'

'No, I mean—'

I would have said more but in a sudden paroxysm of excitement she had locked her legs more tightly around my neck.

'Don't stop!' Her voice was suddenly very throaty.

'Hnngh,' I gasped as the oxygen supply to my brain started to dwindle.

'Don't – please – don't – don't – *don't* – *don't* – *dooonnn'ttt* . . .'

I did. Well, I couldn't breathe, dammit. She hid her disappointment well. Thinking, for some reason, of all-in wrestling's three falls and a submission, I was lying on my back taking deep breaths and discreetly massaging my crushed neck muscles when she nudged me and said: 'What do you mean, you usually do it on your own?'

'It's a yoga position: Uthitha kurmasana. You thread your legs back under your armpits and cross your ankles behind your head. I once saw—'

'Why?'

'Good question. I have no idea. I once saw a woman fall off a hotel roof while I was in that position. The surprise didn't do me any good. Although she didn't come out of it too well either. At all, in fact.'

I looked down.

140

'What are you doing? I'm not one of those five times a night guys – I don't think I'll be able to . . . well, whaddya know?'

I had a feeling it went better this time.

'There's nothing impressive about five times a night,' she said a little later. 'The guy to be impressed by is the one time a night guy.' She gave a dirty chuckle. 'All night.'

Counts me out then.

'So did you and Faye ever fuck?'

'Genevra, that's private. I don't know that I know you well enough.'

'You know me well enough to see my face when I come.'

'You came?'

'Yes, what did you think all that huffing and puffing and moaning and groaning was about?'

'You came.'

'Nick – are you serious? Was this the first time you've made a woman come?'

'Of course not. Don't be silly.'

'So why have you got that daft grin on your face?'

'You weren't faking?'

'Of course I wasn't. Were you? Or was the impersonation of a singing budgerigar your normal response to orgasm?' My face must have dropped. She squeezed me. 'Just kidding, Nick, just kidding.'

She lifted her leg up in the air and flexed her foot. It was a lovely leg.

'We're orphans in the storm, you and I. Bridget told me your mum died when you were three. Mine did too.'

'Did your dad not marry again?'

'Oh yes, I had a stepmother. Camilla. Ghastly woman. Sold off our inheritance, almost destroyed this house renovating it and dressing it up boudoir style – pink ruche curtains everywhere. It was a relief when she cleared off.'

'She abandoned you? Boy, you must have some issues around that.'

Genevra reached up to kiss me on the cheek.

141

'I see you've been reading the right textbooks. Actually, all I felt was relief.'

'Where did she go?'

'South America, I think.'

'You don't know?'

'Never bothered to find out.'

'And she's never been in touch?'

'No, thank Christ.'

I got up bright and early – well, early, anyway – the next morning to do my yoga. As I was cooling off afterwards I looked out of my window and saw Rex crossing the meadows with Neville, the estate manager. Figuring that meant Bridget would be alone, I went down to her room.

She was sitting on the bed messing about with her feet. As I entered she was inserting something rubbery with five prongs on it between her toes on her left foot. A similar device was already in place on her other foot. Her toenails were painted purple.

'I wanted your advice on a couple of things,' I began.

I knew Bridget would listen, being my best friend.

'Oh God, what is it now?' she said grumpily. So much for friendship.

I paused, distracted by the sight of Bridget getting out what looked like a miniature cheese grater and applying it to her heels. I gulped, fascinated and disgusted by the sight of hard skin falling onto the bed cover in thin slices. She caught my look.

'I don't see that the snot-on-a-clothes-line kid – the guy I caught flossing his nostrils with string going up his nose and out of his mouth – can say much about disgusting hygiene habits.'

I plonked myself down on the bed beside her.

'Look, let me take it one at a time.'

'Yeah, but keep it simple, Nick.'

'The bones in the sarcophagus, the ones that don't belong to Arthur and Guinevere – not that any of them probably do belong to Arthur and Guinevere—'

'Simple . . .' Bridget warned.

'The newer bones.'

'The ones that are missing a skull—'

'I'm wondering if they're Faye's brother.'

'Hasn't he been well?'

I looked at her.

'Okay, okay. Does Faye have a view on this?'

'She suspects it might be him, yes. Her brother disappeared at about the right time. But the thing is – and there's no one I can discuss this with except you – Faye's acting pretty strangely both about that time and in general. And Rex is being a bit strange too. Have you noticed? I wonder if they were in something together.'

'You think Faye offed her brother? With my Rex's help?' She dropped her file and sat up straight. 'Fuck you and the Chihuahua you rode in on.'

'Bridget, you're responding to the possible loss of your new – possibly imagined – lifestyle rather than to what I'm saying.'

'Am I buggery. And what do you mean *imagined*? So who chopped off Faye's brother's head? Faye or Rex? And why, for God's sake? Why would they do it?'

'I don't know. The skull could have disappeared after death. I was wondering if it might be something to do with Frome's death.'

The old man's ramblings about Merlin the Duality had led me to think about Bernard Frome's seminars. That in turn had brought to my mind that the outrageously promiscuous gay had died, drunk and very disorderly, at around the same time Ralph had disappeared. Two promiscuous gay men in the same college – surely they must have known each other?

'Frome? Who the fuck is Frome?'

'Don't you listen to anything I say now? God, Bridget, sometimes I despair.'

'First of all, I never have listened to anything you say so

143

why should now be any different? Second, I've been rather preoccupied, in case you haven't noticed, with preparations for the impending nuptials.'

'Who's getting married?'

She gave me a withering look. And a withering look from Bridget is truly withering.

'I am, you pillock.'

'To Rex?'

'Give the man a banana.'

I felt a peculiar twinge.

'When did he propose?'

Bridget avoided my eyes.

'Well, he hasn't yet but I know he's going to.'

'Do you think it's a good idea to make plans on that basis?'

'I can feel it in my water.'

'That's no guarantee of anything good. The last thing I remember feeling in my water was that candiru fish on the Amazon swimming up my urine to lodge in my urethra.'

'You're exaggerating.'

'I didn't know it at the time. It felt as real as if it were actually there.' I crossed my legs at the memory. 'Well, congratulations in advance. But back to the matter in hand—'

'My almost affianced and the love of your life killing her brother. Why do they have to be *his* bones? They could be anybody's.'

'Yeah, but I've read my crime fiction. In this kind of situation you have only a certain number of possibilities to play with.'

'This is real life, Nick.'

'Tell me about it,' I said glumly. I'd had another thought, after my conversation with Genevra the previous night, but that was even loopier than my present theory so I thought I'd keep it to myself.

'So who's this Frome bloke?'

'Bernard Frome was a tutor at college who taught a course on the Arthurian legends. He got drunk, fell down the stairs outside his rooms and broke his neck. He was found with a half full bottle of Scotch by his side.'

'I'm sorry to hear that. Was it good Scotch?'

'That's not exactly the point.'

'So where do you want to go with this?'

I groaned.

'I don't know! I just feel there's something very wrong now and I think the answer may lie back there.'

'Your serial killer goes back that far?'

I stood up and threw my hands in the air. Well, in a manner of speaking.

'Bridget, I don't know! I'd like your input on this. So if you could broaden your attention beyond this – this *madness* about marrying Rex I'd be really, really grateful.'

'Why is it madness?' she said sharply.

'What's the main thing we know about aristos? They're endogamous.'

'That's the main thing we know? I didn't know that's what we know. Thanks for telling me. Now tell me what the fuck *endogamous* means?'

'They marry within the tribe. Keep the bloodline pure. They're never going to marry the likes of you and me.'

'Better break the news to Genevra then. She hears wedding bells every time she sees you. I mean – are you mad? She's gorgeous, she's loaded and, for reasons that are quite beyond me, she's falling madly in love with you.' She peered at me. 'Yet you don't seem keen. What gives?'

'She said she was in love with me? I thought she was just doing that upper-class thing and using me as a stud.'

They say laughter is a release of tension. Bridget must have been excessively tense. When her laughter finally died down, she dabbed her eyes and said: 'I think I can almost guarantee it's more to do with loving you than using your body. Lovely body though it is.'

'I know why you're saying that,' I grumbled.

Bridget knows that I haven't always been a success in bed. For whatever reason, I've had no real trouble getting women to make love with me – once. Repeat sessions, however, have been a little harder to come by.

'So what is the problem, Nick?'

She looked me up and down.

'Is it Frigid Faye? Has she still got your heart in her icy clamp?'

'That's unusually poetic for you,' I said, hoping to change the subject.

'This is like one of those bloody film noirs you make me watch on late-night TV. You're in love with her but you think she might be a murderer. And we both know how that plot always ends. Badly for you. So come on, snap out of it!'

I felt like a schoolboy in front of the head. And just like a schoolboy, I found something to cling onto: the sight of those rubber things still sticking up between her toes like shark's teeth – as if the shark had made an attack on her feet and got the worst of it. Although, thinking about it later, that shouldn't have been comforting at all.

I spent the rest of the morning reading up on the discovery of Arthur's grave back in 1191. Around noon, Bridget came in and plonked herself down in the wing-backed chair.

'Fancy going to the pub for lunch?'

'Only if you leave off the waxed hat and gumboots. Where's Rex?'

'Gone up to London with Bucky Buckhalter,' she said. 'Meeting some money men.'

I put the book I'd been reading down beside the chair.

'Do you remember Genevra talking much about her step-mum?'

'Only what a bitch she was. She'd struggled to get where she was – she'd worked for a hospital trust or something before – and she was determined not to let it slip. I met her once at some "do" years ago. She was loathsome. "Well, of course, until you've run an eighty-five bedroom house you just don't know anything." I worked as a chambermaid in a two hundred-room hotel in Rickmansworth, does that count?'

Bridget pointed at me.

'And she, by the way, proves you're wrong about *endogamy*. Yes, I looked it up. They draft outsiders in if they're getting too inbred.'

'You know she just pissed off and abandoned everybody,' I said. 'Don't you think that's odd?'

'Rex got rid of her.'

'What?' I sat up straight in my chair.

'Not like that, you nelly. She was squandering his money so he paid her off.'

'How could he do that? Didn't his dad control the money? And I bear no resemblance to a seabird.' I saw her look. 'That's what a nelly is.'

'Know-all. Rex had a trust fund of a couple of mill—' She suddenly shrieked and pummelled the chair arms with her fists. 'Sorry. It's just that this is the guy I'm going to marry.'

'But you love him, right?'

'Are you kidding – have you seen his bod? Well, aside from his big feet. But you know what they say about men with big feet – oh, of course you do. Sorry – I forgot the rule has exceptions. No need to hang your head: Genevra obviously finds you adequate.'

'Adequate. Thanks a lot. But you love him, right?'

'Don't be so . . . *bourgeois*, Nick. We can get along.'

'Bourgeois, me? You're the one brought up in Rickmansworth. You know what they say. You can take the girl out of Rickmansworth but you can't take Rickmansworth out of the girl.'

'I thought it was that you can't get the boy out of the Ramsbottom?'

'Ha ha.' I couldn't help coming from a place with such a daft name. It hadn't affected me too badly. I knew a bloke from Mold once who just couldn't handle the embarrassment. Tring has a lot to answer for too.

I smiled at Bridget. I had the same odd twinge again. Jealousy. But how could it be? I'd known Bridget for years. God knows, if I'd wanted to have sex with her or start

something there had been ample opportunity. Well, provided she'd been of the same mind, of course.

'The stepmother went for his trust fund when she was
married to millions more?' I said. 'Doesn't make sense.'

'No, he raised a lot of other money on the basis of what
he was going to inherit and paid her off with that. The deal
was that she'd just disappear. She got about ten mill – less
than she would have squandered.'

'But if she liked the limelight?'

'Nick, how do we know how big a name she is in South
America? She's on the front page of every society magazine
every month out there on the pampas for all we know.'

'But Rex and Genevra would know – aristos nip all over
the world for parties.'

'That's Euro-trash, sweetheart. Trust fund kids. You
mustn't get all your notions of the aristocracy from the style
sections, you know.'

'And you're the expert, I suppose. Rex looks pretty typical
to me. He oozes upper class – all this "old stick" stuff.'

Bridget tutted – she was clearly picking up some strange
habits.

'I thought you were a film buff? He told me he got it from
a villain in an old Paul Newman film scripted by William
Goldman, based on a Ross MacDonald novel. Can't get less
upper class than that.'

'Classy though,' I whispered. I was in shock that she'd
remembered her first bit of film trivia, let alone three bits.

'But I don't get Rex,' I said. 'At all.'

'What's to get? He's a big rich swinging di – eelightful to
see you, Nanny.'

'Am I intruding?' Nanny said, shuffling forward from the
doorway.

'Not in the least,' I said, jumping to my feet and offering
her my chair. I blanched to think how long she might have
been standing at the door listening.

'I won't join you. I have just come in for a book. Did I
hear you discussing Rex?'

148

Bridget and I exchanged glances.

'We come to praise Caesar not to . . .'

Bridget's attempts at quotes were always a little off-key.

'He's a lovely boy. I'd do anything for him. Anything. And woe betide anyone who tries to harm him.'

She looked at me.

'Or Genevra, of course.'

Chapter Nine

I suggested to Bridget we go into Glastonbury for lunch.

'I don't want some lettuce-burger crap,' she warned. 'I want proper food.'

'Vegetarian food is proper food,' I said absently. I was thinking about how I might find the white-haired old man in Glastonbury to tell me about Lucy.

The sky was brighter today. There was even a hint of sunshine. It hadn't rained for forty-eight hours – the first break in the weather for what seemed an age – and the floods were beginning slowly to abate. The water authorities were still predicting hosepipe bans in the summer, of course, since for sound business reasons – i.e. it cost money – they hadn't been repairing leaky pipes and reservoirs. 'Where's the profit in that?' one bewildered millionaire chief executive was quoted as saying.

We drove into Glastonbury past flooded peat beds. Peat is one of the area's major industries. From prehistoric times down to the 1950's it was cut by hand. These days mechanical diggers remove the peat to use not as fuel but as agricultural fertiliser.

It was eerie to look across the flooded fields and see clusters of trees and lines of fencing seeming to float on the water. This whole area, I knew, used to be underwater. Years ago archaeologists found the remains of ancient lake villages west of Glastonbury, with wooden trackways made of planks and poles linking areas of higher ground.

It was people like the inhabitants of those villages who

used to bury their dead in hollowed oaks, not sixth-century Celts, who would use barrow burials. That was one reason I was pretty sure the bones in Arthur and Guinevere's tombs weren't theirs.

'But why would the monks at the abbey pretend to find King Arthur's grave?' Bridget said, tucking into steak and chips in the restaurant of a medieval pub in the town centre.

'They were great marketing men – Buckhalter would've loved them. Relics in those days were like rides now. The more relics you had the better you did. So in the twelfth century, first they claimed they had the three biggest rides – that's to say, three major saints were all buried there: St David of Wales, St Patrick of Ireland, St Gildas of Brittany. Later on they tried to claim another – St Dunstan. That probably came as a surprise to the monks of Christchurch Canterbury, who thought the saint had been buried there for the past two hundred years.'

'So they were con-men?'

'Total rogues. One historian said Glastonbury was a laboratory of forgeries because the monks were infamous for manufacturing stories to bring renown to the abbey – and money in the form of pilgrims' offerings.

'They had pretty much a full set of Last Supper relics: a bit of the table, the pillar Jesus was tied to for scourging, the scourge, a thorn from the crown of thorns. They had both sponges – one filled with wine and myrrh, the other with vinegar and gall – and other odd bits and pieces of the True Cross and Calvary. They didn't have Christ's foreskin from his barmitzvah unfortunately – some other church had that on show.'

Bridget's eyes hadn't started glazing over yet so I carried on.

'I read somewhere that if you put together all the supposed pieces of the True Cross that are scattered in churches throughout the world you'd have a cross the height of Big Ben.'

152

'I can do you one better than that,' Bridget said. 'Rex was telling me about Napoleon's Johnson.'

'Interesting conversations you and your intended have.'

'You'd be surprised. A piece of his penis was the must-have relic in the nineteenth century. It's true. There are bits of it scattered all over Europe. Put them all together and you get a penis about the size of Buck Buckhalter.'

'It may even *be* Buckhalter,' I said. 'What a prick that guy is.'

Bridget pushed her plate away and reached for her cigarettes.

'So finding Arthur was just another money-making scam. Why did they need to find him, though, if they were already doing so well?'

'I'll get back to you when I've done a bit more reading.'

Bridget was having her legs waxed and various other beauty therapies in the afternoon. We were going to meet up later. Before we parted we walked up the main street together. I indicated the sign for the Chalice Well.

'Until 1826 that was known as Chalkwell – it's a medieval well. The water has a reddish tinge, so the owner back then decided to make some money by declaring it to be the well above which Joseph of Arimathea hid the Grail containing Christ's Holy Blood. Hence the Chalice Well.'

'Why is the water red?'

'Iron oxide deposits in the water,' I said. I stopped before the entrance to the abbey. 'I need to find this old bloke. He may be able to shed light on Lucy's death. Sure you don't want to come with me?'

Bridget flashed me a hard look.

'No, I do not. Nick, why don't you leave it to the police? It's going to end in tears.'

I shrugged.

'See you later then.'

I described the old man to the woman at the ticket office. 'Do you know who he is?'

'Why?' she said cautiously.

'Not for anything bad. He just seemed an unusual person when I saw him here the other day.'

She laughed.

'Unusual – he's that all right. He gets a bit carried away but he's harmless. John Crow. He used to be quite a well-known writer in his day. He knows more about the Arthurian legends than anyone else I've met. He's a regular visitor.'

'Is he here now?'

She shook her head.

'He lives over at Wookey Hole. He spends most of his time around the caves and the mill. He used to be a guide there for a few years.' She looked at her watch. 'That's where you'll find him now, I shouldn't be surprised. They don't charge him to go in as long as he doesn't go off on one of his rants and disturb the other visitors. Not that there are many at this time of year.'

'Is he disturbed?'

She laughed again.

'Not really. John's just an old show-off. Likes the sound of his own voice. His family have been lay preachers for generations.'

I thanked her and looked at my watch. Wookey Hole was about fifteen minutes' drive away. I decided I just about had time to go there, speak with him, and get back to meet Bridget.

Wookey Hole is the name given to a series of subterranean caverns through which the River Axe flows. Iron Age Celts lived in some of the caverns and in the Middle Ages an old woman who was said to be a witch made her home there. Of course there's a King Arthur link. One of the Welsh stories had him slaying a black witch who lived in a cave at the head of the Stream of Sorrow on the confines of Hell. Tradition applied the story to Wookey Hole and its witch.

The paper mill which had stood outside Wookey Hole since 1610, using the clean waters of the River Axe to make paper from cotton rags, had been turned some years before into a kind of museum of curiosities. Visitors could explore the caves, tour the paper mill, and check out old penny slot machines from piers and a hall of mirrors. I liked it because it wasn't particularly slick and it wasn't debasing history.

There were about a dozen cars in the mill's car park. Another two pulled in as I was buying a ticket. I followed the tree-lined path up to the cave entrance. Parallel to the path to my right I could see the rushing River Axe, its waters swollen with the rains.

At the cave entrance there was a notice fastened to the wall stating that the next tour started in fifteen minutes. There was nobody around. I didn't have time to wait. I recalled from a visit years before that there was only one way through the caves. I clambered over the metal gate and pushed open the heavy iron door.

There was a short flight of steps cut out of the limestone. The steps were slick with water dripping from the stalactites in the roof above me. It was quite warm – the caves have a constant temperature of eleven degrees centigrade. The river in its flow goes through a series of chambers. Some you can walk through, others are totally submerged and can only be explored in diving gear.

I walked through the first chamber, past a lagoon of tranquil green water and a big rock that was supposed to be the witch turned to stone. The chambers were dimly lit for atmosphere. It was very quiet. I heard a rustling noise behind me and turned to see a pipistrelle bat flitting between the high stalactites.

I walked over a metal bridge and then down into a third chamber. It was almost circular, with a low domed roof. At the far end a short stretch of sand led to another lagoon some ten yards across and twenty yards in length. The old man was sitting on the sand, his knees drawn up to his chin, contemplating the waters.

'John Crow?' I called softly, dimly aware of a noise – something metallic striking rock – back in the tunnel that led into this chamber.

155

He stirred and turned his head. He had the look of Robert Graves: the white hair, burning eyes, strong jaw and nose.

'The water has risen three feet in this chamber in recent weeks,' he said. 'That is nothing. In 1606 the sea rushed in and flooded the Brue Levels to a depth of thirteen feet. Ricks floated away carrying pigs and hogs on top of them. They went on eating. Rabbits jumped on sheep's backs to save themselves but were drowned with them. In the streets of Glastonbury the water was over six feet deep.'

I sat down on the sand beside him.

'Do you know something about Lucy Newton's death?' I said.

'They think they have found the Grail,' he said. 'Ha! Do you remember what Powys said of the Grail? Only those who have caught the secret which Rabelais more than anyone else reveals to us – the secret of the compunction at the particular and extreme grossness of our excremental functions in connection with our sexual functions – are on the right track to encourage this receding horizon where the beyond-thought loses itself in the beyond-words.'

'I don't understand what that means but I'd rather know about you and Lucy Newton. Did you know her? Did you see what happened to her?'

'The meaning is difficult. I think he used the word "compunction" in the sense of guilt rather than regret.' He reached for his stick – it lay on the sand to his left – and, with its help, got to his feet.

'I knew Lucy Newton,' he said. 'Walk with me to the exit.'

I glanced at him. He seemed changed, lucid.

We passed along the narrow gantry into a chamber where a massive wall of rock was streaked with green and red mineral stains.

'She told you of her discovery?' I said, my voice refracting in the high, narrow chamber. He nodded.

'I urged her to get the bones dated. I knew they couldn't

156

be genuine because I've examined the story of their discovery in 1191.'

'Do you know anything about her death?'

We had reached the exit door. Crow pushed it open and we emerged into bright winter sunlight. To our right beneath a rocky overhang the Axe tumbled out from its subterranean world into the valley below. A small lock diverted part of its flow into a narrow canal that ran past the mill buildings some two hundred yards away. Crow and I set off down the path beside the canal.

'Do you?' I repeated. 'Were you there that day?'

He raised his head and sniffed the air.

'And Arthur met with Mordred on that fatal day of battle, pale Death's wings clamouring overhead. And Arthur smote him with his spear that it broke off and daylight could be seen through the wound in Mordred's body.'

I groaned. He was off again.

'Mr Crow—'

He silenced me with a look he must have borrowed from the Ancient Mariner.

'Such force,' he said, his voice vibrating with passion. 'The wrath of the father betrayed by his son. The double betrayal – Mordred and his stepmother Guinevere writhing in unholy embrace.'

He grinned at me. It was almost a grimace.

'Loose talk costs lives,' a voice behind us said.

I swung round. Two men in black balaclavas were standing there. One was tall and slim, the other short and barrel-chested. They were both in jeans, leather jackets and gloves. And they both had baseball bats.

'You!' the barrel-chested one said, pointing his bat at Crow. 'Shut it or have it shut for you.' He pointed the bat at me. 'And you – keep your nose out of other folk's business. If you want to keep it.'

I was trying to think of some witty response – and failing miserably – when he stepped forward and prodded me hard in the chest with the bat. He caught me off-balance and, arms flailing, I fell backwards into the canal.

As I struggled to my feet in the freezing water I saw John Crow raise his stick at the tall man. The tall man hit him on the side of the head. The blow made a horrible, hollow thunking noise and Crow fell down.

'Bastard!' I yelled, trying to haul myself out of the water. The man who had been doing all the talking stepped forward.

'Regard this as a friendly warning,' he growled.

'Friendly?' I gasped just as he belted me round the head with his bat.

It hurt. A lot. Clutching my head I fell to my knees in the water, tipped forward and went under.

I came up again, coughing and spluttering, and dragged myself to my feet, my waterlogged overcoat weighing me down. I clambered out of the canal and stayed on my knees for a moment whilst the water spilled off me.

Crow was lying on his side, unconscious. Or worse? I checked he still had a pulse. His heart was beating strongly, perhaps too quickly. His face was grey. I think he had hit his head hard when he fell. There was a little blood trickling from behind his right ear.

I needed to get help. There was no sign of our attackers but they couldn't have got completely away yet – there didn't seem to be any other way out of the complex other than by going through the mill.

Crow's stick lay on the path beside me. I picked it up and, weighted down by my sodden clothes, squelched along the path after them. Trailing water I hurried through the rooms that showed the paper-making process. I didn't encounter anyone until I reached the gift shop.

'Call an ambulance!' I yelled at the startled assistant. 'There's been an accident.'

I went through into the café. It was empty. The route out of the mill led through the old penny arcade, a couple of rooms full of antique slot machines. I saw a familiar figure at the far end of the first room. He was wearing jeans and a leather jacket.

'You!' I yelled, gesturing with Crow's stick.

The Japanese man I'd seen in Tintagel and in Glastonbury looked back at me. His eyes widened in alarm and he turned and ran.

'You might well be bloody alarmed, you bastard,' I muttered as I squelched in pursuit. This guy had cropped up three times now. I mean, I can only accept so much from the Thomas Hardy Big Book of Coincidences before even I start getting suspicious.

The penny slot machines arcade led into a strange room illuminated by red light with a wall of mirrors at the far end. I could see the Japanese man reflected in one of the mirrors. As a matter of fact I could see about four of him.

Ah, shit. The hall of mirrors. When I reached the wall I looked through into a hall that seemed to go on to infinity. Faux-medieval pillars in faux marble curved up to form a series of arched ceilings only a foot or so above my head. I put my hands in front of me and searched the mirrors for the way into the hall. When my hands touched nothing I advanced.

I could see several Nick Madrids, about a dozen Japanese and multiples of several other people, spread along three corridors.

A hall of mirrors is like a labyrinth, I told myself. It didn't help a lot. I knew vaguely that the illusion was created by sets of mirrors set at specific angles and if I could work out the configuration I could get through this and catch my Japanese friend with no problem.

He looked to be about ten yards away to my left. However, he was also ten yards to my right and some fifty yards straight ahead of me.

A large woman in what looked like a shroud, so voluminous was it, caught sight of me – or a mirror image of me – and started. I could understand that. Although every time I took a step I was now only drizzling rather than shedding water like a mini-Niagara, I was definitely bedraggled. There were unfortunate tendrils of bright green canal growth draped over my head and hanging down my coat.

I smiled cheerily at a pretty woman in a duffel coat and her young daughter as we almost collided. The little girl had mischievous eyes. She looked me over.

'Ugh!' she said, impressively succinct.

The Japanese man, alarm still showing on his face, was looking at me – in one mirrored version, that is. In others he was equally alarmed but facing in different directions. He seemed to be further away than before. But, given the spatial confusion this place was causing me, he could have been standing right next to me for all I knew.

I stuck a hand out – still clutching Crow's stick in the other – and made my way into the next bit of the hall. The problem I faced was that, like any labyrinth, there were wrong turnings and dead ends. My drips acted as a sort of crude Ariadne's thread to let me know where I'd already been.

I'd only recently discovered that the word 'clue', as used in crime stories, comes from the word 'clew', the name given to a ball of thread, like the one Ariadne gave to Theseus so that he could find his way out of the Minotaur's labyrinth. Well, yes, I did think that was quite interesting.

The Japanese guy seemed to be receding from me. Trusting to instinct I rushed through the glass maze as quickly as was safe. It was a hallucinatory experience. Half a dozen times I thought I was going to walk into myself.

Twice I did, smacking my nose against a mirror. At one point I looked down what seemed a long corridor bordered by an infinity of Nick Madrids. Frankly, I had to tear myself away. Twice I reached out to grab the Japanese man and he reached out to fend me off. Both times I hit glass.

The third time I sexually assaulted the woman in the shroud – that's what she said anyway – and that was the end of the chase. By then I was totally befuddled. I could see the Japanese guy a couple of yards away and the woman in the shroud may or may not have been beside him.

160

My hand shot out to check for mirrors and almost immediately came into contact with a large, soft bosom. I thought that, on balance, it was more likely to be hers than his. When she yelled 'Rapist!' and decked me with a straight right to my chin I knew that I was right.

I was up pretty quickly but by the time I'd eluded the woman in the shroud the Japanese guy had disappeared. The woman in the shroud was even worse at figuring out the mirrors than I was, so that although she hollered and pointed at me – and her and anyone else that was around given the nature of the hall – I got out of the building unhindered.

I hurried to the car park in time to see two vehicles disappear round the bend in the road to Wells. One was red, the other green, but I had no idea what make of car they were. I assumed they were the same two that had arrived as I was paying for my ticket.

Plodding back up to the mill, my head throbbing and jaw aching, I reflected that I hadn't been knocked down so often since a misjudged affair with a kick-boxer from Bexhill called Cheryl. What was most memorable about her was that she wouldn't let our relationship end.

'I don't want to see you any more,' I'd say.

'Don't be so silly,' she'd reply.

I was at Wookey Hole for another hour. It gave my clothes a chance to dry out a bit. The police came with the ambulance. John Crow was rushed off to hospital. I told the police we'd been attacked by two men and described the Japanese guy as best I could, saying that I thought he was somehow involved. I didn't go into background details. The woman in the shroud took some calming down but eventually I was able to leave.

When I got into the Range Rover I suddenly remembered Bridget. I was supposed to pick her up an hour ago. Aagh. That was my balls barbecued then. I phoned Wynn House. She'd taken a taxi back. I told her what had happened. She was curt and, of course, totally unsympathetic.

161

Next I phoned the hospital. John Crow was going to be okay but he had been sedated and would probably be staying in hospital for a couple of days. I drove back to Wynn House with the car's heating up high and my clothes gently steaming. Had the Japanese man been the taller of our two attackers?

I got to my room unnoticed, peeled off my sodden clothes and got into a very hot bath. I was dressing when someone knocked on my door. I expected it to be Bridget.

'Why are you cowering?' Faye said.

'Cramp,' I said, straightening up. I stood aside and she entered and sat down in the chair, crossing her legs. She was wearing a shorter dress than usual and a lot of perfume. I sat on the end of the bed. She beamed and leaned forward.

'I saw him this afternoon!' she declared.

'That's great,' I said. 'Who?'

'Ralph! My brother. Just a glimpse but I'm sure it was him. In Wells.'

'That is great, but if it's been so many years are you sure—'

'I'd know my own brother, for goodness' sake! And I think he saw me. He looked right at me.'

'What did you do?'

'I was caught in the bloody one-way system, wasn't I? By the time I'd come back round and parked there was no sign of him. I looked everywhere.'

'Where was this?'

'He was standing in the doorway of the Crown Hotel – in the market square? He wasn't registered at the hotel, though, I checked.'

'I expect he'll be in touch with you soon,' I said.

She looked at my face.

'What's wrong?'

'It just seems odd that the day after you're worried we might have found your brother's remains you should see him alive.'

'You think I'm imagining it was him?' She said fiercely, her face flushing. 'It *was* him, I'm certain of it.'

As she stood up I stood too and moved to her. She allowed me to put my arms around her but her body was stiff.

'I'm sure you're right,' I said, looking over her shoulder at the castle remains I could see through the window.

I was wondering how long her brother had been around and why he hadn't got in touch with her before. Could he have something to do with Lucy Newton's death? Could he have been the man following Faye in Tintagel?

I had a sudden cold remembrance of Faye's husband lurking in a doorway in the college deep in conversation with someone I couldn't see. Could that someone have been Ralph?

Chapter Ten

The police had taken all the bones away for analysis whilst I was out to dinner. Buckhalter was in a foul mood. Rex seemed more relaxed. Indeed, he announced we were all going to Venice in a couple of weeks' time.

'We'll get the opening event out of the way tomorrow then I think we all deserve a bit of a break.'

'Venice?' I said, surprised. 'Why Venice?'

'*Carnivale*, old stick, *carnivale*,' Rex said. 'A few days of dressing up – plebs passing as princes, lords as layabouts – will do us all good. Reggie and I have a bit of business to do over there.'

'Is he coming to the opening tomorrow?' I asked. I wanted a private chat with him.

'Absolutely. Do you know Venice, Nick?'

'A little,' I said.

'You moan about the heritage industry, but look at Venice. The whole city is a museum. It lives on, thrives on, the past. Tourism has been central to the city's economy since the end of the eighteenth century. The Danieli and Café Florian were developed in the nineteenth century specifically for wealthy foreigners. Almost a third of the city's workers are employed in year-round tourism – they revived the carnival in the eighties to get tourists there in February, which used to be a slow time. History with good shopping – what more could anyone want?'

'My take on that is that Venice is eating itself alive,' I said. 'Its economy is set up so that it needs to attract more and more tourists, even though it's sinking under the weight of them. What's Venice best-known tourist product? Glass. The pollution the glass-making process creates is one of the things corroding the city's stonework. It's destroying itself producing tat.'

'Good old Nick,' Rex smiled. 'One can always count on you for the minority point of view.'

'Thanks for the invite but maybe I'll stay in this country,' I said. 'I've got a lot of work to get on with.'

'Nick!' Genevra protested.

'Hey, the guy wants to stay here and sulk, let him,' Buckhalter said, shrugging.

'I am not sulking.'

'He said, sulkily,' Bridget muttered.

'Nick, please come with us,' Genevra said later as she was undressing. When she was naked she pressed herself to me. 'We can have such a time.'

Her voice was breathy and I, as usual, was breathless. I didn't answer right away. In fact I didn't answer at all for some considerable time, being otherwise engaged. Then I did agree to go.

I'd been thinking that I needed to be here to try and solve the various crimes, but I wasn't sure what else I could achieve. It depended on what John Crow could tell me and I wouldn't know that for a couple of days. I'd resolved not to tell anyone at the house what had happened – I couldn't be altogether sure that one of them wasn't behind it.

I touched the scar on Genevra's top lip.

'Tell me about the car accident. It must have been awful for you.'

She looked away.

'Worse for my father,' she said quietly. 'He died in it.'

'What happened?'

Genevra reached for the TV remote control.

'I don't like to think about it.'

I didn't press her. I looked at the TV screen.

'Hey, is this synchronicity or what? *The Natural* is on.'

'That's Robert Redford,' she said.

'Yeah. What a cast – him, Glenn Close, Kim Basinger, the man who would become Michael Madsen . . .'

'So what's the coincidence? It's on loads.'

'It's a retelling of the Arthurian stories as a 1930s base-ball story.'

'Uh-oh,' she said, snuggling up to me.

'It's not exact but there's stuff in there. Assume it's about the search for the Grail – that's to say, the pennant the baseball team is trying to win. Pennant – medieval, huh? The guy who's been trying to get it is called Pop Fisher and his team is called the Knights. Huh? Pop Fisher's team is way down the league – in a wasteland, you could say. He's the Fisher King, see?'

She yawned but I was on a roll.

'Now come to save him is this old player called Roy Hobbs.'

'Roy Hobbs doesn't sound very Arthurian,' she said, stroking my hair.

'Roy – roi – le roi – the king. And he's got a special baseball bat he carved out of a tree struck by lightning. Excalibur by any other name. He sets off at the start of the film to join the best knights in the world – you know, the best baseball team. En route he vanquishes an ogre – the Slugger, played by Joe Don Baker.'

'I haven't seen the film so this is pretty—'

'Dull?' I said. 'You ain't heard nothing yet. Then he meets the Morgan le Fay person who's going after any sportsman that is the best and killing them with a silver bullet. I don't get the significance of the bullet, but she shoots him. And he ends up in the wilderness for years – the team he's been playing for is called the Hebrew Oilers, so he's like the Wandering Jew. It's good against evil. The silver bullet left a wound in his side so he's a bit Fisher King himself – hello?'

Genevra had clambered on top of me and now, nipples brushing tantalisingly against my chest, she set her elbows either side of my head. She looked at me very intently.

'Hey, it's only a hypothesis,' I said. 'You can just enjoy it as a baseball film if you want. That's the thing about great movies, they work on different levels and you just plug into—'

She shushed me.

'What's happening with us, Nick?'

'What do you mean?'

'Call me impulsive but I'm getting really fond of having you around. God knows why.'

'Yeah,' I said uneasily. 'Right.'

She caught the unease.

'What is it? You don't feel the same?'

God, I hate these conversations. But then I'm a man. I would. I tried to think of a way to put it into words without hurting her feelings.

'I like you very much. I love making love with you—'

'But,' she said, hurt in her voice. She rolled off me and lay on her back, her face still turned towards me. 'There always has to be a *but* in life.'

I didn't say anything, hoping in that typical cowardly way men have that she'd figure it out for herself.

'Someone else?' she said. I gave her my helpless look. 'Faye?'

'I know it's crazy, she probably doesn't want me but after all these years I still feel—'

Genevra sat up.

'Faye's not for you, Nick,' she said sharply. 'Trust me.'

'You don't know what it was like in the old days,' I said. 'We were really close.'

'Even with the sex?'

'I hoped one day we might but it never happened.'

'She managed to get over that with Askwith then.'

I'd been thinking about the reference to the Fisher King that Faye had picked up on when we were driving into Glastonbury. His wound is usually held to be a metaphor for impotence.

'I'm not so sure,' I said. 'I think he was impotent.'

168

Genevra allowed the surprise to show on her face. She frowned.

'When did your relationship end?'

'Friday the thirteenth of May, fifteen years ago,' I recited. 'The same day, it turns out, that her brother, Ralph, went missing. Did you know him?'

'Of course. He and Faye lived in the Gatehouse.'

'Did you know he'd gone missing?'

'Yes. There was a rumour he'd gone off with my step-mother. She left around the same time.' She tapped my nose with her finger. 'So did you get *near* to sex with Faye?'

'Okay. We had sex once at the very end. She finished with me the next day.'

'That's tough. And you blamed it on your sexual prowess.'

'It was a disaster so it made me kind of nervy, yes. Why are you so keen to know?'

'Did you wear a condom?'

'Genevra, for God's sake. Why the inquisition?'

'I was wondering who'd fathered her child.'

I tensed.

'What child?'

'You don't know she has a fifteen-year old son?'

'You're kidding me.'

'He's at school down in Sussex somewhere.'

I was surprised but I was also puzzled. I was sure I remembered Faye telling me at the college dinner she had no children.

'And the obvious question is this,' Genevra murmured. 'If Askwith couldn't and you didn't, then who is the father?'

The next day everyone was running around getting things ready for the evening. I phoned the hospital to see if John Crow was up to seeing visitors. The woman at the other end told me he'd checked himself out that morning. She was one of those women who on the telephone suddenly perk up at the end of the conversation.

'Byee!' she said, her voice at a higher pitch than in the rest of the conversation.

'Byee yourself,' I muttered as I put the phone down. Now I had to find him again. I tried directory enquiries but there was no number listed for anyone of his name living in Wookey Hole.

My dinner jacket was back at my flat so I'd rented a tuxedo from a shop in Wells to wear in the casino this evening. I collected it and drove over to Wookey Hole at around eleven. I spent the drive trying to get my thoughts into some kind of order.

First, Askwith. He'd been talking to someone in the quad when Bridget and I arrived at the college. He'd had a meeting with Reggie Williamson in the library and William-son had looked very flustered when he came out. Later I'd seen Williamson in the quad. And Faye.

Then Lucy. She'd been strangled sometime in the after-noon of the Friday I arrived and laid out in a boat as if she were the Fair Maid of Astolet. John Crow might know something about this, although his arthritic hands put him out of the running as her strangler. Lucy had been having an affair with Rex. I remembered Genevra saying that she and her brother had eaten lunch together then he'd been called away. He'd not been seen all afternoon. Williamson was down that day but also out all afternoon. Buckhalter was nowhere to be found either.

Although I presumed the police were satisfied with them since they hadn't hauled anyone in for the third degree. Well, not yet, anyway.

I would have loved a sight of the statements they made to the police.

A stray thought flickered in my mind. What had Rex meant by saying he and Genevra were *so* close? Could they be/have been lovers? It's not unknown, especially where aristos are concerned – normal moral rules don't apply.

I recalled that first evening in Wynn House talking about the incestuous affair between Morgan and Arthur and the complicit look that had passed between Rex and Genevra.

Maybe Genevra was jealous of Lucy? She was certainly strong enough to strangle the slighter woman. I shook my head. How sick could my thinking get? Genevra was one of the most normal women I'd ever met. Except, I mused, in one respect. She seemed to have fallen for me very quickly. Which is quite contrary to my usual experience. My rule of thumb – and it's worked so far – is: if they're nuts about me, what's wrong with them?

'But why would she kill Askwith?' I said aloud. 'And the two deaths must be connected.'

Next, the bones. Whose remains were buried with Arthur and Guinevere in the tomb? If Faye had really seen her brother then they weren't his. I'd thought for one mad moment they might have been Genevra's stepmother until Bridget had told me about Rex paying her off. Whose bones they were I had no idea. Were they somehow connected to Frome's death?

A bunch of men had tried to kidnap Genevra in Bodmin. I didn't really think that was connected to the other things. A man had followed Faye at Tintagel. A man – the same man? – had bopped me over the head in Merlin's Cave and left me to drown. Two men had attacked John Crow and me and warned us off. They could be fifty rather than fifteen years old for all I knew. And that meant they could be *anybodys*.

Then there was the Japanese man. The more I thought about him, the more I was certain he wasn't the taller of our two attackers. So what was he doing at Wookey Hole? And why had he run away?

And finally there was Faye and her brother. How long had Ralph been around and why had he suddenly reappeared? Faye definitely knew more than she was saying. She hadn't even told me about her own son. I'd been puzzling over that and I had only been able to come up with a couple of things that made some sort of sense. Maybe Askwith hadn't always been impotent. Maybe Rex was the father, my other theory notwithstanding.

There was also another possibility. Whilst the one occasion Faye and I made love had been a disaster, the boy could even so be mine.

I found John Crow's house within ten minutes of reaching Wookey Hole. The man in the village shop gave me directions to a detached, three-storey Edwardian villa in a quiet lane a few hundred yards from the mill. As I banged on the front door I reflected that Crow didn't seem to have had need of my largesse. He was obviously worth far more than I was.

There was no reply, and whilst I prowled around the sides and back of the house hoping to see him, I drew the line at breaking in. I scribbled a note, put the Wynn House and my mobile numbers on it and pushed it through the letterbox.

I arrived back at Wynn House to find the courtyard transformed. It was filled with gaudy tents – crimson and purple and green – and caravans faced with polished mirrors. Everywhere pennants fluttered. A canvas awning covered the path from the barn to the entrance of the casino.

I could smell rich, cloying scents. As Mort's travelling players got ready there was laughter and excited screams and strange – very strange – music from high-pitched pipes and discordant woodwind. Two horses, whinnying gently, were having their manes plaited.

I came into the drawing room to find Genevra and Bridget talking to Mort Darthur in his jester's cap and bells. They all turned. Mort stepped forward.

'Nick, I want you to join our Merry Band this evening,' he said. 'I think you have the makings of a travelling player.'

He looked like he was reciting someone else's lines.

'Get stuffed.' I turned to Genevra. 'I'm supposed to be helping out in the casino, aren't I?'

'Leave us a moment, Mort,' she said, with a queenly gesture. Mort made a less than kingly gesture, turned on his heel, stuck his bum out, broke wind and exited.

'His role model was Le Pétomane,' Genevra said.

'Who he?'

'The guy who used to perform, so to speak, before the crowned heads of Europe.'

'Perform what?'

'And I thought you knew everything,' Bridget said. 'He used to fart tunes. The Trumpet Voluntary was his master-work. I think the Flight of the Bumblebee was what did for him in the end.'

'Thanks for sharing that. So what does Mort want?'

'One of the stunt men hasn't turned up. We can manage without you in the casino. You can ride a horse, can't you?'

'That's a matter of opinion,' Bridget interjected. I flashed her a look.

'And you told me you used to fence.'

'Not on horseback.'

'No, no, but you could joust. You fight on horseback then on foot with your broadsword. It's all choreographed.'

'That's hardly fencing,' I said. 'Fencing is all wrist movement.'

'Should come naturally to you then, Nick,' Bridget said, making a frankly unoriginal gesture.

'All right, I'll do it to help out,' I said, though a little voice was telling me that this was not a good idea.

I went to find Mort in the barn to get my instructions. Long banqueting tables had been set out round the perimeter of the space, leaving a fifty-yard strip in the centre for jousting.

About thirty people were getting ready for the evening.

'Hi!' a pretty young woman in a blouse with a very scooped neck said. 'I'm a wench. Can I help you?'

I tried not to fall into her cleavage.

'Yes, I can see that. Who's your friend?'

I indicated the pimply youth beside her with long side-burns and the makings of a moustache. He was sitting with a pair of pliers and a pile of what looked like junk metal.

'I'm just making some chain mail. It's a real pain. You have to use pliers, link by link. Does wonders for your arm muscles.'

173

I looked at his spindly arms.

'Looks authentic,' I said politely.

'It is, although authentic metals rust quickly.' He scratched a pimple, examined his fingernail. 'And it's incredibly heavy. Over two stone. Try to turn sharply while running – the momentum topples you over.'

I went over to Mort, who was waving a pig's bladder round on a stick.

'Who do you want me to be?' I said.

I could see myself as Lancelot to Genevra's luscious Guinevere.

'Oh I don't know – Sir Passing, Sir Gical Truss, somebody like that,' Mort said, his eyes following another of the serving wenches.

'I was thinking perhaps Lancelot.'

He looked over his glasses.

'You do surprise me. He's taken. You're fighting him. The thing to remember is that your opponent is a professional stunt man who knows what he's doing. Even your horse will know more than you – she's circus-trained. When you're jousting, aim for the shield. Just do two passes then get off and fight on foot. When fighting with the broadsword, aim for the shield or the sword, never the man.'

'And I lose, I suppose?'

'Certainly.'

'How will I know when it's time?'

Mort showed his teeth.

'Oh, you'll know.'

He sent me over to an elderly lady who was sitting behind a sewing machine surrounded by racks of clothes. She had permed white hair and spectacles and was wearing her coat and sensible shoes. She looked up.

'Yes, dear, don't tell me, let me guess. I was in the rag trade for fifty years. I can tell you a man's size by looking at him. Just give me a little twirl.'

She looked me up and down, then leaned over the sewing machine to peer at my crotch.

'Alice,' she called, 'bring me a doublet for a forty-two long, hose for a thirty-four inside leg, boots for a size twelve . . .' She peered at my crotch again. 'And better bring one of those padded codpieces.' She flashed her dentures at me. 'Saves embarrassment. People can be very cruel if your pouch looks empty.'

'Thank you,' I said, with as much dignity as I could muster. 'But—'

She glanced again at my crotch.

'Alice, bring one of the half cucumbers too,' she added.

'I think I'm here for a suit of armour.'

'Are you replacing Donald?'

'I'm replacing somebody—'

'So you're going to be the Black Knight. Well, you've got the height for it.' She laughed, although quite why I couldn't say. She pointed into a makeshift changing room. 'It's too heavy to bring out. Alice, forget all that stuff, this gentleman's coming to look at Donald's harness.' She looked back at me. 'That's his suit of armour to you.'

Alice was a plain girl with owl glasses and a poor complexion. She smirked as she indicated the suit of armour. It was spread out on a wooden frame – a full suit of armour from helmet to foot. It was easy to see what Alice was smirking at. In fact you couldn't miss it. An enormous steel codpiece jutted out from the crotch.

'Fancies himself a bit, does Donald,' the elderly lady said, coming up behind me. 'Likes to let the ladies see what's on offer. Mind you, he fills it well enough. He's a big lad.' She glanced at me. 'But *you* could probably keep your sandwiches in there. It's hinged if you get peckish.'

'How am I going to get on a horse wearing all that?' I said, trying to ignore her cackling.

'The helmet is rolled steel and the coif – that's that chain-mail hood – is heavy, but Donald never wore the full hauberk – that's the chain-mail body – under it, and the rest isn't as heavy as it looks.'

'It's all articulated,' Alice said, the smirk still on her face.

175

'That's nice,' I said.

Mort introduced me to my opponent, a quietly spoken bloke called Philip who had long hair and a beard. We spent half an hour going through the broadsword fight, working out the basic routine. Which seemed to be that I bashed his shield – excuse me, buckler – then he bashed mine and we did that until one of us got bored, at which point we took turns at whacking each other's swords.

'We'll do it a bit harder, obviously, when we get the armour on,' Philip said. 'We can improvise a bit.'

I was more concerned about the joust. The broadsword was heavy enough but I assumed the lances, which were about fifteen feet long, would be heavier. How I was going to keep mine pointed at the target whilst galloping, I hadn't a clue.

'We won't be at full gallop,' Philip said. 'And the horse knows what she's doing. The spears are fine once you've got their fulcrum. You won't have any trouble keeping on target.'

'How long have you been doing this?' I said.

'Not long down here. I've been living in Northumberland. I used to do Viking re-enactments up there. On foot.'

'Bit of rape and pillage, eh?'

Something flickered behind his gentle eyes.

'The Vikings got a bad press. They were essentially settlers, but because they weren't Christians they saw nothing wrong in stealing from churches and abbeys. Since it was the churchmen who wrote the histories, it's understandable the Vikings have been presented in the worst light possible.'

'Point taken, Philip.'

I excused myself and went into the house. Genevra and Rex were standing in the drawing room over by the long windows looking out at the dying day. They were standing side by side, each with an arm round the other's waist, their heads leaning together.

I withdrew before they noticed my presence. Hey, nothing wrong with affection between brother and sister. Especially when they have no living parents. Nothing wrong at all.

176

I was back in the barn at six. The banquet was due to start at seven thirty. Outside one of the barn's entrances an enormous barbecue had been set up, piled high with steaks, chops and, of course, Excaliburgers. The chef had dressed the barbecue fire with rosemary, thyme and other herbs so a wonderful aroma drifted into the barn.

I was surprised to see half a dozen other knights in suits of armour standing to attention at intervals along each side of the barn. I was having a pleasant conversation with the nearest one when Mort came over, lifted the front of the knight's hinged helmet and showed me there was nobody inside it.

'Easy mistake,' I said. Mort shook his head wearily.

Philip and I were supposed to stay out of sight until it was time for our joust but we needed to get the armour on. A stage had been erected at one end of the barn and the space behind curtained off as a changing room.

He showed me how to put the armour on over the loose pair of leggings and long cotton tunic I'd been given. There were about a dozen different bits and mostly I had to fasten them on with leather straps and buckles. I started with the greaves – the shin armour. They stopped about six inches below my knee.

'Armour's made to measure,' Philip said. 'Donald had that made to fit him perfectly. You'll just have to make do as best you can.' I'm sure he looked at my crotch as he said that. Bastard.

I strapped the knee armour on – called poleyn for some reason. The gap between the big metal knee-pads and the greaves made me look as if I was wearing soccer shin-pads. The cuish was armour that went right round my thighs. It hung off a kind of suspender belt at my waist.

I thought I'd better get the foot armour – two long sheaths of metal called sabatons – on next whilst I could still bend. They pinched my toes a bit but I thought I could manage. Everything was going okay until I put the coif on. That was the chain-mail hood and it was seriously heavy. By the time Philip had tied on my backplate and breastplate and I'd added the armour for my arms I was feeling weighed down and hot. The armour on my arms was the wrong length, too, so there was a gap between the elbows and the metal strips running down my forearms. My gauntlets – steel gloves – were a tight fit.

I picket up the helmet. Philip's had a long pointed snout sticking out in front. Mine, he'd told me, was a barrel helm. It was a cross between an inverted waste-paper bin and a colander and covered my entire head. There were two horizontal slits to see through. The bottom half had a dozen or so breathing holes punched in it. A brass cross reinforced the face and the eye-slots.

'Sixteen grams of cold-rolled steel,' Philip said. 'Made to measure by craftsmen.'

'It's the made to measure that's the problem,' I said, my voice muffled. The problem being that my eyes were about half an inch too high for the eye slits. I could see down immediately in front of me but if I wanted to see ahead of me I had to tilt my head back.

'You'll be fine,' Philip said. 'Now if you'll excuse me I need some time alone to prepare spiritually for our combat.'

'Spiritually?' I said, twisting my body to see how articulated this armour actually was. Not very, was the answer.

'It's something we special troops used to do in the Viking army,' he said, clanking out of the changing room by the barn's side exit, his helmet under his arm.

'What kind of special troop were you?' I called after him.

'What?' he said, turning.

I shouted the question again.

'A berserker,' he said, disappearing into the night.

I would have slumped if the armour hadn't held me so rigid. Fucking great. Berserkers were the most feared men in the Norse armies. We get the word berserk from them. A berserker would fight in a mad frenzy, unable to feel pain, never getting tired, never stopping until either he or his opponent was dead.

178

'I've got to see Mort about this,' I muttered. I tilted back my head and peered through the curtains. People were already crowding in. Mort was down at the far end of the barn. He was . . . I believe the word is *capering*, in a jester's cap and bells, shaking a pig's bladder on the end of a stick. He still had his glasses on.

I was supposed to keep out of people's view until the joust, but I figured that I could nip round the outside of the barn and catch his attention at the entrance.

I made slow progress. The armour was clunky – not to mention clanky – so I had to walk in that legs spread, simian-roll-of-the-hips way beloved of yobs everywhere. My neck was starting to ache with tilting my head back but I discovered that I could see out of one eye-slit at a time if I tilted my head to the left and the right. To anyone watching, my head must have resembled a golf ball circling the rim but refusing to drop in the hole.

It was cold out there and I soon discovered that walking around in a tin suit exaggerated the coldness. In short, I needed a pee. Urgently. I *know* I should have gone before, but putting a suit of armour on isn't something I do every day and I hadn't thought it through.

My gauntlets seemed to have contracted in the cold. There was no way I was going to get them off. I fiddled around with the catch under the codpiece with cumbersome fingers, the urgency increasing by the moment. At last I managed to lift the lid.

The next problem was actually extracting my virile member – I can have an opinion, can't I? – with a set of chilly metal digits, I'll say only that it really didn't want to come out but I managed to relieve myself. After a fashion.

I had turned and was closing the lid of the codpiece, hoping there was some kind of rust warranty on the armour, when I heard Reggie Williamson's voice.

'If he can't shag it, shoot it or bet on it, he's not interested' he said, laughing loudly.

I was standing right at the corner of the barn. I peered

round the corner. Reggie was standing with Rex some ten yards from the entrance. His upraised voice had obviously drawn attention from people going into the banquet because Rex took his arm and drew him away from the entrance. Towards me.

I jerked my head back and stood stock still, confident that I was completely hidden from view.

'What's that?' Williamson said.

Well, almost completely. As I looked down through the eye slits I realised that the codpiece was jutting out past the end of the barn.

Although the helmet muffled my hearing as well as my voice, I could hear footsteps crunching on the gravel as they approached. A moment later I could see two pairs of dress shoes standing before me.

'A suit of armour,' Rex said. 'Don't be so paranoid, Reggie. Mort has them scattered all over the place. I must say, he might be an irritating little man, but he knows his business.'

Williamson tapped my codpiece. Damned cheek.

'I'd like to have known the fellow that fitted this.' He chuckled. 'It's nice to meet someone you can see coming a mile off.'

'Yes, well, if you can keep your prick in your pocket for a minute, we've got more urgent matters to discuss. If this deal doesn't come through, I'm finished, you know that. So no slip-ups.'

'You're finished? I think I'm in a rather more vulnerable position than you, *old stick*. I'm looking at jail if anything goes wrong.' He paused. 'Or am I not the only one with that prospect in mind?'

'Rex! Cooey! There you are.'

It was Bridget's voice, but I wondered for a moment if she'd been taken over by some alien pod person. *Cooey*? What was wrong with her usual shout: 'Hey, fuck-face'?

I had to stand there for five more minutes whilst Bridget, Rex and Williamson were joined by other people. Neville, the estate manager, turned up with a bloody great wolf-hound. I knew this when I heard a noise like rain on a tin roof and felt something hot and liquid running into the gap between my left leg's greave and sabaton.

When it was safe to make a move I set off back to the other end of the barn. My metal joints had stiffened in the cold so progress was slow. My mind was racing over what I had heard. Williamson being gay was neither here nor there. But Rex being in financial difficulty certainly was.

I was helped onto my horse by two blokes dressed as peasants. My shield was strapped to my arm. One of the serfs sniffed suspiciously at my left leg.

'Smells like a dog's pissing post,' he said with a guffaw.

I pulled on the horse's reins. It stepped to the left, barging the peasant to the floor.

'So sorry,' I said.

I'd been having bad experiences with horses in the past couple of years so I was wary of this one, trained or not. And the lance was heavier than I expected, Philip's remarks notwithstanding. So for that matter was I. The coif and armour really dragged me down. I tilted my head and tried to see down to the other end of the barn where Philip/Lancelot would be entering. I had the sound of the sea in my ears, which I took to mean that the banquet was appropriately boisterous.

Mort, in cap and bells, was a few yards away from me on stage. I tilted my head so that I could see him.

'Lords and ladies, serfs and wenches, let us put on the motley,' he declared. His voice reverberated through the barn out of speakers hooked on wooden posts. He leered at one of the wenches bending low over a table.

'I'd like to firkytoodle her. You know, I'm a great traveller me. I'd like to visit her Low Countries. Her Netherlands, if you get my meaning. I'm not saying she's easy, but most men around here know her old hat – I call it that because it's frequently felt. How are you, sir? You're looking a little pale.

181

Have you been playing the one-holed flute, galloping the maggot? Come on, we all like to flog the bishop once in a while. No? Is that why you're pinching the cat now?'

I was wondering who wrote his script – Chaucer? – when I heard him announce the joust. My horse heard too. She moved forward of her own volition. I clanked a little. I was sweating heavily. I knew the horse was a professional and I was just along for the ride, but I had visions, therefore, of her rearing up to do little two steps on her hind legs, her front hoofs pawing the air whilst I slid down her tail. I reassured myself. All I had to do was cling on, point the lance at Philip's shield and, after two passes, dismount.

It was probably because I couldn't see out of my slits as I set off that I didn't angle my shield properly to receive the first blow. I felt my lance jar against his shield and slide away then I felt this jarring pain in the side of my head and the next thing I knew I was flat on my back on the ground.

I could hear the cheering but I could see bugger all. My head was pulsing. I supposed I should get up, although I wasn't sure how I'd get to my sword. I assumed that me falling off meant that we'd move on to the sword-fight. That was the next part of the tourney. *Tourney* – see, I was getting into it now.

When I tried to sit up, I couldn't. My fall from my horse had been sudden and unexpected. I'd been as relaxed as a drunk falling over – no cheap comments, please – so I didn't think I'd done myself much damage. But the weight of the chain mail and the helmet was holding me down.

I rolled onto my side, then got slowly onto all fours. I stood up and looked around, which was a waste of time because I couldn't see anything. I felt a big dent in my helmet just above the left ear, where I'd been walloped.

I was wrestling with the helmet when I heard the audience start to boo. Tilting my head and squinting, I saw Philip – excuse me, Lancelot – lumbering towards me, broadsword in hand, clearly about to whack me whether I was ready or not.

182

Oh shit. He was in berserker mode.

I still had my shield attached to my right arm – it felt like it was welded to me – but my sword was hanging from its scabbard on the horse, which was standing about twenty yards behind me.

I guessed that if I called she was trained to come. The problem was what to call. Lancelot was ten yards away. I backed towards the horse. Lancelot got nearer. I backed faster. Nearer. I stood my ground and held up my shield and he swung his sword at me two-handed. When he was committed to the swing, I jumped back.

Actually, jumped back is too ambitious a term for what I did. Given the weight I was carrying around, I sluggishly got one leg back and then the other. It was enough. The sword arced down in front of me and cut a large groove in the sawdust.

I turned and ran – excuse me, lumbered – for the horse, to the sound of laughter and applause. I was half expecting her to edge away from me when I got close. But she really was a trouper. She stayed as I pulled the broadsword out of its scabbard and turned to face Lancelot.

My impression was that playing pat-a-cake with swords and shields was no longer an option. Phil was in frenzied mode. But if I was to stand a chance I needed to get my helmet off so that I could see what he was up to. I'd worry about him lopping my head off once I could see him.

I dodged round the back of the horse and tugged at my helmet with my free hand, the one with the shield stuck on its forearm. I gave it an almighty wrench and it popped off as if it had been greased. I've never rated ears much anyway.

Philip had followed me round the horse. He wasn't going to strike at me whilst I was near it. I immediately thought about marrying the horse but remembered we were putting on a show. I backed away from my mount, holding my sword two-handed up against my right shoulder. Philip put his sword in the same position and stepped towards me.

PETER GUTTRIDGE

Having decided all bets were off as far as play-fighting was concerned, I went for his legs, swinging my sword down and across at the level of his knees. I knocked his legs from under him.

The crowds cheered but I didn't dare look at them. I should have brained the guy there and then but I let him get up. He swung his sword high at my unprotected head. I parried desperately but his attack was just a feint. He did to me what I'd done to him. I buckled at the knees.

He didn't let me get up. Instead he swung again, aiming at my head. I rolled and he overbalanced with the power of his attack.

Getting to my feet proved harder than expected. I soon realised why. He'd dislodged my knee guard. What was the proper name? Right – who gives a fuck? The knee guard had slipped down and so had the thigh armour. That meant I couldn't bend my right knee.

I hobbled back and parried another swing to my head as best I could. The power of the two swords connecting vibrated down my arm and through my body. The other knee pad dropped and the thigh armour dropped with it, right over my other knee.

Terrific. This was exactly the moment I wanted to move like a stiltwalker.

I took a swing at his midriff and connected. He grunted then swung at me. I parried but, given my inflexible legs, struggled to keep standing. He closed in on me. Breastplate to breastplate, he tried to bash me in the face with the snout of his helmet.

'You don't fucking learn, do you?' he shouted.

Startled, I stepped back a pace. That didn't sound like Philip. It sounded like the man who had attacked Crow and me at Wookey Hole.

Chapter Eleven

'Pinching the cat?' Bridget said.

'Means he was palping his genitals,' I croaked.

'*Palping?*'

'You know,' I said wearily. 'Playing pocket billiards.'

Bridget sighed.

'Palping his genitals. Nick, how come you're such a tosser but I still love you?'

'Would you still love Rex if he was skint?' I said. Or did I? Perhaps I only thought I did, for she didn't seem to register the question, and the next moment Rex, smiling, came into my field of vision. He lowered a large glass of wine in front of my face.

'I believe knights brave in battle received a goblet of wine,' he said, grinning. 'And, of course, a beautiful damsel.'

Genevra's head replaced his in my line of vision. She leaned over and kissed me softly on the lips. It was okay, if you like that sort of thing. Woof.

I was lying flat on my back on the sofa in the drawing room. Mild concussion, the doctor said. Yeah, well, I'd lost but I'd lived. When the armour on my arms had slid down so that I couldn't bend my elbows either the fight had become even more ridiculous. I must have looked like Pipe-cleaner Man, legs stiff, arms stiff.

Fortunately, as I was flailing around, dazed, trying to keep both my balance and Lancelot away, Mort, ever the showman, decided we were boring. So he sent in jugglers, fire-eaters and a couple of exotic oriental dancers to break us up. My opponent managed to get in a couple of heavy blows with the flat of his sword to the top of my head before being absorbed into the motley group of performers. Thank Christ he hadn't wanted to kill me – if he'd delivered those blows with the edge of the sword, chain-mail hood or not, it would have been goodnight, sweet ladies, goodnight.

I learned later that Philip had gone to the chapel to prepare spiritually and somebody had locked him in. Nobody knew who the man was who'd replaced him. Philip's armour was found abandoned.

The doctor had recommended I stay in bed for a couple of days.

'Alone,' Bridget said as, later that evening, she and Genevra tucked me in. Genevra pouted. I was obscurely relieved.

I was pretty much out of it for the next forty-eight hours. I'd been walloped on my head so many times in the past few days I was sure my skull was beginning to resemble the one in Arthur's tomb. In my delirium I had many strange thoughts about Rex and Genevra. I kept remembering the way Rex had told me that they were, '*So* close.'

I had a little dream. I was wandering in an unfamiliar part of the house and came to a half-open door. I knew what I would find on the other side even before I pushed it open. The soft candlelight. A black woollen dress discarded on the floor beside a man's trousers and shirt. Genevra and Rex, coiled on the bed, asleep in each other's arms.

I felt no jealousy. They were both beautiful in their nakedness. My eye fell on Genevra's lean thigh, crossed her belly to her breasts. When I looked at Rex's face I saw a flicker of movement behind the curtain of his eyelashes. He was examining me as I examined him.

'Join us.' Whispered so softly. I looked again at Rex. His lips were parted. Had he made the invitation? Had I imagined it? I stayed a moment longer, the tableau before me, then silently withdrew, closing the door behind me.

Everybody else flew off to Venice whilst I was still laid up. I was to follow two days later, still in time for the main carnival event on Fat Tuesday. Genevra came to my room the night before her departure and slipped into bed beside me. I wasn't in any shape to do anything physical and the dream still lingered in my mind, so I lay unmoving and pretended to be asleep. She stayed beside me quietly for a time then I really did fall asleep. When I awoke I was alone.

Only Nanny and I remained in the house and I rarely saw her. Neville seemed to be around the house more than before – I'd scarcely seen him since my arrival until the night of the banquet. Occasionally I caught him looking at me speculatively.

I lay in bed in a darkened room and listed to the radio a lot. On the Today programme one morning they reported that a group of Scottish art students had come upon scores of bodies of sixth-century warriors in a mass grave thought to be the site of Arthur's last battle, the Battle of Camlann. Strong claims had often been made in the past that Arthur's kingdom was in Scotland.

On the next morning's programme, however, a solemn-voiced man from the Scottish Archaeology Society reported from the site that there were not scores of bodies, there were six. And that given the fact they were made of plastic they were most likely not sixth-century warriors. They were more likely to be a group of Action Men dressed in tiny kilts. When the art students protested that the wounds on one Action Man's skull were consistent with him having been in a battle, the archaeologist responded that in fact the 'wounds' were consistent with the plastic head having been gnawed at by a dog.

There was a report about the two messiahs and King Arthur too. The Wiltshire Christ was now being investigated for child abuse but was nevertheless going ahead with plans to open a number of therapy centres around the country.

The next item reported that the East End Messiah and

King Arthur had met for secret talks that had ended in violence. The East End Messiah had links to various far-right nationalist groups. They included those paradoxical ones who express a fervent loyalty to England and hatred of foreigners whilst worshipping Adolf Hitler, who they presumably believe came from Leytonstone.

Those nationalist forces brought him into contact with the Welsh King Arthur, who was backed by Little Englanders. They met secretly in a motorway eatery off the M6 to discuss a merger, maybe using Joseph of Arimathea and the Grail as the glue.

But soon the Son of God and the Once And Future King were at loggerheads, each claiming the other was stealing part of their message. The reporter speculated that the problem was that they were competing for the same market of credulous idiots.

The ensuing dust-up was broken up by police, called by the manager of the soft-drinks-only eatery because the Messiah had been caught swigging alcohol with his burger and fries. The Messiah's claim that it was a miracle because the alcohol had started out as water didn't impress anybody. Police made thirty arrests and charges were pending.

Later that day, the day before I was due to fly to Venice, I went looking for John Crow. Again without success. He wasn't at home and he hadn't been seen at Glastonbury Abbey or Wookey Hole.

'He has a brother over in Herefordshire – Hergest Ridge,' the man at Wookey Hole said. 'Happen he's gone there.'

I called in at the police station to report Crow missing. The desk sergeant, a bulky man with kind eyes behind horn-rimmed glasses, took the details briskly enough but obviously thought the old chap was going to turn up. When I suggested breaking into Crow's house he demurred.

'Expensive business that when you get down to repairs,' he said gnomically.

When I referred him to the attack that had been made on Crow and me he paused and took his spectacles off.

188

'Now funnily enough we've got some news on that. You're Mr Madrid, I take it?' I nodded. 'We were going to call you today. Your Japanese gentleman has turned up.'

'Where?'

'We tracked him to a hotel in Salisbury.' The sergeant looked stern. 'His version of events is that he was visiting Wookey Hole mill when he was attacked by a madman who looked like he'd had a shower fully clothed. He said this madman, who was trailing various bits of marine life off his hair, waved a stick, shouted in a threatening manner and chased him into the hall of mirrors, making strenuous efforts to do him an injury. Is that true?'

'Sort of,' I mumbled. 'But did he say why he'd been in Tintagel and Glastonbury Abbey when I was there?'

'There was no reason why he should – it's a free country. But in fact he's an academic with an interest in the Arthurian legends and has been visiting all the sites. Are you saying he was following you?'

'I thought he might have been,' I said quietly, picturing in my head how the events in Wookey Hole mill could bear this other interpretation. 'And he hadn't seen me before?'

'I asked him that,' the sergeant said. 'He said we all look the same to him.' The sergeant put his spectacles back on. 'Fortunately for you, he doesn't want to press charges.'

I took the train to Gatwick next morning and was in Venice just after lunch. I hadn't been there for years. On the plane I recited to my neighbour my two favourite witticisms connected to the city. When Robert Benchley visited he sent back a telegram to Dorothy Parker and the Algonquin set that read: 'Streets full of water, please advise.' And Woody Allen used to tell a one-liner about a streetwalker who went to Venice – and drowned. My neighbour excused herself and went to sit somewhere else.

Venice stunned me. It was cold but bright when I came out of the airport and got into the water-taxi Rex had sent for me. I sat in the rear, baggage piled at my feet. Within twenty minutes the taxi had crossed the lagoon and entered the canal system. With tired eyes I surveyed the wash, rushing the walls of the ancient buildings and flopping back towards the boat.

We passed beneath the Rialto Bridge, past vaporettos edging into their landing stages, the filthy water churning madly behind them. People waved from the bridge, tourists sipped drinks outside the restaurants on the waterfront. Wandering among them in a surreal manner were a number of people already in carnival costume, dressed as harlequins.

Rex had rented a grand old palace called the Ca' Dario which had been empty since the early nineties. The Gothic palace had belonged to Giovanni Dario, the Venetian chancery secretary who negotiated peace with the Turks in 1479. In the twentieth century it had had a flamboyant history.

A colourful American owner in the sixties had held outrageous homosexual orgies there and had been expelled from the city. Kit Lambert, the manager of the Who, had owned it for a time but sold it in the early seventies. He was murdered in a dispute with a drug dealer not long afterwards and the superstition grew that the palace was somehow bad luck. In the nineties Woody Allen had apparently considered buying it.

The Ca' Dario was only a couple of hundred yards up the Grand Canal from the Rialto. It was a beautiful Gothic structure, its façade intricately patterned with roundels, plaques of marble and porphyry and bits of oriental tracery. It was tall, with living quarters on three floors.

The taxi pulled into its watergate and nudged to a halt against tall blue mooring posts with golden caps. A porter was waiting at the bottom of a flight of steps. He took my luggage and led me up two flights of stairs to a wood-panelled room. It had a large four-poster bed and a terrific view of the Grand Canal.

There was a note on top of my chest of drawers: 'We're attending a carnival ball in the Ca' Rezzonica tonight. Cocktails at six, in costume (look in wardrobe).' It was signed Genevra with a couple of kisses and there was a postscript: 'Out shopping.'

I looked in the wardrobe. Hanging there was a silk shirt with ruffles down the front, knee-length black trousers, long white stockings, a full-length black coat, a white papier-mâché face-mask and a three-cornered hat. In the bottom of the wardrobe was a pair of buckled black shoes.

Of course I wanted to try it all on, but I thought I'd explore the house first. I made my way down into a silk hung drawing room. It had a coffered ceiling from which were suspended several ornate chandeliers of Murano glass. I was looking up so much I didn't at first notice Faye sitting by the window gazing out at the Grand Canal, inexpressibly sad.

'Faye?' I called gently.

She turned her head, a sudden expectant look on her face. Her disappointment when she saw who it was stabbed at me, although she quickly covered it with a warm smile.

'Nick,' she said, getting to her feet and coming over to me. 'You made it.'

She offered her cheeks to kiss. I looked down at her. Her small, conical breasts were draped in silk, and a clinging, full-length skirt of some velvet material outlined the smooth curve of her hips.

'We need to talk,' I said.

Her expression became wary.

'Nick, not—'

'Yes, now.'

She looked up into my eyes for a moment then glanced towards the door.

'All right, but not here. Let's go for a drink.'

The water taxi's engine made too much noise for conversation to be possible. It dropped us at a mooring a few hundred yards from St Mark's Square and Faye led me down a narrow alley into a chic bar once frequented by Ernest Hemingway – one of the many.

'Yes?' the barman said peremptorily, in English.

'I think you mean "yes, please",' I said, amiably enough.
He looked down his nose.
'I'm very busy.'
'I'm your job,' I said. 'Don't forget that.'
Don't tell me I can't be assertive.
He walked off down the bar and started polishing glasses.
We got drinks eventually – well, Faye did – and took a
table on a narrow mezzanine gallery with a view over the
lagoon.
'What do you want to talk about?' she said quietly.
'Where to start? Well, how about the son I didn't know
you had?'
She leaned back and ran her fingers through her hair.
'First, there's something else I have to tell you. About the
letter.'
'What letter?'
'The letter from the university to Lucy about the dating
of the bones.'
'Go on.'
'I have it. I took it from her body.'
'But why?'
'Not for any suspicious reasons—'
'It sounds pretty suspicious to me.'
'I didn't know about any third set of bones!' she pro-
tested. 'I just wanted to see what the letter was about.'
'How did you know about it?'
Faye looked down.
'She c-called that morning to talk to either Rex or
Buckhalter. Rex hadn't been taking her calls since they'd
stopped having sex. She'd been quite bitter about that. I
remember her saying, "Tell him he'd better take this call.
I've got a letter that makes very interesting reading." '
'And did he?'
'What?'
'Take the call.'
'No, he wasn't around. I phoned him on his mobile to tell
him Lucy had phoned.'

192

I recalled Genevra saying that their lunch had come to an abrupt end when Rex got a call on his mobile.

'What time did you call him?' I said casually.

'About ten thirty. Why?'

Oh well.

'What was his reaction?'

'The phone was switched off. I left a message on the voice-mail.'

'And what about Buckhalter?'

'He was in the office. I told him.'

'And what did he do?'

'I – I don't know. I think he said he would call her back.'

I had an image of Buckhalter calling Lucy and arranging to meet her in the chapel, then strangling her when she turned up. But why the Maid of Astolet bit? And why didn't he take the letter?

'Do you still have the letter?'

'Yes. I realised it was a stupid thing to do, but I needed to know what it said. I thought it might be about . . . other things. And having got it I didn't know what to do with it.'

'What other things? Your brother?'

She looked away.

'I've heard from him,' she almost whispered. 'He's here. In Venice.'

'Heard from him? How?'

'He wrote to me at the Gatehouse. He's been living in Tangiers for the past fifteen years – it's a g-good place for gays.' She grimaced. 'He comes over to Venice regularly. He's staying at the Danieli.'

'He must have done well for himself.'

Faye didn't respond. We suddenly heard in the distance the wailing of a siren, like an air-raid warning. We looked at each other. Faye shrugged.

'So was it Ralph you saw in Wells?'

'*Rafe*. Oh, I don't know. I don't care. What's important is that my brother is alive and I'm going to see him.'

'When?'

'He's going to be at the carnival ball in Ca' Rezzonica this evening.'

'Everyone will be masked – how on earth will you recognise him? Why don't you go to see him at the Danieli?'

She shook her head.

'He doesn't want me to. He said I'd know him when I saw him at the ball.'

She looked at her watch.

'Nick, I need to be getting back. I've still got things to do before this evening.'

'Ten more minutes. I must say, the prospect of seeing your brother doesn't seem to have filled you with unalloyed joy.'

'When someone you care about lets you think they've been dead for fifteen years, it's a little difficult to cope with the discovery that they're alive and well.'

'Faye, why exactly did *Rafe* leave so abruptly?'

'I can't—'

'Could it be anything to do with Bernard Frome's death?'

She looked out at the lagoon.

'It's raining again,' she said. 'We've had terrible rain these past couple of days.'

'Faye! For God's sake, just tell me. You can trust me.'

'Can I?' she said, adding, but without real force, 'I trusted you before.'

She was referring to my infidelity.

'It was just sex. Christ, I was only twenty. I got horny if the wind changed direction. And you wouldn't, couldn't. Except that once, that crazy night we finished.'

'Why didn't you tell me you'd been unfaithful before you slept with me? Or is that a male thing? You knew that if you did I wouldn't let you.'

'You didn't exactly let me then.'

She laughed, despite herself.

'Oh God,' she said. 'That was so awful. I'd just heard my brother had disappeared after Frome's death. He left me a note.'

'Saying?'

'That he couldn't handle things. He was off, I mustn't try to find him, he'd be in trouble.' She looked at me anxiously. 'Nick, there's a lot you don't understand. Your views of those days . . . you don't know the full story.'

'I'd like to,' I said gently. 'Tell me what happened.'

'Ralph was having an affair with Bernard. That afternoon they got into a drunken squabble – you know how much Ralph used to put away, and Bernard was never sober. Ralph started to leave. Bernard tried to stop him. They were standing at the top of the stairs . . .' She shook her head. 'I'm sure it was an accident. But Ralph ran off anyway.' There were tears in her voice now. 'He was never very good at facing up to his responsibilities.'

She spent a couple of minutes looking for a handkerchief in her bag and blowing her nose.

'I've got to ask you about us,' I said. 'You finish with me. Next thing, I now discover, you're marrying Askwith. Had you been having an affair with him whilst you were with me?'

'Come on, Nick, this is old history.'

'There's a lot of it about at the moment.'

'No, I wasn't having an affair with him. He was just part of that crowd – Reggie and Rex and the others – that my brother hung out with.'

'So why'd you marry him? And have his baby so fast?'

She was wringing the handkerchief in her hands. I felt inclined to do the same, because now we were coming to it.

'Except you implied that Askwith couldn't do it. Were you already pregnant?'

She continued to look at her hands.

'We never used any precautions that night.' I blushed. 'In the circumstances I didn't quite . . . but maybe . . . Faye, whose baby was it?' I squeezed her arm. 'Was it mine?'

There, I'd said it. W.C. Fields was once asked: 'Do you like children?' He replied: 'I do if they're properly cooked.' Though not quite so extreme, I'm essentially in his camp when it comes to the little brats. But at the same time something about them intrigues me.

195

'Nick, I wasn't thinking straight. I'd wanted to be fair to you, you'd been so patient. But with my brother in all this trouble and then when we made love and then you telling me about that girl . . .'

'I know, I know.' I turned her face to mine. Inhaled her perfume. 'But why didn't you tell me you were pregnant? I'd have—'

Well, what would I have done? I was full of plans to write the Great Novel. I didn't want to settle down. The last thing I wanted was a steady job. And the very last thing I wanted was some mewling kid.

'Whose son is it, Faye?'

She smiled. An odd smile.

'If you saw him you wouldn't even need to ask.'

She left a few minutes later. Leaning over she pecked me on the cheek, then sighed and looked at her watch.

'I really have to go.'

'I'm going to stay here,' I said. 'Be on my own for a little while.'

When the barman came to clear the table I ordered another drink. Then another. When I tried to leave the bar, my initial instinct was to blame the drink for the fact that I was about to step into a canal.

I was standing at the door I thought I'd entered by, except there was milky green water lapping against a plank some two feet wide wedged lengthways across the bottom of the doorway. I looked back into the room to see if there was another door. The barman was still ignoring me. I looked back down at the water and could see paving stones some two feet beneath it. I recalled the siren like an air-raid warning.

Oops. Venice was flooding.

196

Chapter Twelve

Apparently, in winter, it happens all the time. The lagoon rises and for a few hours Venice is under two or three feet of water. Once I'd waded down the alley – trousers rolled up to my knees, overcoat tucked round my waist, shoes and socks in my hand – and entered a main thoroughfare I could see the Venetians were well used to it. It was time for the early evening promenade when the locals put on their furs and wander the streets greeting friends. A bit of flooding wasn't going to stop that.

Clad in smart wellingtons, fur-coated women and trimly-dressed men made their way along raised walkways, constructed from what looked like a long series of trestle tables on metal supports. One or two looked askance at me, up to my shins in canal water.

'*Turistici*!' I heard one snigger with a shake of his head.

'Yeah?' I muttered. 'Fuck off you neatly-dressed Italian.'

I was a little concerned about my predicament myself. The sewerage arrangements for the city left a lot to be desired. If people weren't discharging all kinds of toxic shit straight into canals, it was sent out through piping to be discharged in the lagoon, where the next tide brought it back in.

Byron swam the width of the Grand Canal and survived. But by the nineteen fifties, when it came time for Katherine Hepburn to fall into a canal in David Lean's *Summer Madness*, the filmmakers had to pump the canal full of disinfectant to make sure she didn't catch anything.

Aside from being very cold, therefore, I was sure the water around my legs was even now stripping my skin off. Although surprisingly, there was no smell. I hoisted myself onto the walkway and went in search of a pair of wellingtons.

It took me a while to find a shop with a pair big enough to fit me. Eventually I had to buy an enormous pair of waders. They weren't ideal. They'd been made to measure for some super-model with my size feet but very skinny legs. She'd never collected them.

I had to take my trousers off to get them up my legs. I figured I could keep my overcoat closed, but even then it was like wearing a pair of thick rubber gloves, except at their tops where they curved out like bugles. When I left the shop I discovered I squeaked at every step since my thighs rubbed.

I looked at my watch. I had an hour before I needed to be back for cocktails. I thought I'd explore a little.

Some of the narrower alleys had no walkways, but in my waders I could go anywhere. I quite enjoyed it, except on the couple of occasions I mistook canals for alleys again and almost stepped in.

St Mark's Square was submerged to a depth of some two feet and photographers were busy getting arty photos of the reflections in the water of the campanile and the gorgeous basilica with its Byzantine onion domes. Walkways had been set up going all the way into the basilica.

I followed the street that ran behind the church and soon found myself in a warren of much quieter alleys. The shops and restaurants had closed until the flooding subsided. I could see water standing on their marble floors.

I was heading roughly in the direction of the Danieli, the opulent hotel to the east of the Doge's Palace. I wasn't sure what I would do when I got there but I had a number of questions to ask Ralph. Like, was he the Camelot serial killer?

As I headed there, and twilight came, I got increasingly melancholy and not a little spooked. There is a Venice more primitive than the Doge's Palace or the elegance of San

Marco square. Perhaps I was still a little concussed, but walking through dingy alleys and lonely squares, past dark, dead stretches of water, the city seemed to sigh with redolences of past misery.

Voices echoing from hidden rooms took on sinister overtones. Occasionally I would hear footfalls or on the edge of my vision catch a glimpse of some masked figure, dressed for the carnival, flitting by.

I'd got myself into serious *Don't Look Now* mode when I walked onto a low, humped bridge. Off to the right the canal broadened enough for three or four gondolas to pass together around a bend. A small quay with two steps down to the water had been constructed at the outer edge of the curve. Beside the quay was the Danieli.

By now it was dark. Yellow pools of light from a lamp beside me swayed on the water below the bridge. I heard the gondola first, the gondolier calling as he reached the blind corner, his voice echoing off the walls of the crumbling palace beyond.

Then the gondola's dark shape approached, silent but for the rhythmic plash of the oar in the water. I peered down at the passenger as the boat passed beneath the lamp. The face was concealed by a tricorne hat but the long, thin limbs were clothed in what looked like a death shroud, drenched with something dark and sticky. Something that could very well be blood.

I stepped back. I suppose my waders must have squeaked. The masquerader tilted his head back to look up at me. I swallowed hard but held his look. His mask had been designed so closely to resemble the face of a stiffened corpse, it would have been difficult to tell the difference. The mask too was splattered with what I took to be blood.

The gondola passed under the bridge. The masquerader twisted to have another look at me then said something I didn't catch to the gondolier. The gondolier guided his boat to the dock at the Danieli. Two more masqueraders, women in long gowns and small black dominoes, stepped in.

I knew my Poe. I recognised that the masquerader was in the costume worn by the unwelcome reveller – the Red Death itself – in the 'The Masque of the Red Death'. Even so, the sight of him spooked me. I suddenly wanted to be among people again.

I got back to Ca' Dario at about seven. I'd taken the vaporetto to the Rialto and walked through the flooded alleys to the back gate of the palace. The waders were killing me. The streets were by now thronged with boisterous people dressed for the carnival.

Carnival in history has always been a time of licence and of inversion – as Rex had said, lords dressing as layabouts, plebs as princes. Inversion in another sense too – in the costumes, in masks, gender became ambiguous, sexuality even more so. Masks encouraged another kind of licence – outrageous behaviour and a lot of sex. Ordinarily I would have been light-headed at the thought but I was determined that by the end of this long night – the city would be partying until dawn – I would know exactly what had been going on back in England.

I could hear voices on the ground floor but I went straight to my room to change into my costume and get the damned waders off. They felt as if they'd been welded to my knees and calves.

Half an hour later I joined the others. Except that it wasn't just the others. There were about forty people in various exotic costumes, and masks that ranged from simple white dominoes to golden half moons, silver devils and various animals' features. Some women wore half masks, so that their mouths were visible. Most people in the room, however, had masks that covered the entire face. They had coloured straws to allow them to drink their cocktails.

The most unsettling were a couple of tall men dressed as Punchinellos, in white costumes with humpbacks. Their cruel white masks were etched with lines across the forehead and dominated by grotesque hooked noses. The mouths were set in lewd grins. They both wore tall, conical hats and carried clubs.

I was wondering how I was going to identify Bridget, Genevra and the rest when two women wearing black dominoes and with full bosoms spilling from their *very* décolleté dresses headed towards me.

'Hello, poppet,' one of them said, kissing me on my papier-mâché cheek.

'My chevalier,' the other said, kissing the other cheek. 'How excitingly mysterious you look.'

Bridget and Genevra, both smelling strongly of alcohol.

'But how did you know it was me?' I said.

They both pointed down.

'Who else is going to turn up to the society party of the year in bright yellow wellingtons?' Genevra said. 'Do you have an irrational fear of floods?'

'I can't get the bloody things off,' I said.

'You must be boiling in your cloak,' Bridget said. 'Why don't you ditch it until later?'

'No, I'm fine thanks—'

But Bridget had already taken the two sides of the cloak and tossed them back over my shoulders.

'That's how you – Nick, you pervert!'

I suppose I must have looked odd, bright yellow waders almost up to my crotch, but what was I supposed to do?

'Oh dear, not just wellingtons then,' Genevra said, hiccuping with laughter.

'Do you have a pair of scissors?' I said to her. 'Then I can cut them off.'

'Ah, someone from the s/m scene in Venice, I see,' another voice said dryly. One of the Punchinellos was standing between Bridget and Genevra. He sounded like Reggie Williamson, but the Reggie Williamson I'd heard outside the barn, not the public one.

I pulled the edges of my cloak together with as much dignity as I could muster.

'Hands off, Reggie,' Genevra said, rather sharply. 'He's taken.'

'Genevra,' he said loudly. 'It's carnival. Everything is permissible.' He leaned towards me. 'But do I gather you to mean this is your chap, Madrid?'

I nodded.

'Indeed.' He looked me up and down. 'People always say to be yourself. In your case, I'd avoid that.' He laughed. 'You put up a good fight in the joust, however. Though your armour looked rather familiar. Eh?'

'The taxis are here,' I heard Rex bellow. He was dressed in braided frock coat, buckled shoes and a white mask covering his whole face. I looked around wondering which of these people was Buckhalter. There was a stout chevalier on the other side of the room who could have been him. He was facing me and I had the uncomfortable feeling he was staring at me from behind his white mask.

'Come on, Nick,' Genevra and Bridget said, taking an arm each.

'What about those scissors?'

'No time for that now,' Genevra said.

'Nobody will notice,' Bridget added, before the pair of them burst into a fit of giggling.

They dragged me across the room. In one of its many ornate mirrors I saw Williamson standing alone, watching us go.

Outside the watergate a flotilla of gondolas were rolling and dipping in the swell, their black lacquered prows reflecting the blazing torches atop the mooring posts.

'Rex is with some business people, so you're stuck with me for the time being,' Bridget said as she followed Genevra and me into one of the boats.

The palaces flanking the Grand Canal were shimmering with lights and the canal itself was thronged with many small craft, all with lights ablaze fore and aft, and all crammed with partygoers in costume. Music drifted across the water and there was a hubbub of conversations, shrieks and laughter.

Both my escorts were affectionate, cuddling up to me on a seat intended only for two. I wanted to ask what Faye was wearing but in the circumstances felt that would be rather tactless.

The Ca' Rezzonica, I knew, was now a museum. It had a distinguished history and had once belonged to Robert Browning's son.

'Robert Browning died here,' I said as the gondolier steered into the watergate.

'Robert Browning?' Bridget echoed.

'The poet,' I said. Then, hurriedly, 'Forget it.' I've been through that with her before.

There was a short dock actually in the courtyard of the palace. We disembarked and made our way up a flight of wide, worn steps. I looked back in time to see a Punchinello get out of a gondola. Whether he was Williamson or the other one I had no idea.

A second flight of stairs brought us to a lavishly decorated entrance. Noise and heat came out from it in blasts.

On the high canopied ceiling and down the walls were painted elaborate incidents from Roman mythology, intersected by golden cornices and cherubim. Waiters were standing with trays of drinks. Bridget's and Genevra's shoes clattered on the marble floor. I merely squeaked, which set them off giggling again.

The room we entered was packed with revellers in a giddy range of costumes. There were far too many slave girls in brief bikinis to be good for a young man's equilibrium. A number of men were dressed as I was and there were half a dozen harlequins in diamond-patterned costumes and hats.

To counter the hubbub everyone was screeching, which only made things worse. The members of a string quartet in front of an immense carved fireplace were sawing furiously at their instruments in a hopeless effort to make themselves heard.

Genevra, Bridget and I stationed ourselves beside one of two ferocious, giant marble blackamoors, with ivory teeth and eyes, who guarded the entrance to a second room with heavy clubs. Dance music wafted through from a third room we could see beyond the second.

'I'm going to check out the dancing,' Bridget said. 'Don't move from here. I'll be back.'

My priority was to find Faye and her brother, since I believed them to be the key to everything. How I was going to know them, I couldn't figure out. I was scanning the two rooms when Genevra touched my arm.

'Nick, are you okay? You seem a bit off with me.'

I took her hand and squeezed it.

'Still feel a bit weird from the concussion.'

'You're looking for Faye, aren't you?'

I nodded.

'Well, you're a bloody fool,' she said, anger in her voice. 'What has she told you about her son?'

'Enough,' I said.

'Who the father is?'

An eastern potentate in gold turban and mask and long scarlet cloak went by, a slave girl draped over each arm.

'She implied . . .' I said.

'That it was you?' I nodded. 'The cow,' Genevra added vehemently.

'Hey, steady.'

'What were her exact words?'

'That if I saw him I'd know immediately.'

Genevra nodded slowly. She spoke more gently.

'And you took that to mean it was you? Nick, I've seen him. It's not your child. And if it's not yours and it isn't Askwith's, who does that leave?

'Rex,' I said, looking at her blank porcelain face. 'And that's why you're so against her.'

'It isn't Rex, I assure you. Faye is one of the few he hasn't managed to bed. So who's left?'

'I don't know!' I shouted, causing a nearby harlequin to

look our way. I was angry because I wasn't sure I wanted to know. My fear was that I was about to have my youth snatched away, a part of my personal history rewritten.

'What about her brother?' Genevra said.

'Her *brother*?' I recoiled, felt the marble statue at my back. 'Don't be putting yours and Rex's stuff on Faye.'

'Mine and Rex's stuff?' she said stiffly. 'What exactly do you mean?'

'It's pretty obvious you and he are – well, that you have been—'

'You think we're having an affair?' Her voice trembled with emotion. 'You think I'd sleep with my own brother? What kind of person do you think I am?'

'The same kind of person you think Faye is,' I spat, equally angry. 'Except you're an aristocrat – you have different rules to the rest of us.'

I blocked her swing at my face pretty easily. It was the knee to the groin that got to me, even though my cloak took most of the force.

'What have I ever said or done to give you that idea?' she said, both hurt and anger in her voice.

I didn't answer until I could stand again. I glanced round the room. Nobody seemed to have noticed a thing.

'I saw you cuddling in the window at Wynn House. There's something secretive between you. When you were talking about all that Arthur and Morgan le Fay stuff I saw the way you were looking at each other.'

'We often cuddle. He's my brother. But it doesn't mean anything. And the secret we were keeping was Faye's, not ours, you great charlie.'

'That's a ruder word than you think – it's rhyming slang.'

'I don't give a flying fuck.' She took a deep breath and touched her mask where the scar was on her lip.

'Remember you asked me about the accident my father was killed in?' I nodded. 'It was a family celebration. Nothing grand – only down the pub. We had quite a jolly time. Everybody had a lot to drink. Except Rex. He was on antibiotics for something, I forget what. Father was reeling. Rex drove us back in Father's car. Father never wore a seat belt. On principle.'

She paused for a moment. Looked down.

'Rex wasn't used to father's Bentley,' she continued. 'Big, heavy old thing. There's a road a couple of miles from Wynn House that is really treacherous when it's been raining. It's been closed because of flooding for the past few weeks. Going down that, Rex skidded off the road. Hit a tree. Father was in the front passenger seat. Went through the windscreen. I was in the back. I went face first into the seat in front. Caught my mouth on a metal ashtray . . .'

I fished a tissue out of the top of my left wader. Well, I didn't have any pockets.

'What were you celebrating?'

When she had composed herself, Genevra said: 'Father had invited Rex and me to meet his new fiancée. An actress from Bath called Felicity. Sweet, but Rex and I thought "Here we go again – ruche curtains".'

She moved closer to me.

'Nick, Faye used you,' she said fiercely. 'All the time you were at Oxford. She and her brother have been lovers since she was fourteen. She avoided going out with boys at Oxford by pretending to have a boyfriend at home. Then her parents grew suspicious so she needed someone to fool them with – you. She never slept with you because – and I'll give her full marks for fidelity – she was sleeping with her brother.

'What she didn't know, at first, was that her brother was pretty much pansexual. You might have guessed that from the fact he seduced his own sister. Ralph would sleep with anything with a heartbeat. He tried it on with me when I was sixteen. But he was also screwing around with most of the blokes in their group.'

'They were all gay?' I said numbly.

'It was very fashionable to be bi back then, don't you remember?'

206

I remembered. All the boys were at it. And whilst I didn't want to appear provincial it didn't appeal to me. I only wanted to have sex with girls, albeit every girl I saw.

'Nick?' Genevra said. 'Focus. When Faye told Ralph she was pregnant by him he pissed off because, child that he was, he couldn't handle that.'

I recalled Faye saying wistfully earlier in the day that Ralph had never been good at facing up to his responsibilities.

'Hang on,' I said. 'He went because he'd pushed Bernard Frome down the stairs in an argument.'

'Sez who?'

'Faye told me.'

'Who actually saw it?'

'I don't know. Nobody had to see it if Ralph admitted it to her.'

'Did he?'

'How else would Faye know? Who told you?'

'That's not important. We all know about that version of events.'

I thought for a moment. There was a lot going on at the time that I had no idea about. The problem was I didn't know if I wanted to know.

'Nick, I'm sorry to be the one to tell you these things, but I care about you and I think you should know. Even though it means you'll want to shoot the messenger and I'll lose you. And I don't want to lose you.'

'So how *does* everyone know Faye's brother knocked off Frome?'

'Do you remember what staircase Frome was on?'

'Staircase A, West Quad.'

'Do you know who else was on that staircase?'

'After all this time – come on.'

'It was alphabetical, wasn't it – rooms for students were parcelled out in alphabetical order starting at staircase A?'

'Askwith,' I said, not because I knew but because it suddenly all made sense. 'Askwith saw it and promised to keep quiet about it if Faye would marry him – the bastard.'

207

Genevra was quiet for a few moments but I could see her eyes behind her mask. She was watching me intently.

'What?' I said. 'There's more?'

'You tell me,' she said cautiously.

I shrugged.

'I'm out of my depth and my rubber ring has a hole in it.'

'In light of all that's been happening since, do you think Askwith's death was an accident?'

She continued to look at me intently.

'What are you getting at?' I said. 'You mean that Faye offed her husband? But why would she do it now? She'd been married to him for years.'

Bridget chose this moment to burst in on us.

'You dancing?' she shouted, grabbing Genevra's arm.

'Not just now . . .' Genevra started to say but Bridget didn't hear her and continued to tug.

'You'd better stay there until they do the rowing boat song, Nick,' Bridget called back, cackling. Cackling. She was drunk then.

Genevra looked back over her shoulder.

'Wait for me,' she called.

I waited and watched, hoping for a sign that would show me Faye or her brother. I was conscious that others too were merely watching. And because they, like me, were masked, there was something unsettling about their blank-faced stillness.

My mind was spinning from the things Genevra had told me and the sure feeling that she was probably right. I was leaning my head against the marble statue behind me and looking up at the massive chandelier suspended from the middle of a fierce battle scene when I became conscious of a slight commotion at the main entrance. I looked over.

The blood-bedewed masquerader I'd seen in the gondola some hours before had entered, walking stiffly between the two companions I had seen board the boat at the Danieli. People parted to let him pass. There were some murmurs of disapproval – the blood looked very fresh – but the party soon swallowed him up.

Except that I kept a watch on him. He toured the room, walking in his stiff, frail way. He passed within two yards of me and I could see his two companions lightly supporting him. I noticed the stubble beneath the powder and rouge of the one who passed closest to me.

I had no doubt the person who had come as the Red Death was Ralph, and I was equally certain that I knew why he had got in touch with Faye after all these years.

As I watched Ralph I saw a tall, slender harlequin detach himself from a small group of people and follow him. The harlequin walked neatly, almost heel to toe. I'd found Faye too.

I followed at a distance. In a room with a brightly decorated ceiling and walls hung with vast, doomy canvases I saw the harlequin approach the Red Death. They spoke for a moment then moved off together. Ralph's two companions watched them go through a door in the far wall.

I skirted the room and, when I was sure the two (wo)men weren't watching, also slipped out of the door.

I was in a stairwell with steps going both up and down. I listened and thought I heard shuffling footsteps above me. I mounted the stairs after them, as quietly as my squeaking waders would allow.

The floor above had not been open to the public for some years but the rooms were still laid out as in a museum. Security lights glowed dimly. The rooms were arranged in a complex way so that passage from one to another meant continual turns and twists. For the most part they were bedrooms, private chambers and studies.

From the windows I occasionally caught a glimpse of the Grand Canal. Fireworks were arcing into the sky and bursting in enormous showers of colour. But the walls of the Ca' Rezzonica were thick and it was like watching a silent film. More usually the windows looked over dank alleys or narrow, dark canals. I took my mask off.

209

I found Faye standing by a four-poster bed in a small bedroom. The short bed covered with a richly embroidered counterpane and drapes of fading chenille was on a shallow platform. Faye had taken her mask off. She was staring at the bed, tracing with her finger a delicate convolvulus of golden thread along the bolster. She was unaware of me until I stepped closer. She heard the squeak and jerked her head round.

'Where's Ralph?' I said.

'*Rafe*,' she said automatically.

It was very hot in the room. I loosened my cloak and dropped it on the bed.

'Faye, I know about you and Ralph, and about you and Askwith.'

'Know what?' she said, looking up then suddenly bursting out laughing. There was a tinge of hysteria to her laughter.

'It's okay,' I said. 'I know they look weird. I can't get them off.'

'You need scissors.'

'Why, Faye?'

'Have you seen Ralph?'

I nodded.

'He's . . .'

'I know. I'm sorry.'

Hot tears spilled from her eyes. I felt like crying too. Instead I stood watching her, keeping the bed between us.

'Askwith claimed he'd seen what happened. I thought that was why Ralph had gone. Askwith said he'd go to the police if I didn't agree to be his . . . companion. Even then, he couldn't . . . but there were other things . . . Then, worse than that, when Ralph tried to get in touch with me Askwith forbade it. All these years wasted. I thought he was dead. And now . . .'

'I figured something like that had happened,' I said. 'And I'm really sorry. But what you're saying gives both you and Ralph a pretty strong motive for killing your husband. Which one of you did it?'

'I don't think I'm capable of killing anyone,' a frail voice said. I turned. It was Ralph in his blood-bedewed costume. He'd taken his mask off but, aside from the blood, his ravaged face didn't look much different without the mask. It had a ghastly pallor. Faye looked at him then looked away, tears still falling.

'Nor have I ever been. I came back to see Faye. And my son. Before I . . .'

'Die,' I said.

Ralph smiled briefly.

'Hello, Nick. Nice waders.' He took a step closer. 'You look well.'

'I wish I could say the same,' I said with feeling.

He shrugged.

'I'm just a boy who can't say No.'

I gestured at the bloody outfit.

'Pretty crude metaphor, isn't it?'

'Spoken like a true Englishman,' he said. 'AIDS is a pretty crude disease. Sorry if it offends you, *old chap.*'

'I didn't mean that—'

'I've been reading all day of deeds of valour,' he said. 'Of the fatal love of Lancelot for Guinevere and the incestuous passion of Arthur and Morgause, Queen of the Orkneys.' He looked at Faye. 'I wanted to find a way to make amends to her. I did see Askwith at the college. To confront him. He just laughed.'

'But why didn't you come forward earlier and deny killing Frome?'

'I didn't know until I heard from Faye that people had been thinking I'd somehow killed dear old Bernard.'

'But—'

'Askwith was around that afternoon,' Ralph said. 'He told me he'd take care of everything. I didn't *quite* realise what he meant.'

'But—' I said again.

'Don't you understand, Nick?' Faye said. 'No, you have no family, why would you know? How could you?' She

211

raised her hands and let them fall wearily. 'Family secrets, Nick. So much is kept hidden. It simply wasn't talked about. Ever. By anybody. The official verdict on Bernard was accidental death and we all maintained that, just as we all maintained the fiction that Joseph was mine and Askwith's child.'

'Then if Ralph didn't kill Askwith—' I began.

Faye looked at me sorrowfully. I heard a door slam somewhere.

'Then it must have been me?' She shook her head. 'I thought of killing *myself*. Often. But never Askwith. And I couldn't kill myself because of Joseph, my son.' She looked at Ralph. 'Our son.'

'Then Askwith did die accidentally?' I said. 'He and Frome both?'

'No,' Ralph said, sinking down on the bed. 'Just as Frome's death was not accidental.'

'You did kill Frome?'

Ralph shook his head.

'Look,' I said. 'I feel like a ping-pong ball here being bounced all over the table. Could you just tell it straight?'

'Of course, Nick, of course.' Ralph paused as if to gain his strength. 'I was with Bernard when he died. We'd spent the afternoon together. A large amount of alcohol had been consumed. We were disturbed by a violent banging on the door and demands that we open up. I assume the racket was what drew Askwith from his room on the floor above.

'Frome wasn't my lover, I was just one of his seductions. The irony was I'd gone to see him because he was my moral tutor – immoral tutor would be more accurate – to ask what I should do about Faye and the baby. I needed a confessor but I couldn't see the padre understanding. Frome, naughty man, poured drink down my throat and then offered me comfort.

'It was my regular male lover at the door. He was a very jealous person. Frome answered the door but went outside, to protect me, I suppose. There were harsh words and I went to the door just in time to see my lover deliberately push Frome down the stairs. Frome cracked his head on one of the steps as he went down. When he stopped falling, he just lay crumpled in the angle of the stairs, in a pool of blood, his head at a terrible angle. It was awful, terrible. I used to faint at the sight of blood.'

He twisted his mouth into a grimace and indicated his blood-bedewed gowns.

'Ironic, eh?'

He paused.

'Askwith found us on the stairs. Told me he would sort it. I left that evening, promising my lover I wouldn't say anything. The police knew Frome had been with someone but not who that someone was. The college wanted to hush it up – they could see the newspaper headlines – Immoral Tutor in Love Trysts with Student Lovers and so on – so no one made much of a fuss when the verdict of accidental death came in.'

I expelled my breath slowly.

'You seem to be missing one thing out,' I said. 'Who was your lover?'

Ralph looked surprised.

'Sorry, Nick, I thought you knew. Everybody else did. It was Reggie. Reggie Williamson? Lord Williamson of Fleming?'

Chapter Thirteen

Reggie Williamson had killed Bernard Frome. But if Askwith had really seen what happened, why hadn't he put the bite on Williamson? Ah. Things began to click into place. I recalled bumping into Williamson as he came out of his meeting with Askwith in the college library. He looked rattled. Askwith had tried to blackmail him.

Suddenly Williamson seemed the likeliest candidate for Askwith's murderer. I recalled seeing him alone in the quadrangle. And what about Lucy? I'd thought he and Lucy might have had an affair. The fact that he was gay didn't necessarily negate that theory. Everybody was being so bloody polymorphously perverse.

If Williamson had killed Lucy too, then he was my serial killer. I shivered. From Williamson's comment about the armour, I assumed he realised that I'd heard that snippet of conversation between him and Rex outside the barn on the night of the joust.

Given his evident ruthlessness, that put me right in the firing line. I looked at Faye and Ralph. And I wasn't the only one.

'Does Williamson know you're back in circulation?' I said to Ralph. He and Faye exchanged glances. Before they could speak we all heard the clatter of footsteps on the corridor behind us.

'Come on,' I said, grabbing my cloak and leading the way into the next room. It was a hexagonal changing room with a mirror on each wall and behind the mirrors

215

hanging space for gowns and dresses.

'Faye, you two hide in one of these,' I whispered. 'I'll lead him away.'

Faye shook her head.

'We're in this together.'

'Well, put your masks back on then. He might not realise who you are.'

Ralph looked down at his distinctive costume.

'Good idea,' he said.

I caught sight of myself in the yellow waders in one of the mirrors. I definitely wouldn't bother.

'Why can't we just see what he has to say?' Ralph complained. 'I'm sure he doesn't mean us harm.'

'I'm sure he does,' I said, going through into a passage some fifteen yards in length. 'We can hear what he has to say when we're back downstairs with everyone else.'

We tiptoes past a series of disturbing paintings of a masked ball. Each featured tall, gaunt harlequins at a masquerade looking almost as if they were warders. In one, masqueraders, frozen in postures of alarm, turned to stare at an open door where a harlequin passed by. What stood out in all the pictures was the lack of gaiety in this masquerade. There was no dancing, no drinking, no movement.

We passed through a short T-shaped apartment filled with glass cabinets displaying examples of eighteenth-century costume, complete with dominoes and stiff masks like the ones depicted in the paintings we had just seen. I paused to listen for signs of pursuit. All I could hear was the rain as it began a light rataplan across the palace windows.

We came into a chamber decked out as an alchemist's laboratory. Two red emergency lights glowed dimly in the ceiling. They cast a curious glow on the benches loaded with primitive chemical apparatus: crucibles, cupels, flasks, retorts and bowls. Books lined one wall; jars and bottles lined another. Some of the jars were marked: cinnabar, argentive, azoth, white water and aqua fortis. On the floor were bellows, wooden casks, a pelican. A small furnace was set into one wall.

Faye and I were supporting Ralph, our pace dictated by his slow shuffle. We entered a suite of small rooms, each room no more than six feet square but some fifteen feet in height. They led one into the other. The sixth room was hexagonal and seemed to be a dead end.

I looked back anxiously, then surveyed the room. A perverse hand had etched an army of hunchbacks across the ceiling and down the walls: hundreds of Punchinellos dancing a strange, rickety step, hobbling over bare hills, limping in blind procession, clinging one to the next in single file. Humped backs, bent heads, vicious leering faces.

I shivered. The rain increased in intensity, hammering on the narrow window.

I spotted a tiny ring set in one wall. I pulled it and a door opened onto a large apartment, some twenty yards in length. Through a long window set halfway along one wall I saw, with a lifting heart, fireworks exploding over the Rialto Bridge. Their bursts of light fitfully illuminated the shadowy room.

We advanced cautiously into the apartment. All was quiet except for Ralph's ragged breathing, the heavy tock of a clock and, of course, the squeak of rubber on rubber. Ralph was weakening, leaning more heavily on my arm. We reached a small stage, with heavy tasselled drapes closed around it. A puppet theatre. There was a large, glass-fronted cupboard to the left of the stage. In the bursts of coloured light from the fireworks outside we could see that it contained the puppets, each some four feet in height.

They were the stock characters from the commedia dell'arte, in ancient, tattered garments: the pirate, the blackamoor, the sultan, the Chinaman, the serving man, the rich lord, the fair maiden, the brave chevalier, the doctor. Suspended by their strings over a long rail, they hung limply, sagging at the knees.

217

The eyes in the shiny, grotesquely painted faces were white balls with black staring pupils; their lower jaws hung open in slack grins. In the irregular light, the puppets seemed to be swaying, very slightly. Two, I noticed, were not on the rail. At one side of the cabinet Lucifer stood, horned and black cloaked. At the other side, in shadow, stood a Punchinello with a long bulbous stick.

I peered at the Punchinello, my heart thumping, half expecting the eyes to swivel and peer back at me. There was no movement. I looked round the room. The shadows pressed in on us.

I freed myself from Ralph and stepped over to the stage to open the curtains. The fireworks had been diminishing in intensity for the past minute or two. Now, abruptly, with a final fitful flicker, they stopped altogether. We were plunged into darkness. I heard Faye's sharp intake of breath. I paused, my arms outstretched, my fingers touching the heavy drapes.

A sliver of light shot across the floor of the room. I looked back to the door we had come through from the last hexagonal room. It was ajar. I could glimpse the hunched Punchinellos in procession over the pale hills.

Something brushed my left hand. I jerked back to face the curtains. A white shape loomed between them. As my eyes adjusted to the darkness I could make out, through the dim motes of light from the window, the hooked nose and the horrible, frozen leer of a Punchinello.

'Evening all,' Williamson said.

I fell back involuntarily. Faye gasped. Williamson pushed open the curtains and hopped to the floor, his club swinging in his left hand. He looked Ralph up and down.

'Bit OTT, isn't it?' he said. 'But then you always were a bit of a poser.'

'Hello, Reggie. Can't say I'm mad about the hat.'

Williamson lifted the club.

'This is rather more titillating though, don't you think?'

Ralph was still leaning on Faye's arm. I saw her clutch him more tightly.

'Game over, I think, Reggie.'

He looked at me.

'Lord Williamson to you, you oik. And I assure you, my game is far from over.'

'You're going to kill all three of us? I don't think so.'

I said this with more confidence than I felt.

'Nor do I. Why would I wish to? Did you know, Madrid, that the Venetian secret police used daggers made of glass for their assassinations? When inserted into a victim's body the glass point would snap off and leave virtually no trace of the fatal wound.' Williamson waggled the club. 'If I were to do what you suggest I would have to be less discreet.'

'Not sure you'd want my blood splashing around, Reggie,' Ralph said. 'In the circs.'

'Why don't we go downstairs and talk about this?' I said, rather optimistically I admit.

'No, no, we're fine here,' Williamson said. 'I need to think for a moment. No offence, Ralph, but I was hoping never to see you again. As long as you were out of the way, my little secret was safe.'

'Except with Askwith.'

'That piece of slime! Sorry, Faye, I know he was your husband.'

A burst of light abruptly illuminated us. The fireworks had begun again. I saw an odd tableau. The harlequin and the blood-bedewed masquerader clinging onto each other, the Punchinello standing before them, his club threatening. I felt we were in one of the paintings we'd passed earlier.

'I'm inclined to agree with your estimation,' Faye said quietly.

'He tried to blackmail you, that night at the college dinner?' I said.

'Askwith had been blackmailing me for years. He came to see me the day after Frome's death and agreed to keep it quiet. And he did. But I knew it was only a matter of time

until he called in the note. I guessed that once I was
ennobled he'd come looking for me. He'd kept in touch over
the years, checking on my progress. It wouldn't do him any
good to expose me earlier in my career and I wasn't earning
enough – he took an annual stipend, index-linked to my
salary. You could tell the bastard was an accountant.'

'And that night?'

'Yes, he approached me and demanded serious money.
Money I simply didn't have.'

'He'd lost a lot of our money on the stock market, sunk
the last of it in Rex's venture,' Faye said.

'And that excuses him?' Williamson said coldly.

'I wasn't trying to—'

'But how could he say what he knew after all these years,'
I said, 'without being accused of withholding evidence?'

Williamson tapped the club on the floor impatiently.

'He just needed to speak to a few people in your profes-
sion.'

'Accusing you of murder? You could have argued it was
an accident.'

'What difference would that make to my reputation? A
government minister, a married man with children, involved
in a scandal at university concerning his lover and the gay
don – can't you just see it?' His voice was bitter, indignant.
'Even without a murder accusation my reputation would
have been in tatters.'

'Publishing that wouldn't have been in the public interest.'

Williamson laughed. It echoed harshly in the bare room.

'When has that *ever* made a difference?'

'But it would have meant exposing his own wife's
brother.'

'That wouldn't concern my husband in the least,' Faye
said.

'And, frankly, I didn't give a sod about that,' Williamson
said impatiently. 'I'd worked hard to get where I am and I'd
be damned if one little mistake was going to get in my way.'
He looked at me. 'I still feel the same.'

'But it's more than one little mistake now. You killed Askwith.'

'Accidental death, actually. I believe that was the coroner's verdict. Lovely funeral, by the way, Faye. So *final*, a cremation, don't you think? I mean, I know we're all going to make our fortune out of digging up Arthur's bones but I'm pleased Askwith's body can never be dug up.'

'You poisoned him?'

'No, no. Merely helped him drink some port. Quite a lot of port actually. But holding him down was difficult. He struggled, A black tie doesn't make an ideal wrist restraint. I could have done with two but his, of course, was a slip-on. Anyway, there were some marks on him that could be . . . *reinterpreted.*'

I wanted to ask about the significance of the Holman Hunt painting but there was a more pressing question.

'Weren't you worried that he and Faye were in it together?'

'I thought it unlikely – I knew the state of their marriage – but I did have a chat with Faye. Just to make sure that she and everyone else still thought Ralph here had killed Frome.'

'When was this?' I said. But I realised I already knew the answer. 'In Tintagel?'

Faye looked towards me. She took her mask off with her free hand.

'I'm sorry, Nick. I wanted to tell you. He offered to help Ralph if he needed money. I thought he was being kind but now I realise he was just trying to find out if Ralph was still alive and if I suspected anything.'

'This is all fascinating stuff,' Ralph said shakily. 'But I'm afraid I'm going to have to sit down, if that's okay with you, Reggie.'

He let go of Faye and shuffled over to the edge of the stage. He lowered himself onto it, breathing hard. He tore at his mask then sat there, gasping for air.

Williamson seemed transfixed by Ralph's face.

'You used to be so beautiful,' he said, shaking his head.

I was remembering the man who followed Faye up onto Tintagel Island. The man who clobbered me and left me to drown in Merlin's Cave. I threw my cloak over Williamson's head.

'You tried to kill me, you bastard!' I said, grabbing him in a bear hug and trying to kick his legs out from under him. He writhed and tried to raise the club but I held on and we fell to the floor together. He tried to roll back on top of me but I resisted strenuously. As we struggled he managed to free the arm with the club in it. He was raising it to hit me when Faye darted in and, with surprising strength, dragged it from his grasp.

He subsided then and I moved away and got to my feet. Faye handed me the club as he started to rise.

'Stay down or I'll use this bloody thing,' I gasped. 'I owe you.'

Williamson poked his head through the cloak.

'Look, I couldn't be seen down in Tintagel,' he said, his voice wheedling. 'I had no reason to be there and I was supposed to be elsewhere on government business. I didn't know if you'd overheard our conversation or what else you knew. I knew you'd gone into the library when Askwith was there. How did I know you weren't in this thing with him? The unfortunate incident in the cave . . . It was nothing personal, I assure you.'

'Sure. But why Lucy? Why kill her? What had she stumbled on?'

'Lucy?' he said, surprised. 'I didn't kill Lucy. I liked the poor lamb.'

I frowned.

'No, that one is a mystery to me, Madrid. I expect we'll probably find out one day. I—'

With a groan, Ralph slid sideways and fell off the stage to the floor. Faye clutched her throat, pinching the skin between her fingers. She moaned then rushed towards him.

'Ralph!' she cried.

My attention was distracted for only a moment but the next thing I knew my cloak was spreading before me then falling around my head. I was punched hard in the stomach. I heard the clatter of feet running the length of the apartment.

I wrestled the cloak from around my head. Faye was cradling Ralph in her arms. I looked round for Williamson. Skidding on the polished floor, he had almost reached a door I hadn't noticed before at the far end of the apartment. The flashing lights from the fireworks sent his looming, distorted shadow up the wall and along the ceiling. I looked back at Faye. She saw my indecision.

'We're all right alone. Go after him.' Her voice was tender. 'We're all right.'

I took off down the room. The waders weren't exactly ideal for sprinting but at least the rubber soles gripped the polished floor. The door opened onto a narrow flight of stairs. Down all its twists and turns it was lit only by dim electric lights set at intervals on the rough walls.

As I ran down, hearing Williamson descending pell-mell ahead of me, I was aware of the increasing smell of damp and mildew. I heard the screech of wood on stone and when I turned the next corner saw an open door and, beyond it, the Grand Canal. I reached the door just as a motor boat, moored some yards to my left, roared into life.

I lunged for it as it started to move. I got the top half of my body into the boat; my legs were dangling over the side in the water. Williamson was standing at the wheel, his back to me. As the boat dipped with my weight, he looked back over his shoulder. He snarled and pressed a button. The boat shot forward with a thrust of acceleration obviously intended to dislodge me.

I threw myself onto the deck of the boat. After a moment I got unsteadily to my feet. Now I could hear as well as see the cascade of fireworks bursting over the city. The Grand Canal was brightly lit and choked with flotillas of all shapes and sizes. Boats, I saw with alarm, that we were heading towards at alarming speed.

223

The thrust of the boat had taken Williamson by surprise too and I saw him stagger back from the controls. Directly ahead of us was a long, slender boat, pulled by a dozen oarsmen in ruffs and caps. At one end two men were sitting, at the other two women. All were looking at the motorboat about to plough into them.

One of the men was Rex. I recognised Bridget and Genevra. Rex started to rise.

Williamson grabbed the wheel and spun it frantically. The motor boat seemed to stop dead in its tracks before veering sharply to the left, its rear slewing round and sending up a huge fan of water which crashed down on the occupants of the other boat.

Our boat continued to slew and a moment later the back end collided with the rear of the long boat. I saw an oar fly up and catch Williamson on the side of the head, pitching him over the side of the motor boat. A moment later I saw Rex topple over the far side of the long boat. Then something hit me across the side of the head and I too toppled into the water.

Chapter Fourteen

I don't recommend having your stomach pumped. I mean, it's one thing ingesting a piece of milky gauze to sop up bile for fifteen minutes, but having a tube stuck down inside you for half an hour, turning your innards inside out, definitely ain't pleasant. However, if you've swallowed half a gallon of the Grand Canal and want to live, you've really got little choice.

I woke in the hospital feeling as if my throat had been flayed. I was in a private room. Next door on the left was Rex, on the right Bridget and next to her Genevra. Williamson hadn't made it. A tragic accident, the British newspapers were calling it. I saw no point in raising other matters.

It was a day or so before I found out what had happened, Bridget came in – with her usual exquisite timing I was having an injection in my backside at the time – and flopped down in the chair.

'If I'd known what having my stomach pumped was going to be like,' she croaked when the nurse had gone, 'I'd have let you drown.'

I recalled hitting the water, woozy and pretty much a dead weight. Then, as I was gulping in water and sinking – the wide thighs of the waders were filling up with water – I felt somebody grab me under the arms. A palm cupped me under the chin.

I was lifted up to the surface but I could feel the weight of the water in the waders dragging me back down. Then I heard a familiar voice close to my ear.

'This dress cost me an arm and a fucking leg to hire. It's ruined so I'm already *really* pissed off. If you don't start making an effort to stay afloat I'm just going to let you sink.' I felt the smack of lips against my cheek. 'All right, poppet?'

'You saved me,' I whispered. 'But what about Rex? I would have thought you'd have gone to the aid of your future husband.'

'Yeah, well . . . anyway, Genevra went in after him. Not that she needed to – he could swim.'

'I can swim! Something hit me on the head—'

'I know, dear. Even so, can I suggest that next time you're drowning you're a bit more proactive.'

'Righty-ho,' I said.

I smiled at her.

'Save the gloopy look,' she said. 'It doesn't mean anything.'

We flew home the next day. All except Faye. She stayed on in Venice to care for Ralph. She intended to stay until the end. Their son would join them during the Easter holidays.

I stared blankly out of the window on the flight home. If Williamson was telling the truth about Lucy, then there was still an unsolved murder. I wanted to question Buckhalter about any meeting he might have had with Lucy on the day of her death, but when we landed in Britain he went straight up to London to find a replacement investor.

Genevra and I had been awkward with each other in recent hours. However, back at Wynn House that evening, she whispered to me to come to her room that evening. We talked and we made love but I sensed that my accusations had broken something that couldn't be repaired.

Later that night I was lying in bed preening – I seemed finally to have got the hang of this sex lark – when Genevra picked up the remote and put on the TV. There was a local news report about how archaeologists were in hog heaven because the now receding floods had brought so much new material up from the depths of the earth to the surface.

226

'How far have you got with the research about our tomb?'
she said.

'Far enough to know the whole discovery back in the
twelfth century was a fake.' I told her what I'd told Bridget
about the greed of the Glastonbury monks. I listed the
relics.

'So why did they need one more?' she said.

'I couldn't figure that out at first. Then I discovered that
in 1184 their ancient wattle and daub church burned down.
They'd been claiming it was the first church in Britain and it
had been a popular attraction for pilgrims. King Henry II
agreed to pay for a replacement and, because of his lead,
lots of other lords and ladies chipped in. The monks
planned the rebuilding of the whole abbey on a vast scale.'

I glanced over at the television. It was showing pictures of
skeletons and pieces of pottery.

'Do you remember when the monks found Arthur's
grave?' I asked.

'1191.'

'Henry died in 1189. Know who succeeded him?'

'History wasn't my thing, I'm afraid.'

'Richard the Lionheart. He's another one who got all the
glory for being a shit whilst King John, who stayed home
and held it all together, became a byword for badness.
Anyway, Richard wasn't going to cough up any money. He
was spending all he had on preparations for the Third
Crusade – it wouldn't be long before he instigated the
massacre of the Jews in York to pay for his adventures.

'So suddenly the money for Glastonbury dried up. If the
monks were going to build their big abbey they needed
another money-spinning attraction.'

'Cue Arthur and Guinevere's grave,' Genevra said, gazing
blankly at the television screen.

'The grave was found, by the way, in a spot that had been
mysteriously curtained off a few days prior to the discovery.
The bones went first to a chapel in the south aisle of the
new church, then later into the black marble tomb. Funds

227

poured in and the monks rebuilt the abbey bigger and better than ever before. At the Dissolution, Glastonbury was the richest abbey in the country.'

'Didn't you say the tomb got moved again?'

'Edward I and his wife Queen Eleanor visited Glastonbury in 1278. Edward, aside from being quite taken with Arthur, had been fighting the Welsh and he needed to impress upon them that Arthur was really dead. They opened the tomb. The contemporary witness said that Arthur's left ear had been cut off "with the marks of the blow which slew him visible".

'Edward insisted they moved the tomb into the choir of the church, immediately in front of the high altar. They kept out the "heads and cheeks" – I have no idea what the cheeks were – as relics.'

The news report was saying that the most recent find had been in a peat bed just outside Glastonbury. The head of a woman had surfaced, perfectly preserved for God knows how many centuries. Peat bed discoveries are great because remains, aside from being a bit leathery, look almost as if they might have been buried yesterday. They're almost impossible to date for that reason.

'What do you mean,' Genevra said, stifling a yawn, 'Edward was taken with Arthur?'

'He used to hold chivalric tournaments. More practically, later on in his reign he based his claims to Scotland on the rights of King Arthur to the whole of Britain, as recorded in Geoffrey of Monmouth.'

A photo of the woman's head appeared on screen. Genevra stiffened.

'Good God,' she said. 'That's my stepmother.'

'I don't understand,' Genevra said.

'I do. You've got a matching set of bones for that head in your crypt.'

Genevra blanched.

'Oh my God. What could have happened?'

I sat up and slid out of bed.

'Let's find out. We'll go and ask Rex.'

'Why Rex?'

I pulled on my trousers. My brain seemed to be working very quickly but very clearly. And everything, all the disparate elements of the past few weeks' events, was clicking into place.

'Didn't Rex pay your stepmother off by borrowing against his trust fund? Seems to have wasted his money, don't you think. Unless—'

'You think my brother killed her.' She jumped out of bed and stormed across to me. 'What is it with you and my family, Nick? Have you got that much of a chip on your shoulder?'

I shook my head. I was still figuring permutations.

'Nick, what does it matter to you anyway? You're not involved.'

'There have been attempts on my life at least twice and you say I'm not involved?'

'But that was Williamson. That's all finished.'

'Not all Williamson.' I looked around for my shoes. 'Look, I'm sure Rex has got a perfectly simple explanation.'

'She was a dreadful woman,' Genevra said.

'I'll be back shortly,' I said, moving to the door.

'Don't be,' she replied.

I hammered on Rex's door. I hoped he and Bridget weren't mid-sex. This kind of coitus interruptus Bridget could do without. I glimpsed Genevra coming down the corridor.

'Jesus, come in!' Rex shouted, 'No need to knock the frigging door down.'

When he saw me, with Genevra standing at my shoulder he shrugged.

'If you want me to referee a fight, I'm not sure I'm the best person—'

'What happened to your stepmother?' I said.

Rex was sitting up in bed, bare-chested, his hair hanging loose down to his shoulders. The bed was rumpled but he was alone.

229

'What? You burst into my bedroom at this time of night – what the fuck has it to do with you, Nick, what happened to *our* stepmother?'

'Nothing. Except that her head turned up on the eleven o'clock news and we seem to have the rest of her stacked in the crypt.'

He looked at me for a moment.

'Come in,' he said. 'Sit down.'

It was a huge bedroom. He was lying in a big four-poster bed. There was a sofa and a couple of chairs in a bay window. A lavatory flushed behind a door to the right of the bed.

Genevra sat down in one of the chairs. I sat on the sofa.

'Look, you have my sympathy,' I said. 'Really. I'm one of those people who believe that bad taste should be punished and Camilla sounds ghastly. But even so, to kill her . . .'

The bathroom door opened. Bridget was standing there in a pair of men's pyjamas.

'Nick. A word.'

'This is not the time—'

'Please.'

I went into the bathroom. Bridget started to close the door but I held it open so that I could keep an eye on Rex.

'Why are you doing this?' she hissed. 'This is my big chance. Why are you trying to destroy what could be good for me?' She looked at me. 'I know – because you never had a proper family.'

'No,' I said wearily, tired of the bullshit. 'I never had a proper family so I don't know what it's like and that fucking upsets me. But all I can say is, if the people we've been mixing with are what family life is like then I don't think my out-of-it dad did too badly. I'm after the truth, Bridget. I think Rex is a bad man and I don't think you – when you're thinking straight – would want to be involved with him.'

She glared at me fiercely for a long moment then scowled.

'Shit. I've a horrible feeling it's back to the bloody dinner party circuit.'

230

We came out of the bathroom and sat together on the sofa. Rex looked calmly at Bridget. Genevra stared at me.

'We were talking about the death of your stepmother,' I said to Rex.

'Why would you understand?' Rex said. 'I've told you before that I have a duty to the country. I'm a member of the patrician elite. The management of a landed estate brings responsibilities.'

'Yeah, yeah,' I said. 'So why'd you kill her?'

'I'm not saying I did. But would you stand by whilst some totty from Tunbridge Wells lived off the fat of your inheritance? She'd already persuaded Father to sell things off.'

'But you tried to buy her off?' Genevra said. She looked miserable and out of her depth.

'With what?' Rex said. 'Babe, like most of the aristocracy we're land-rich, cash poor.'

'What about the sixteen mill?' Bridget said.

Rex laughed softly.

'I'm skint. If this development doesn't work, I've lost everything.'

'*We've* lost everything,' Genevra said.

'Sure, babe, but I'm the head of the household.'

'Look,' I said, 'I don't really care about your stepmother. I'm not even concerned about your father—'

'My father?' Genevra flashed a look at me. 'What's he got to do with this?'

Rex looked at me sullenly. I should have kept it to myself, but what was it I'd been told? Family secrets – better to get them out in the open.

'I'm dancing in the dark here,' I said. 'But didn't you tell me your father had got serious about some other woman just before he died? Some actress? And your dad died in a car accident, in a car driven by Rex. If Rex offed your stepmother because she was squandering his inheritance, I would think he'd be seriously pissed off if he saw his dad about to let someone else into the happy home – to do exactly the same.'

'You sick bastard,' Genevra said, half rising. I stood too. Just in case. She was a strong woman.

'There's no way to prove it,' I said. 'But I wonder who chose that particular route home that day and how fast Rex was going? You said Rex hadn't been drinking with the rest of you – almost as if he knew he was going to be breath-alysed after an accident.'

Genevra looked over at Rex and then back at me.

'Damn you,' she said. 'Are you determined to destroy everybody's life?'

'It's not me that's doing the destroying,' I said. 'And aside from the hurt it causes you, I'm not really concerned about your father. He seems to have lived off the fat of the land for the years he had.'

Genevra started to speak but I put up my hand.

'I'm concerned about a more recent death. The death of someone who didn't deserve to die but was killed by Rex to keep her quiet. I'm talking about Lucy Newton.'

'Lucy?' Genevra said. 'I thought Williamson killed her.'

'An easy assumption. I was tempted to make it too.'

Genevra looked at Rex.

'Why would Rex kill her?'

Rex shrugged, then reached down and pulled the blankets up around him. I looked round. I had the floor. I felt like Poirot. Except I was groping blindly in the dark. I would have killed for a waxed moustache.

'Rex had a problem – didn't you, Rex?' I said. 'When you killed your stepmother, where better to put the body than in the crypt? Nobody had been down there for years. And in a couple of years, she'd just be a pile of bones like all the other piles of bones. But you knew a bit about archaeology.'

I looked at Bridget and Genevra. Both were staring at Rex with very similar expressions. Love tinged with great sadness.

'Rex knew that if there was some suspicion later on – and if, by chance, someone found his stepmother's remains – it would be possible to reconstruct her skull, to put her face

232

back together. He didn't want to take the risk. So he severed the head and chucked it away.'

I looked at Rex. 'What I don't understand, given his knowledge, is why he disposed of it in a peat bog, peat being such an amazing preservative.'

Rex met my look but said nothing.

'He'd chosen the easiest sarcophagus in the crypt to dump the bones in. The one with the broken marble lid.'

I turned to Rex again.

'I imagine you checked from time to time over the years that nobody had been fiddling about down there and that the body had decomposed. When it came time to make your theme park the crypt seemed an obvious place for the Grail Chapel. By then you weren't worried about moving the coffins out. This may have been a sarcophagus with only two skulls in, but how many people know how many bones there are in the human body? What's a few more?'

I was aware of movement in the doorway. Nanny was standing there in a long dressing gown.

'I heard a commotion,' she said.

'Come in, Nanny,' Rex said. 'We're hearing a nightmare from Nick here.'

'I've always been here to soothe your nightmares, my lord,' she said, stepping into the room. 'You know that.'

I watched her speculatively as she went to sit on the edge of Rex's bed. I sat back down on the sofa. Bridget put a hand out and squeezed my leg. I addressed Rex again.

'I imagine you were a bit more concerned when Lucy, enthusiastic Lucy, told you that a black marble tomb – one you were very familiar with – was the tomb from Glastonbury purporting to be that of Arthur and Guinevere. What bad luck that you'd dumped your stepmother's body in there.

'What a weird dilemma. A discovery that could be worth millions, but at the risk of the discovery of the crime you'd committed. You knew enough about archaeology to know the bones needed to be dated – and if that happened to your stepmother's, you'd be in deep doo-doo.

233

'You probably thought about getting the bones out – but how could you figure out which they were? Maybe swap all the bones for those in another coffin – but they'd be tested too, wouldn't they? It must have been a difficult decision – earning power from the coffin versus the risk of the bones being dated. As it turned out—'

I stopped mid-sentence because Nanny was staring fixedly at me. And another possibility had been occurring as I spoke. Rex saw me looking at Nanny. He reached over and squeezed her hand. They both looked at me. I recalled Nanny saying she'd do anything for Rex and Genevra. Anything.

As if reading my mind Rex said: 'She'd spill blood for me.'

I nodded.

'I think she already has.'

Nanny was sitting very erect on the bed. She'd relinquished Rex's hand.

'I killed them both,' she said. 'I wasn't sorry at all about that dreadful woman, Camilla. But I quite liked Lucy.' She looked pointedly at Bridget. 'As far as his totties go.' She looked away to one side, Method actor style.

'Lucy came down into the crypt when I was guarding the bones. I used to go down there a lot. I think I startled her. She started to say that she'd had some bones analysed and now she needed to send the rest of them away for testing – but I knew why she was there, she didn't need to say. I offered to help her. When she was reaching in to pick up some bones I took her by the throat.'

Nanny paused for breath.

'It wasn't difficult – she was only a little thing. I went and got the boat.'

I asked her the question that had been tormenting me almost since the beginning of all this.

'Why did you lay her out in the boat like that, like Elaine of Astolet, then leave her out there?'

Nanny looked at me and laughed scornfully.

'I just laid her out the way that seemed decent. And I didn't leave her there deliberately, you idiot. I'd gone back into the chapel and the boat drifted away. Then you turned up so I was stuck.'

I was actually relieved rather than disappointed that there wasn't some weird symbolism going on. That only really happens in books. I was pleased I hadn't missed anything.

'Okay,' I said. 'But tell us about killing Genevra and Rex's stepmother. What about the head?'

'I'm not educated, dearie. I wouldn't know nothing about bones. When I put her in the tomb I thought: well, bones is bones. It's only recently I've heard Rex talking and realised you can guess the age of anything these days. There wasn't much I could do about the head.'

'But why did you cut it off in the first place? If you're not educated, you wouldn't know it could be recreated.'

Nanny looked stumped. She looked at Rex for help.

'Enough!' Genevra screeched, erupting from her seat. She rounded on me. 'Can't you hear yourself? You've been implying all the way along the line that we're somehow dysfunctional, and we probably are. But what about you? You ask so calmly about severed heads? You're so ruthless about working out who did what to whom. What is it with you?'

The vehemence of her attack startled me. I looked at her for a long moment. Emotions raced through me. I took a deep breath.

'I'm going to call the police,' I said. I looked over at Rex. 'I don't know which of you did what, so I'll let them work it out. Although I think Lucy went to the crypt to meet you. Your phone rang whilst you were having lunch. I think it was your answering service telling you that you had a message. And that message was from Faye saying that Lucy was pressing to see you. I guess the phone records will show whether you phoned her that day.'

Rex sat, huddled in blankets, his hand in the Nanny's. I was half-expecting a tussle but he looked at me and said nothing. I looked at Genevra.

'I'm sorry.'

She glanced my way, worked her mouth, then spat on the Persian rug at my feet. It was an act I found more shocking than if she'd spat in my face. I was aware that, suddenly, Bridget was by my side.

As we walked down the corridor together she reached for my hand. Squeezed it.

'I'm sorry about this,' I said.

'Forget it,' Bridget said. 'I get discontented if I'm too content.' She slowed us down. 'I know a part of you is wondering whether I'm walking away with you now because Rex said he's not worth the sixteen million he told me about,' she said.

'Hey—'

She squeezed my hand again.

'And to tell you the truth, I don't know. But something happened between you and me in Venice . . .' She leaned against me. 'Nick, you know I'll always be there for you.'

'What if you meet a guy worth *twenty* million?' I said.

She reached up to peck me on the cheek.

'Hey,' she said. 'Let's not spoil a soppy moment with hypotheticals.'

Bridget and I left the next morning. Genevra kept out of sight. The police had taken Rex and Nanny away in the night. I was pretty sure Nanny was covering for Rex, that he had done both murders, but whether that could be proved I didn't know. Bridget wanted to get straight back to London so I took her to the nearest station then drove into Glastonbury. I parked the car and walked down the high street in the rain. It was jammed with people, umbrellas jogging, heads down. I was threading a way through them when I glanced into a café window, streaked with runnels of rain. A face that had been pressed against it quickly withdrew. I walked on, then, stopping at the corner, retraced my steps.

When I entered the café the heat hit me like a wave. I

closed the door carefully behind me, wiped my face free of raindrops, shook water from my coat, rubbed my cold wet hands on a handkerchief, then together. Finally I looked up, scanned the room.

I couldn't see him at first. Then I saw a distinctive pair of arthritic hands loosely clasped round a cup of coffee. I walked down the aisle. He had tried to shrink into the corner. He was looking down at the table, continued to look at the table, even though he knew I was standing over him.

He didn't look as magnificent now. He seemed shrunken. Aged.

'John Crow,' I said.

'I'm an old man,' he said when I sat down. 'I abhor violence.'

'Me too,' I said, touching his mottled hand. I looked at the long scab on his head. The wound inflicted when he'd fallen at the hands of the thugs was slowly healing. 'I don't blame you for going into hiding. I was just worried. I came into town today to try to find you.'

'Visited my brother in Hergest Ridge.'

'I guessed. Tell me, do you know Faye and Ralph, from the Gatehouse?'

He looked at me for the first time.

'Did you used to see them in Hergest Ridge?'

'Once or twice, when I visited my brother. Years ago now.'

I'd guessed that when Faye went off to visit a 'boyfriend' in Hergest Ridge in the old days she was actually going for assignations with Ralph, far away from anyone they might know. But Crow had seen them. That's why she'd been so twitchy whenever she came across him. She knew he knew her secret.

I remembered the evening Crow had appeared on the other side of the flooded river below Wynn House and we'd been talking. He'd seen somebody behind me and suddenly hurried away. I was guessing that he'd seen Faye and that in the past she had warned him to keep quiet.

A warning I felt sure she'd had the two thugs who attacked us repeat at Wookey Hole. I didn't know who they were. I suppose I should have cared, but I didn't. I felt so utterly betrayed by her – used by her – all the way along the line. But I knew it all came out of the tragedy of her obsessive love for her brother. She'd suffered enough.

Crow tilted his head to one side, winked at me.

'I'll share a secret with you if you like.'

'Feel free,' I said.

'I'm looking after King Arthur.'

He was off again.

'Good for you.'

'Want to meet him?'

'Er, absolutely.'

He got to his feet and reached for his stick. He looked down at me.

'Well, come on then!'

I got to my feet wearily.

'Sure, John.'

He led the way down the high street at a brisk pace, oblivious to the rain that still teemed down, clearing a way through the other pedestrians with his stick. He turned into the abbey gates, waved his stick at the woman at the ticket office.

'Just want to show my young friend something. Only be five minutes.'

He took me through to the ruins and walked towards the sign indicating where Arthur and Guinevere's bones had been found. It was the place where I had first seen him a couple of weeks before. It felt like an age ago.

He walked past the sign and on down to the abbot's kitchen. Instead of entering, however, he went round the side and down a couple of steps. He looked up.

'Come on, come on!'

I followed him down.

He was crouching over a cardboard box. I looked over his shoulder. I could see a lot of straw and leaves.

238

'You can hold him if you like.'

'King Arthur?'

'Who else?'

'Yeah, who else. Silly me.'

He picked up something round and brown in his arthritic hands. He twisted and handed it to me.

'My liege, this is a young friend of mine. Nick, this is King Arthur.'

I took the brown object gingerly. It had a little snout, black sleepy eyes, sharp little feet and a lot of quills. It probably also had fleas. King Arthur was a hedgehog.

'I found him sitting on the site of his own grave,' Crow said, standing up.

'So that's why you called him King Arthur?'

Crow frowned.

'I called him King Arthur because he *is* King Arthur.'

I sighed.

'John, this is a hedgehog.'

'Do you not know the Mabinogion, in which it is recorded that when Arthur returns it will be in animal form? It might be a bear, a wolf, a swan—'

'Or a hedgehog?'

Actually, I'm rather fond of hedgehogs. They used to come into our garden when I was a kid in Ramsbottom. We'd leave out milk for them all year. I learned then that their winter hibernation was not total. Quite often they would wake up and walk around a bit or eat some more food.

The hedgehog wriggled a little in my hands.

'Unfortunately, Arthur's got a bit of a tummy upset,' Crow said.

'Really,' I said, immediately straightening my arms and leaning over the box to put the hedgehog back in it.

The other thing I know about hedgehogs is that they have salmonella bacteria in their intestines and are prone to food poisoning. A hedgehog suffering the consequent diarrhoea is quite something – able to project a substantial spray of bright green shit a distance of some twenty feet.

Twenty feet. Hence my eagerness to get King Arthur back in his box.

I was too slow.

And only three feet away.

Epilogue

There was a moment in Venice, during our stay in the hospital, when Bridget and I straddled the border between best friends and lovers.

Bridget was in the chair by my bed. She was wearing a hospital shift and very little underneath. I was sitting up, pillows plumped behind me. I looked at her and had that strange feeling again.

'Why have we never made love?' I said, as casually as I could.

'Because you're lousy at it, I suppose – why would I waste my time?'

'Genevra thinks I'm adequate – she told you.'

Bridget showed her teeth.

'Adequate doesn't cut it with me, honey.'

She examined my face.

'Are you asking me for a shag?'

'No, of course not!' I flushed. 'Well, not right now. I thought maybe we could go out on a date.'

'Why?'

'To see what happens.'

Bridget tilted her head as if to get a better look at me.

'I'm confused. First because Genevra is down the corridor panting for you. Second because I thought this was a no-go area for us.'

'So did I,' I said glumly.

'Hmm. Is this a mercy shag because something's happened between you and Genevra?'

241

'No! And I'm talking about making love, not *that*.'

'Yeah, yeah. Tell you what. Let me think about it. And whilst I am, since you're already embarrassed, why don't you tell me about your disastrous night with Faye all those years ago?'

I groaned.

'Not a chance.'

'Suit yourself.'

Bridget studied her nails.

'It's the most embarrassing thing that's ever happened to me. And only now do I realise why it happened.'

'Now you've got to tell me – you can't give it a build-up like that then walk away.'

'The why? Because it's clear that Faye was forcing herself to make love with me when all she could think about was her brother.'

'I don't want the why, I want the how.'

'The last time I confessed everything about Faye you fell asleep.'

'You were rambling. You're a journalist – you know to put the sexiest bit at the top of the article. So tell me.'

'You'll laugh.'

'I sincerely hope so.'

'Okay,' I said, sighing. 'Faye came round to my flat in Summertown in a very strange mood. I shared it with four girls but only one of them – Ros – was in. She let Faye in as I was on my way to the loo. I took Faye into the bedroom and almost immediately she jumped on me. She was being very passionate but there was something about it that seemed a bit forced.'

After a couple of minutes lying tangled on the bed she'd started tugging at my zip.

'Come on then,' Faye said, her voice tense and urgent.

'What?' I whispered.

'You know what. You've always wanted to.'

'You sure?' I said, rearing back to look at her face. It was flushed, her eyes filmy. I could smell drink on her

242

breath. She gave a jerky little nod.

'Honestly?'

'For God's sake, Nick, stick it in!' she said through gritted teeth.

I excused myself for a moment.

'Loo,' I mumbled. Well, I was bursting. I was also nervous. To be honest I'd only had one full sexual experience before and I don't think the girl I slept with thought that had been particularly full.

'Is that it?' had been her succinct remark.

I knew that in the bathroom my flatmates had put, as a joke, one of those sprays men are supposed to use to prolong the sexual act. They make you go numb or something. The sprays, not my flatmates – so far as I knew, which, sadly, wasn't far at all. I also thought, since I didn't know what Faye and I would be getting up to, I should freshen up a bit.

I dabbed my aftershave on my cheeks and under my arms. As an afterthought I pulled the waistband of my underpants away from my stomach and poured the rest down there.

It's the kind of mistake a man will only make once in his life.

I don't think I've ever felt pain like it. The alcohol in the aftershave felt like acid. Choking back my screams, legs crossed, hopping from foot to foot, I tried to wash the aftershave off in the sink.

Given my height and the shape of the sink, this wasn't easy.

'Where have you been?' Faye said sharply when I finally got back to my room. She was lying on the bed, looking distinctly like a sacrificial virgin, her body was so taut.

'Are you sure you want to do this?' I said, sitting beside her on the bed and casually putting the spray can on the floor. She gazed at me.

'I'm sure. I'm just n-nervous.'

'Me too,' I said.

We undressed rather formally, sitting on opposite sides of the bed.

'What's that?' she asked when she heard the quick hiss of the spray canister.

'Deodorant,' I said, pushing the can under the bed.

Naked, we embraced. She clung tightly to me and put her lips to my ear.

'Hurry, Nick, hurry,' she whispered.

'That was my problem last time,' I thought but didn't say. However I did as she requested.

And got stuck.

'I'm sorry there was no way to say that delicately. Faye tensed – oh how she tensed – and suddenly I couldn't move. At all.

Faye had gone totally rigid. Arms clasped tightly round my shoulders, legs stiff against my thighs, every other muscle – and I do mean every – taut.

I now know this is quite common. It's even got a name: Honeymoon Disease. It's just nerves. Problem is, to relax those nerves requires a trip to the hospital and an injection of a muscle-relaxant. As I was soon to discover.

'I can't, Nick, I'm sorry, I can't,' she gasped.

'It's okay,' I said. 'But could you just . . .'

She couldn't.

Ten minutes later I began to realise we had a problem.

'Can't you make it go down?' she said impatiently.

'Apparently not,' I said into the pillow, quietly impressed by the potency of the spray. I could hear Ros moving about outside. I knew if I was going to enlist her help it would need to be before she smoked her first joint of the evening.

'I think we need a doctor,' I said. 'Let me call Ros.'

'No bloody way,' she said.

It was another twenty minutes before she reluctantly agreed.

Ros circled the bed.

'Wow,' she said.

'I don't think you two have been formally introduced,' I said to Ros, twisting my head to see her. 'Faye this is Ros, Ros this is Faye.'

'This is formal?' Ros said.

The doctor wouldn't come out. Whilst we were waiting for the ambulance my other flatmates – Sally, Angela and Ruth – arrived home.

'Wow,' they said, pulling up chairs to join Ros, who was sitting by the bed.

'Hi, girls, I don't think you know—'

'I think we can skip the introductions,' Faye hissed. 'Don't you, Nick?'

The ambulance arrived soon after.

Bridget was howling with laughter. When she'd finally ground to a halt, breathless, she got up and climbed onto the bed. She reached round behind my head and cupped it, her face in front of mine. She looked at me intently. Her voice was gruff.

'C'mere, you big lug.'

Author's Note

My view of the heritage business is shaped by Robert Hewison's *The Heritage Industry* (Methuen, 1987). I've tried to make the history in this novel – particularly in my account of the discovery of Arthur's grave – as accurate as possible. I have made good use of the summary of arguments about this 1191 discovery presented in *Glastonbury* by Philip Rahtz (Batsford, 1993).

CITYSPOTS
HELS

Barbara Radcliffe Rogers
& Stillman Rogers

GW00362996

Written by Barbara Radcliffe Rogers & Stillman Rogers
Updated by Tero Puha

Published by Thomas Cook Publishing
A division of Thomas Cook Tour Operations Limited
Company registration No: 1450464 England
The Thomas Cook Business Park, 9 Coningsby Road
Peterborough PE3 8SB, United Kingdom
Email: books@thomascook.com, Tel: +44 (0)1733 416477
www.thomascookpublishing.com

Produced by The Content Works Ltd
Aston Court, Kingsmead Business Park, Frederick Place
High Wycombe, Bucks HP11 1LA
www.thecontentworks.com

Series design based on an original concept by Studio 183 Limited

ISBN: 978-1-84157-903-0

Series Editor: Kelly Anne Pipes
Production/DTP: Steven Collins

Printed and bound in Spain by GraphyCems

Cover photography (Statue of Tsar Alexander II in front of Helsinki's
Lutheran Cathedral) © Fred Bjorksten/Getty Images/Gorilla RM

CONTENTS

SYMBOLS KEY

The following symbols are used throughout this book:

ⓐ address ☎ telephone ⓕ fax ⓦ website address ⓔ email
🕒 opening times 🚍 public transport connections ⓘ important

The following symbols are used on the maps:

𝒊	information office	▪	points of interest
✈	airport	◯	city
➕	hospital	◯	large town
🛡	police station	○	small town
🚌	bus station	═	motorway
🚆	railway station	▬	main road
Ⓜ	metro	▬	minor road
✝	cathedral	▬	railway
❶	numbers denote featured cafés & restaurants		

Hotels and restaurants are graded by approximate price as follows:
£ budget price ££ mid-range price £££ expensive

▶ *Rooftops view towards the Lutheran Cathedral*

Introduction

Helsinki's beauty hits you right between the eyes, not least because some of the greatest architects in the world designed its buildings, which are set amid parks and against watery backdrops. Its beauty deserves a closer look, whether it's into shop windows filled with smart Finnish design or inside buildings whose interiors match their stunning outside views. But Helsinki is much more than just another pretty face. It is a friendly, exciting, warm-hearted place filled with people whose wry attitude to life will make you laugh and whose nightlife will keep you dancing into the early hours of the morning. It is blessed by almost round-the-clock sunlight in the summer, when no-one ever seems to sleep, and a population that knows how to make the most of the long snowy winter. Join them on skis or snowshoes in the parks, on paths that glitter with lights reflecting in the snow, or skate across the frozen bay of Töölönlahti. Warming up is no problem: take a sauna (you can choose from traditional wood-fired or modern state-of-the-art spas), knock back a steaming cup of *glögi* (mulled wine), go to a jazz club to hear authentic Dixieland, or dance to whatever moves your shoes.

The fastest-growing capital in the European Union, Helsinki seems to be always on the move, with a star-studded line-up of festivals celebrating everything from samba and world cultures to heavy metal and Gay Pride. Downtown streets rock at night, and the buzz comes from people having a good time, not trying to impress one another with their dress or their oh-so-cool attitudes. Maybe that's because they know – and know the world knows it, too – that they have a great deal to declare at the customs of fashionable good taste. Whatever's new, you'll see it here first, not because the Finns have rushed out to buy it, but because they have designed it themselves. Here, you'll sense that you are on the cutting edge, whether you're dining on the latest plates from Arabia, drinking out of the newest Iittala stemware, lounging in an Alvar Aalto chair or simply chatting on your super-stylish mobile.

It's hard not to have a good time in Helsinki, especially when things heat up at night. Perhaps that's the city's biggest surprise – and it's certainly what makes it so much fun to visit.

⬤ *World-famous Finnish design*

When to go

SEASONS & CLIMATE

With northern perversity, Helsinki's climate brings the most rain during the warm summer months, and the best chance of sparkling sunny days in winter. Summer temperatures hover around 20°C (68°F) and winter averages around -4°C (25°F). The winters can be cold sometimes, with temperatures dropping as low as -20°C (-4°F). The most popular months to visit are between May and September, but the city is pleasant year-round, as long as you remember a raincoat in the summer and warm coat (and boots) in the winter.

Snow is frequent in winter, but rarely deep in the city centre, often melting away quickly. In the rural areas there is permanent snow for the whole winter and it can get deep, especially in northern Finland. Light reflecting on the snow makes the city lighter during the short mid-winter days from November to January, when the sun doesn't rise until late morning and sets by around three in the afternoon.

● *Heavy snowfalls in the park don't deter Helsinki walkers*

ANNUAL EVENTS

January

Art Meets Ice (International Ice Sculpture Competition)
Competitors from around the world gather to carve ice into artistic forms, which are left on display until they melt. Advance booking is recommended: pre-book from **Tiketti** 🄰 Helsinki Zoo, Korkeasaari Ⓦ www.korkeasaari.com (Tickets Ⓦ www.tiketti.fi) 🄱 Bus: 11 (from Herttoniemi metro station), 16; Metro: Kulosaari (from where it's a 1.5 km (1 mile) walk to the zoo).

DocPoint This documentary festival, which runs over into February, features films not only from Finland and the Baltic states but also from around the world. 🄰 Fredrikinkatu 23 🄣 (09) 672 472 Ⓦ www.docpoint.info

March

Church Music Festival Kirkko Soikoon Churches honour Finnish and other Scandinavian religious music genres with orchestral, choral and solo performances in beautiful, contemplative surroundings. 🄣 (09) 709 2498 Ⓦ www.kirkkosoikoon.fi (Tickets Ⓦ www.lippupiste.com or on the door)

Musica Nova Helsinki Hear important new music at this showcase for Finnish and international contemporary composers. The festival is generally held every other year; the next event is scheduled for 2009. 🄰 Lasipalatsi, Mannerheimintie 22–4 🄣 (09) 6126 5100 Ⓦ www.musicanova.fi

April

April Jazz/Big Band Jazz Festival Finnish and international performers do their best to avoid the melody in concert halls, restaurants and other relaxed (and even ad hoc) venues. 🄰 Ahertajantie 6 B, Espoo 🄣 (09) 455 0003 Ⓦ www.apriljazz.fi

Vappu (30 April) This is Walpurgis Night, cue for one of the biggest parties in Finland, when students gather around Havis Amanda, the mermaid symbol of Helsinki, to drink champagne.

May
Evening Markets Evening markets at the head of the harbour begin in mid-May, luring locals and visitors alike with beautifully presented stalls of foods, handicrafts and other goods.
Vappu päivä (1 May) The Ullanlinna and Kaisaniemi quarters are the main sites for the lively May Day celebrations, with lots of family-oriented fun, including carnivals.

June
Helsinki Day (12 June) (see page 47) One of the few European capitals that knows its exact birthday, Helsinki marks the occasion with free concerts at Kaivopuisto Park, plus children's events, sports, tours and a market. Ⓦ www.hel.fi
Midsummer Eve Finns celebrate at country homes with huge bonfires and *juhannussalko* poles decorated with ribbons and flowers. Also expect traditional folk music and dance. Tickets are sold at the Seurasaari bridge and in advance from the Tomtebo Folklore Centre. ❸ Tamminiementie 1, Seurasaari Ⓦ www.kolumbus.fi

July
Jazz Espa Free daily jazz performances on the Esplanadi.
❶ (09) 757 2077 Ⓦ www.jazzfin.com
Tuska Open Air Metal Festival Major bands from across Europe and the UK play in Kaisaniemi Park. Ⓦ www.tuska-festival.fi (Tickets Ⓦ www.lippupiste.com and www.tiketti.fi)

○ An audience party at a May Day event

August

Art Goes Kapakka (mid-August) Ten days of music and entertainment right across the city, totalling 250 performances and events in clubs, bars, restaurants, theatres and streets. Ⓦ www.artgoeskapakka.fi

Helsinki City Marathon Scandinavia's biggest marathon begins at the Paavo Nurmi statue and winds along the shore and hillsides. ⓐ Radiokatu 20 ⓣ (09) 3481 2405 Ⓦ www.helsinkicitymarathon.com

Helsinki Festival (late August–early September) Featuring prominent international artists in various venues and a festival tent. The Night of the Arts brings a wide range of street music and art. ⓣ 0600 900 900 Ⓦ www.helsinkifestival.fi and Ⓦ www.lippu.fi

Koneisto Electronic Music Festival More than one hundred artists have gathered every year for this event since 2001. ⓐ Cable Factory, Tallberginkatu 1 ⓣ 0600 1 08 00 Ⓦ www.koneisto.com (Tickets Ⓦ www.lippupiste.com

September

Helsinki International Film Festival Finland's largest film festival draws upwards of 14,000 people to see movies of all types from all over the world. ⓐ Mannerheimintie 22-24 ⓣ (09) 6843 5232 Ⓦ www.hiff.fi

October

Herring Market (early October) Fishermen gather in Kauppatori (Market Square) to sell traditional herring products. A great opportunity to sample local foods and boost your Omega 3 intake.

November

Winter Circus (November–early January) The Hurjaruuth Dance Company at Boiler Hall (Pannuhalli) brings expertise in dance and an

array of performing arts. Tickets from Ⓦ www.lippupalvelu.fi ⓐ Cable
Factory, Tallberginkatu 1 ⓣ (09) 565 7250 Ⓦ www.hurjaruuth.fi

December
Independence Day (6 December) This date kicks off the holiday
season, and is also an occasion for processions, visits to cemeteries
and gatherings in churches and public places for concerts (which
always include Sibelius's *Finlandia*).
St Thomas Christmas Market The finest crafts, foods and arts line
the Esplanadi, set out in colourful tents to engage the interest
of the passer-by.
Turku Christmas Market Held in the Old Great Square, with crafts
and foods.
Women's Christmas Fair An astonishing variety of fine crafts,
all created by Finnish women, fill a market hall at the
Wanha Satama.

PUBLIC HOLIDAYS
New Year's Day 1 January
Epiphany 6 January
Easter 21–4 March 2008, 10–13 April 2009
May Day 1 May
Ascension Day 1 May 2008, 21 May 2009
Midsummer Eve & Midsummer Day 20 & 21 June 2008,
19 & 20 June 2009
All Saints 1 November 2008, 31 October 2009
Independence Day 6 December
Christmas 24–6 December

The National Romantics

Finland's version of Romantic Nationalism was similar to other countries' in that it sprang from a desire for independence. By the turn of the 20th century, the people we know as the Finns were reacting against years of control, first by the Swedes, and then by Russia. Their wish for an identity and cultural heritage of their own focused primarily on the *Kalevala*, a national saga that was a compendium of folk tales from the rural heartland of Karelia. These stories' motifs and themes, which are evident in Finnish culture today, were met by an influx of new ideas that came from the European Arts and Crafts Movement and the art nouveau aesthetic; this synthesis of ancient and modern cultural phenomena resulted in the emergence of a group of brilliant young artists. Among them were Jean Sibelius (whose *Finlandia* is a pure expression of national pride) and the painters Akseli Gallen-Kallela and Helene Schjerfbeck.

Pre-eminent among them, though, were the architects Herman Gesellius, Armas Lindgren and Eliel Saarinen, who met at Helsinki's Polytechnic Institute, formed a consultancy, and soon began to wield an immense influence on the local, national and international stages. The trio developed Jugendstil (Finnish for 'art nouveau') architecture into a style called National Romantic, a form that was directly influenced by the Karelian architectural heritage. They designed some of Helsinki's most prominent buildings, such as the Ateneum and Helsinki Railway Station (see pages 64–5). Finnish National Romantic really came to the world's attention at the Paris World Exposition of 1900 (at which time Finland was still a Grand Duchy of the Russian Empire), thanks to the sensation caused by the drama, dynamism and dash of Saarinen's Pavillion. In fact, Paris 1900 almost certainly marks the birth of what the world would come to admire as Finnish design, which, despite the fact that the Finns' independence has removed the catalyst of artistic urgency, has prospered and evolved, and, some might allege, reached its zenith thus far with the Nokia 7600 phone. Or was it the Oma lemon squeezer?

🔺 The elegance of 19th-century Finnish architecture is best seen on Esplanadi

History

At a latitude of 60° north, Helsinki is the northernmost of all continental European capitals, with a prime location on the Baltic. Its historical position as the bridge between Russia and the West made Finland a pawn between the rulers of Sweden – Scandinavia's most aggressive power – and Russia. During Swedish rule the provincial capital was at Turku; it was Swedish King Gustav Vasa who established a trading port at Helsinki in 1550.

This busy port settlement gradually grew in importance, until the early 1700s dealt it a double blow: in 1710 the plague nearly wiped out its 2,000 inhabitants; then, in 1713, the Swedes burned it down to keep it from falling into the hands of Peter the Great. To protect the harbour from future attacks, Sweden built the great Suomenlinna Fortress (see pages 112–13). However, Russian harassment continued to slow the city's growth.

A century after the plague, two more events changed Helsinki irrevocably. A fire in 1808 devastated most of the city and, before it was rebuilt, the province was ceded to Russia in 1809, ending Swedish rule. Finland became the semi-autonomous Russian Grand Duchy of Finland, and Tsar Alexander I lavished attention on his new city on the Baltic. He brought in the German-born architect C L Engel, who had designed much of St Petersburg. Engel remodelled Helsinki, especially around Senate Square, and gave it the elegance that it retains today. In 1812 Alexander I moved the capital of the Grand Duchy from Turku to Helsinki, and the city has been the capital ever since.

Rapid industrialisation from the 1860s to the beginning of the 20th century meant equally rapid population growth, and with it came the need for new neighbourhoods. Building after building sprang out of this boom, especially at the turn of the century, when Helsinki acquired a remarkable number of art nouveau structures by such luminaries as Eliel Saarinen, Alvar Aalto and their contemporaries. At the same time, a feeling of growing nationalism pushed the country toward independence.

Finland seized the moment when revolution rocked Russia in 1917: Parliament declared independence on 6 December and, after a short period of civil unrest, a republic was declared in 1919, with Helsinki as its capital. Since then, with the exception of the period of Soviet invasion in the 1940s, Helsinki has grown as an industrial and innovatory centre at the forefront of the Scandinavian design phenomenon. Since the 1952 Olympics it has also been a centre for major sporting events, and a prime location for the development of international diplomatic initiatives. Since 1995 Finland has been a member of the European Union. In 2001 the country elected (and in 2006 re-elected) its first female President, Tarja Halonen.

⬥ The ordeal of World War II is commemorated at Hietanemi Cemetery

Lifestyle

It was the Finns who invented the sauna, despite what jealousy may lead other Scandinavians to allege. For most Finns, the chance to relax in extreme heat is one of life's civilising rituals, and they're likely to fit one in at any time of day, as the urge takes them. Saunas are the venues for business meetings, family gatherings and all kinds of social interplay, which explains why they're found all over the city, sometimes in the unlikeliest of locations. Proximity to a lake

○ *Out and about in the occasional snowstorm*

is a definite bonus, since the Finns are great believers in a quick plunge into cold water after – or during – a sauna.

Though often believed to be taciturn, the Finns can actually be quite voluble in social situations, especially when loosened up with a little alcohol. They also have a wicked sense of humour, which is often very dry and sly, along with a keen sense of the ridiculous. They can laugh at themselves, and their apparent self-deprecation is a popular national joke with them. It is true, however, that a group of Finns can sit in a room together quite happily without uttering a word, and be quite comfortable. So don't be alarmed if silence appears to descend the very minute you enter almost any social setting. And expect silence in the sauna, unless you're in a business meeting. By the way, saunas are always gender-divided, except for those owned or popularly used by families. The same is true of the nude beaches in Helsinki, which you will find at Seurasaari and on Pihlajasaari. Women and men each have separate sections of beach on which to frolic, giggle and go all shrivelled.

Finns are generally easy-going and have a live-and-let-live attitude, so although Helsinki doesn't have the gay scene of, say, Stockholm, gays are welcome and excite little attention. There are several gay clubs in the city, but at most of them heterosexual couples are welcome. When it comes to clothes, Finns are usually casual, though they like to put their glad rags on for a big night out. They dress for the climate, so it's not unusual to see boots and thick ski jackets in the cloakrooms of upmarket restaurants in the winter. The Finns are pretty sensible people, who don't get huffy over dress codes or have bouncers to protect self-consciously cool venues from the criminally under-preened. The Finns go out to have a good time, and they are happy for you to have a good time, too.

Culture

The fact that Finland has such a distinct culture of its own is remarkable, considering that this small country spent so much of its past being tossed back and forth between two other – and very strong – cultures. That the Finnish language has remained distinct and in steady use is equally surprising. Today, just enough of the Russian and Swedish flavours remain in Finnish culture to make things interesting.

What does predominate is the Finnish sense of style. Leaders in modern design, the Finns are the epitome of the Scandinavian aesthetic – clean lines, fresh concepts and functional designs that look sharp and work well. Whether it's a building, a mobile phone, sportswear or a kitchen appliance, if it's designed in Finland, it will combine the often-conflicting needs of form and function into one graceful whole. Interest in design is more than a trade commodity, it's a national passion, because the Finns genuinely revel in being surrounded by well-designed things, whether they are the world's most comfortable scissors (Fiskars) or stylish home accessories (Marimekko or Arabia).

Helsinki's Design District is the place to revel in this Finnish phenomenon. There, in the space of a few streets, you'll find the Designmuseo (Design Museum) (see page 73), the Museum of Finnish Architecture (see page 74) and the Design Forum (see page 75), as well as galleries and designers' shops.

Other arts hold a high place in Finnish culture, too. Foreigners may be surprised to see enthusiastic fans of all ages in audiences at the opera or symphony. Finns are likely to have the works of Finnish artists hanging on their walls. Finland's architects are world famous, and the Finns value their creativity just as much as the rest of the

Marimekko is one of the most famous Finnish design brands

A RACE APART
Although Finland is most definitely a Scandinavian country,
and culturally has gained a lot from its long connection with
Sweden, the Finns are not primarily of the same northern
Germanic stock as their Scandinavian neighbours, and their
language is also distinct. No-one knows for sure how long
the Finns have been living in the Baltic or exactly where their
ancestors came from, but the Finnish language belongs to
a group that includes Estonian and Hungarian, and is entirely
unrelated to the Indo-European languages that nearly all of
the rest of Europe speaks.

world, so you'll see examples of their work at every turn. Helsinki
residents are far more likely to know the name of a local building's
architect than residents of any other city in Europe.

Helsinki is filled with performance venues for everything
from opera and dance to rock concerts and sports competitions.
Tickets are refreshingly well priced – those for the Philharmonic
Orchestra concerts cost between €5 and €15, for example. For
tickets to various concert and theatre venues, contact Lippupalvelu
(① 0600 1 08 00 or 0600 10 020 Ⓦ www.lippupalvelu.fi), or Tiketti
(① 0600 1 16 16 Ⓦ www.tiketti.fi). For schedules of everything
from music and theatre to sports events, see *Helsinki This Week*
(Ⓦ www.helsinkiexpert.fi/helsinkithisweek_eng). To learn about
art galleries and shows, pick up an English copy of *Taide-Art*,
a brochure that also has a map to help you find them.

◗ *Tourists admiring the Helsinki view from the steps of the Lutheran Cathedral*

Shopping

The streets bordering Esplanadi and the parallel Aleksanterinkatu lead to Mannerheimintie, forming the centre of Helsinki's most fashionable (and pricey) shopping district. Just beyond lies the Design District (don't miss the Design Forum for the hottest new looks in everything from paper clips to coffee pots) and Fredrikinkatu, lined with boutiques and music shops. In the morning market at the harbour, you'll find fresh local farm products, crafts and Russian fur hats, with more foods sold in the striped market hall. Another market is at Hakaniemi, which has crafts on the upper floor. At the western edge of the city is the restored Hietalahti market hall and a giant flea market, where you can get anything from last year's clothing to family heirlooms – all at cheap prices.

Shops are generally open from 09.00 or 10.00 to 18.00 or 20.00 Monday to Friday and 09.00 to 14.00 Saturday. Most close Sundays, though major department stores often open on Sundays from June to August and before Christmas.

Distinctive Finnish products to look for are glassware (big names are Iittala, Nuutajärvi and Arabia), clothing of fur and leather, traditional and contemporary jumpers and jerseys, and beautiful wooden utensils and furnishings. Exquisite kitchenware, carved in graceful and flowing forms of velvet-smooth local woods, includes spoons, spatulas and cake servers. Foods you may want to take back with you after you've tasted them are cloudberry or lingonberry preserves, smoked reindeer or salmon, and the incomparable Finnish honey.

Local crafts, found in handwork and museum shops and in markets, vary widely. Rustic reindeer made of bundled straw or hand-knitted traditional woollen hats, socks and mittens are sold alongside the sleek, modern designs for which Scandinavia is so well known. In Helsinki's shops you'll find Sámi crafts from Lapland, such as reindeer-bone jewellery and carved birchwood cups. Look for the *duodji* label, guaranteeing that these are genuine Sámi crafts.

VAT REFUNDS

Finland's 22 per cent VAT is often refundable for those who are not residents of the European Union. The easiest way to avoid receiving separate euro cheques from each shop (these may cost you more than their value to cash) is to use Global Refund Service. Ask for a refund cheque at any shop displaying a 'Tax Free' logo. At the airport, have these stamped at the Global Refund Desk and collect your refund in cash.

USEFUL SHOPPING PHRASES

What time do they open/close?
Milloin se avataan/suljetan?
Mil-loin she ervertahn/suljehtahn?

How much is it?
Paljonko se maksaa?
Perlyonko she merksah?

I'd like to buy ...
Haluaisin ostaa ...
Herlu-aisin ostah ...

Eating & drinking

It's true that Finnish cuisine has not yet rocked the European charts, but several of Helsinki's chefs certainly have. The best of them revel in the ingredients of the surrounding water and land – seafood from the Baltic and from Finland's lakes, vegetables and berries whose flavours have concentrated as they ripen in the long hours of summer sun, wild berries from the north, mushrooms gathered from the forests, and game from the tundra and fells. A number of Helsinki's restaurants offer special seasonal menus of these local ingredients at the height of their season, as part of an initiative called HelsinkiMenu.

Complicated preparations are shunned in favour of those that let the natural flavours of fresh ingredients shine through. Chefs draw on the traditional influences of Finland, Russia and Sweden, as well as an eclectic mix that ranges from Asian to Mediterranean. While you can find French, Italian, Chinese, Thai and even Irish pub food here, you'll eat best when you seek Finnish chefs working with their own native ingredients.

LOCAL FARE

Meals are normally served in three courses, often beginning with a warming hearty soup in the winter. Pork, lamb and beef are common

PRICE CATEGORIES
Price ratings for restaurants in this book are based on the average cost of a main course for one person.
£ up to €15 **££** €15–25 **£££** over €25

⬤ *Finns make the most of the summer by eating outdoors as much as possible*

main-course meats, and many menus offer reindeer in some form. Bear is usually served in Russian restaurants (Helsinki's are known for being better than those in St Petersburg), as a stew or smoked.

Baltic herring, *silakka*, is the favourite fish, fried, grilled, baked with layers of potato and cream or pickled as a snack. Herring is also smoked or marinated in a way similar to *gravadlax*, which is made with salmon. Arctic char, trout, salmon and whitefish are popular, and crayfish are in season during August and September.

In the autumn, markets are piled high with woodland mushrooms (mostly) from Lapland, and chefs take full advantage of this bounteous supply. Chanterelles are the tastiest of these, but you'll see all sorts, in meat dishes or served on their own.

Sausages (*makkara*) are the snack food of choice, and you'll find them sizzling on grills in markets and street stalls. They may be made from pork or any other meat, and are always delicious. *Mustamakkara* is a black sausage from Tampere, and is usually served with sweet-tart lingonberry jam.

Lingonberries and the earthy-sweet cloudberries ripen in the autumn, but you'll find them as jams and condiments and in desserts any time of year. Cloudberries are an especially rare delicacy, but they will be on the menus of better restaurants, frequently as a topping for puddings and ice cream. Pastries and baked goods are excellent, and the Finns enjoy these with their coffee at cafés and bakeries. Sweet coffee breads are popular, as is *karjalanpiirakat*, a savoury pastry from eastern Finland, with a filling of rice. Breads are varied and very good, ranging from dark rye to a snowy-white bread made with potatoes. Crisp flatbreads are usually made of rye flour.

Breads are always part of a full breakfast (a meal that is usually quite hearty), with a hot dish of eggs and meat and often porridge, or a buffet of cold cuts and cheeses – and plenty of coffee, although tea will always be available.

DRINKS

Wine is available at most restaurants, and some, such as Ravintola Carelia (see page 103) and Sundmans (see pages 82–3), have outstanding wine lists. Local alcoholic drinks include vodka, schnapps and liqueurs made from local berries. Look especially for *lakka*, made of cloudberries, and *mesimarja*, made of highly flavoured Arctic brambleberries. Or try Salmari, a potent and extremely popular pre-mixed vodka cocktail. If you prefer beer, a good local one to try is Lapin Kulta. In the winter you'll be offered *glögi*, a tasty blend of red wine, spices, raisins, almonds and blackcurrant juice. There are as many recipes for this as there are people making it, some using white wine. At any winter market, you'll find at least one steaming black cauldron of *glögi*.

MEAL TIMES

Breakfast is normally served from 07.00 to 10.00, and lunch begins early, at 11.00. The evening meal is also served early, often from 16.00 or 17.00, but continues late into the evening, with many restaurants serving until 23.00. The midday meal may be a light lunch or a full meal. The latter is often a bargain, at a set price as low as €8. Advance booking is wise for popular restaurants, especially on Wednesday, Friday and Saturday evenings. If meeting Finnish friends for a meal (or any other occasion), remember that they are prompt and value punctuality. If you are delayed for more than five minutes, phone them – they will be carrying a mobile.

TIPPING

Service charges are usually included in restaurant bills, but a modest tip is always welcome if service has been attentive. Give this directly to the server in cash, rather than adding it to the bill. Smoking is banned in public places.

USEFUL DINING PHRASES

I would like a table for ... people, please
Saadaanko me pöytä ...
Sahdahnko meh per-ewta ...

May I see the menu, please?
Voisinko nähdä menun?
Voi-shinko nahkh-da mehnun?

I am a vegetarian
Olen kasvissyöjä
Olehn kers-vis-sewer-ya

May I have the bill, please?
Saisinko laskun?
Sai-sinko lerksun?

Where is the toilet (restroom) please?
Missa on vessa?
Mis-sa on vehs-ser?

Entertainment & nightlife

With almost ten per cent of its population being university students, Helsinki is among Europe's hippest cities, with non-stop nightlife that's all the better for being largely undiscovered by foreigners. Don't worry about feeling left out, though, since almost everyone under 40 speaks excellent English. Variety is the name of Helsinki's game, with everything from clubs run by film directors to jazz clubs, gay clubs, raucous pubs and heavy-metal karaoke bars.

CLUBS & BARS

Without, perhaps, the pretension of Stockholm, but with all its variety and cool, Helsinki's night scene is user-friendly. There are no dress codes here – you'll want to be smartly dressed, but no ties are required and, as we've said, no bouncers will be at the door selecting clientele on the basis of their designer labels. Age is another matter, since clubs set their own rules. If you're over 24, you're home free; between 20 and 24 you may not be allowed into some clubs, especially on busy nights. A few places welcome anyone over 18, especially in the area around the Kamppi metro station, a popular area for under-20s.

The hot nights are Friday and Saturday, but Wednesday is also often busy. Expect to pay about €5 for admission to clubs, more for those with live music, plus another €1–2 for the compulsory coat check. A glass of beer or wine is usually about €4–5.

Nightlife is hottest in the streets around the centrally-located railway station (forget the grungy areas around railway stations in many other cities – in Helsinki this is prime real estate), along the Esplanadi and immediately south, between Mannerheimintie and Fredrikinkatu, west of Mannerheimintie between Finlandia Hall (see page 64) and the opera, and in the streets south of Uudenmaankatu, as far as Kapteeninkatu.

Do be aware that Finns can become belligerent when drunk, and fights may break out as night fades into morning. So if the atmosphere begins to take on an angry tone, slip quietly away, and under no circumstances engage a drunk in an argument or take chances with a potentially insulting remark. And if someone insults you, ignore them and leave as soon as possible.

PERFORMANCES

Clubs are not the only place young Finns spend a night out. Live performances are everywhere: arena rock shows, experimental metal, pop and a summer packed with festivals that always include music, often free. Besides the highbrow halls for opera, ballet and classical music (all well attended by people of all ages), venues include the Savoy Theatre for stage performances by Finnish and touring companies that range from classical theatre to contemporary and occasional musical shows; Olympic Stadion (Stadium) (see pages 88–90), home to all the big summer concerts; and the somewhat smaller Hartwall Areena, where even headliners like Metallica, Depeche Mode and Elton John perform. At the smaller House of Culture you'll hear metal, rock and pop.

Hartwall Areena ➌ Areenakuja ❶ (0) 204 1997
Ⓦ www.hartwall-areena.com
House of Culture ➌ Sturenkatu 4 ❶ (09) 774 0270
Ⓦ www.kulttuuritalo.fi
Savoy Theatre ➌ Kasarminkatu 46 ❶ (09) 169 3703

CINEMAS

Cinema programmes are available from hotels and the tourist office. The widest choice is at Tennispalatsi, with 14 screens, and Kinopalatsi, with ten. The selection is international and all films are shown in their original language with Finnish subtitles. Soundtracks are very rarely dubbed. The Orion is home to the Finnish Film Archive, which shows three films every day except Mondays. Tickets at the major cinemas are about €10 for evening; smaller venues cost less. Book ahead for Friday and Saturday evenings.

Kinopalatsi ❸ Kaisaniemenkatu 2 ❶ 0600 944 44 ❿ www.finnkino.fi

Orion ❷ Eerikinkatu 15 ❶ (09) 615 400 ❿ www.sea.fi

Tennispalatsi ❸ Salomonkatu 15 ❶ 0600 007 007 ❿ www.finnkino.fi

TICKETS & INFORMATION

Helsinki City Tourist & Convention Bureau (see page 153) has up-to-date information on what's happening at all venues, including clubs. Before you go, visit ❿ www.hel2.fi/tourism, and click on 'brochures' to download three publications filled with the latest news on what's hot in entertainment and clubs: *Groovy Nordic Oddity*, *Bohemian Nordic Oddity* and *Smooth Nordic Oddity* each contain insider tips.

Pick up a copy of the monthly *City Lehti* for listings of current happenings – it's free at most shops and hotels. *Helsinki This Week* (❿ www.helsinkiexpert.fi/helsinkithisweek_eng), the tourist office's magazine in English, is also free, and available everywhere. It is stronger on restaurant information and has a good calendar of events for the current month, in addition to seasonal features. For a complete listing of the many summer music festivals in Finland, see ❿ www.festivals.fi

Tickets for events at most major venues are available through Lippupalvelu Ticket Service (❶ 0600 1 08 00 ❿ www.lippupalvelu.fi).

---

❿ *Helsinki has a wealth of exciting live performance venues*

Sport & relaxation

Don't abandon your fitness routines in Helsinki – this is an exercise-friendly, go-for-it town, with parks and paths everywhere. The Finns are great walkers, runners, skiers, skaters and cyclists, so this is a good way to mingle with locals, too. The most popular running and walking routes are around Töölö Bay and the shore at Old Town Rapids. To enjoy the network of bike paths between sights, borrow a free City Bike (€2 deposit) from the green racks or rent a bike (or skateboard) from Töölö Bay Recreational Centre.

In winter, you can also rent ski equipment and snowshoes at the Töölö centre and go on your own or take a guided hike (❶ 09 228 81500 ❾ www.helsinkiexpert.fi). The Paloheinä Recreational Centre also offers rental skis, boots and poles. Trails, lit after dark, open as early as November and may have snow into April. Skating rinks are everywhere, but the Kallion Tekojäärata at Brahen Kenttä has music and rental skates.

Kallion Tekojäärata ❸ Helsinginkatu 23 ❶ (09) 710618 ❶ 08.00–20.00 Mon–Fri, 10.00–20.00 Sat & Sun, 20 Nov–11 Mar ❷ Tram: 8

Paloheinä Recreational Centre ❸ Pakilantie 124 ❶ (09) 8775 2281

Töölö Bay Recreational Centre ❸ Mäntymäentie 1 ❶ (09) 4776 9760

All that sparkling clean water surrounding the city will tempt anglers, and all they need is a traveller's fishing permit from Stockmann department store (see page 79) or a fishing shop. The shore around the Old Town Rapids is reserved for fishing. See ❾ www.ahven.net for further information.

The best beaches are at Seurasaari, Suomenlinna and Pihlajasaari. The Olympic-size pools at the Swimming Stadium and the Mäkelänrinne Swimming Centre are open to the public, or you can combine swimming with a real cultural fix at Helsinki's oldest traditional swimming hall. The recently restored Yrjönkatu Swimming Hall opened in 1928, and is used by people of all ages. Bathing suits are not worn, so men and women swim at different times; the schedule is available at most hotels.

Of course, you shouldn't miss the most Finnish of all activities – a sauna. Combine it with swimming at Yrjönkatu Swimming Hall, use your hotel's or enjoy the traditional experience at the 70-year-old Kotiharju, Helsinki's last old-fashioned wood-burning (as opposed to electric) sauna; the cost is €7, plus €1.50 for a towel. To find more options, visit ⓦ www.sauna.fi. Or for the ultimate luxury, steal away for a day or two of sauna and aromatic aquatherapy at Naantali Spa, a beautiful resort near Turku (see page 140).

Kotiharju ⓐ Harjutorinkatu 1 ⓣ (09) 753 1535

Mäkelänrinne Swimming Centre ⓐ Mäkelänkatu 49 ⓣ (09) 3484 8800
ⓕ (09) 3484 8809 ⓦ www.urheiluhallit.fi ⓛ 06.15–21.00 Mon–Fri,
08.00–20.00 Sat, 09.00–20.00 Sun ⓝ Tram: 1, 1A, 7

Swimming Stadium ⓐ Hammerskjöldintie 5 ⓣ (09) 310 87854

Yrjönkatu Swimming Hall ⓐ Yrjönkatu 21 ⓣ (09) 310 87401

● *All of Helsinki's large parks have ski trails*

Accommodation

For a Scandinavian capital, Helsinki offers some surprisingly moderate hotel rates. Of course, you can luxuriate in grandeur, but there are more budget options here than in many other Nordic cities. Even the finest hotels, such as the Hotel Kämp, offer special promotions, especially at weekends. Always ask about these when booking.

Most hotels are centrally located, and nearly all are close to public transportation. Unlike in many other cities, you needn't worry about staying close to the railway station, since this is an excellent neighbourhood in the midst of the best shopping and attractions.

Kaivokatu, a booking service located at the railway station, handles hotels, hostels and smaller guest houses. For information on hostels, contact the Finnish Youth Hostel Association.

Finnish Youth Hostel Association Ⓦ www.srm.fi

Kaivokatu ❶ (09) 228 81400 ❶ (09) 228 8149 Ⓦ www.helsinkiexpert.fi ❷ 09.00–19.00 Mon–Fri, 09.00–18.00 Sat, 10.00–18.00 Sun, June–Aug; 09.00–18.00 Mon–Fri, 09.00–17.00 Sat, Sept–May

HOTELS

Finn £ Just over half a kilometre (a third of a mile) from the railway station, this is a small but comfortable hotel and reasonably priced. All 27 rooms have private facilities, TV and phone, and some have a shower. A pool and saunas are next door. ⓐ Kalevankatu 3 B ❶ (09) 684 4360 ❶ (09) 684 43610 Ⓦ www.hotellifinn.fi Ⓝ Metro: Kamppi

Arthur £–££ A handsome and recently refurbished small hotel within 300 m (330 yd) of the railway station and the best shopping.

PRICE RATING
Price ratings for accommodation are based on the average rate for a double room for one night (usually including breakfast).
£ up to €80 ££ €80–175 £££ over €175

Weekend rates for a standard double are under €100. The on-site restaurant is well regarded. ❸ Vuorikatu 19 ❶ (09) 173 441 ❶ (09) 626 880 Ⓦ www.hotelarthur.fi Ⓝ Metro: Kaisaniemi

Helka £–££ Rooms at this centrally located hotel were recently refurbished with funky décor and furniture; all have private bathrooms, TV and phones. Further facilities include saunas and a whirlpool for relaxation, and a bar and restaurant. It's a business hotel, so rates are reduced at weekends. ❸ Pohjoinen Rautatiekatu 23 ❶ (09) 613 580 ❶ (09) 441 087 Ⓦ www.helka.fi Ⓝ Metro: Kamppi

Crowne Plaza Helsinki ££ The Crowne Plaza is a large, multi-storey, modern, glass-fronted building at the very heart of city life. The beautifully appointed modern rooms have everything, including high-speed internet connections. The fitness facilities, including a large pool, are impressive, too. ❸ Mannerheimintie 50 ❶ (09) 252 10000 ❶ (09) 252 13999 Ⓦ www.crowneplaza-helsinki.fi Ⓝ Metro: Rautatientori

Cumulus Kaisaniemi ££ Another business travel hotel, close to downtown. Clean, comfortable and friendly. ❸ Kaisaniemenkatu 7 ❶ (09) 172 881 ❶ (09) 605 379 Ⓦ www.cumulus.fi Ⓝ Metro: Kaisaniemi

Cumulus Olympia ££ A sister hotel to the Kaisaniemi, this is a good choice if you're interested in athletics. It's near the Olympic Stadium, and bowling, swimming and ball games are available at the Urheilutalo Sports Centre next door. It's also close to Linnanmäki Amusement Park and the Sealife Aquarium. ⓐ Läntinen Brahenkatu 2 ⓣ (09) 691 51 ⓕ (09) 691 5219 ⓦ www.cumulus.fi ⓝ Tram: 4, 10

Haaga ££ Large and modern, this recently renovated hotel is about 5 km (3 miles) from the centre, about halfway between downtown and the airport but handy for Central Park, Korkeasaari Zoo, the National Opera and the Finnish National Museum. Golfers note: Tali golf course is only 2 km (1 mile) away. ⓐ Nuijamiestentie 10 ⓣ (09) 580 7877 ⓕ (09) 580 78386 ⓦ www.bestwestern.com ⓝ Bus: 453

Palace ££–£££ This is a charming boutique hotel located right on the waterfront; many rooms have harbour views. It was built in the 1950s and retains much of the feel of Scandinavian modernism of that period. It is small (37 rooms) and intimate, and only minutes by foot to the Market Square, ferries and downtown shopping. ⓐ Eteläranta 10 ⓣ (09) 134 56656 ⓕ (09) 654 786 ⓦ www.palacekamp.fi ⓝ Tram: 4, 7B

Scandic Grand Marina ££–£££ This hotel, in a brilliantly converted 1913 warehouse designed by architect Lars Sonck, boasts elegant modern rooms. Excellent location on the harbour, opposite the ferry terminal. ⓐ Katajanokanlaituri 7 ⓣ (09) 16 661 ⓕ (09) 664 764 ⓦ www.scandic-hotels.fi ⓝ Tram: 4

● *Hotel Glo is one of the city's best hotels*

Sokos Hotel Torni ££–£££ Well situated, near the city centre and close to the train and bus stations, the 152-room Sokos is classed as a four-star but has reasonable rates. Rooms have wireless internet and other facilities include four saunas, multiple restaurants and bars. ⓐ Yrjönkatu 26 ⓣ (020) 123 4604 ⓕ (09) 433 67100 ⓦ www.sokoshotels.fi ⓜ Metro: Rautatientori

Glo £££ This new boutique hotel offers 144 sleekly designed, generously sized rooms with trendy extras such as flat-screen TVs and Wi-fi. Staff go out of their way to accommodate special requests. The restaurant, La Cocina, serves Northern Spanish cuisine. ⓐ Kluuvikatu 4 ⓣ (0) 10 3444 400 ⓕ (0) 10 3444 401 ⓦ www.palacekamp.fi ⓜ Metro: Kaisaniemi

Hotel Kämp £££ Stunningly restored, this grand hotel dating from 1887 has service to match, with facilities such as a day spa. The location, near the Esplanade, is superb, and the breakfast buffet outstanding. ⓐ Pohjoisesplanadi 29 ⓣ (09) 5840 9520 ⓦ www.hotelkamp.fi ⓜ Metro: Kaisaniemi

Rivoli Jardin £££ Close to the Esplanade and to the activities of the central district, this elegant, family-run boutique hotel has 55 rooms, plus a wide range of business features including internet access. There's also an on-site sauna. Apartments are available and you can even bring your dog. ⓐ Kasarmikatu 40 ⓣ (09) 681 500 ⓕ (09) 656 988 ⓦ www.rivoli.fi ⓜ Tram: 4

HOSTELS
Eurohostel £ This hostel has 255 beds in 135 rooms; singles, doubles, triples and family rooms are available. The recently repainted rooms

have TVs and new furniture, and there are self-catering facilities on each floor. Rates include a morning sauna. Shared bathrooms. ❸ Linnankatu 9 ❶ (09) 6220470 ❺ (09) 655044 Ⓦ www.eurohostel.fi Ⓝ Tram: 4

Hostel Suomenlinna £ If the idea of staying in a fortress appeals, this is the place for you. A fascinating sight in itself, the island fortress (see pages 112–13) was built by the Swedes and reinforced by the Russians as a primary defence for the city. The hostel has 40 beds, in rooms from two to ten people, plus a café and self-catering kitchen. Showers and toilets are shared. It's only a 15-minute ferry ride from the city centre. ❸ Suomenlinna C 9 ❶❺ (09) 684 7471 Ⓦ www.leirikoulut.com Ⓝ Ferry from Kauppatori

Stadion Hostel £ This friendly, comfortable hostel is part of the Olympic Stadium. There are 162 beds, available in dormitories or in private rooms. Breakfast is served in the café from 06.30; guests have a kitchen available and a choice of nearby restaurants. ❸ Pohjoinen Stadiontie 4 ❶ (09) 477 8480 ❺ (09) 477 84811 Ⓦ www.stadionhostel.com Ⓝ Tram: 3B from the railway station, 3T or 7A from Mannerheimintie, 3B or 3T from Silja Lines ferry and 4 from Viking Lines ferry. Ask the driver to let you off at Aurora Hospital, from where it's a 200-m (220-yd) walk.

CAMPSITE

Rastila Camping Camping in the city is possible here, a 15–20 minute ride from the railway station. The on-site restaurant is open in summer. ❸ Karavaanikatu 4 ❶ (09) 310 78517 ❺ (09) 310 36659 Ⓦ www.camping.fi Ⓝ Metro: Rastila

THE BEST OF HELSINKI

If you only have a few days to spend in Helsinki, you may be tempted to concentrate on the eastern half of the city centre, but you should try to make time to take in some of the sights of the western and northern areas and definitely take a harbour trip to see this fascinating metropolis from a different angle.

TOP 10 ATTRACTIONS
Here are ten sights and experiences you won't want to miss on any visit to the city.

- **Suomenlinna Fortress** One of the world's largest sea fortresses and a World Heritage Site to boot on an island out in the harbour (see pages 112–13)

- **Boat trips around the archipelago** Admire the city from all angles on an excursion boat or a ferry trip to the islands (see pages 106–8)

- **Uspenski Cathedral** The Russian presence of western Europe's largest Orthodox church still makes an impression (see page 72)

🔻 *The Pohjola Building, design by Eliel Saarinen, sculptures by Hilda Flodin*

- **Kauppatori (Market Square) and Harbour** The real heart of Helsinki, where locals, visitors, craftspeople and traders meet (see page 68)

- **Designmuseo (Design Museum)** The evolution of style periods expressed in numerous materials and objects. Brilliant design, brilliantly displayed (see page 73)

- **Art nouveau buildings** The beginnings of the Finnish love affair with architecture – architecture – kick your tour off at Saarinen's central railway station (see pages 66–7)

- **Seurasaari Open-air Museum** Historic buildings from all over Finland are here at this island museum with its working farm (see page 111)

- **Korkeasaari Zoo** Snow leopards, Amur and Siberian tigers, Asian lions: big cat heaven (see pages 110–11)

- **Temppeliaukio** The church in a rock – come here for wonderful concerts (see pages 91–2)

- **Finnish design shops** The latest and coolest – see it in the Design District around Diana Park first (see page 20)

Suggested itineraries

HALF-DAY: HELSINKI IN A HURRY

If you're unlucky enough to have only half a day free, you can still use it to absorb a lot of the sights and sounds of the city. Begin at the market, right at the head of the harbour, for a look at what you'll see on tonight's menu and to mix with the hearty, good-humoured Finns. Make a detour east to see the interior of Uspenski Cathedral (see page 72) before heading uphill from the market to Senaatintori (Senate Square) (see page 71). Head west on Aleksanterinkatu, past the smart shops, stepping into no. 44, the Pohjola Insurance Building (see page 70), for a sampling of Finnish Jugendstil. Don't miss the big square bordered by the National Theatre (see page 70), the Ateneum (see pages 72–3) and Saarinen's landmark railway station (see page 64). Beyond the station, take a left on Mannerheimintie, then left again to circle back to the harbour along the Esplanadi (see page 62). This walk will take you to some landmark sights, the best of Helsinki's shops and some great cafés (Engel on Senate Square or Café Kappeli on the Esplanadi (see page 81) are local favourites).

1 DAY: TIME TO SEE A LITTLE MORE

If you have completed the morning's whistle-stop tour and have acquired a feel for the architecture, design and lively buzz of the city, use the afternoon to take a boat to the fortress island of Suomenlinna (see pages 112–13). The 15-minute trip gives good city views, and once you're on the island you can explore the fortress buildings, watch the excellent film, visit the museums and craft studios, and walk the island paths for views of the city, surrounding islands, and the ships in the Gulf of Finland. In the evening, treat yourself to a dinner in one of Helsinki's restaurants specialising in local ingredients. Then hit the streets around Fredrikinkatu to learn what real nightlife is.

2–3 DAYS: TIME TO SEE MUCH MORE

You can add a lot more experiences if you have another day or two. The first stop should be the Design Museum (see page 73), after which you will want to wander in the city's exciting Design District to see what's at the cutting edge before it hits the shops all over Europe. Don't miss the Design Forum (see page 75), where you can find top designers' work in all price ranges. Window-shop your way north on Fredrikinkatu or take a bus to Temppeliaukio, carved out of solid rock. Head back east toward the unmissable tower of the National Museum (see page 74) and Finlandia Hall (see page 64), opposite, before returning to the centre along busy Mannerheimintie. If you have another day, spend it visiting some of the excellent museums or head for the islands: either the open-air museum of Seurasaari (see pages 111–12) or the Korkeasaari Zoo (see pages 110–11) to see rare big cats, including snow leopards and Siberian tigers.

LONGER: ENJOYING HELSINKI TO THE FULL

A longer stay gives enough time to head out of the city for a day in old Porvoo or one of the many cruises among the islands. Or combine the two by cruising to Porvoo. After a few days' walking the pavements, you'll be ready to relax in one of Helsinki's parks, where you can snowshoe or ski in the winter and walk or cycle in the summer. After that, you'll be ready for the other Finnish obsession, a sauna. If your hotel doesn't offer one, choose one of the city's public saunas and join the Finns as they relax.

Something for nothing

Attending one of Helsinki's free festivals doesn't just save on money, but it's also a great way to mingle with locals, enjoy music and be part of Finnish life. However, since the majority take place during the most popular tourist season, you need to book accommodation early.

The ultimate in syncretism is the confluence of Walpurgis Night (itself coinciding with pagan rites of spring), May Day, International Workers' Day and Finland's Student Day (celebrating graduation).

● *Students crowd into Senate Square to celebrate Student Day*

The city welcomes spring (even if the day brings a late snowstorm) in a most un-Finnish way, by becoming one giant block party, with champagne, picnics and bands of liberated students wearing white hats. A cap is placed ceremoniously on the statue of Havis Amanda on the evening of 30 April, and champagne flows – along with the goodwill – well into the night and all the next day.

The last weekend in May brings the World Village Festival (ⓦ www.maailmakylassa.fi), two days of free stage performances, exhibitions, street musicians and sports in Kaisaniemi Park. Several stages feature performers from all over the world, many of them emerging artists that go on to become famous. Past performances have included Sengalese hip-hop, Chilean reggae, Finnish folk rock and a Spanish ska/rock/flamenco/Rai group. Exotic food, folk crafts and exhibition booths add to the atmosphere, with an international buzz filling the city.

Helsinki-päivä, Helsinki Day, celebrates the city's birthday on 12 June, with free concerts, a three-day samba and dance festival with cruises, tours and free entrance to museums. It ends with a rock concert in Kaivopuisto Park, (close to the British and United States Embassies, off Puistokatu). There are market stalls on the Esplanadi, free performances on the Espa stage all day and free admission to Suomenlinna Fortress. Especially good for families with children, it is relatively alcohol-free and admission is free all day at Linnanmäki Amusement Park (you'll need to pay for the rides, though).

Each August a large stage is built below the sloping lawn of the Kaivopuisto Park observatory for the Kaivopuisto People's Festival, forming an amphitheatre for a free performance (genres vary, as do performance times). The last Thursday in August is Night of the Arts (see page 11), when museums and galleries stay open until late at night and the streets are alive with free musical performances.

When it rains

Helsinki is such an outdoor city, filled with leafy parks, broad avenues, street markets and pedestrianised shopping streets, that most travellers spend much of their time outside enjoying the long daylight hours. Three of its most famous sights – the islands of Suomenlinna, Seurasaari and the zoo – are open-air attractions. But a whole layer of the city is so hidden that even multi-time visitors might not know it exists under their feet. Beneath the streets of the city centre, from the railway station to the Esplanadi, under Mannerheimintie to the Forum, and as far west as the Kamppi bus station, lies a maze of connected underground passages lined with shops, cafés, restaurants, bakeries and food markets. Street musicians play, and escalators and stairs connect to the department stores, shopping centres and services above.

The tunnels even offer direct access to transportation, connecting the train and bus stations and city transit lines. In cold or rainy weather you can spend a whole day shopping or browsing in the subterranean shops, the department stores of Stockmann and Sokos, the trendy shops of the Forum, and even the Academic Bookstore, without ever emerging above ground.

The two department stores and the Forum shopping centre have their food stores on the subterranean level, which are better places to look for typical foods than in the tourist shops. Browse the shelves for wild-berry preserves and the coolers for smoked fish and venison. Both departments stores have good sections for Finnish design, in both fashion and home furnishings, as well as sections for typical local products, including genuine Sámi-made goods. The new Kamppi shopping centre offers designer shops and a variety of restaurants and cafés. If you feel adventurous take the eastbound metro from the train station to Itäkeskus, where you'll find two huge shopping centres.

The underground routes access at least two of Helsinki's architectural landmarks, the interior of Eliel Saarinen's railway station and the Academic Bookstore, designed by Alvar Aalto. And close to their exits are two art museums well worth exploring on a rainy day: the Ateneum (see pages 72–3), with the country's best collections of Finnish and foreign art, and Kiasma, the Museum of Contemporary Art (see page 74), featuring post-1960 Finnish works. (Without the visible landmarks of the world above, it is easy to lose your bearings in the tunnels, so signs help you find your way.)

The Academic Bookstore is a destination in its own right

On arrival

TIME DIFFERENCE
Helsinki follows Eastern European Time (EET). During Daylight Saving
Time (end Mar–end Oct) the clocks are put forward one hour.

ARRIVING
By air
Vantaa International Airport is 19 km (12 miles) north of the city
centre. The two-terminal (domestic and international) airport has
three shopping centres and numerous bureaux de change and
ATMs. Finnair operates a shuttle (30 minutes) to Helsinki Railway
Station (€5.20) every 20–30 minutes, daily 05.00–24.00. Public
buses (about 40 minutes) depart 06.00–01.00, every 10–30 minutes
(€3.40). Taxis deliver you and your luggage directly to your hotel for
about €30. An alternative gateway used by low-cost airlines such as
Ryanair is Tampere. Buses connecting with arrivals run to Helsinki
(railway station); the one-way fare is €25 and journey time 2½ hours.
Tampere-Pirkkala Airport ❶ (03) 283511 Ⓦ www.finavia.fi
Vantaa International Airport ❶ (09) 82 771 (09) 61 511
Ⓦ www.helsinki-vantaa.fi

By rail
Rail passengers arrive at one of Helsinki's great architectural
landmarks, Eliel Saarinen's 1911 granite railway station. This busy
terminus has a wealth of facilities – including restaurants and coffee
shops, ATMs, public card phones and its own shopping centre – and
is right in the centre of the city. Unlike many other large European
stations, it is located in a busy, safe and upmarket area. Ⓦ www.vr.fi

By road

In Helsinki, traffic is light, roads are well marked (and free of tolls) and drivers polite. But unless you plan to travel outside the capital and into the countryside, a car is really not necessary because public transport is so good.

If you are from a left-hand-drive country, be especially aware that in Finland driving is on the right, and cars overtake on the left. Drivers bringing their own cars from the UK should be sure their lights are adapted to right-hand driving. Drivers from outside the EU should carry an International Driving Permit (available from local automobile clubs before leaving home), along with their national licence. Unless otherwise posted, the speed limit is 80 kph (50 mph) outside the city, 50 kph (30 mph) within city limits and 100–120 kph (60–75 mph) on motorways (the limit increases with the number of lanes). In the city, trams, bicycles and pedestrians have right of way over cars. Seatbelts are compulsory everywhere.

If you intend to travel by car in the winter, you should be familiar with handling a vehicle on snow-covered and icy roads and driving in winter storm conditions. Winter wheels are mandatory in every car between November and March. Anywhere outside the city, be aware that reindeer and elk are formidable obstacles that can appear suddenly in the road at any time. Hundreds of people are killed in wildlife collisions annually, so slow down whenever you see one, and be especially careful at dusk or in the dark.

By water

The ferry and cruise ship docks are right in the centre of the city, within a few steps of the market, the Esplanadi, shopping streets and hotels.

FINDING YOUR FEET

Few capital cities are as compact or as easy to get around in as Helsinki. The central sites surround the harbour, and the city is laid out in a tidy grid with broad avenues. Some of Helsinki's most outstanding architecture is visible from the harbour, and its streets are lined with elegant old buildings. The city is clean, well lit and safe, with drivers who are careful of pedestrians.

The neat, sensible street plan makes finding addresses easy (and house numbers are marked on most local maps), although street names may seem to defy pronunciation. Pick up a free map at the tourist office, either at the airport or at Pohjoisesplanadi 19, near the harbour (see page 153). Here you can buy a Helsinki Card, economical if you plan to visit many sites or use public transport often (see Getting Around, pages 56–7, for price comparisons). A great source of neighbourhood maps is *See Helsinki on Foot*, downloadable via Ⓦ www.hel2.fi/tourism

ORIENTATION

The city wraps around the harbour, with Senaatintori (Senate Square) (see page 71), which is easy to identify thanks to the round dome of the Lutheran Cathedral, behind it. To the east the golden domes of Uspenski Cathedral (see page 72), on a second hill, provide another useful landmark, and to the west stretches the Esplanadi (see page 62), a wide park bordered by elegant buildings. From the end of the Esplanadi, the broad Mannerheimintie heads northwest, alongside the railway station and the bay of Töölönlahti. Between those are the unmistakable Finlandia Hall (see page 64) and Opera House (see page 85), with the Parliament House (ⓐ Mannerheiminte 30) and the tall tower of the National Museum (see page 74) as landmarks on Mannerheimintie's western side.

From this walkable nucleus, other neighbourhoods are easy to find: the art nouveau Katajanokka beyond Uspenski Cathedral, Kallio north of Senate Square, Sibelius Park and Hietaniemi to the west, Bulevardi to its south and the neighbourhoods and parks of the southern end of the peninsula. The three islands – Seurasaari, Suomenlinna and Korkeasaari – are respectively west, south and

● *Trams in central Helsinki*

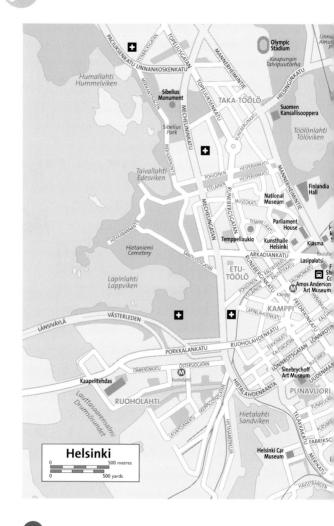

Helsinki

0   500 metres

0   500 yards

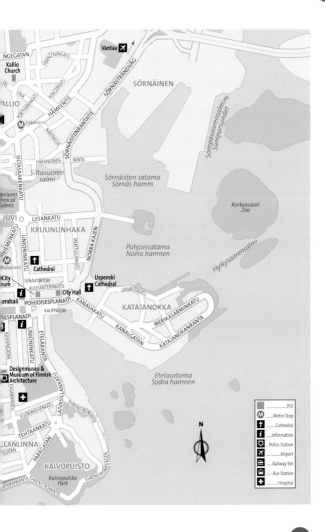

NGEGATAN
Kallio
Church
FRANZÉNINKATU
Vantaa ✈
PORTHANINKATU
LINJA
PENGERKATU
SÖRNÄISTENRANTATIE
SÖRNÄSTRANDVÄG
SÖRNÄINEN
ÄS
HÄMEENTIE
ALLIO
ALLIO
M Hakaniemi
NÄGINKUJA
SÖRNÄISTENRANTATIE
Sompasaarensalmi
Sumparsundet
SILTASAARENKATU
HAKANIEMEN-
RANTA
Siltavuoren
salmi
Sörnäisten satama
Sörnäs hamm
niemi
nical
dens
Korkeasaari
Zoo
JUVI
LIISANKATU
UNIONINKATU
KRUUNUNHAKA
MARIANKATU
NORRA KAJEN
METTILINKATU
Pohjoissatama
Norra hamnen
Hylkysaarensalmi
NIEMENKATU
M Kaisaniemi
City
eum
SENAATINTORI
Cathedral
Uspenski
Cathedral
ALEKSANTERINKATU
City Hall
LAIVASTOKATU
endsali
POHJOISESPLANADI
KANAVAKATU
KAUPPATORI
KATAJANOKKA
MERIKASARMINKATU
AESPLANADI
KANALGATAN
KATAJANOKANRANTA
UNIONINKATU
ETELÄRANTA
KASARGENKANA
Etelasatama
Sodra hamnen
Designmuseo &
Museum of Finnish
Architecture
KASARMINKATU
LAIVASILLANKATU
EHRENSTRÖMINTIE
VUORIMIEHENKATU
TEHTAANKATU
N
LANLINNA
SCATAN
PARKGATAN
⊕
KAIVOPUISTO
Kaivopuisto
Park
TAMANRANTA EHRENSTRÖMINTIE

POI
M .....Metro Stop
.....Cathedral
i .....Information
.....Police Station
✈ .....Airport
.....Railway Stn
.....Bus Station
⊕ .....Hospital

east of the city. The handy website ⓦ kartta.hel.fi will locate any street address for you.

GETTING AROUND
Public transport

Buses, trams and trains make covering long distances easy, and the website ⓦ journey.fi has a Journey Planner section that gives you exact bus and tram connections between any two points, including scheduled times. *Helsinki This Week* has a transport map showing the lines by colour. Buy tickets (€2.20) at stations or from the driver on the bus or tram; the ticket is good for transfers within an hour. If you expect to use public transport often, a tourist ticket for 24 hours costs €6; for three days it's €12 and for five days it's €18. You can buy these at the railway station, ticket machines or from the tourist office.

IF YOU GET LOST, TRY ...

Excuse me, do you speak English?
Anteeksi, puhutko englantia?
Erntehksi, puhutko ehnglerntier?

How do I get to ...?
Miten mä pääsen ...?
Mi-ten mah pa-a-sen ...?

Can you show me on my map?
Voitko näyttää minulle kartasta?
Voytko na-ewt-ta-a mul-leh ker-terster?

Another option is the Helsinki Card (one day €33, two days €43, three days €53), which also includes free admission to museums and attractions. But this is only a good value if you plan to visit several attractions, since admissions to most major sights are €5–8 each. Entrance to all the separate museums on Suomenlinna plus the ferry trip adds up to more than a 24-hour Helsinki Card, but that assumes that you would tour every little museum in the complex.

Ferries shuttle continuously between the harbour and Suomenlinna (€3.80 return) and a little less frequently to Korkeasaari Zoo from the harbour or Hakaniemenranta.

Taxis

Hail taxis from the street (the yellow sign will be lit if it is available), or at busy times go to a taxi rank or phone ➊ 0100 0700. The base rate is €4; most city destinations are €6–10. Tipping is not necessary, but if you do, add €1 to the fare.

Cycling

In good weather, consider cycling as a way to get between sights. The city is relatively flat and 900 km (over 500 miles) of cycle lanes and paths follow the major streets. Look for the free City Bikes in green racks, available for a €2 deposit.

Outside Helsinki

Getting around Finland is easy and efficient using buses, trains or internal flights, but it can be expensive unless you fall into one of the discount groups. The fastest trains are the Pendolinos, connecting major points, such as Helsinki and Turku. Express trains connect to northern cities, such as Rovaniemi, which is an 11-hour journey. Eurail and other passes are valid in Finland (see page 143). Bus services

Pikku Huopalahti (10)

Kuusitie

Jalavatie

(4) (4T) Munkkiniemi

Paciuksenkaari

Töölön tulli

Meilahden sairaala

Humallahti

Kansaneläkelaitos

Töölön Halli

Ooppera

Töölöntori

Apollonkatu

Caloniuksenkatu

Perhonkatu

Marian saiaala

(8) Salmisaari

Ruoholahti

(M) Ruoholahti

Kalevankatu

(6) Hietalhti

Köydenpunojankatu

Hietalahdentori

Pasila Sörnäinen

Maistraatintori (7A)

Palkkatilanportti (7B)

Eläintarha

Karjalankatu

Auroran sairaala

Alppila

(3B)

Linnanmäki

Kansaneläkelaitos

Kaupungin-puutarha

Ooppera

Töölönlahti

Hesperianpuisto

(3T)

Kansallismuseo

(3B)

Sammonkatu

(7B)

Eläinmuseo

Kauppakorkeak

Lasipalatsi

Yliopistalo

Kamppi

Erottaja

Itämerankatu

Fredrinkatu

Aleksanterin Teatt

Hietalahdentori

Iso roobertinkatu

Hietalahdentori

Viiskulma

Eira

(1A) Perämieh

St. Petersbur

Metro	Tram Lines	Finnish Railways
	1, 1A	
	3B, 3T	
	4, 4T	
	6	
	7A, 7B	
	8	
	10	

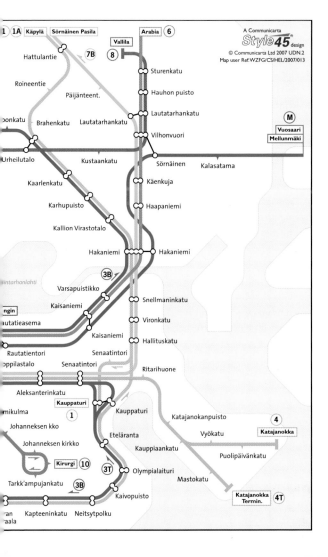

1 1A Käpylä Sörnäinen Pasila
Arabia 6
Vallila
7B 8
Hattulantie
A Communicarta
Style45 design
© Communicarta Ltd 2007 UDN.2
Map user Ref:WZFG/CS/HEL/2007/013
Roineentie
Sturenkatu
Päijänteent.
Hauhon puisto
Lautatarhankatu
onkatu   Brahenkatu   Lautatarhankatu
Vilhonvuori
M
Vuosaari
Mellunmäki
Urheilutalo
Kustaankatu
Sörnäinen   Kalasatama
Kaarlenkatu
Käenkuja
Karhupuisto
Haapaniemi
Kallion Virastotalo
Hakaniemi
Hakaniemi
3B
iintarhanlahti
Varsapuistikko
Snellmaninkatu
ngin   Kaisaniemi
Vironkatu
autatieasema
Kaisaniemi
Hallituskatu
Rautatientori
Senaatintori
oppilastalo   Senaatintori
Ritarihuone
Aleksanterinkatu
Kauppaturi
mikulma   1   Kauppaturi
Katajanokanpuisto
4
Johanneksen kko
Vyökatu   Katajanokka
Eteläranta
Johanneksen kirkko
Kauppiaankatu
Kirurgi 10   Puolipäivänkatu
Tarkk'ampujankatu   3B   3T   Olympialaituri
Mastokatu
Katajanokka
Termin.   4T
Kaivopuisto
ran   Kapteeninkatu   Neitsytpolku
aala

are scheduled to be compatible with trains, reaching out into the countryside and smaller towns. Finnair flies to Rovaniemi and other points in the north.

Bus information Ⓦ www.journey.fi

Finnair ❶ 0600 140 140 Ⓦ www.finnair.com

Train information ❶ 0600 41 902 Ⓦ www.vr.fi

CAR HIRE

All major companies are represented in Helsinki, most with desks at Vantaa Airport. Check car-hire rates before making air reservations, since you can often save with an air-car package from the airline.

If you plan to visit Helsinki before travelling elsewhere, consider picking up the car as you leave, instead of on arrival, to save city driving and parking charges. The minimum age for car hire is 18, and you must present (and carry while driving) your own home driver's licence. Non-EU residents should also have an International Driving Permit, obtained from an automobile club (you needn't be a member) before leaving home. In addition, you will need to show a credit card, even if you are not charging the car to one. If you plan to take the car on the ferry to Estonia or Sweden, be sure you have the necessary documentation (you should ask for this when you book).

❶ *Helsinki Railway Station*

THE CITY OF
Helsinki

Esplanadi & the Harbour

So many of Helsinki's most popular sights are in the streets
surrounding the harbour that it would be easy to spend several
days in the city without venturing any further. Outstanding
architecture, churches, museums, dining and shopping are
all within a few steps of the busy waterfront, which, given the
number of ships and boats that seem to be constantly moving
in and out, is itself a scenic attraction.

SIGHTS & ATTRACTIONS

Half the fun of visiting Helsinki is the variety of sights and experiences.
High on that list is just ambling around the harbour and through
the city's markets, enjoying the architecture and the constantly
changing waterscape. Each time you approach the harbour, it looks
different, as the huge Baltic ferries and cruise ships come and go,
and little boats sail in and out.

Esplanadi

Stretching west from Kauppatori (Market Square), the open swath
of the Esplanadi is bordered by elegant buildings. The pavilion at the
beginning of the park is the Café Kappeli, and the nearby bandstand
is the scene of free summer concerts. Before Christmas, the entire
Esplanadi is lined with booths selling crafts and food. Between it
and Market Square, a statue of Helsinki's symbol, Havis Amanda,
emerges from a fountain. The fountain is the work of Eliel Saarinen,
and Havis Amanda is by Ville Vallgren. On summer evenings, all of
Helsinki seems to congregate and stroll in the park.

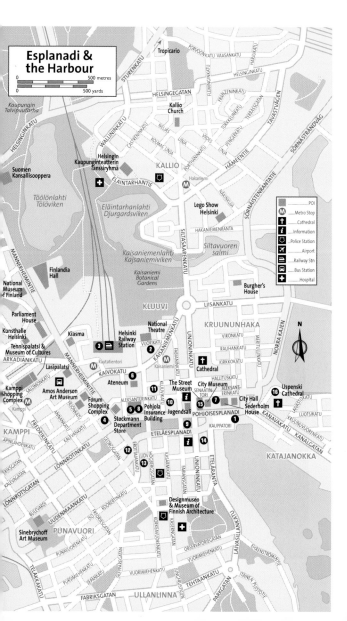

Esplanadi &
the Harbour

0   500 metres
0   500 yards

Tropicario

Kallio
Church

HELSINGEGATAN

Suomen
Kansallisooppera

Helsingin
Kaupunginteatterin
Tanssiryhmä

ELÄINTARHANTIE

KALLIO

Töölönlahti
Tölöviken

Eläintarhanlahti
Djurgardsviken

Lego Show
Helsinki

HAKANIEMENRANTA

Kaisaniemenlahti
Kajsaniviken

Siltavuoren
salmi

Finlandia
Hall

Kaisaniemi
Botanical
Gardens

Burgher's
House

National
Museum
of Finland

KLUUVI

LIISANKATU

KRUUNUNHAKA

Parliament
House

VIRONKATU

RAUHANKATU

Kunsthalle
Helsinki

Kiasma

National
Theatre

Helsinki
Railway
Station

Cathedral

KIRKKOKATU

HALLITUSKATU

Tennispalatsi &
Museum of Cultures

ARKADIANKATU

VUORIKATU

Rautatientori

Kaisaniemi

The Street
Museum

City Museum
SENAATIN-
TORI

ALEKSANT-
ERINKATU

Uspenski
Cathedral

Lasipalatsi

KAIVOKATU

Ateneum

City Hall
Sederholm
House

Amos Anderson
Art Museum

ALEKSANTERINKATU

KLUUVIKATU

POHJOISESPLANADI

Kamppi
Shopping
Complex

Forum
Shopping
Complex

Pohjola
Insurance
Building

Jugendsali

KAMPPI

Kamppi

Stockmann
Department
Store

KAUPPATORI

ETELÄESPLANADI

KATAJANOKKA

APINLÄHDENKATU

FREDRIKINKATU

KALEVANKATU

EERIKINKATU

GEORGSGATAN

FREDRIKSGATAN

ETELÄRANTA

UNIONINKATU

FABIANINKATU

LÖNNROTINKATU

LÖNNROTSGATAN

KALEVAGATAN

ANNANKATU

YRJÖNKATU

ROOBERTINKATU

KASARMINKATU

Designmuseo
& Museum of
Finnish Architecture

BULEVARDI

UUDENMAANKATU

PUNAVUORI

Sinebrychoff
Art Museum

PUNAVUORENKATU

KORKEAVUORENKATU

PUKINMÄENHENKATU

SEPÄNKATU

OBSERVATORIEGATAN

VUORIMIEHENKATU

VUORIMIEHENKATU

TEHTAANKATU

ULLANLINNA

LAIVASILLANKATU

TELAKKAKATU

FABRIKSGATAN

PARKGATAN

Legend

	POI
Ⓜ	Metro Stop
✝	Cathedral
🛈	Information
▣	Police Station
✈	Airport
🚆	Railway Stn
🚌	Bus Station
✚	Hospital

N

Finlandia Hall

Famed architect Alvar Aalto's best-known work in Helsinki is the enormous concert hall overlooking Töölö Bay. It's no accident that its white Carrara marble and black granite remind you of a piano keyboard. Tours of the 1970s building are given when the hall is not in use. ⓐ Mannerheimintie 13 E ⓣ (09) 402 41 ⓦ www.finlandiatalo.fi ⓛ 09.00–16.00 Mon–Fri ⓝ Bus/tram: 4, 4T, 7A, 7B, 10. Admission charge for tours

Helsinki Railway Station

For visitors arriving by rail or airport bus, the first stop is Helsinki's art nouveau railway station, designed by Eliel Saarinen (father of Eero). Its tower was the first of several designs that culminated in Saarinen's 1922 Chicago Tribune Tower, so it could be called the model for America's first skyscraper. Be sure to go inside to see the

monumental arched halls, with walls ornamented in surprisingly delicate carved panels. ❸ Rautatientori

Kaisaniemi Botanical Gardens

The iron-framed glass Palm House was designed by Gustaf Nyström in 1889, and today more than 900 labelled plant species grow in rainforest, desert, Mediterranean and water environments. Go in the winter to be among orchids, African violets and water lilies with massive leaves. The flowerbeds, fountains, pools and rose borders are beautiful in June, when the park hosts the Helsinki Pride festival. ❸ Enter from Unioninkatu 44 or Kaisaniemenranta 2, near the railway station ❶ (09) 1912 4453 ❹ Gardens 07.00–20.00 Mon–Fri, 09.00–20.00 Sat & Sun, Apr–Sept; 07.00–17.00 Mon–Fri, 09.00–17.00

🔻 *Finlandia Hall is home to the Helsinki Philharmonic*

Sat & Sun, Oct–Mar, Glasshouses 10.00–17.00 Tues–Sun, Apr–Sept; 10.00–15.00 Tues–Sun, Oct–Mar. Admission charge to glasshouses

Kallio Church

One of Finland's great architects, Lars Sonck, designed this great church in the National Romantic style in 1912. The bells inside its distinctive tower play a piece by Sibelius. Go inside the granite building to see the sculpted relief and other works of art, and go for a Sunday service or a concert to hear the great organs. ❷ Itäinen Papinkatu 2 ❶ (09) 2340 3620 ❶ 12.00–18.00 Mon–Fri, 10.00–18.00 Sat & Sun ❶ Bus/tram: 3B, 3T, 51

ART NOUVEAU

At the turn of the 20th century, a unique combination of events, ideas and talents propelled Finland and its capital city into the spotlight of European design. Finland's rising intellectual and artistic community, already seeking its own national identity (see pages 14–15), was further inspired by the Arts and Crafts Movement popular in Europe at the time. Today, the results of that Golden Age of Finnish Art make Helsinki a living museum of art nouveau, or Jugendstil, as it was known in German-speaking countries.

The primary architects were Lars Sonck, Sigurd Frosterus, Selim Lindqvist, Valter Thomé, Herman Gesellius, Armas Lindgren and Eliel Saarinen. Helsinki was in a rapid growth spurt, so housing and public buildings were in great demand – and so were these brilliant young architects to design them. Dozens of their landmark buildings cluster in easy-to-visit neighbourhoods.

One of Europe's signature buildings in this style is Saarinen's Helsinki Railway Station, whose dramatic straight lines are accented by stylised figures holding lamps. The interior is a triumph of art nouveau, combining elegantly simple structure with flowing lines of natural ornamental designs.

In the nearby downtown streets are several other noteworthy structures; one of the most outstanding is the Pohjola Insurance Building at Aleksanterinkatu 44 (see page 70). You can't miss its rusticated stone exterior, and its interior mixes stone with the local wood, using designs of local plants and animals. Climb the curving stairs to see art nouveau balustrades, doors, hinges, panels, even the newel post.

Just beyond the Uspenski Cathedral (see page 72) are some of the city's best residential examples. Katajanokka was the first neighbourhood of this type in Europe, and is also Europe's best preserved. Walk along the streets of this five-block quarter, looking for details of stone ornament as well as surprising doorways, fanciful hinges, fairytale towers, balconies and other architectural details.

To see the best of Helsinki's art nouveau, sign up for the 'Pearls of Jugend' tour with Archtours. Architect Marianna Heikinheimo or one of her associates will take you to the best art nouveau neighbourhoods and hard-to-reach out-of-town sites. **Archtours** ① (09) 4777 300 ① (09) 4777 3010 Ⓦ www.archtours.fi

Katajanokka

The city's best concentration of art nouveau architecture can be found in the streets beyond Uspenski Cathedral, across the harbour from

67

Kauppatori (Market Square). Built within a decade, at the height of Jugendstil's popularity, this is Europe's best preserved art nouveau residential neighbourhood. Each new apartment building, for the wealthy middle class who could afford quality design and construction, was designed to outdo its neighbours. The castle-like Aeolus building and the turreted Tallbergin Talo, across the street, form a gate to the quarter, at either side of Luotsikatu, which is lined with fine examples. Behind Tallbergin is another signature building, Eol, with a projecting balcony, corner turret and outstanding wooden door with elegant iron fittings and carved mythic creatures. The most exquisite doorway, however, is on the 1902 **Kataja building** (❸ Kaupiaankatu 2 ❷ Bus/tram: 4, 4T, 13).

Kauppatori (Market Square)

At the harbour's edge, with some of its merchants selling directly from boats, is the colourful market, a daily gathering of locals, visitors, farmers, fishermen, craftsmen and traders. Impromptu cafés, enclosed by plastic in the winter, serve everything from juicy sausages to salmon fillets grilled on cedar planks. At the Esplanadi side of the harbour is Gustaf Nystrom's 1889 market, worth visiting for the market stalls of honey, smoked fish, local cheese and other delicacies. ❸ Helsinki Harbour ● 08.00–19.00 Mon–Fri, 08.00–16.00 Sat. Outdoor market 06.30–14.00 Mon–Fri, 06.30–15.00 Sat, 09.00–16.00 Sun (summer only) ❷ Tram:3B, 3T

Lego Show Helsinki

Adults have just as much fun at this Lego theme park as kids do. Admissions are ticketed in these time slots: 10.00–14.00, 14.00–17.00

▶ *Katajanokka is an outdoor museum of art nouveau domestic architecture*

and 17.00–20.00. Entrance for each is limited, so the activities are never too crowded to enjoy, and there is plenty of Lego – enough to go round for all the kids, large and small. ⓐ Jaffa Station, Sörnäisten rantatie 6, at Hakaniemi Market Square ① 020 710 9902 ⓦ www.leikkiluola.fi ⓛ 10.00–20.00 May–Aug ⓝ Bus/tram: 68, 23N, 97N. Admission charge

National Theatre
The focal point of the north side of the Helsinki Railway Station Square is the National Theatre, built in 1902. The façade is in granite and sandstone, while the interior is almost entirely worked in curved lines. The foyer is decorated with frescoes. ⓐ Suomen Kansallisteatteri, Läntinen Teatterikuja 1 ⓝ Metro: Rautatientori

Pohjola Insurance Building
The interior motifs used in this 1901 office building by Saarinen, Lindgren & Gesellius are clearly Finnish, but the style shows the influence of French art nouveau. The dramatic sweeping staircase is asymmetrical, bordered in graceful balustrades. Art nouveau elements decorate these, as well as the walls and doorways of each landing. To see the interior, go during weekday business hours, wait until someone opens the door and simply walk in. ⓐ Aleksanterinkatu 44 ⓝ Tram: 3B, 3T

Privatbanken Jugendsali (Jugend Hall)
Jugendstil meets medieval in this 1904 interior by architect Lars Sonck. Romanesque churches seem to inspire the banking hall's low vaulting and three 'naves', but the similarities end there. Sonck uses the stone itself as a decorative material, sometimes rough-surfaced and rusticated, or polished to a high gloss in the

muscular pillars. Relief carvings in their capitals are reminiscent of Viking ship prows, a popular Scandinavian theme but not frequently seen in Finland. Today the building houses the tourist office. ⓐ Pohjoisesplanadi 19 ⓣ (09) 310 13800 ⓛ 09.00–17.00 Mon–Fri, 11.00–17.00 Sun, Aug–June; 09.00–16.00 Mon–Fri, July ⓝ Tram: 3B, 3T

Senaatintori (Senate Square)

Up the hill behind the market, its dome visible above the row of intervening buildings, the majestic neoclassical Lutheran Cathedral is the focal point of Senate Square. The buildings at its adjoining sides, also by C L Engel, create an unusually unified public space – and one of Europe's finest squares. It's a well used one, too, for celebrations that range from Finland's Independence Day to the start of the St Lucia Parade before Christmas. The early 19th-century cathedral, with its tall green dome, stands high above the square, at the top of a long flight of steps. Sederholm House, the oldest stone building in Helsinki, faces the lower corner of the square. ⓐ Intersection of Unioninkatu and Aleksanterinkatu streets ⓛ Cathedral 09.00–24.00 summer; 09.00–18.00 winter ⓝ Tram: 3T, 7A, 7B

Tropicario

This is the most modern and exciting tropical terrarium in Scandinavia. It boasts fantastic examples of some amazing flora and fauna, including crocs, snakes and lizards of all types, with which you can interact up close and personal. This plot of Finnish jungle really isn't one for the phobic, but everybody else will have a roaring good time. ⓐ Sturenkatu 27 ⓣ (09) 750 076 ⓦ www.tropicario.com ⓛ 10.00–20.00 Sept–Apr; 10.00–18.00 May–Aug ⓝ Metro: Sörnäinen; tram: 1, 1A, 7A, 7B

Uspenski Cathedral

Dominating the far side of the harbour is western Europe's largest
Orthodox church, an ornate brick pile whose dome and towers are
crowned by 13 gold cupolas. The interior is a wondrous cavern of
icons, crosses, altars and gleaming gold, its intricately decorated
arches offset by black marble columns. Along with serving the large
Russian population, the church marks Helsinki's long-standing Russian
influence. ⓐ Kanavakatu 1 ⓣ (0) 207 220 683 ⓛ 09.30–16.00 Mon–Fri,
09.30–14.00 Sat, 12.00–15.00 Sun, May–Sept; 09.30–16.00 Tues–Fri,
09.30–14.00 Sat, 12.00–15.00 Sun, Oct–Apr ⓝ Bus/tram: 4, 4T, 13

CULTURE

A high concentration of the city's many museums lies in this central
area; all are within easy walking distance of each other. The Helsinki
Card admits visitors to nearly all of these, as well as to other attractions.

Amos Anderson Art Museum

This features mainly 20th-century Finnish art and furnishings from
Amos Anderson's private collections. There is also Finnish and foreign
art from the collection of the architect Sigurd Frosterus. As one would
expect, both exhibit excellent taste. Watch out for special exhibitions.
ⓐ Yrjönkatu 27 ⓣ (09) 684 4460 ⓛ 10.00–18.00 Mon–Fri, 11.00–17.00
Sat & Sun ⓝ Metro: Rautatientori

Ateneum

The building is a beautiful setting for Finnish painting, sculpture,
graphics and drawings, as well as international art. Internationally it
is strong in works from the 19th and early 20th centuries, including
those of Gauguin, Modigliani and Degas. ⓐ Kaivokatu 2 (opposite

railway station) ☎ (09) 1733 6401 Ⓦ www.ateneum.fi 🕐 09.00–18.00
Tues & Fri, 09.00–20.00 Wed & Thur, 11.00–17.00 Sat & Sun
Ⓜ Metro: Rautatientori. Admission charge

Design District Helsinki
The area around Diana Park is full of design and antique shops,
fashion stores, museums, art galleries, restaurants and showrooms.
Here you can find fascinating examples of the work of the people
who really matter. For an immediate immersion into the aesthetic
that governs Finnish design, one could do a lot worse than pay
a visit to this area. Guided walking tours of the Design District
Helsinki are organised by a company called Helsinki Expert.
Walks start from the Esplanade Park on Mondays and Fridays
at 14.00. For an up-to-date list of participating venues and
artists check Ⓦ www.designdistrict.fi

Designmuseo (Design Museum)
Nowhere is the evolution of decorative styles better illustrated
than in the ground-floor gallery of this Design Museum.
Decorative arts in ceramics, glass, metal, fabrics, furniture,
utensils, and décor show how various style periods interpreted
these items. So if you are unclear just how Victorian gave
way to art nouveau and how that morphed into art deco and
modernism, you can see side-by-side examples. Although the
primary focus is on Finnish design, special exhibitions may feature
other designers or themes. The shop is a treasure box of quality
design gifts and books. ⊙ Korkeavuorenkatu 23 ☎ (09) 622 0540
Ⓦ www.designmuseo.fi ✉ info@designmuseo.fi 🕐 11.00–20.00
June–Aug; 11.00–20.00 Tues, 11.00–18.00 Wed–Sun, Sept–May
Ⓝ Bus: 17; tram: 10. Admission charge

Kiasma (Museum of Contemporary Art)

The home of Finnish modern art is, like the city's other art museums, as much about the building as its contents. Designed by the American architect Steven Holl, the curvy Kiasma opened in 1998, and is considered one of Finland's paramount works of modern architecture – no small feat in the native land of so many well-known architects. It contains a theatre for experimental drama, dance and music, as well as collections of post-1960 Finnish art. Mannerheiminaukio 2 (09) 173 36501 www.kiasma.fi 09.00–17.00 Tues, 10.00–20.30 Wed–Sun Metro: Rautatientori. Admission charge

Museum of Finnish Architecture

Special exhibitions highlight Finnish architects past and present, as well as the styles they created and influenced. Kasarmikatu 24 (09) 8567 5100 www.mfa.fi 10.00–16.00 Tues & Thur–Sun, 10.00–20.00 Wed Bus: 17; tram: 10. Admission charge

National Museum of Finland

Your first stop to learn about Finnish culture and traditions, the museum also covers Finland's history from prehistoric to the present. Historical artefacts and ethnographic collections illustrate daily life as well as events. Like the Ateneum, the building itself is a landmark, designed by the pre-eminent firm of Saarinen, Lindgren & Gesellius in 1902. Mannerheimintie 34 (09) 4050 9544 www.nba.fi 11.00–20.00 Tues & Wed, 11.00–18.00 Thur–Sun Bus/tram: 4, 4T, 7, 10. Admission charge

Sederholm House

Overlooking Senate Square, this is the central city's oldest stone building (built in 1757). It contains exhibitions from various city

74

museums. Aleksanterinkatu 16–18 (09) 3103 6529 11.00–17.00 Wed–Sun Bus/tram: 1, 3T, 3B, 4. Admission charge

RETAIL THERAPY

The Esplanadi and the streets north – Mannerheimintie, Aleksanterinkatu and Kaisaniemenkatu – are lined with the smartest shops, featuring the best in Finnish design. Just browsing their stunningly arranged windows is an art experience. On Senate Square and the streets around it you will find boutiques selling handicrafts and folk arts. In good weather, Market Square is filled with stalls of crafts and other local goods. You could shop till you drop without leaving this small area of Helsinki – take tram 4 or 10 here then explore on foot.

Aarikka Finland Clever, irresistible creations from wood include Christmas decorations, home décor, jewellery and whimsical utensils. Pohjoisesplanadi 27 www.aarikka.com

Artek Furniture designed by Alvar Aalto forms the centrepiece, with other interior décor including rugs, linens, decorative fabrics and tableware. Eteläesplanadi 18 (09) 6132 5277 10.00–18.00 Mon–Fri, 10.00–16.00 Sat

Design Forum To see – and buy – what's new and hot, shop at Design Forum, where useful items from notebooks to kitchen appliances are practical, as well as beautiful and stylish, proving that Finnish design isn't just another pretty face. Erottajankatu 7 (09) 6220 8130 www.designforum.fi 10.00–19.00 Mon–Fri, 10.00–18.00 Sat, 12.00–18.00 Sun

CHRISTMAS MARKETS

Every Finnish school child knows that Santa lives in Finland, just south of Rovaniemi, near the Arctic Circle. Many have visited him there. The village where he lives with his elves and reindeer, is open all year, except 24 December, but you don't have to go all the way to the Arctic Circle to find the Finns celebrating the Christmas season.

It begins early in December with the Christmas market that springs up like a little village on the Esplanadi. Helsinki's St Thomas Market forms a double row of bright tents, each outlined in tiny twinkling white lights. Step inside each one to find a tiny, brightly lit shop filled with beautiful hand-made gifts: woodcarvings, knitted hats and mittens, gingerbread, wrought ironwork, fanciful candles, woven scarves, wooden toys, fur hats, blown glass or jars of shimmering lingonberry jelly.

Designers Gallery This is the place to be inspired by top quality modern fashion for women as envisaged by prize-winning Finnish designers such as Iris Aalto, Ilona Pelli and Tarja Niskanen ⓐ Kauppatori, Eteläesplanadi 4/Unioninkatu 26 ⓣ (050) 340 8290 ⓛ 11.00–18.00 Mon–Fri, 11.00–15.00 Sat

Hakaniemi Market Hall Textiles and handicrafts fill the small shops on the upper floor above the food hall. A daily open-air market lines the square outside. ⓐ Hakaniemi ⓛ 08.00–18.00 Mon–Fri, 08.00–16.00 Sat ⓝ Bus/tram: 68, 23N or 97N

Brightly painted wooden puzzles come in shapes of fish, turtles, rabbits and hedgehogs. Velvet-smooth wooden cooking utensils – spatulas, forks, spoons and spreaders – are carved in graceful flowing shapes, from richly grained woods. Cups are formed from the gnarly-grained tree burls and cutting boards show off a variety of local woods in contrasting stripes. More rustic are the Christmas elves made of small angle-cut logs, with beards of curly yarn and peaked caps of bright felt. Smaller elves of wool perch everywhere.

A warmer venue for a craft show is the **Women's Christmas Fair**, at the Wanha Satama, across Helsinki's harbour (🕐 10.00–19.00, 2–6 Dec 🚊 Tram: 4, 4T). The variety is astonishing, from stacks of beeswax candles and creamy Finnish honey to elegant painted silks, hobby-horses, finger puppets, fashionable knitwear and cheery little red-hatted elves, all created by Finnish women.

Marimekko Famed for striking decorator fabrics, Marimekko also leads the design world with tableware, bags and wearables. 🅰 Pohjoisesplanadi 2 and 31, and other locations 🅰 Kamppi Shopping Centre, Urhu Kekkosen Katu 1 🕐 (0) 10 344 3300 🌐 www.marimekko.com 🕐 variable, so phone to check

Sokos Slightly less rarified than Stockmann, but with a wide variety of high-quality Finnish and Scandinavian goods, from fashions to furnishings, Sokos is near the railway station. 🅰 Mannerheimintie 9 🕐 (0) 10 766 5100 🕐 09.00–21.00 Mon–Fri, 09.00–18.00 Sat, 12.00–21.00 Sun

⬘ *The Design Forum is Finland's shop window to the world*

Stockmann Even an entire city block can't hold all the merchandise, which overflows into the Academic Bookstore, across Keskuskatu (and connected by a tunnel), in a building designed by Alvar Aalto. ⓐ Corner of Aleksanterinkatu and Mannerheimintie Ⓦ www.stockmann.fi Ⓛ 09.00–21.00 Mon–Fri, 12.00–18.00 Sat & Sun

TAKING A BREAK

Central Helsinki is filled with cafés, from elegant Old World settings to cafés in shops, museums and even a ship in the harbour. In the summer many of them move outdoors to enjoy the long daylight hours.

Kauppatorin Kahvila £ ❶ In a bright orange tent in the market, but warm inside even on blustery snow-filled days, this is a favourite of local politicos, who come for the coffee and the outstanding meat pies. ⓐ Kauppatori Ⓣ (09) 411 10284 Ⓛ 06.00–14.00 Mon–Sat Ⓝ Tram: 4, 10

Kipinä £ ❷ Unreserved atmosphere, cosy interior, excellent home-made food and the friendly and professional service will guarantee an unforgettable time. ⓐ Vuorikatu 16 Ⓣ (09) 670 089 Ⓛ 11.00–24.00 Mon–Wed, 11.00–02.00 Thur–Fri, 15.00–02.00 Sat Ⓝ Tram: 10

Restaurant Eliel £ ❸ You might not choose a railway station for a meal, but this café is very popular with locals and visitors for good food and low prices. Breakfast is served until late morning, the buffet lunch until late afternoon; there's a full evening menu. ⓐ Rautatieasema Ⓣ (09) 707 4943 Ⓛ 07.00–24.00 Mon–Sat, 08.00–24.00 Sun Ⓝ Metro: Rautatientori

Baker's Bar & Restaurant ££ ❹ Baker's is a versatile restaurant complex in the heart of Helsinki. On the international menu you'll find season's specialities as well as Finnish classics. During the week, a delicious buffet lunch is set from 11.00 till 14.00. A mouthwatering selection of different kinds of breads awaits all the gourmets.
ⓐ Mannerheimintie 12 ❶ (09) 6126 330 ● 11.00–23.00 Mon & Tues, 11.00–24.00 Wed–Fri, 13.00–24.00 Sat, 13.00–04.00 Sun ⓝ Tram: 10

Café Aalto ££ ❺ On the balcony of the Academic Bookstore, the café overlooks the interior designed by Finnish design-meister Alvar Aalto. Relax with a book over coffee or have lunch here. The pastries are baked in-house. ⓐ Pohjoisesplanadi 39 ❶ (09) 121 41 ● 09.00–21.00 Mon–Fri, 09.00–18.00 Sat ⓝ Tram: 4, 10

▲ *Café Kappeli – a landmark on the Esplanadi*

Café Ateneum ££ ❻ The smoke-free café in the Ateneum museum serves inexpensive vegetarian dishes at lunch, along with soups, sandwiches and pastries. . ❷ Rautatientori ❶ (09) 1733 6231 ❸ 10.00–17.30 Tues & Fri, 11.00–19.30 Wed & Thur, 11.00–16.30 Sat & Sun ❹ Metro: Rautatientori

Café Engel ££ ❼ In the dark days of a northern winter, this cheering café is brightly illuminated with 'daylight' bulbs. The coffee menu is long and the lingonberry pie is mouthwatering. ❷ Aleksanterinkatu 26 ❶ (09) 652 776 ❸ 07.30–24.00 Mon–Fri, 09.30–24.00 Sat, 11.00–24.00 Sun ❹ Bus/tram: 1, 3T, 3B, 4

Café Esplanad ££ ❽ You'd expect high prices at this Esplanadi terrace, but the sandwiches, pastries, soups and salads are quite reasonable. Add smokeless air and occasional live jazz, and it's no wonder the place is popular. Minimum age is 20 in the evenings. ❷ Pohjoisesplanadi 37 ❶ (09) 665 496 ❸ 08.00–22.00 Mon–Sat, 10.00–22.00 Sun ❹ Tram: 4, 10

Café Kappeli ££ ❾ The beautiful building is a Helsinki landmark, and in the summer its terrace is always filled – especially during concerts on the adjacent Espa stage. Cakes are stunning (and stunningly pricey), and the cellar pub serves the café's own beer. ❷ Eteläesplanadi 1 ❶ (09) 681 2440 ❹ Tram: 4, 10

Karl Fazer Cafe ££ ❿ The venerable Fazer specialises in Franco-Russian cuisine. If you want to go posh, try the French delights; if you want to go modern, the lunch menu is for you. The desserts are peerless. ❷ Kluuvikatu 3 ❶ 020 729 6702 ❺ www.fazer.fi ❸ 07.30–22.00 Mon–Fri, 09.00–22.00 Sat ❹ Metro: Kaisaniemi

Memphis ££ ⑪ This venue presents a hotch-potch of cuisines that's rather too complex to be termed as fusion: the major influences are Indian, American and Latin, and it's the skill with which they're combined that really makes everything work. ⓐ Kluuvikatu 8 ⓣ (09) 4332 6310 ⓛ 11.00–24.00 Mon & Tues, 11.00–01.00 Wed & Thur, 11.00–03.00 Fri, 12.00–03.00 Sat, 13.00–24.00 Sun ⓝ Metro: Kaisaniemi

AFTER DARK

Friday and Saturday are the big nights for partying, but Wednesday is also popular for clubs. Book ahead for dinner at the more sought after restaurants in the city centre at weekends or in the summer.

RESTAURANTS

Filmitähti ££ ⑫ This, Finland's first movie restaurant, has had great reviews for its traditional fare and imaginative drinks. ⓐ Erottajankatu 4 ⓣ (020) 7704 712 ⓛ 11.00–23.00 Mon–Thur, 11.00–23.00 Fri, 12.00–03.00 Sat ⓝ Tram: 10

Via ££ ⑬ Here you'll find Italian and Asian cuisine served in the suavest of atmospheres. The star offering is the antipasti, and there are excellent vegetarian meals, too. ⓐ Ludviginkatu 6–8 ⓣ (09) 681 1370 ⓦ www.viaravintola.com ⓛ 11.00–24.00 Mon–Sat, Wine bar 15.00–24.00 Mon–Thur, 15.00–02.00 Fri & Sat ⓝ Tram: 10

G W Sundmans £££ ⑭ One of Finland's oldest restaurants, and still one of its best, Sundmans occupies a beautifully restored former mansion. Art nouveau interior details are soon forgotten as the food arrives, from the heavenly terrines with woodland mushrooms to the dessert of Arctic cloudberries. ⓐ Eteläranta 16 (facing the

harbour) ❶ (09) 622 6410 ⏰ 11.00–23.30 Mon–Fri, 18.00–24.00 Sat
🚋 Tram: 4, 7B

Sasso £££ ⓯ From the smart, stylish doorway on Market Square to the
stunning presentation, Sasso combines Italian cooking with Finnish
design. It's a happy mixture, and the food is always paramount,
as Nordic ingredients join imported Italian. ➌ Pohjoisesplanadi 17
❶ (09) 1345 6240 🚋 Tram: 4, 7B

Sipuli £££ ⓰ The skylight looks straight up at the domes of Uspenski
Cathedral. Nordic ingredients from the sea and forest are elegantly
prepared – a frothy pumpkin soup is sprinkled with roasted nuts,
and fried scallops are paired with fennel purée and pomegranate
vinaigrette. ➌ Kanavaranta 7 ❶ (09) 622 9280 ⏰ 18.00–24.00 Mon–Fri
🚋 Bus/tram: 4, 4T, 13

BARS & CLUBS
Bar and Library, Hotel Kämp The Hotel Kämp is the classiest place in
town, and this is its classiest place for a drink. Forbes voted it among
the best hotel bars in the world and you won't disagree. Kamp Brasserie
and Wine Bar is a nice venue for a glass of wine, with 100 varieties
sold by the glass from €4. ➌ Pohjoisesplanadi 29 ❶ (09) 576 1111
🚇 Metro: Kaisaniemi

Gaselli Patrons here can enjoy an extensive range of tapped
beers and over 40 bottled products. Finnish pop and rock is
often played in this relaxed venue, but don't let that put you off.
➌ Aleksanterinkatu 46 ❶ (09) 8568 5760 ⏰ 16.00–21.00 Tues,
16.00–02.00 Wed–Thur, 16.00–03.00 Fri, 18.00–03.00 Sat
🚋 Tram: 4, 7B

Helsinki Club Large and stylish, the nightclub of the Hotel Helsinki has five bars and a dance floor. Occasional live music replaces the usual DJ playing Euro hits. Pay admission on busy nights; minimum age 24. Yliopistonkatu 8 (020) 1234601 www.helsinkiclub.com 23.00–04.00 Sun–Tues, 22.00–04.00 Wed–Sat Tram: 4, 7B

Mecca This joint positively exudes soul, and the vast selection of cocktails only helps this spiritual dimension. There's a DJ from Wednesday to Saturday. Korkeavuorenkatu 34 (09) 1345 6200 www.mecca.fi 16.00–24.00 Mon & Tues, 16.00–02.00 Wed & Thur, 16.00–04.00 Fri & Sat Tram: 4; bus: 42

Redrum Name the type of music that gets you going and you'll find it in this wood-panelled club that boasts superb acoustics and a nifty sound system by Funktion-One. Vuorikatu 2 www.redrum.fi 22.00–04.00 Tram: 4, 7B

ENTERTAINMENT
Finlandia Hall Classical music fills the programme at Finlandia Hall, home venue of the Helsingin kaupunginorkesteri (Helsinki Philharmonic Orchestra) and the Radion sinfoniaorkesteri (Radio Symphony Orchestra). Mannerheimintie 13 E (09) 402 41 www.finlandiatalo.fi 09.00–16.00 Mon–Fri Bus/tram: 4, 4T, 7, 10

Helsingin Kaupunginteatterin Tanssiryhmä (Contemporary Dance Theatre)
Finland's largest modern dance ensemble performs at various city stages, but mostly at the Helsinki City Theatre. Eläintarhantie 5 in Hakaniemi, across Eläintarha to the north of the railway station.

Tickets: ⓔ Ensi linja 2 ⓔ Eläintarhantie 5 ⓣ (09) 394 022 ⓦ www.hkt.fi
ⓛ 12.00–19.00 Sat ⓝ Tram: 1, 1A, 3T, 3B, 7A, 7B

Kinopalatsi For American mainstream and occasional European films, check the ten screens at this new multi-level cinema complex near the railway station. Tickets are discounted for weekday matinées. Cafés, Wi-Fi, shops and game arcades complete the centre. ⓐ Kaisaniemenkatu 2 ⓣ (09) 0600 94444 ⓦ www.kinopalatsi.fi ⓛ from 11.00 daily ⓝ Metro: Kaisaniemi

Lasipalatsi This has become a magnet for all cultural and creative phenomena, and it also doubles as a multimedia shopping centre. It boasts a great library. ⓐ Mannerheimintie 22-24 ⓣ (09) 6126 570 ⓦ www.lasipalatsi.fi ⓝ Metro: Rautatientori

Suomen Kansallisbaletit (National Ballet) Performances are at the Opera House, a state-of-the-art performance venue completed in 1993. Ballet favourites as well as lesser-known works are performed, with leading choreographers. ⓐ Helsinginkatu 58 ⓣ (09) 4030 21 ⓦ www.operafin.fi ⓛ Box office 09.00–18.00 Mon–Fri, 15.00–18.00 Sat ⓝ Tram: 3B, 3T, 4, 7A, 7B, 10

Suomen Kansallisooppera (National Opera) The dozen productions each season include many classical favourites. The modern stage is among Europe's finest, with revolving floor, flexible mirrored ceiling and other techno tricks. Behind-the-scene tours are offered Tuesday and Thursday at 14.30. Tickets begin as low as €12, and some performances are free. ⓐ Helsinginkatu 58 ⓣ (09) 4030 21 ⓦ www.operafin.fi ⓛ Box office 09.00–18.00 Mon–Fri, 15.00–18.00 Sat ⓝ Tram: 3B, 3T, 4, 7A, 7B, 10

Western & northern Helsinki

The broad Mannerheimintie slices the part of Helsinki lying north of the Esplanadi neatly in half. Although it may seem as though everything you could want is on the harbour (eastern) side of that line, there is a lot more to see if you cross it. Fewer museums and attractions, perhaps, but more of the city's colourful nightlife and a great deal of its shopping lie in the streets adjoining Uudenmankatu, Lönnrotinkatu and the shopping street of Frederikinkatu. Some of the city's most frequently visited attractions are in this area. Among these are the Temppeliaukio (Church in the Rock), the Olympic Tower and Finland's most popular amusement park.

SIGHTS & ATTRACTIONS

Hietaniemi Cemetery

On All Saints, Christmas and Independence Day, Finns visit cemeteries not only to remember loved ones, but also to honour national heroes and those fallen in wars. Along with the public observations, it's a personal thing with many Finns to remember those who died for their country or who contributed to culture or public life. Hietaniemi is especially busy on 6 December, Independence Day, when the march of students to Senate Square begins here. Buried in its elegant park setting, along with a clutch of presidents in Statesman's Grove, is Marshal Mannerheim, Commander-in-chief of Finnish forces in the war that gained Finland freedom from Russia in 1939. Architects Alvar Aalto and Engel, and artist Albert Edelfelt rest on Artists Hill.
ⓐ Mechelininkatu ⓝ Tram/bus: 8, 15A

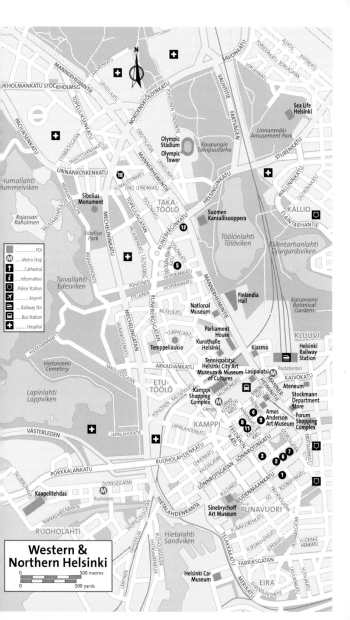

Western & Northern Helsinki

0 ————— 500 metres
0 ————— 500 yards

POI
Ⓜ ....Metro Stop
✝ ....Cathedral
ℹ ....Information
🛡 ....Police Station
✈ ....Airport
🚉 ....Railway Stn
🚌 ....Bus Station
✚ ....Hospital

Sea Life Helsinki

Linnanmäki Amusement Park

Olympic Stadium
Olympic Tower

Kaupungin Talvipuutarha

Sibelius Monument

TAKA-TÖÖLÖ

Suomen Kansallisooppera

Sibelius Park

Töölönlahti Tölöviken

Eläintarhanlahti Djurgardsviken

Rajasaari Raholmen

Humallahti Hummelviken

Taivallahti Edesviken

Finlandia Hall

Kaisaniemi Botanical Gardens

KLUUVI

National Museum

Hietaniemi Cemetery

Parliament House
Kunsthalle Helsinki

Kiasma

Helsinki Railway Station

Temppeliaukio

Lapinlahti Lappviken

Tennispalatsi, Helsinki City Art Museum & Museum of Cultures

Lasipalatsi

Ateneum

Stockmann Department Store

ETU-TÖÖLÖ

Kampp Shopping Complex

Amos Anderson Art Museum

Forum Shopping Complex

KAMPPI

VÄSTERLEDEN

Kaapelitehdas

Ruoholahti

Sinebrychoff Art Museum

PUNAVUORI

RUOHOLAHTI

Hietalahti Sandviken

EIRA

Helsinki Car Museum

Kaupungin Talvipuutarha (Winter Garden)

Near the Olympic Stadium, this vast collection of glasshouses is a tropical paradise perfect for a winter's day. Step inside to stroll beneath towering palms and Norfolk Island pines, and to revel in the passion flowers and camellias that bloom through the winter. Christmas and Easter bring indoor displays of flowers and in the summer the outdoor rose gardens are spectacular. ⓐ Hammarskjöldintie 1 ⓘ (09) 166 5410 ⓒ 09.00–15.00 Tues, 12.00–15.00 Wed–Fri, 12.00–16.00 Sat & Sun ⓝ Tram 8

Linnanmäki Amusement Park

From the original 1951 wooden roller coaster to the latest in high-tech thrills, Linnanmäki is fun for all ages. In addition to the 17 major rides and 14 kiddie rides, the park has a fun house, hall of mirrors and a toy museum. The park is run by group of children's charities and ticket money goes to a good cause. Live shows are performed daily on the outdoor stage and a free play area, Fairytale Valley, is always there for children. ⓐ Tivolikuja 1 ⓘ (09) 773 991 ⓦ www.linnanmaki.fi ⓒ hours vary, May–early Sept ⓝ Tram: 3B; bus: 17. Rides charged separately or with general pass

Olympic Stadion (Stadium)

Built in 1938 by functionalist architects Yrjö Lindegren and Toivo Jäntti, for the 1940 Olympics, the stadium was not used because World War II intervened and the Games were cancelled. It was not until the summer of 1952 that the Olympics finally came to the stadium, which is now a venue for athletic and music events. Outside is a statue of runner Paavo Nurmi, 'The Flying Finn', who

---

⏵ *The Olympic Tower is the epitome of 1930s style*

won the gold medal, and carried the Olympic torch the last lap into the stadium for the 1952 Olympiad. The stadium's 72 m (236 ft) tower gives a panoramic view of the city and over the Gulf of Finland, and also at the stadium is the Museum of Finnish Sports. ❸ Paavo Nurmentie 1. Tower ❶ (09) 436 601 ❿ www.stadion.fi ◷ 09.00–20.00 Mon–Fri, 09.00–18.00 Sat & Sun (closed during events). Museum ❶ (09) 434 2250 ❿ www.urheilumuseo.org ◷ 11.00–19.00 Mon–Fri, 12.00–16.00 Sat & Sun ❻ Tram/bus: 3T, 3B, 4, 4T, 7A, 7B. Admission charge

Sea Life Helsinki

The underwater world of the local Baltic waters, the Arctic and the tropical seas are explored in this series of underwater exhibits. A transparent tunnel takes visitors through these underwater

◔ *Some like it, some don't, but you can't ignore the Sibelius Monument*

worlds to see creatures from starfish to sharks. Environmental impact of human activity is a major theme, dealing with issues such as pollution and the unrestrained harvesting of fish. Be there for the feeding times at 12.30 for tropical reef (Wednesday 18.00) and 14.30 for the ocean tank. ⓐ Tivolitie 10 ⓣ (09) 565 8200 ⓦ www.sealife.fi ⓛ 10.00–17.00 Thur–Tues, 10.00–20.00 Wed, Oct–Apr; 10.00–19.00 Mon–Sat, 10.00–17.00 Sun, May & June and Aug & Sept; 10.00–20.00 July ⓝ Tram: 3B; bus: 17. Admission charge

Sibelius Monument

The great Finnish composer once said that 'Nobody erects a monument to a critic' – and thus expressed a frustration of artists everywhere. He needn't have worried about his own legacy – not only a monument, but an entire Sibelius Park to accommodate it – although the critics had much to say about the monument. Designed by Eila Hiltunen, it was unveiled in 1967, and was immediately subjected to a barrage of criticism. Composed of a collection of large metal pipes that catch the wind, the monument creates its own music. Later, in response to the complaints that people didn't 'identify' with the composer through this monument, a more conventional statue of him was added. The park is a nice place to stroll or take a picnic. ⓐ Sibelius Park, Mechelininkatu 38 (Taka-Töölö) ⓛ daylight hours ⓝ Bus: 18, 24, 42

Temppeliaukio (Church in the Rock)

Nowhere is the Finns' fascination with architectural experiments more evident than in the Church in the Rock, one of the city's most visited attractions. The notion of carving an entire church out of solid rock is not new, but such troglodyte chapels are rarely cut into a relatively small outcrop in the middle of a city. However, that's exactly what architects Timo and Tuomo Suomalainen did, covering the

excavation with a roof of woven copper connected to concrete spokes. The rounded copper roof offsets the deadening effect of the granite walls, creating extraordinary acoustics for concerts, which can range from Christmas chorales to klezmer groups.
ⓐ Lutherinkatu 3 ❶ (09) 494 698 ❷ 10.00–17.00 Mon & Wed, 10.00–12.45 & 14.15–17.00 Tues, 10.00–20.00 Thur & Fri, 10.00–18.00 Sat, 11.45–13.45 & 15.30–18.00 Sun. Hours may vary to accommodate services and concerts ❷ Bus: 18, 24; tram: 3T

❷ *The city's most unusual church was hollowed out from granite*

CULTURE

Three art museums and one highlighting Finland's relation to other
world cultures are located in the streets west of Mannerheimintie,
an area more known for its shopping and nightlife than its
traditional attractions.

At the far western edge, the Kaapelitehdas (Cable Factory)
is a multi-faceted complex of small museums, with a theatre
and restaurant.

KAAPELITEHDAS (CABLE FACTORY)

The renovated factory overlooking the western docks, a combination of sights under one roof, houses the following trio of small museums and two dance theatre groups, as well as a restaurant. ❸ Tallberginkatu 1 ❶ (09) 4763 8300 Ⓦ www.kaapelitehdas.fi Ⓝ Bus/tram: 8, 15, 20, 21, 65A, 66A. Admission charge

Dance Theatre Hurjaruuth This theatre specialises in children's dance performances. ❶ (09) 565 7250 Ⓦ www.hurjaruuth.fi

Finnish Museum of Photography This museum explores the history and artistry of photography from 1840 to the present. ❶ (09) 686 63621 Ⓦ www.fmp.fi ❶ 11.00–18.00 Tues–Sun

Hotel and Restaurant Museum Take a look at Finnish food and drink traditions. ❶ (09) 6859 3700 Ⓦ www.hotellijaravintolamuseo.fi ❶ 12.00–19.00 Tues–Sun

Theatre Museum This museum offers special exhibits on the history and art of the stage, but its primary focus is on interaction, so visitors can play with the exhibits and try their hand at various forms of theatre art. ❶ 0207 961 670 Ⓦ www.teatterimuseo.fi ❶ 11.00–18.00 Tues–Sun

Zodiak Centre for New Dance This centre is a repertory company that explores trends in dance though regular performances. ❶ (09) 694 4948 Ⓦ www.zodiak.fi

Helsinki Car Museum

If model cars race your engines, don't miss Europe's largest collection of over 3,000 miniature autos. The real things are there, too, and the collection of vintage autos – everything from a 1931 taxi to the cars of Finnish presidents – is enlivened by wax figures of the famous Finns who owned them. ⓐ Munkkisaarenkatu 12 ⓣ (09) 667 123 ⓛ 12.00–15.00 Tues–Sun, Apr–Oct; 12.00–15.00 Thur–Sun, Nov ⓝ Tram: 6. Admission charge

Helsinki City Art Museum

Special exhibitions of Finnish and international art are shown here, often part of an international circuit. ⓐ Tennispalatsi, Salomonkatu 15 (near the bus station) ⓣ (09) 310 87001 ⓦ www.taidemuseo.hel.fi ⓛ 11.00–20.30 Tues–Sun ⓝ Metro: Kamppi. Admission charge

Kunsthalle Helsinki

Changing exhibitions of contemporary art highlight young artists as well as those who have already established a reputation. Taidehallin Klubi, the gallery's restaurant, is open for lunch and evening meals Monday–Saturday and through the evening. The bar is open Monday–Saturday until 02.00. ⓐ Nervanderinkatu 3 ⓣ (09) 454 2060 ⓦ www.taidehalli.fi ⓛ 11.00–18.00 Tues–Fri, 12.00–17.00 Sat & Sun, mid-June–Sept ⓝ Bus: 24. Admission charge

Museum of Cultures

The 'Fetched from Afar' exhibit, new in 2005, is a permanent feature of this museum of ethnic cultures, and it makes the museum more interesting to visitors, since it explores the Finno-Ugric peoples (see page 22), as well as telling the story of other cultures through the work of early Finnish explorers and anthropologists. Part of the exhibit is the early China collection, brought to Finland by traders and seafarers in the early 19th century. ➌ Tennispalatsi, Eteläinen Rautatiekatu 8 ❶ (09) 405 09806 ❹ 11.00–20.00 Tues–Thur, 11.00–18.00 Fri–Sun ◍ Metro: Kamppi. Admission charge

Sinebrychoff Art Museum

Finland's finest collection of Old Masters and other European art from the 1300s to the 1800s is displayed in the furnished mansion of the museum's donors. The rooms, although used as galleries, have fine parquet floors and other interior features. Miniatures and porcelain collections are especially impressive. ➌ Bulevardi 40 ❶ (09) 1733 6460 ❻ www.sinebrychoffintaidemuseo.fi ❹ 10.00–18.00 Tues & Fri, 10.00–20.00 Wed & Thur, 11.00–17.00 Sat & Sun ◍ Tram: 6. Admission charge

RETAIL THERAPY

The lovely Fredrikinkatu and the streets adjoining it are known for their fashion and interior-décor boutiques. Stroll Bulevardi to browse or buy art and antiques. Forum is the biggest shopping complex in the city centre, with more than 100 shops, facing onto Mannerheimintie (number 20) and filling the entire area between it and Yrjönkatu. Kamppi shopping complex has a variety of designer shops, restaurants and cafés. Access to underground bus terminals.

Aero Find a piece of vintage Alvar Aalto, or the work of other Finnish designers in this shop that specialises in 1930–1970 Finnish design and furnishings. ➌ Yrjönkatu 8 ❶ (09) 680 2185 ❻ www.aerodesignfurniture.fi ◍ Bus: 17

Antiq Bulevard It won't be cheap, but it will be good if you find it in this high-class antiquerie. Hours are eccentric, so call or just stop in if it's open. ❸ Vuorimiehenkatu 10 ❶ (09) 647 286 ❻ Bus: 17; tram: 10

Bisarri Here you'll find modern Finnish design alonside glassware, ceramics, textiles and gorgeous utility items. ❸ Annankatu 9 ❶ (09) 611 252 ❿ www.bisarri.fi ❻ Tram: 10

Galerie 1900 Art nouveau's back with a 'V' and, of course, Helsinki's the place to find it. The shop offers lighting fixtures and decor items in Jugendstil and art deco style. ❸ Annankatu 11 ❶ (09) 649 152 ❻ Tram: 10

Helsinki 10 Trendy shop of vintage designer clothes, music and art books. ❸ Eerikinkatu 3 ❶ (01) 05 489801 ❿ www.helsinki10.com ❻ Tram: 10

Hietalahti Flea Market Be prepared to bargain for everything from cut-price clothes to antiques. The latter may include the family treasures of someone settling an estate or just cleaning house, as well as regular dealers. ❸ Hietalahdentori ❶ 08.00–14.00 Mon–Fri, 08.00–15.00 Sat ❻ Tram: 10

Hietalahti Market Hall Architect Selim Lindqvist's historic building, across the square from the flea market, is filled with shops and stalls selling local handicrafts, plus cafés. ❸ Hietalahdentori ❶ 08.00–14.00 Mon–Sat ❻ Tram: 8; bus: 15

Irja Leimu Boutique The clothes that spring from the thimble of Irja Leimu represent uncomplicated Scandinavian design and carefree elegance. Yrjönkatu 34 (09) 694 4611 11.30–17.30 Mon–Fri, 11.00–15.00 Sat www.irjaleimu.fi Bus: 17

Ivana Helsinki Campus Visionary stylish clothes for an easy lifestyle, Ivana's clothes are rich in outdoor themes and designed to be lived in. Uudenmaankatu 15 (09) 622 4422 www.ivanahelsinki.com 11.00–19.00 Mon–Fri, 11.00–16.00 Sat Tram: 10

Le Slip Shop for undergarments at uber-prices, all from the best designers. Annankatu 6 (09) 640 762 11.00–18.00 Mon–Fri, 11.00–15.00 Sat Bus: 17

Limbo Shop Limbo's easy styles flow with the season, from comfortable sundresses in cheery colours to sweats and t-shirts with a sense of humour. Hip clothes don't get more comfortable. Annankatu 13 (09) 644 060 www.limbo.fi Tram: 10

Lux Shop This shop sells one-of-a-kind fashions by creative young designers, including the fashion pieces rich in printing, embroidery and applique by Rinne Niinikoski. Uudenmaankatu 26 (09) 678 538 www.lux-shop.fi 12.00–18.00 Mon–Sat Tram: 3T

Miun You like Finnish designer clothing, jewellery, accessories and ceramic statues? Come here now. Uudenmaankatu 14 (050) 303 0530 www.miun.fi 11.00–18.00 Mon–Fri, 11.00–15.00 Sat Tram: 10

Myymala2 A plain-jane environment where young artists can show their work, Myymala2 has launched several talents, as well as creating a venue for gallery-goers. The boutique is a gold-mine of groovy gifts and funky finds. 🅐 Uudenmaankatu 23 🕿 (041) 7832 327 🅦 www.myymala2.com 🕒 12.00–18.00 Wed–Sat, 12.00–17.00 Sun 🚊 Tram: 10

Popparienkeli Whatever you need in new or used vinyl from the 1950s and 60s or CDs from the 80s onwards, you're likely to find it here. But ask, since not everything is displayed. Look for other music shops in this vicinity. 🅐 Fredrikinkatu 12 🕿 (09) 661 638 🅦 www.popangel.fi 🕒 10.00–18.00 Mon–Fri, 10.00–16.00 Sat 🚊 Tram: 3T

Punavuoren Peikko The coolest shop in Helsinki for kids' clothes and toys. Small labels from Scandinavian designers 🅐 Uudenmaankatu 15 🕿 (045) 120 0823 🅦 www.punavuorenpeikko.fi 🕒 11.00–18.00 Mon–Fri, 11.00–15.00 Sat 🚊 Tram: 10

Stupido Shop If it's on DVD, tape, CD or vinyl, and it's alternative, from humppa to the latest Aavikko, just ask the Stupido guys. 🅐 Iso Roobertinkatu 23 🅦 www.stupido.fi 🕒 09.00–20.00 Mon–Fri, 10.00–18.00 Sat 🚊 Tram: 3T; bus: 17

TAKING A BREAK

The mega-malls Forum and Kamppi both have a number of cafés and small eating places. It's a good rule that wherever shoppers congregate, there will be places to stop for coffee and compare finds.

Belly ££ ❶ If you have a licence to enjoy a bag of nuts and a mocktail, this 1960s- and 1970s-style restaurant has its own James Bond bar. If you like soul and funk, you'll be in double-O heaven. ⓐ Uudenmaankatu 16–20 ⓣ (09) 644 981 ⓦ www.belly.fi ⓛ 10.30–02.00 Mon–Thur, 10.30–04.00 Fri, 18.00–04.00 Sat

Café Bar no. 9 ££ ❷ Cool and trendy place to eat during the day. Good for drinks in the evening as well. ⓐ Uudenmaankatu 9 ⓣ (09) 621 4059 ⓦ www.bar9.net ⓛ 11.00–02.00 Mon–Fri, 12.00–02.00 Sat–Sun ⓝ Tram: 10

Café Ekberg ££ ❸ Helsinki's oldest café, Ekberg isn't just a period piece, it's a bit of romantic old Europe. Reminiscent of between-the-

● *People enjoy drinks at an outdoor café on Aleksanterinkatu*

wars Vienna, it's the kind of place you expect to see writers working on their books. They serve a breakfast buffet, lunch, light meals and tasty pastries or a glass of something in between. ③ Bulevardi 9 ① (09) 605 269 ● 07.30–20.00 Mon–Fri, 08.30–17.00 Sat, 10.00–17.00 Sun ⊗ Tram: 3T

O'Malley's ££ ④ A Finnish take on an Irish pub, but a good stop for a pint if you're over 20. ③ Sokos Hotel, Yrjönkatu 26 ① (09) 4336 6330 ● 16.00–01.00 Mon–Thur, 16.00–02.00 Fri & Sat, 18.00–midnight Sun ⊗ Bus: 17

Tin Tin Tango ££ ⑤ Something for everyone in this combination bar, self-serve laudromat, art gallery and sauna in the Töölö neighbourhood. ③ Töölöntorinkatu 7 ① (09) 2709 0972 ● 07.00–24.00 Mon–Fri, 10.00–02.00 Sat & Sun ⊗ Tram: 37; bus: 42

AFTER DARK

Along with having some of the hottest clubs and entertainment venues in the city, the neighbourhoods away from the Esplanadi are also the 'low rent district' for bars and pubs. Iso Roobertinkatu is known for its restaurants, pubs and bars, which fill almost the entire street. While a number of places have age limits that cut out those below 20 or 24, most of the places around the Kamppi metro station do not, so traditionally, this is where the under-20s hang out.

RESTAURANTS

Rafla ££ ⑥ Modern European cuisine with a touch of French and Scandinavian home cooking. Excellent espresso, good wines

and nice atmosphere. ⓐ Uudenmaankatu 9 ⓣ (09) 6124 2244
ⓦ www.ravintolarafla.fi ⓛ 11.00–02.00 Mon–Fri, 13.00–02.00 Sat
Ⓝ Tram: 10

Demo ££–£££ ❼ High-class home-made food combined with
personal and friendly service. Recently awarded a Michelin star.
ⓐ Uudenmaankatu 9–11 ⓣ (09) 2289 0840 ⓦ www.restaurantdemo.fi
ⓛ 16.00–23.00 Tues–Sat Ⓝ Tram: 10

Helmi ££–£££ ❽ The stylish décor sets the tone for equally well
designed dishes. The inspiration is global and eclectic, and the
vegetarian dishes are as well planned and original as the other choices
– taro chips and mushroom mousse might accompany a tofu steak.
Even the plain-sounding dish of chicken and vegetables is a winner.
Minimum age is 24. ⓐ Eerikinkatu 14 ⓣ (09) 612 6410 ⓛ 17.00–24.00
Tues–Thur, 17.00–04.00 Fri & Sat Ⓝ Metro: Kamppi

Lappi ££–£££ ❾ Not just Finnish, but only those dishes originating
in Lapland are the speciality of this cosy restaurant. Reindeer and
other game meats are featured, along with salmon in several forms
and boutique farm-made cheeses. The authentic atmosphere of
natural wood furnishings and soft lighting is pleasant, too.
ⓐ Annankatu 22 ⓣ (09) 645 550 Ⓝ Tram: 10

Lehtovaara ££–£££ ❿ The menu speaks for itself at this exceptional
restaurant near the Sibelius Park: fillet of beef with deep-fried garlic
potatoes, garlic butter and fried fresh mushroom slices, lightly
smoked Arctic char with lobster ravioli or snowgrouse breast with
a cake of root vegetables and potato. Vegetarians might be offered
cheese polenta with ginger-braised vegetables. ⓐ Mechelininkatu

39 (09) 440 833 ◔ 11.00–24.00 Mon–Fri, 16.00–24.00 Sat,
13.00–21.00 Sun ⓝ Bus: 18, 24, 42

George £££ ⓫ This restaurant earns its international renown
by virtue of customer service alone. The food will win inter-planetary
praise if there's anybody out there. ⓐ Kalevankatu 17 ☎ 010 270 1702
◔ 17.00–24.00 Mon, 11.00–15.00 Tues–Fri, 17.00–24.00 Sat,
18.00–24.00 Sun ⓝ Metro: Kamppi

Ravintola Carelia £££ ⓬ The wine list alone is staggering, with over
300 varieties, including 50 different champagnes, making it a good
place to stop before or after the opera, just across the street. Menu
choices are just as difficult. Begin maybe with cep soup with thyme
foam, then go on to guinea fowl breast with truffle risotto and bacon.
ⓐ Mannerheimintie 56 ☎ (09) 2709 0976 ◔ 11.00–01.00 Mon–Fri,
16.00–01.00 Sat ⓝ Tram: 7A, 10; bus: 42

BARS & CLUBS

DTM No-one has disputed DTM's claim to be the biggest combo of
gay café, bar, disco and nightclub in Scandinavia. Taking it from the
top, the upstairs has a cruise ship-style dance floor with disco and
traditional dance music on Friday and Saturday. The street level is
a café, with internet access. Downstairs, the nightclub has live
music, dance and shows, with a killer sound system and over-the-
top lighting and video tech. Special nights bring from top drag
shows, bubbling foam parties and more. Minimum age 18 between
18.00 and 21.00; after 21.00 it's 24 (those younger will be ejected).
ⓐ Iso Roobertinkatu 28 ☎ (09) 676 314 ⓦ www.dtm.fi ◔ 09.00–04.00
Mon–Sat, 12.00–04.00 Sun ⓝ Tram: 3B, 3T; bus: 17. Admission charge
from 24.00 Sat

Highlight Nightclub The building has come a long way from a 1878 church to a raucous dance floor with three storeys of nightclub. The second floor has a full view of the centre stage and dance floor. The music has wide appeal, so expect a queue. One of the few popular clubs that admit guests at age 18. ➌ Fredrikinkatu 42 ➊ (09) 694 7775 ➍ www.ravintolahighlight.com ➋ 22.00–04.00 Fri & Sat ➍ Metro: Kamppi. Go between 22.00 and 23.00 for free admission

Labyrinth The jewel in this venue's crown is the large terrace, which, during the summertime, is popular with a football-loving crowd. ➌ Iso Roobertinkatu 3 ➊ (09) 6123 415 ➍ www.barlabyrinth.com ➋ 01.00–02.00 Mon–Thur, 11.00–03.00 Fri & Sat, 18.00–24.00 Sun ➍ Tram: 3T; bus: 17

Lost and Found Gay, straight, whatever. Everyone is welcome and feels at home in this modern restaurant/club/bar/disco. Call it Lostari, to feel like a local. Best to go early, since queues form on the big party nights – Wednesday, Friday, Saturday – before midnight. Age 22 and over. ➌ Annankatu 6 ➊ (09) 680 1010 ➍ www.lostandfound.fi ➋ 16.00–04.00 Sun–Thur, 15.00–04.00 Fri & Sat ➍ Bus: 17

Onnela Big disco, table-dancing and a section for metal, this place is especially popular because the €5 membership card buys you beers for €1 from 23.00 to 01.00 most nights. ➌ Fredrikinkatu 48 ➊ (020) 7759 460 ➍ www.ravintolaonnela.fi ➋ 23.00–04.00 Mon–Wed, 22.00–04.00 Thur–Sat, 23.00–04.00 Sun ➍ Metro: Kamppi

Rose Garden When the others close, everyone heads to this underground club/restaurant for groove, soul, hip-hop, techno and house by DJs and big-name guest performers. Three bars, two dance floors, one cool place to be. ❷ Iso-Roobertinkatu 10 ❶ (09) 678 010 ❿ www.clubrosegarden.com 🕑 22.00–04.00 Fri & Sat Ⓝ Tram: 3T; bus: 17

Stockholm Diskotek This vast new venue (seven bars, no less) is right in the middle of Helsinki, and already it knows how to party. ❷ Simonkatu 8 ❶ (045) 110 3210 🕑 22.00–04.00 Wed–Sun Ⓝ Metro: Kamppi

Storyville The city's premier jazz club, Storyville offers live jazz in an environment that favours listening to the New Orleans-style music and enjoying a drink. The pub upstairs provides a place to wait for the crowd to thin on weekends. ❷ Museokatu 8 ❶ (09) 408 007 🕑 20.00–04.00 Ⓝ Tram: 10; bus: 42. Admission charge

Tavastia You can witness the country's major bands in action at Finland's leading rock venue. ❷ Urho Kekkosen katu 4–6 ❶ (09) 774 67423 ❿ www.tavastiaklubi.fi 🕑 21.00–02.00 Sun–Thur, 21.00–03.00 Fri & Sat Ⓝ Metro: Kamppi

The Club This has become an in-place with the youngsters as it has three bars and reasonable prices. ❷ Simonkatu 6 ❶ (020) 775 9365 ❿ www.theclub.fi 🕑 21.00–04.00 Tues–Sat Ⓝ Metro: Kaisaniemi

ENTERTAINMENT
Tennispalatsi The indoor tennis stadium was built in 1938 for the Olympics that never happened, but the Finns have put it to good use as a sports area and entertainment venue. One of its 14 cinema screens is northern Europe's largest. Look here, too, for cafés and restaurants. ❷ Salomonkatu 15 🕑 Box office from 10.00 Ⓝ Metro: Kamppi

The islands & outskirts

Helsinki sits in an archipelago, and some of its most outstanding attractions are on the islands, including the excellent zoo, an outdoor historical museum and the World Heritage Site of Suomenlinna Fortress. Fortunately, getting to them is quite easy, thanks to ferry and bus services. The ferries to these islands make inexpensive sailing excursions, and are covered by the Helsinki Card (see page 57).

SIGHTS & ATTRACTIONS

Perhaps Helsinki's foremost place to visit is the island fortress of Suomenlinna and the museums, craft studios, restaurants and cliff-edged island itself. Animal lovers will enjoy the zoo, where rare animals have plenty of room to roam. Between the ferries and various excursion boats, there are several ways to view the city from the water and to explore the archipelago.

Boat trips
You can enjoy the views of elegant Helsinki and get a cheap mini-cruise, by taking any of the several ferries that shuttle between Kauppatori (Market Square) and the islands of Suomenlinna and Korkeasaari, where the zoo is located.

The ferry to Korkeasaari continues on to Hakaniemenranta quay in the Kallio neighbourhood behind the railway station, where there is another daily market. Ferries leave Market Square for Suomenlinna 06.00–02.20 daily, and Katajanokka (east of Market Square), and the harbour 07.25–15.25 Mon–Fri. Another ferry leaves from the southern tip of the city (in the Eira neighbourhood), bound for Pihlajasaari, a beach-ringed island west of Suomenlinna. For further information, call **Helsinki City Transport** (❶ (09) 010 0111).

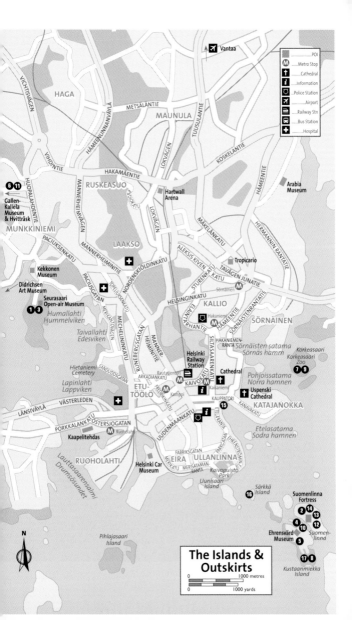

	POI
M	Metro Stop
⊕	Cathedral
i	Information
⊙	Police Station
✈	Airport
☱	Railway Stn
☷	Bus Station
✚	Hospital

▲🚲 **Vantaa**

HAGA

MAUNULA

HAGA
METSÄLÄNTIE
HÄMEENLINNANVÄYLÄ
METSÄNTIE
TUUSULANTIE
LOKVÄGEN
KOSKELANTIE

VICHTISVÄGEN

VIHDINTIE

HAKAMÄENTIE

RUSKEASUO

Hartwall
Arena

HÄMEENTIE

Arabia
Museum

6 11
Gallen-
Kallela
Museum
& Hvitträsk

MANNERHEIMVÄGEN
MANNERHEIMINTIE
LOKVÄGEN

LAAKSO

✚

MÄKELÄNKATU
HERMANNIN RANTATIE

MUNKKINIEMI

PACIUKSENKATU

MANNERHEIMINTIE
NORDENSKIÖLDINKATU

ALEKSIS KIVEN KATU

🚲 Tropicario

TAVAGEN JUNATIE

**Kekkonen
Museum**

PACIUSGATAN
TOPELIUSGATAN
MECHELININKATU

STURENKATU
ELÄINTARHANTIE

STUREN KATU

Sörnäinen **M**

SÖRNÄINEN

Didrichsen
Art Museum

HELSINGINKATU

ELÄINTIE
HÄMEENTIE **M**

1 3

**Seurasaari
Open-air Museum**

KALLIO

Hakaniemi 🚲

SÖRNÄISTENRANTATIE

Korkeasaari
Korkeasaari
Zoo

*Humallahti
Hummelviken*

RUNEBERGSGATAN
RUNEBERGINKATU
MANNER
HEIMINTIE

HÄMEENTIE **M**
HAKANIEMEN-
RANTA

*Sörnäisten satama
Sörnäs hamn*

7 9

*Taivallahti
Edesviken*

**Helsinki
Railway
Station**

SILTASAARENKATU

Cathedral **⊕**

*Pohjoissatama
Norra hamnen*

*Hietaniemi
Cemetery*

SANDUDSGATAN

Rautatientori **M**
ARKADIANKATU
KAIVOKATU

Kaisaniemi

Uspenski
Cathedral **⊕**

*Lapinlahti
Lappviken*

MANNER
HEIMINTIE
HELSINGINKATU

Kamppi **M**
i

KATAJANOKKA
KANAVAKATU

LÄNSIVÄYLÄ
VÄSTERLEDEN

ETU-
TÖÖLÖ

KAUPPATORI

15

*Etelasatama
Sodra hamnen*

✚

UUDENMAANKATU
i

ETELÄRANTA
EHRENSTRÖMIN

PORKKALANKATU
PORKKALAGATAN

Ruoholahti **M**

FABRIKSGATAN

EIRA
ULLANLINNA

*Kaivopuisto
Park*

Kaapelitehdas

FABRIKINKATU
MERISATAMAN
RANTA
MERIKATU

*Uunisaari
Island*

RUOHOLAHTI

**Helsinki Car
Museum**

*Lauttasaarensalmi
Drumsösundet*

16 *Särkkä
Island*

Suomenlinna
Fortress

2 14
13

*Pihlajasaari
Island*

4
10
12

N

**Ehrensvärd
Museum**

*Suomen-
linna*

5

The Islands &
Outskirts

17 8

0				1000 metres
0				1000 yards

*Kustaanmiekka
Island*

A number of traditional cruises ply the waters around Helsinki. **Sun Lines** explores the tree-lined Degerö Canal, Korkeasaari Zoo, the Finnish icebreakers and the cruise ship harbours, along with circling Suomenlinna sea fortress, in comfortable cruisers that offer a coffee and drink bar. ℗ (020) 741 8210 ⓦ www.sunlines.fi ⏰ May–Sept

IHA Lines offer à la carte dining on their boats as they cruise through the archipelago on trips that last from 90 minutes to three hours. Three different routes, each beginning at Market Square, cover the eastern islands or the fortress and surrounding islands. Booking is essential for dining cruises. ℗ (09) 6874 5050 ⓦ www.ihalines.fi ⏰ May–Sept

Along with archipelago cruises, Royal Line offers daily trips to the medieval town of Porvoo in July and August (see page 124).

● *Escape from the city to the tranquility of the forested islands*

Ehrensvärd Museum

The museum, in the former home of the fort's designer and commander Augustin Ehrensvärd, depicts the earliest Swedish period with models, arms, furniture and paintings. The Doll and Toy Museum displays dolls, dollhouses, teddy bears and other toys from 1830 to the present, set in an old Russian villa, well worth seeing in its own right. The 250–ton submarine *Vesikko* was commissioned by the German Navy, but was used by the Finnish Navy from 1936 until the end of World War II. ⓐ Suomenlinna Fortress 🕐 10.00–17.00 mid-May–Aug; 11.00–16.00 Sept Doll and Toy Museum ❶ (09) 668 417 🕐 11.00–17.00

Hvitträsk

If the artistic buzz of the Arts & Crafts and art nouveau period fires your imagination, it's worth the 30 km (18 mile) bus ride to visit the

local shrine to this style, built as home and studio to some of its
most illustrious lights. Designed by architects Herman Gesellius,
Armas Lindgren and Eliel Saarinen, the log-and-stone home is the
epitome of the National Romantic style. The architects all lived and
worked there at some point, and it was here that the plans were
drawn for the Helsinki Railway Station and others of the firm's most
famous works. This was the boyhood home of Eliel's son, Eero Saarinen,
known for designing American buildings and monuments such
as the Gateway Arch in St Louis, Missouri. **❸** Hvitträskintie 166,
Luoma **❶** (09) 4050 9630 **Ⓦ** www.nba.fi **🄻** 11.00–18.00 Apr–Oct;
11.00–17.00 Tues–Sun, Nov–Mar **Ⓝ** Bus: 166 from Kamppi bus
terminal, bay 55, to Hvitträsk. Admission charge

Kekkonen Museum

The home of Finland's most famous president, Urho Kekkonen,
is a fine villa set in a park estate adjacent to the island of Seurasaari.
Tamminiemi Villa was his official residence during his presidency,
from 1956 to 1981. The villa is furnished with outstanding examples
of Finnish design and art, as well as gifts of state. In the summer, the
tour includes the sauna, which was the scene of a number of high-
level meetings between Soviet and Western diplomats during the
Cold War. **❸** Seurasaarentie 15 **❶** (09) 4050 9650 **Ⓦ** www.nba.fi
🄻 11.00–17.00 mid-May–mid-Aug; 11.00–17.00 Wed–Sun,
mid-Aug–mid-May **Ⓝ** Bus: 24. Admission charge

Korkeasaari Zoo

More than just a place for visitors to view exotic wildlife, Helsinki's
zoo is a well-respected leader in the preservation and breeding of
endangered species. Their snow leopard successes are legendary
in zoo annals, and they continue to have rare species of the big cats.

Currently these include, in addition to the snow leopards, Amur tiger, Siberian tiger, of which there are only a few hundred remaining, and the exceedingly rare Asian lion from India. Rare Arctic species include the polar fox and musk ox, whose protection from icy winters includes hair a metre (3 ft) long. Environments represented include tropical rainforests to arctic tundra, and the collections include 200 species of animals, with 1,000 species of plants to make them feel at home. Founded in 1889, it is one of the oldest zoos in the world. ⓐ Korkeasaari ① (09) 169 5969 Ⓦ www.korkeasaari.fi ⓛ 10.00–20.00 May–Sept; 10.00–16.00 Oct–Feb; 10.00–18.00 Mar–Apr. Closed Christmas Eve Ⓝ Ferry from Market Square or Hakaniemi Market May–Sept; bus: 11 summer and winter weekends; on winter weekdays, bus: 16 or metro to Kulosaari, then a 1.5 km (1 mile) walk. Admission charge

Pihlajasaari Island

To get away from it all and luxuriate in the sun on an island in the Gulf of Finland, take the boat to the rocks and beaches of Pihlajasaari. Rent a private changing cabin or bare it all on the nudist beach. (You'll need clothes for the café, and for the boat ride!) ① (09) 534 806 Ⓦ www.jt-line.fi ⓛ May–Sept Ⓝ Boats depart Merisatamanranta.

Seurasaari Open-air Museum

Historic buildings from all over Finland have been moved to this outdoor museum, beautifully insulated from modern-day Helsinki on its own island. The village of 87 buildings centres around the farmstead, a working farm where livestock and crops are raised using old methods. Grander by far is the 18th-century Kahiluoto manor house, with its well-preserved interior, and the parsonage from Iisalmi. The oldest building preserved here is the wooden Karuna church from the 1600s. A regular series of workshops and

programmes highlight folk life and traditional skills for visitors.
ⓐ Seurasaari, FI-00250 ⓣ (09) 4050 9660 ⓞ 09.00–15.00 Mon–Fri,
11.00–17.00 Sat & Sun, late May & early Sept; 11.00–17.00 (until
19.00 Wed), June–Aug; 11.00–17.00 Sat & Sun, mid-Sept–late Nov
ⓝ Bus: 24. Admission charge

Suomenlinna Fortress

One of the world's largest sea fortresses, the 18th-century fort on
Suomenlinna has a fascinating past and an interesting present.
A 15-minute ferry ride from Market Square brings you to the group
of connected islands, where there is enough to occupy an entire day
– and in the summer, an evening, too. It was built in 1847 by the
Swedes, who owned Finland then, to scare off the Russians, who
eventually captured both it and Finland, turning the island's guns
figuratively to the west. The impressive fortifications became
a UNESCO World Heritage Site in 1991.

In the visitor centre a wide-screen show, 'The Suomenlinna
Experience', explores the fortress's long history, in English. Sign up
here for guided walks that help bring all the sites into a whole
picture. In the same building is the museum, which paints a picture
of how officers and soldiers lived during the Swedish and Russian
rules. The fortress was also used by the Finns after independence as
a prison for Communist detainees, a military garrison, a submarine
base and the Valmet shipyard, which made ships as reparations for
the Soviet Union after World War II.

Walking and cycling paths (you must bring cycles from the
mainland as none are hired out here) lead along the cliffs and
to small beaches. Be careful on the cliff paths, since these are
not fenced, and when on the beaches with children, because of
dangerous sudden ship wakes and currents. Various buildings house

studios and shops of glassblowers, potters and other craftsmen.
📞 (09) 684 1880 🌐 www.suomenlinnatours.fi 🕐 10.00–16.00 daily
⛴ Ferries leave Market Square for Suomenlinna 06.00–02.20; Boats
also leave Katajanokka (beyond Uspenski Cathedral) 07.25–15.25 Mon–Fri

Uunisaari Island

Just off the southern tip of the city and reached by boat from
Kompassitorilta (mid-April–mid-Nov) and Ponttoonisilta (mid-Nov–
mid-Apr), both near Kaivopuisto Park, Uunisaari offers sand beaches
with lifeguards, café, restaurant and sauna. The well-protected beach
is a good one for children. 📞 (09) 636 870 🌐 www.uunisaari.com

CULTURE

Arabia Museum

The Arabia company began in 1874, and moved into the design of
modern tableware in the 1930s. But it was not until the 1960s that
it became a worldwide name in smart dinnerware and porcelain
design. Follow the history of this well-known company, along with
the development of Finnish and modern design in home furnishings
in the museum, where 1,600 examples of utility and decorative
porcelain from the past 125 years are shown. You'll also find the
company's factory outlet shop here, with excellent bargains on
imperfect and overstocked items. 📍 Hämeentie 135 📞 (0)204 3910
🌐 www.arabiamuseum.fi 🕐 12.00–18.00 Tues–Fri, 10.00–16.00
Sat & Sun 🚊 Tram/bus: 6, 52, 68, 71, 71V, 73B, 74, 77S, 503 or 735K

Didrichsen Art Museum

A couple's private collection is now a museum rich in 20th-century
art, along with specialised collections of Asian antiquities of the

Shang and Ming dynasties and pre-Columbian art of the Olmec, Jalisco and Mayan cultures. Primary here is the Finnish art from the 20th century, including works by Edelfelt and his contemporaries. Non-Finnish modern art includes works by Picasso, Kandinsky and Miro. ⓐ Kuusilahdenkuja 1, Kuusisaari ⓣ (09) 477 8330 ⓦ www.didrichsenmuseum.fi ⓛ 11.00–18.00 Tues–Sun ⓝ Bus: 194, 195 from Elielsquare (bay 25), 503, 506. Admission charge

Gallen-Kallela Museum

The most important Finnish artist of the early 1900s, Gallen-Kallela had a rich and varied career in painting, drawing, graphics, sculpture, posters, photographs and applied art, all of which are represented in this museum. It also tells about the artist's colourful life and times, as well as his friends. Gallen-Kallela designed this Jugendstil home and studio, built 1911–1913. The wooden Tarvaspää villa, built in the 1850s, houses a café. ⓐ Gallen-Kallelantie 27, Espoo ⓣ (09) 849 2340 ⓦ www.gallen-kallela.fi ⓛ 10.00–18.00 mid-May–Aug; 10.00–16.00 Tues–Sat, 10.00–17.00 Sun, Sept–mid-May ⓝ Tram: 4 to Munkkiniemi, at Laajalahden aukio, then walk 2 km (1½ miles) through Munkinpuisto Park (Mon–Fri bus service from Munkkiniemen puistotie). Admission charge

RETAIL THERAPY

Outside the busy and trendy shopping streets of downtown Helsinki, the islands and outer suburbs nonetheless offer some quality shopping. The fortress of Suomenlinna houses a number of excellent artisan studios, and museum shops offer unique speciality gifts. And Arabia's factory outlet is a mecca for bargain hunters with a taste for fine dinnerware.

Arabia Factory Shop One of Scandinavia's best-known brands of porcelain and dinnerware, Arabia spans all ages and tastes with its classic lines and functional style. The outlet offers discontinued styles and seconds at deep discounts. Along with the Arabia label are goods in Iittala and other company brands. See page 113 for further details.

Arts and Crafts Summer Shop Selected traditional and modern crafts in all media. ⓐ Suomenlinna B 34 ⓣ (050) 408 2902 ⓛ 10.00–17.00 mid-May–Sept

Bastion Hårleman, Susisaari Artisans' studios, some open to the public in the Summer. Esa Toivanen, woodworking studio. ⓐ Suomenlinna B 31 ⓣ (040) 533 7903

Hvitträsk Museum Shop A source of the beautiful Kalevala and Kaunis *koru* jewellery, based on designs from Finnish folklore, this outstanding museum gift-shop also carries art and architecture books and prints, and crafts made by the Friends of Finnish Handicrafts. The work of local artists includes glass art, jewellery, ceramics, sculpture, knitted woollens and linen tablecloths. ⓐ Hvitträskintie 166, Luoma ⓣ (09) 4050 9630 ⓦ www.nba.fi ⓝ Trains: L and U to Luoma

Hytti ry This studio is a place where one can worship at the altar of the glass-blower's art. Phone to check opening times. ⓐ Suomenlinna B 48 ⓣ (09) 668 727

Jetty Barracks Gallery Operated by the Helsinki Artists' Association, the gallery shows exhibitions of juried contemporary art in the rooms of the Jetty Barracks. ⓐ Iso Mustasaari, next to the Main Quay, Suomenlinna ⓣ (09) 673 140 ⓦ www.helsingintaiteilijaseura.fi ⓒ 12.30–18.00 Tues–Thur, 11.30–16.00 Fri–Sun

Pot Viapori Ceramics Studio ⓐ Suomenlinna B 45 ⓣ (09) 668 151 ⓒ 12.00–17.00 mid-July–late Aug

⬇ *Hand-made souvenirs are sold at the Kappatori market*

Safari Shop The Korkeasaari Zoo's own brand of animal-themed and environmentally friendly products, as well as Fair Trade products and crafts from cooperatives in developing countries, are sold in the zoo's shop. ⓐ Korkeasaari ⓣ (09) 696 2370 ⓛ 10.00–20.00 May–Sept; 10.00–16.00 Oct–Feb; 10.00–18.00 Mar–Apr

Seurasaari Museum Shop Traditional Finnish handicrafts, authentic sauna products, books and other historical items are available in the museum store. ⓐ Seurasaari ⓣ (09) 4050 9662 ⓛ 11.00–17.00 June–Aug; 09.00–15.00 Mon–Fri, 11.00–17.00 Sat & Sun, late May & early Sept

TAKING A BREAK

Nearly every museum has its own café, usually open at least the same hours as the museum itself. Suomenlinna is well supplied with eating places, several of which are listed under After Dark below, since they are open for evening meals, as well. For travel directions, see under the corresponding museum or attraction.

Café Antin Kaffeliiteri £ ❶ In a little shed building next to Antti farmstead, the café bakes traditional Finnish pastries and otherwise hard-to-find old-fashioned regional treats, including Karelian rice pastries and pancakes from the Aland Islands. The cinnamon rolls are addictive. ⓐ Seurasaari ⓣ (09) 4050 9660 ⓛ 11.00–17.00 June–Aug; 09.00–15.00 Mon–Fri, 11.00–17.00 Sat & Sun, late May and early Sept

Café Vanille £ ❷ Opposite the church in the Russian merchants' quarter, cosy modern Café Vanille serves soups and sandwiches, along with fresh-baked pastries, cappuccino, tea, hot cocoa and beer. ⓐ Building C 18, Suomenlinna ❶ (040) 556 1169 ❷ 11.00–17.00 Fri–Sun, May; 11.00–18.00 June–Sept; 11.00–16.00 Wed–Fri, 11.00–18.00 Sat, 11.00–17.00 Sun, Oct; 11.00–17.00 Sat, 12.00–17.00 Sun, Nov–Dec

Seurasaari £ ❸ Several historic kiosks serve food and offer tables for those with picnics. The kiosk by the bridge (❷ 11.00–16.00 June–Aug) used to be in central Helsinki, and the kiosk in the Festival Grounds (❷ 11.00–16.00 Sat & Sun) has a grill available where you can barbecue your own food. ❶ (09) 484 511

Café Bar Valimo ££ ❹ The grass-roofed ammunition foundry that houses this summer café is located on the docks near an old wooden sailing vessel and the guest harbour. Valimo serves soups, pasta dishes, snacks, sandwiches and soft drinks, as well as having a full alcohol licence. ⓐ Building B 13, Suomenlinna ❶ (09) 692 6450 ⓦ www.valimo.org ❷ 11.00–22.30 Mon–Thur, 11.00–22.30 Fri & Sat, 11.00–18.30 Sun, May–mid-June; 10.30–22.30 Mon–Sat, 10.30–20.30 Sun, mid-June–mid-Aug. Closes earlier late Aug

Café Piper ££ ❺ In a charming old wooden villa set in a park, with a terrace overlooking the sea, Café Piper serves soup, savoury snacks, pastries and drinks including beer. ⓐ Building B 56, Suomenlinna ❶ (09) 668 447 ❷ 10.00–17.00 May; 10.00–19.00, June–mid-Aug; 10.00–17.00, mid-Aug–mid-Sept

Hvitträsk ££ ❻ Located in the estate's Little Villa, the Café Hvitträsk offers sandwiches and pastries, coffee, tea and alcoholic drinks in a charming atmosphere. On the second floor of the villa, the upmarket restaurant has a terrace for summer dining. An à la carte menu is offered in the evening. ➋ Hvitträsk, Hvitträskintie 166, Luoma ➊ (09) 297 6033 ➌ Café 11.00–18.00, Restaurant 11.30–23.00 Mon–Sat, 11.30–22.00 Sun

Korkeasaari Zoo ££ ➐ A variety of kiosks and cafés serve snacks and lunches in the summer, including Café Coco and kiosks by the Bear Castle and Café Safari near the Mustikkamaa entrance. ➌ 10.00–20.00 May–Sept; 10.00–16.00 Oct–Feb; 10.00–18.00 Mar–Apr. Closed Christmas Eve

Pizzeria Nikolai ££ ➑ Inside the stone casemates of the fortress at King's gate, Nikolai serves good pizza. In the summer, you can enjoy it on the terrace with a sea view. The waterbus goes directly to King's Gate, or you can take the ferry and stop here on your walk around the connecting islands. ➋ Building A 10, Suomenlinna ➊ (09) 668 552 ➌ 12.00–22.00 Sat, 12.00–20.00 Sun, early May; 12.00–20.00 Sun–Thur, 12.00–22.00 Fri & Sat, mid-May–Aug

Pukki Restaurant ££ ➒ Serving meals and hot snacks in the daytime, Pukki also offers an à la carte dinner menu and live music some summer evenings 19.00–24.00. ➋ Korkeasaari Zoo ➊ (09) 2705 1150 ➌ Year-round

Restaurant Café Chapman ££ ➓ Near the Visitor Centre, the year-round café with a courtyard terrace is a lunch spot, and summer evenings an à la carte restaurant. ➌ Building B 1, Suomenlinna ➊ (09) 668 692 ➌ 10.30–15.00 Mon–Fri, Jan–early May; 11.00–21.00 Mon–Fri, 12.00–21.00 Sat, 12.00–18.00 Sun, late May–mid-Sept; 10.30–15.00 Mon–Fri, mid-Sept–Dec

Tarvaspää ££ ⓫ The villa was Gallen-Kallela's summer house until 1913, when the studio was completed. The caféteria is now there, serving traditional fresh-baked Finnish pastries, including cinnamon buns, called *korvapuusti*. ⓐ Gallen-Kallelantie 27, Espoo ⓣ (09) 849 2340 ⓦ www.gallen-kallela.fi ⓛ 10.00–20.00 Tues–Thur, 10.00–18.00 Fri–Mon, mid-May–Aug; 10.00–16.00 Tues–Sat, 10.00–17.00 Sun, Sept–mid-May

Toy Museum Café ££ ⓬ Tucked into the wooden Russian villa with the Toy Museum, this cosy tearoom and terrace serves Russian-style tea, real lemonade and fresh-baked pastries, including wonderful apple pie. ⓐ Building C 66, Suomenlinna ⓣ (09) 668 417 ⓛ 11.00–16.00 Sat & Sun, Apr; 11.00–16.00 late May; 11.00–17.00 June; 11.00–18.00 July; 11.00–17.00 Aug; 11.00–16.00 Sat & Sun, Sept

AFTER DARK

Apart from the islands of Suomenlinna, most of the 'museum islands' are daytime destinations. One or two restaurants might offer evening meals, but the city's nightlife is centred in its in-town neighbourhoods. That said, if you plan to be at one of the outlying museums, such as Hvitträsk, in the late afternoon, their restaurants are well worth considering for their charm and their unhurried ambience.

RESTAURANTS
Suomenlinna Petty Officers' Club £–££ ⓭ Not fancy, but a favourite place for locals to meet, the club is in one of the old wooden buildings near the ferry landing. The terrace overlooks the city, across the

water. **③** Building C 8, Suomenlinna **❶** (09) 668 273 **🕓** 16.00–22.45 Mon–Fri, 12.00–23.45 Sat, 12.00–20.45 Sun, Jan–mid-Dec

Suomenlinna Panimo Brewery Restaurant ££ ⑭ The brewery, brewpub and restaurant are inside the high-vaulted casements of the Jetty Barracks, built during the Russian control of the fort. Sample the brewery's own Höpken Pils, Coyet Ale and the dark Helsinki Portteri. Booking is wise in the summer. **③** Building C 1, Suomenlinna **❶** (09) 228 5030 **🕓** 15.00–22.00 Wed–Fri, 12.00–22.00 Sat, 12.00–18.00 Sun, Jan–Mar; 15.00–22.00 Mon–Fri, 12.00–22.00 Sat, 12.00–18.00 Sun, Apr; 11.00–23.30 Mon–Sat, 12.00–18.00 Sun, May–Aug; 15.00–22.00 Mon–Fri, 12.00–22.00 Sat, 12.00–18.00 Sun, Sept–Dec

Helsinki by Sea Dinner Cruise ££–£££ ⑮ Enjoy a changing land and seascape over dinner on board a sightseeing boat with a full kitchen. The à la carte menu offers starters such as forest mushroom cream soup or salmon soup, and main courses including grilled breast of chicken in a gorgonzola sauce. Book in advance for these popular evening excursions. IHA Lines. **❶** (09) 6874 5050 **🕸** www.ihalines.fi **🕓** 19.00 Tues–Sat, May–Sept

Restaurant Särkänlinna £££ ⑯ On the island of Särkkä between Suomenlinna and the southern tip of the city, the summer restaurant in a stone fortress offers stunning sea views and a setting rich in history. If you think the floor of the long dining room tilts a bit, you're right; it was designed to make it easier to get cannonballs to the cannons at the far end. **③** Särkkä **❶** (09) 134 561 **🕸** www.palace.fi **🕓** 17.30–24.00 Mon–Sat, May–Sept **🚢** Reached by ferry from the Ullanlinna quay on the mainland at the southern end of the city

Walhalla Restaurant £££ 🔟 King's Gate is at the far end of the small island of Kustaanmiekka, attached to Suomenlinna, and Walhalla is set in the stone-arched interior of the fortress there. It's worth the waterbus ride – an enjoyable evening trip – to savour such starters as mousse of smoked Arctic char with whitebait roe, or main courses such as fillet of reindeer with morel sauce. You can end a meal with equally traditional local ingredients: try cloudberry charlotte with cloudberry melba. The views from the terrace bar are just as outstanding. Be sure to book ahead. ⓐ Building A 10, Suomenlinna ① (09) 668 552 Ⓦ www.restaurantwalhalla.com ① 18.00–24.00 Mon–Sat

ENTERTAINMENT

Suomenlinna Summer Theatre Productions are in Finnish, but the programme is based on movement, action, dance and music, so the words are not essential to enjoying the performance. These take place on both Suomenlinna and Seurasaari islands. Tickets from **Lippupalvelu** (① 0600 1 08 00 or 0600 10 020 Ⓦ www.lippupalvelu.fi), Stockmann department store (see page 79) or Sokos department store (see page 77). ① 0600 108 00 Ⓦ www.lippupalvelu.fi ① June–Aug

● *The forbidding keep of Finland's largest castle is one of the sights of Turku*

OUT OF TOWN
trips

Porvoo

Dating from the 1500s, Porvoo is Finland's second-oldest town, and lies 50 km (30 miles) east of Helsinki. Today the town is known for its small shops specialising in crafts and antiques, enough reason for a day trip here. Royal Line offers daily trips to Porvoo in July and August. Departing from Market Square at 10.00 the cruise goes through the archipelago while guests enjoy lunch on board. After travelling up the river past the colourful old town, with its riverside storehouses, there are about two hours to explore the town's cathedral, wooden buildings and narrow lanes lined with shops and cafés, before the return voyage to Helsinki. See below for details to make your own plans.

Porvoo Tourist Office ⓐ Rihkamakatu 4 ⓣ (0) 19 520 2316
ⓦ www.porvoo.fi ⓛ 09.00–18.00 Mon–Fri, 10.00–16.00 Sat & Sun, June–Aug; 09.30–16.30 Mon–Fri, 10.00–14.00 Sat, Sept–Jan
Royal Line ⓣ (09) 612 2950 ⓦ www.royalline.fi ⓛ Mid-May–mid-Sept

GETTING THERE

Porvoo is very close to Helsinki; it is only about thirty minutes away by car, on Highway E18. There are also regular buses from Helsinki to Porvoo. The main bus terminals are underground at Kamppi bus station (bays 1–4). One-way tickets cost between €9–12, and there are buses every 20–30 minutes. For more detailed timetables, consult ⓦ www.matkahuolto.fi. Of course, you can also take a ferry from Helsinki Market Square, which affords a wonderful opportunity to see the beautiful archipelago (do book in advance). The boats have cafés and fully licensed restaurants and run twice a day. Return tickets are around €35. **J L Runeberg** (ⓦ www.msjlruneberg.fi) and **Royal Line** (ⓦ www.royalline.fi) are the two operating ferry companies.

◆ *Porvoo's many boutiques make it a popular day-trip destination*

Around Helsinki

0   20 km

0   10 miles

Gulf of Finland

Sibbofjarden

○ City
○ Large Town
○ Small Town
■ POI
━ Motorway
━ Main Road
━ Minor Road
✈ Airport
━ Railway

SIGHTS & ATTRACTIONS

Porvoo's picturesque riverfront is lined with little red wooden buildings that were once storehouses for the city's mercantile trade. The land rises from these to the old town, a charming tangle of old streets lined with ochre-coloured wooden houses in typically Karielian architecture. Two museums face the market square of the old town, one with historical collections and the other an art museum featuring the work of several art nouveau-era artists.

Cathedral

Topping the hill is the cathedral, parts of which date from the 14th century, although it was largely reconstructed a century later and became a cathedral in 1723. Highlights are the ornate 1764 pulpit and wall paintings from the 15th century. ⓐ Kirkkotori 1 ⓣ (0) 19 661 11 ⓘ The cathedral is closed for renovation until further notice. For more information, please contact the parish register office

Albert Edelfelt Studio Museum

This is where the great man painted many of his most important works. Examples of his various periods are hung liberally all over the museum, and this is a must for art-lovers. ⓐ Edelfeltinpolku 3 ⓣ (019) 577 414 ⓛ 10.00–16.00 Tues–Sun, June–Aug; 10.00–14.00 Tues–Sun, May & Sept. Admission charge

Runeberg Museum

Even before Sparr and Edelfelt made Porvoo into an art colony, it had been a centre of creative talent. Finland's national poet,

Johan Ludvig Runeberg, lived and wrote here for more than two decades from 1852 onwards, drawing other talent of his times to Porvoo. The home has been a museum since 1882.
ⓐ Aleksanterinkatu 3 ❶ (0) 19 581 330 Ⓦ www.runeberg.net

TAKING A BREAK

The following represent just a small selection from the wide choice of cafés and restaurants in Porvoo.

Café Fanny £ Friendly café in an 18th-century building on the Town Hall Square in old Porvoo, serving good coffee and fresh-baked cinnamon buns. ⓐ Välikatu 13 ❶ (0) 19 582 855

Old Town Café £ Sandwiches and pastries to eat in or take out.
ⓐ Välikatu 1 ❶ (0) 19 580 201

Porvoon Paahtimo ££ This red-tiled converted warehouse in the old historic centre of Porvoo is easy to spot. Excellent coffee choice and a river-facing terrace. ⓐ Mannerheiminkatu 2 ❶ (0) 19 617 040
Ⓦ www.nexthotels.fi

ACCOMMODATION

Hotel Seurahovi ££ Centrally located, the modern building offers nicely appointed rooms, saunas, a sports bar and restaurant. Close by the 19th-century steam ship *Glückauf* is another dining choice. ⓐ Rauhankatu 27 ❶ (0) 19 547 61 ❶ (0) 19 524 9329
Ⓦ www.seurahovi.fi

Turku

Finland's oldest city at almost 800 years old, Turku was the capital until 1812. It is the most traditional medieval town in Finland, with a castle, marketplace, cathedral and a river harbour. In Turku you will see architecture ranging from the 1200s to art nouveau and the stunning modern Sibelius Museum by Woldemar Baeckman. Charming, if quiet, Turku proclaims itself as Finland's Christmas City. Visit then, or during the midsummer Medieval Festival, when the old square regains its medieval air, with craft stalls and food vendors. The Turku Card (€21 for 24 hours) gives free admission to all city museums and transport, worthwhile if you plan to see a lot of museums. Frequent trains and buses from Helsinki take about two hours to Turku.

Turku Touring Stop here for tourist information and maps of the southwest coast. ⓐ Aurakatu 4 ① (02) 262 7444 ⓦ www.turkutouring.fi ⓔ turku.touring@turku.fi ⓛ 08.30–18.00 Mon–Fri, 09.00–16.00 Sat & Sun, Apr–Sept; 10.00–15.00 Sat & Sun, Oct–Mar

GETTING THERE

The easiest way to get to Turku is to take the hourly, quick Pendolino-train from Helsinki Railway Station (a journey of about two hours). Train travel in Finland is not cheap, but it is reliable, modern and comfortable. Although the train is the most popular method of travelling, you can also fly (ⓦ www.finnair.fi), or take a bus (ⓦ matkahuolto.fi).

SIGHTS & ATTRACTIONS

The Aura river is alive in summer as historic boats line the shore, ferries cross, families picnic and lovers stroll alongside the water.

Music drifts from the restaurant boats and the whole town seems to gather there in the long evenings. In winter, lights fill the trees and reflect off the snow in a glittering fairytale world as skaters skim along its frozen surface.

Boat trips

Opportunities to explore the River Aura and the archipelago include everything from a free ferry to dinner-dance cruises and day-long sails. The City Ferry (*Föri*) crosses the Aura from early morning until midnight, year round. From June to August the Pikkuföri river ferry plies the river from the Forum Marinum (€2). M/s *Ruissalo* cruises daily June–August between Turku and Ruissalo Island.

Airisto Line Oy ⓘ (040) 593 0200 Ⓦ www.airistoline.fi

Forum Marinum

A combination of museum, shipyard and maritime research facility, the Forum includes two buildings (and 3,500 exhibits) and two historic vessels to tour, the full-rigger *Suomen Joutsen* and the minelayer *Keihässalmi*. Exhibits feature navy and commercial ships, local coastal boats and culture. A second building contains boats and tools for boatbuilding. ⓐ Linnankatu 72 ⓘ (02) 282 9511 Ⓦ www.forum-marinum.fi Ⓛ 11.00–19.00 May–Sept; 10.00–18.00 Tues–Sun, Oct–Apr. Ships: 11.00–19.00 June–Aug Ⓝ Bus: 1. Admission charge

Kuralan kylämäki (Village of Living History)

A working 1950s farm on the eastern outskirts of city takes visitors back half a century to smell fresh goodies baking in the farmhouse kitchen and pet baby animals in the barns. Hands-on activities bring the farm to life for children, who can make a whistle from a willow

stick or play shops using real items from the period. At weekends in December the farm is decorated for the holidays and hosts a craft market, with prices far below those of street markets. ❷ Jaanintie 45 ❶ (02) 262 0420 ❸ 10.00–18.00 Wed–Sun, June–Sept ❹ Bus: 28

Luostarinmäki Handicrafts Museum

An entire neighbourhood of 40 homes, the only ones saved from the fire that destroyed Turku in 1827, is preserved as a museum village, showing how ordinary people lived. Homes and workshops open onto little courtyards, surrounded by stables and small rooms built as families grew. About 30 artisans demonstrate period crafts, from wire weaving and printing to carving shaved-wood ornaments, and you can buy from them or from the shop (see page 136). ❷ Luostarinmäki ❶ (02) 262 0350 ❸ 10.00–18.00 mid-Apr–mid-Sept; 10.00–15.00 Tues–Sun, mid-Sept–mid-Apr ❹ Bus: 3, 12,18, 24, 30. Admission charge

Moomin World

Finland's most famous cartoon characters, the Moomins, will please even children who did not grow up with their adventures. Moomins cavort in the story settings, such as Moominhouse, Moominpapa's Boat, Hemulens House and the Witch's Labyrinth. At the Pancake Factory children make their own pancake and choose favourite toppings. ❷ Naantali ❶ (02) 511 1111 ❺ www.muumimaailma.fi ❸ 10.00–18.00 mid-June–late Aug ❹ Bus from Turku harbour. Admission charge.

The Old Great Square

The ensemble of old buildings near the river was the historic centre of power, both church and state, when Turku was the capital. Brinkkala mansion was the residence of the Russian Governor General, and the stables in its courtyard are now artisans' studios. The entire square becomes a marketplace before Christmas and during the Medieval Market from late June to early August. ⓦ www.keskiaikaisetmarkkinat.fi

Turku Castle

Built between 1280 and 1650, Finland's largest castle is a defensive pile with outer walls 3 m (10 ft) thick. Enter its maze of stairways and passages through a picturesque courtyard to find towers, banqueting halls and a chapel with medieval woodcarving. Historical exhibits highlight events, customs and dress. ⓐ Linnankatu 80 ⓣ (02) 262 0300 ⓔ maakuntamuseo@turku.fi ⓛ 10.00–18.00 mid-Apr–mid-Sept; 10.00–15.00 Tues–Sun, mid-Sept–mid-Apr; 10.00–17.00 Sat, Oct–mid-Apr ⓝ Bus: 1. Admission charge

Turku Cathedral

In 1229, the Pope ordered a church to be built here, and the cathedral remained Catholic until the mid-16th century, when it became Finland's Lutheran mother church. Burned or pillaged 30 times throughout its history, it has been rebuilt each time, and remains a landmark of Finnish architecture. Although its lines are familiar perpendicular Gothic, the interior is entirely plastered, without visible stonework. ⓐ Tuomiokirkkotori 20 ⓣ (020) 261 7100 ⓛ 9.00–19.00 (summer till 20.00)

CULTURE

Along with the historic buildings and ships, Turku has three museums well worth seeing. Two of these occupy different levels of the same site.

Aboa Vetus & Ars Nova

Built around an excavated city block of medieval Turku, Aboa Vetus

⬤ *The atrium of the Sibelius Museum doubles as a concert hall*

explores not only the history of the site, but the archaeology of its discovery and preservation. The foundations have been dug 7 m (22 ft) deep to disclose glimpses of the medieval town, where artefacts, the stones themselves and exquisite models combine to tell the story. Guided tours are in English, daily July–Aug at 11.30.

Above, in the same building, Ars Nova couldn't be in sharper contrast to the medieval world below. More than 500 works by major contemporary and 20th-century artists from Finland and elsewhere trace movements and styles in modern art. ⓐ Itäinen Rantakatu 4–6 ⓣ (02) 2500 552 ⓦ www.aboavetusarsnova.fi ⓛ 11.00–19.00 late Mar–mid-Sept; 11.00–19.00 Tues–Sun, Jan–late Mar & mid-Sept–mid-Dec ⓝ Bus: 13, 30, 55. Admission charge

Sibelius Museum

See this for the building, even if Sibelius and music leave you cold. Built in 1968, it was Finland's first glass and concrete building, and the concrete simulates rough-cut wood, its organic sand colour enhanced by lighting. Museum exhibits include rare musical instruments, sheet music and memorabilia, with signage in English. The atrium is a beautiful setting for Wednesday evening concerts. ➋ Piispankatu 17 ➊ (02) 215 4494 ⓦ www.sibeliusmuseum.abo.fi ⓛ 11.00–16.00 Tues–Sun, also 18.00–20.00 Wed ⓝ Bus: 4, 28, 30, 50, 51, 53, 54. Admission charge

RETAIL THERAPY

Kiosks in the central square sell fresh produce, sizzling sausages, flowers and crafts, changing with the seasons, from early morning until 18.00 Monday to Friday, until 14.00 on Saturday. Overlooking this is the large Sokos department store (➋ Eerikinkatu 11 ➊ (010) 765 020) and from the square's upper corner runs Kauppiaskatu, the main shopping street. Small shops are scattered through the central streets around the market square and two shopping centres – Hansa and Forum – are close by.

Antiikkiliike Wanha Elias Shop or browse for antique furniture and decorative pieces. ➋ Eerikinkatu 29 ➊ (0400) 84 6817 ⓦ www.antiikkiliikewanhaelias.fi

Arabia Hackman Iittala Finnish design, from glassware and china to cooking pots, in a factory outlet store. ➋ Hämeenkatu 6 ➊ (020) 439 3547

Au-Holmberg Oy This provides a fascinating insight into a goldsmith's workshop and shop. ➋ Itäinen Rantakatu 64 ➊ (02) 2316419 ⓦ www.au-holmberg.fi

Boreus Everything for the outdoors – fishing gear, all-weather clothes, boots – as well as everyday wear. @ Yliopistonkatu 11 ☎ (02) 251 9409

Christmas Market & Medieval Market The Old Great Square comes alive with people shopping for crafts and munching hearty traditional foods in the first three weeks in December and from late June to early August.

Fatabur The museum shop at Turku Castle sells a well-chosen selection of tasteful gifts, including historic glassware and jewellery reproductions, as well as traditional crafts (see Sights & Attractions for access details).

Föritupa Traditional and contemporary Finnish crafts.
@ Sairashuoneenkatu 1 ☎ (02) 233 1073 🕑 10.00–14.00 Mon–Fri, 10.00–17.30 Thur

Piha-Puoti (Luostarinmäki Handicrafts Museum Shop) The products of these authentic workshops – candlesticks and wall hooks woven from wire, framed stained-glass panels, straw wreaths, round wooden boxes and birds made of shaved wood – are sold in the museum's shop (see page 132 for access details of the museum).

Turku Market Hall In a traditional indoor market atmosphere, 50 merchants offer speciality foods, produce and crafts.
@ Eerikinkatu 16 🕑 07.00–17.30 Mon–Fri, 07.00–15.00 Sat

TAKING A BREAK

Stop at the Market Square for sausages or other quick foods. You'll also find food stalls in the market hall and at the two big open-air markets that fill Old Great Square in December and July.

Koulu £ Set in a restored school (*Koulu* means 'school'), the brewery serves house beers and others, along with lunch and dinner. ⓐ Eerikinkatu 18 ⓣ (02) 274 5757 ⓦ www.panimoravintolakoulu.fi ⓛ 11.00–02.00 Sun–Thur, 11.00–03.00 Fri & Sat. Food served 11.00–24.00 Mon–Fri, 12.00–24.00 Sat

Pub Old Bank £ Everyone meets at this popular pub in an historic Jugendstil bank building, where they serve 150 different beers in an English-style bar atmosphere. The food is good, too. ⓐ Aurakatu 3 ⓦ www.oldbank.fi ⓣ (02) 274 5700 ⓛ From 12.00 daily

Puutorin Vessa £ Sometimes it helps if you don't speak Finnish, especially when a pub's name translates to 'The Toilet'. This one is in a much-converted WC, hence the name – another example of the Finns' wicked sense of humour. They're serious about the food, though, and the good selection of beers. ⓐ Puutori ⓣ (02) 233 8123 ⓦ www.puutorinvessa.fi

Caffe Panini £–££ Italian panini sandwiches, pasta, pizza, salads and other light dishes, in the sophisticated setting of Casagrande House, near the river. ⓐ Linnankatu 3 ⓣ (02) 251 5310 ⓛ 11.00–22.00 Mon–Fri, 12.00–22.00 Sat & Sun

Börs Café ££ Light meals in a bright window-surrounded café just off the Market Square. ⓐ Sokos Hotel Hamburger Börs, Kauppiaskatu 6 ⓣ (02) 337 381

Café Marinum ££ Stay in the maritime spirit at the Forum Marinum, with lunch at this cheery café-restaurant. ⓐ Linnankatu 72 ⓣ (02) 251 0898

Café Restaurant Aula ££ For a break to separate the two very different worlds of medieval life and 21st-century art, stop for coffee at this tidy little museum café. ⊚ Aboa Vetus & Ars Nova, Itäinen Rantakatu 4–6 ⊕ (02) 279 4936 ⊕ 11.00–19.00 Tues–Sun

Cafeteria Domcafé ££ Tucked into the brick vaults below the Cathedral, this café serves excellent coffee and cakes from historic recipes. ⊚ Entrance at the Cathedral steps ⊕ (02) 261 7100 ⊕ Daily in summer, first three weekends in December

AFTER DARK

Along with several outstanding restaurants well worth spending an evening in, Turku has a rich cultural scene, with theatres, two orchestras, jazz and rock bars. The Turku Music Festival and Rockfestival Ruisrock are among the oldest in Scandinavia.

RESTAURANTS

Pavilion Vaakahuone £–££ Go for the fish, go for the swing and Dixieland, go for the summer scene at the river. Choose from several menus all grouped around the same terrace – seafood, pizza, giant Bratwurst or a coffee shop. Live music every night. ⊚ Linnankatu 38 ⊕ (02) 515 3300 ⊕ daylight hours May–Aug (which means most of the night)

Cindyn Salonki ££ Uncomplicated dishes, many based on local seafood, are served in a boat moored on the river. ⊚ Itäinen Rantakatu ⊕ (02) 250 2300 ⓦ www.cindy.fi ⊕ 11.00–23.00 Mon–Fri, 12.00–24.00 Sat, 13.00–21.00 Sun

Blanko ££–£££ In the vaults of an old building near the Aurasilta Bridge, Blanko serves fusion cuisine drawn from everything from tapas to sashimi. Creative dishes include chanterelle and pumpkin lasagna or beetroot risotto. ⓐ Aurakatu 1 ① (02) 233 3966 ⓒ from 11.00 daily

Enkeliravintola ££–£££ The name of this restaurant translates as 'angel' and the food is indeed heavenly. Begin with a cup of warming *glögi*, while you look around at the playful décor. Then order dishes based on creative interpretations of Finnish cuisine: game terrine with lingonberries, creamy soup of forest mushrooms, *pot-au-feu* of lightly smoked pork or vegetarian mushroom pie. ⓐ Kauppiaskatu 16 ① (02) 231 8088 ⓦ www.enkeliravintola.fi

Linnankatu 3 ££–£££ The presentation is worthy of the outstanding cuisine and surroundings; seafood dishes are superb, and the pâté is memorable. ⓐ Linnankatu 3 A ① (02) 233 9279 ⓦ www.linnankatu3.fi ⓒ 11.00–24.00 Mon–Fri, 17.00–24.00 Sat

Rocca £££ Fresh local ingredients are brilliantly treated by famous Finnish chef Antti Vahtera in dishes such as roast goose over a savoury ragout of mixed beans, and desserts such as espresso crème brulée or gingerbread sorbet. ⓐ Läntinen Rantakatu 55 ① (02) 284 8800

ENTERTAINMENT

Galax Sleek dance/restaurant with better-known Finnish performers. Minimum age is 24. ⓐ Aurakatu 6 ① (02) 284 3300

Sibelius Museum Chamber Concerts Chamber music concerts are held each Wednesday evening in the atrium (except in summer). ⓐ Piispankatu 17 ① (02) 215 4494 ⓦ www.sibeliusmuseum.abo.fi

ACCOMMODATION

Best Western Hotel Seaport £ Located in a charming converted customs warehouse right in the dock area, this makes a good choice if you are cruising in or out of Turku on a Baltic ferry. The rooms are attractive and comfortable; the whole place was updated and renovated in 2004. ➌ Matkustajasatama ➊ (02) 283 3000 ➐ (02) 283 3100 Ⓦ www.bestwestern.com

Ruissalo Spa Hotel ££ Pamper youself at this elegant spa on Ruissalo Island. A large, modern resort, its rooms are smart and there are several restaurants. The sport and spa facilities are superb. It sits amidst walking, jogging and cycling trails and beaches and is close to an 18-hole golf course. ➌ Ruissalon puistotie 640 ➊ (02) 445 5100 ➐ (02) 445 5101 Ⓦ www.ruissalospa.fi

Naantali Spa Resort ££–£££ Saunas and aromatic aquatherapy are only the beginning of the facilities offered at this state-of-the-art resort spa near Turku. From the huge indoor pool, dive under the glass wall and stare at the winter sky from a steaming outdoor pool. ➌ Naantali ➊ (02) 445 5100 Ⓦ www.naantalispa.fi

Sokos Hotel Hamburger Börs ££–£££ You could hardly find a hotel closer to the centre of activity in this handsome town than the 346 rooms overlooking Market Square. These are nicely appointed in modern Scandinavian style. There are three saunas, a pool and other leisure facilities for guests, as well as seven restaurants. ➌ Kauppiaskatu 6 ➊ (02) 337 381 ➐ (02) 23 1010 Ⓦ www.hamburgerbors.fi

---

▶ *Helsinki Railway Station has Eliel Saarinen's most famous interior*

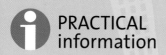

PRACTICAL
information

Directory

GETTING THERE

Helsinki can be reached by direct daily flights from major European hubs. Its location on the Baltic makes ferries a popular method of transport from Stockholm and from ports in Estonia and Germany. Most of these ferries also carry cars, so Finland can be incorporated into a driving holiday.

By air

From the UK and Europe Finnair offers the most options, with several daily flights from Heathrow to Vantaa and some direct flights from Manchester. Ryanair flies from Stansted to Tampere. SAS and British Airways also have daily flights direct to Vantaa from Heathrow. Blue 1 has direct flights from Stansted. Finnair operates

⬤ *Vantaa is Helsinki's modern gateway*

daily direct flights from JFK in New York and in the summer, from Toronto. SAS flies from several US gateways, but always connecting through Stockholm or Copenhagen.

Blue 1 Ⓦ www.blue1.com
British Airways Ⓦ www.britishairways.com
Finnair ⓘ +358 600 140 140 Ⓦ www.finnair.com
Ryanair Ⓦ www. ryanair.com
SAS Ⓦ www.scandinavian.net

Many people are aware that air travel emits CO_2, which contributes to climate change. You may be interested in the possibility of lessening the environmental impact of your flight through Climate Care, which offsets your CO_2 by funding environmental projects around the world. Visit Ⓦ www.climatecare.org

By rail

Train travel is possible as far as Stockholm, from which point you must take a ferry. The trip from London's St Pancras International to Stockholm takes just over 18 hours, by Eurostar to Brussels, with changes in Cologne, Hamburg and Copenhagen, and the trains boarding ferries for the water crossings. The monthly *Thomas Cook European Rail Timetable* has up-to-date schedules for European international and national train services. Travellers from outside Europe who plan to use trains should investigate the various multi-day and multi-country train passes offered by Rail Europe. Eurail Selectpass includes rail travel in all four Scandinavian countries (or any combination of them) plus Germany, with even greater savings for two or more people travelling together.

Eurostar ⓘ (UK) 08705 186186 Ⓦ www.eurostar.com
Rail Europe Ⓦ www.raileurope.co.uk
Thomas Cook European Rail Timetable ⓘ (UK) 01733 416477; (USA) 1 800 322 3834 Ⓦ www.thomascookpublishing.com

By road

Next to a lucky hit for rock-bottom air fare, the cheapest way to Helsinki from the UK is by bus, again via Stockholm, about 35 hours from London's Victoria Coach Station via Eurolines. From Stockholm you must take a ferry to Finland.

Eurolines ☎ 08705 143219 Ⓦ www.gobycoach.com or Ⓦ www.eurolines.com

Car trips to Finland from the UK must include at least one crossing by car ferry, which adds significantly to the cost. But this remains a budget-friendly option if several people are travelling together. The shortest route, the Via Baltica, is to Tallinn, Estonia, making the final short crossing on one of the several daily car ferries to Helsinki.

Finland, like the rest of the continent, drives on the right-hand side of the road. Keep a sharp eye out for elks and/or reindeer on the road outside urban areas. Serious – many of them fatal – accidents occur each year when vehicles hit animals, sometimes weighing several hundred kilos.

By water

Sweden, Germany, Estonia and St Petersburg are all connected to Finland by ferry links. The main shipping lines operating these are Viking, Silja, Tallink and Superfast Ferries, which operates the route from Rostock, Germany, to Hanko, 90 minutes from Helsinki. Service from Rostock and Stockholm is offered daily, year-round. DFDS in Newcastle operates ferries to other Scandinavian ports, from which connections to Finland are possible, but time-consuming.

DFDS ☎ (UK) 0871 522 9955 Ⓦ www.dfdsseaways.co.uk
Superfast Ferries Ⓦ www.superfast.com
Tallink Silja Ⓦ www.tallinksilja.com
Viking Ⓦ www.vikingline.fi

ENTRY FORMALITIES
Passports & visas
Citizens of the UK, Republic of Ireland, USA, Canada and Australia need only a valid passport to enter Finland and do not require visas. Citizens of EU countries other than the UK need only a valid national identity card, or a passport. Citizens of South Africa must have a passport and visas to enter. Visa forms can be obtained from your nearest Finnish embassy or consulate.

Customs regulations
EU citizens can bring goods for personal use when arriving from another EU country, but must observe the limits on tobacco (800 cigarettes) and spirits (ten litres of alcohol over 22 per cent proof, 20 litres of wine). Limits for non-EU nationals are 200 cigarettes and one litre of spirits, two litres of wine.

MONEY
The currency in Finland is the euro (€), which is divided into 100 cents. Notes are in € 5, 10, 20, 50, 100, 200 and 500 denominations and coins are € 1 and 2, plus 1, 2, 5, 10, 20 and 50 cents. The best means of obtaining local currency is by using a debit card. Although many banks charge a fee for this, these are usually less than cash advances on credit cards, and are at a more favourable exchange rate than cash transactions or travellers' cheques. ATMs (cashpoints) can be found nearly everywhere, easily recognised by yellow hoods. Finns call an ATM an *otto*.

Credit cards are very widely used in Helsinki, even by taxis, and you can often pay by credit card in pubs and get cash back if you're short. Travellers' cheques can be cashed at banks, post offices and in most hotels, and are widely accepted in major shops and stores in Helsinki.

Currency exchange services are in airports and near Helsinki Railway Station. There is a Travelex exchange booth at the Vantaa Airport International Terminal (① (09) 6151 3852). Helsinki's main bank is Nordea (most central branch ② Aleksanterinkatu 52 ① (02) 003 000) ③ Banking hours are usually 09.30–16.15 Mon–Fri

HEALTH, SAFETY & CRIME

Finnish medical care is excellent, with English-speaking doctors and modern clinics and hospitals. Free emergency service is available to all visitors. Those from EU (and a few other European countries) are treated free if they have brought an EHIC card. Obtain this from a local post office before leaving home. Those without an EHIC must

pay for services. EU residents are recommended, nevertheless, to take out adequate travel insurance before departing, and for non-EU travellers it is an absolute necessity.

If you are there in the winter and take part in winter sports, remember that the thickness of ice on lakes and bays is hard to judge. Skate or walk on ice only with a trained guide or where a number of others are also on the ice. Never venture onto ice alone, even if you think you are sure of its strength.

Finland is one of the safest countries to travel in, but remember that wherever tourists gather, there will be occasional pickpockets

⬤ *Gigantic art nouveau guardians of Helsinki Railway Station*

(perhaps visitors themselves). Lock valuables in the hotel safe or leave them at home. You are not likely to need your diamond tiara in Helsinki.

OPENING HOURS

Most shops are open 09.00–16.00 Monday to Friday and 09.00–14.00 Saturday. Very few are open Sunday. Banks are open 09.00–16.00 Monday to Friday and close at weekends. Other types of venue vary individually.

TOILETS

Public facilities are common in Helsinki, but they may not be open all hours. Those inside buildings such as the public markets close with the market. Those in parks may be open limited hours and closed Sunday and in the winter. Those in hotels and cafés are a good alternative when others are closed.

CHILDREN

Finns are fond of children and frequently take their own out and about, so most hotels and restaurants are prepared. Those with music and entertainment, as well as other nightspots, do not welcome children, any more than their equivalents would in any city. However, Helsinki has plenty of family-friendly attractions.

- **Korkeasaari Zoo** is worthwhile for the entire family, with rare cats (including snow leopards), red pandas, a specialist collection of animals indigenous to the Arctic and, by contrast, many Amazonian species in the Amazonia micro-climate house. The trip there by ferry is fun for children, too. ⓐ Korkeasaari ⓣ 0600 95911 ⓦ www.korkeasaari.fi ⓛ 10.00–20.00 May–Sept; 10.00–16.00 Oct–Feb;10.00–18.00 Mar & Apr ⓝ Ferry daily,

May–Sept from Market Square, or Hakaniemi Market; bus: 11
(summer and weekends winter) or, on winter weekdays, bus: 16
or metro to Kulosaari, then a 1.5 km (1 mile) walk. Admission charge

- **Lego Show Helsinki** You'll like playing in this Lego wonderland just
  as much as the kids do. Plenty of access to all the hands-on activities
  is assured by timed ticketing. Choose your three-hour time slot,
  at 11.00–14.00, 14.00–17.00 or 17.00–20.00. 🚉 Jaffa Station,
  Sörnäisten rantatie 6, at Hakaniemi Market Square 🛈 020 710 9902
  🌐 www.leikkiluola.fi 🕐 10.00–20.00 May–Aug 🚍 Bus/tram: 68,
  23N, 97N. Admission charge

- **Linnanmäki Amusement Park** and its Sea Life Centre are close
  to the centre of Helsinki and especially designed for children,
  with rides, a monorail, an open-air theatre, eating places that
  welcome children, and a free playground. Sea Life Centre explores
  marine life with aquatic adventures. And to make you feel good
  about every euro you spend on rides, all the income goes to the
  national child welfare organisations that run the park. 🚉 Tivolikuja 1
  🛈 (09) 773 991 🌐 www.linnanmaki.fi 🕐 Apr–Sept, hours vary with
  season 🚍 Tram/bus: 3T or 23. Admission charge, according to
  child's age and height, at each ride

- **Serena Waterpark** is a bit out of town, but reachable by bus.
  This is a good diversion if the weather turns hot in the summer,
  or when you need a breath of the tropics on a wintry day. Children
  won't believe that a water park stays open in the winter. It's a low-key
  splash park, but good for young children. 🚉 Tornimäentie 10, Espoo
  🛈 (09) 8870 5557 🌐 www.serena.fi 🕐 11.00–20.00 🚍 Bus: 339 from
  Helsinki bus station. Admission charge

Performances for children are staged on Suomenlinna Island during the summer, with a variety of shows and theatre companies participating. The Helsinki City Tourist &Convention Bureau (see page 153) will have schedules. Older children will enjoy exploring the fortress and, as with the zoo, the boat ride there is an adventure itself. They will also enjoy the hands-on activities at Seurasaari Open-air Museum, as well as the unusual old buildings.

COMMUNICATIONS
Internet
Public internet access is widely available in larger towns, with public libraries offering access, in addition to internet cafés. Many hotels have internet available for guests. Stockmann department store has computers in its cybercafé Brutal, but there are often long queues waiting to use them. Other internet cafés include:

Mbar Internet café with DJs and performances at night.
ⓐ Lasipalatsi/Mannerheimintie 22–24 ❶ (09) 6124 5420
🕒 09.00–24.00 Mon & Tues, 09.00–02.00 Wed & Thur, 09.00–03.00 Fri & Sat, 12.00–24.00 Sun
Waynes Coffee ⓐ Kaisaniemenkatu 3 ❶ (09) 6843 2310
🕒 08.00–21.00 Mon–Fri, 10.00–21.00 Sat, 12.00–21.00 Sun

Phones
Mobile phones are almost universal, and European, New Zealand and Australian mobiles can link to several GSM networks after changing the band. US and Canadian mobile phones do not work in Finland unless they are specially equipped before leaving North America. Because of the high use of mobile phones in Finland (the highest per capita in the world), public telephones are getting harder and harder to find. The best places to find them are the

railway and bus stations, shopping centres and large department stores. Phone cards are still available from the main information desks in the railway and bus stations and in large department stores and at some hotel reception desks.

The country code for Finland is 358. The city code for Helsinki is 09, for Turku 02, for Porvoo 019. To call from outside Finland, dial the international access code of the country you're calling from (usually 00), then 358 and then the Finnish city code (omitting the first 0), e.g. 00 358 9 for Helsinki, and then the number. From inside Finland, dial the city code and number. To make an international call from Finland, dial 00, then the country code (UK 44, Republic of Ireland 353, USA and Canada 1, Australia 61, New Zealand 64, South Africa 27) and the area code (omitting the initial zero in UK area codes) and then the number.

Post

Finnish post is not only prompt, it is safe; the Finns are honest to their toes, so what you mail will arrive safely and quickly. Each city or town's main post office has poste restante service, so letters and parcels can be sent to the post office with the recipient's name and post office address marked 'Poste Restante'. Mail will be held for a month before being returned. Helsinki's main post office is Posti Central Office ❸ Elielinaukio 2 ❶ 9800 7100 (free within Finland) ❶ 07.00–21.00 Mon–Fri, 10.00–18.00 Sat & Sun. A postcard should arrive within three to four days in the EU and a week in North America.

ELECTRICITY

Current in Finland is 220V AC, at 50 Hz. Australian, New Zealand, US, Canadian and some South African and UK appliances will need adapters to fit Finnish wall outlets. If you are travelling in other

Scandinavian countries, note that outlets are not all the same. Appliances using only 110V will need transformers, as well as plug adapters.

MEDIA

Helsinki's newspaper *Helsingin Sanomat* publishes an English-language version, good for local news and events. International newspapers are available at news-stands and in hotels. For events, see the free weekly magazine in English, *Helsinki This Week*.

TRAVELLERS WITH DISABILITIES

Lifts provide access to all floors (including the subterranean tunnels that connect much of the central area) in the major department stores

● *Ferries drop their passengers right into the very heart of Helsinki*

and shopping centres, as well as the railway station and Kinopalatsi Cinema Centre. When using the tunnels, you can access street level through these buildings or by a number of lifts throughout the system. For a listing of these locations, as well as excellent maps, see Ⓦ http://esteeton.teho.net. This handy site also lists public toilets with full access, car parks and tourist sights with access information, in English. The zoo, Suomenlinna Fortress, the Atheneum and a number of other tourist sights have disabled access to most of their facilities, as do the Opera House and Finlandia Hall. The outdoor areas of Seurasaari Open-air Museum are accessible, but the historic buildings are not.

There is normally space in Finnish trains for wheelchairs, as well as special tables, allowing for wheelchair manoeuvres. These spaces need reservations, but there is normally no extra charge.

For specially equipped taxis, call one of the following:

Helsingin Invakuljetus Oy ⓐ Helsingin Palveluauto ❶ (09) 350 5200
Invataxi Iiro's Taxi Service Ltd ❶ (09) 4114 2070 or (040) 500 6070

TOURIST INFORMATION

Embassy of Finland ⓐ 38 Chesham Place, London SW1X 8HW
❶ (020) 7838 6200 ❶ (020) 7235 3680 Ⓦ www.finemb.org.uk
Finnish Tourist Board ⓐ PO Box 33213, London W6 8JX
❶ (020) 7365 2512 ❶ (020) 8600 5681 Ⓦ www.visitfinland.com
Finnish Tourist Board ⓐ 655 Third Ave, New York, NY 10017
❶ (212) 885 9735 Ⓦ www.visitfinland.com
Helsinki City Tourist & Convention Bureau ⓐ Pohjoisesplanadi 19,
Helsinki ❶ (09) 169 3757 ❶ (09) 169 3839 Ⓦ www.hel.fi/tourism
🕒 09.00–20.00 Mon–Fri, 09.00–18.00 Sat & Sun, May–Sept;
09.00–18.00 Mon–Fri, 10.00–16.00 Sat & Sun, Oct–Apr

Emergencies

Police, ambulance or fire emergency number ❶ 112

MEDICAL SERVICES

Should you become ill in Finland, you have several sources of
information on English-speaking doctors – although you will find
that most speak rather good English. The consular office of your
embassy can provide a list. You can also go prepared with the
appropriate pages from the directory published by the International
Association of Medical Assistance for Travellers (IAMAT), a non-profit
organisation that provides information on health-related travel
issues all over the world, as well as lists of English speaking doctors
Ⓦ www.iamat.org

24-hour medical and dental treatment can be obtained at:

Hospital Mehiläinen ❸ Pohjoinen Hesperiankatu 17

❶ (010) 414 4210

EMERGENCY PHRASES

Help!   **Help me, please!**
Apua!   Voitko auttaa!
Erpuer!   *Voytko owttah!*

Call an ambulance/Call a doctor/Call the police!
Soittakaaa ambulanssi/Kutsukaa lääkäri/Soittakaaa poliisi!
Soi-terkah ermbulernsi/Kutsukah lahkari/Soi-terkah polleesi!

POLICE
Main police station For non-urgent police assistance
🅐 Punanotkonkatu 2. The most central precinct is at
🅐 Pieni Roobertinkatu 1–3 ☎ (09) 1891

Lost property
Police Lost Property Office 🅐 Punanotkonkatu 2 ☎ (09) 189 3180
🕐 08.00–16.15 Mon, Tue, Thur, Fri 08.00–16.15 Wed Ⓝ Tram: 7B
Transport Lost Property For items lost on trains, buses, trams
and at the airport. You can make enquiries by telephone.
🅐 Kauppiaankatu 8–10 ☎ 0600 410 06 🕐 09.00–18.00 Mon–Fri

EMBASSIES & CONSULATES
Consulates and consular sections of embassies handle emergencies
of travelling citizens. After reporting it to the police, your consulate or
embassy should be the first place you turn to if a passport is lost or stolen.
British Embassy 🅐 Itäinen Puistotie 17 ☎ (09) 228 65100, 228 65210 or
2286 5216 (for emergencies outside normal hours, call ☎ (0500) 817 242)
🌐 www.britishembassy.fi 🕐 08.30–15.00 Mon–Fri, late June–late Aug;
09.00–17.00 rest of year
Canadian Embassy 🅐 Pohjoisesplanadi 25 B ☎ (09) 228 530
📠 (09) 601 060 🌐 www.canada.fi
Irish Embassy 🅐 Erottajankatu 7 A ☎ (09) 646 006
New Zealand Consulate 🅐 Kohdematkat Oy, Hietalahdenranta 13
☎ (09) 615 615
South African Embassy 🅐 Rahapajankatu 1 A 5 (3rd Floor)
☎ (09) 6860 3100 🕐 Consular hours 09.00–14.00 Mon–Fri
United States Embassy, Consular Office 🅐 Itäinen Puistotie 14 B
☎ (09) 616 250 🌐 www.usembassy.fi 🕐 09.00–12.00 Mon–Thur.
Phone hours 08.30–17.00 Mon–Fri

WHAT'S IN YOUR GUIDEBOOK?

Independent authors Impartial up-to-date information from our travel experts who meticulously source local knowledge.

Experience Thomas Cook's 165 years in the travel industry and guidebook publishing enriches every word with expertise you can trust.

Travel know-how Contributions by thousands of staff around the globe, each one living and breathing travel.

Editors Travel-publishing professionals, pulling everything together to craft a perfect blend of words, pictures, maps and design.

You, the traveller We deliver a practical, no-nonsense approach to information, geared to how you really use it.

SPOTTED YOUR NEXT CITY BREAK?

Then these lightweight CitySpots pocket guides will have you in the know in no time, wherever you're heading. Covering over 80 cities worldwide, they're packed with detail on the most important urban attractions from shopping and sights to non-stop nightlife; knocking spots off chunkier, clunkier versions.

Aarhus	Genoa	Paris
Amsterdam	Glasgow	Prague
Antwerp	Gothenburg	Porto
Athens	Granada	Reykjavik
Bangkok	Hamburg	Riga
Barcelona	Hanover	Rome
Belfast	Helsinki	Rotterdam
Belgrade	Hong Kong	Salzburg
Berlin	Istanbul	Sarajevo
Bilbao	Kiev	Seville
Bologna	Krakow	Singapore
Bordeaux	Kuala Lumpur	Sofia
Bratislava	Leipzig	Stockholm
Bruges	Lille	Strasbourg
Brussels	Lisbon	St Petersburg
Bucharest	Ljubljana	Tallinn
Budapest	London	Tirana
Cairo	Los Angeles	Tokyo
Cape Town	Lyon	Toulouse
Cardiff	Madrid	Turin
Cologne	Marrakech	Valencia
Copenhagen	Marseilles	Venice
Cork	Milan	Verona
Dubai	Monte Carlo	Vienna
Dublin	Moscow	Vilnius
Dubrovnik	Munich	Warsaw
Düsseldorf	Naples	Zagreb
Edinburgh	New York	Zurich
Florence	Nice	
Frankfurt	Oslo	
Gdansk	Palermo	
Geneva	Palma	

Available from all good bookshops, your local Thomas Cook travel store or browse and buy on-line at

Thomas Cook Publishing

Editorial/project management: Lisa Plumridge
Copy editor: Paul Hines
Layout/DTP: Alison Rayner
Proofreader: Wendy Janes

The publishers would like to thank the following companies and individuals for supplying their copyright photographs for this book: A1 Pix, pages 33, 108–9 & 152; Dainis Derics/iStockphoto.com, page 18; Finnish Tourist Board, pages 27, 35, 46, 89 & 142; Olli Laine/iStockphoto.com, page 11; Tero Puha, pages 7, 21, 39, 42–3, 53, 61, 100 & 116; Rūta Saulytė-Laurinavičienė/Dreamstime.com, page 5; Stillman Rogers Photography, pages 1, 8, 15, 17, 49, 64–5, 69, 78, 80, 90, 92–3, 116, 123, 125, 134, 141 & 146–7.

Send your thoughts to
books@thomascook.com

- Found a great bar, club, shop or must-see sight that we don't feature?
- Like to tip us off about any information that needs a little updating?
- Want to tell us what you love about this handy little guidebook and more importantly how we can make it even handier?

Then here's your chance to tell all! Send us ideas, discoveries and recommendations today and then look out for your valuable input in the next edition of this title.

Email the above address (stating the title) or write to: CitySpots Project Editor, Thomas Cook Publishing, PO Box 227, Coningsby Road, Peterborough PE3 8SB, UK.